The Reckoning

Also by Jane Casey

The Burning
The Missing

The Reckoning

Jane Casey

Minotaur Books
New York

THE RECKONING. Copyright © 2012 by Jane Casey. All rights reserved. Printed in the United States of America. For information address St. Martin's Press, 175 Fifth Avenue, New York, N.Y. 10010.

www.minotaurbooks.com

ISBN 978-0-312-62200-8 (hardcover)
ISBN 978-1-4668-0085-4 (e-book)

First published in Great Britain by Ebury Press, an imprint of Random House Group, Ltd.

First U.S. Edition: May 2012

10 9 8 7 6 5 4 3 2 1

For James

The Reckoning

The light isn't good. It's hard to see much, at first.

The image on-screen flickers and fades out as the camera struggles to make a picture out of what it can pick up in the dim interior. Handheld, the video jumps and wobbles, catching details that hint at a narrow space, a low ceiling, a dirty tarpaulin laid on the floor. Nineteen seconds in, the curve of a wheel arch tells the viewer that the scene is being filmed inside a van, and not a large one.

When the camera turns to what is lying on the tarpaulin, the person holding it fumbles for a second before switching on a light. It's bright enough to send the shadows shrinking blackly to the edges of the picture. This is important. This must be seen in detail.

This is the reason for the film.

The camera starts at her feet, which are streaked with dirt and trussed in high-heeled sandals. It tracks up, lingering on thighs exposed by a white dress that was short to begin with. The pleated skirt is pulled up almost to her hips. She's lying on her side, her hands loose and relaxed, her face veiled in loose curls of fair hair. Tiny artificial flowers wind through the strands. A dusting of glitter winks here and there on her skin, her limbs gleaming in the light. On the tarpaulin, next to her face, a jeweled mask lies abandoned. The long pink ribbons that once tied it spiral in curling disarray. It takes a moment to register that the shading on one is not a trick of the light, but dark-red liquid that has seeped into the fabric.

On the folds of her dress are minute specks of dark red in droplets shaped like comets.

And on the full lower lip, just visible through a skein of her hair, a plump bead of dark red swells and slides downward even as the camera focuses on it, running to join the small pool that spreads under her head.

It's the details that are important, and the view isn't good enough, not with her hair over her face. The camera jerks sideways and a hand enters the shot for a second, reaching out to gather a handful of curls and throw them to one side. Now you can see.

Now you can see everything.

Now you can see the bruise that darkens one cheek. Now you can see the eyelashes brittle with mascara, the traces of color in the creases of her mouth. Now you can see the curve of her breasts. Now you can see that she's pretty but not perfect, her nose too short and wide, her mouth too full, her jaw just a shade too square. Now you can see that she's young.

A tremor, too slight to be called movement, and the camera retreats a pace or two, the focus staying on her face. A frown tugs her eyebrows together, pulls the corners of the full mouth down; her face, for a moment, is that of a sulky cherub in an Old Master's sketch. And then the eyes blink open, unfocused at first, hazy blue.

The camera wavers, up and down, uncontrolled. It's laughter. The person holding the camera is laughing.

All at once there is sound on the recording, an extra dimension to the viewing experience. A rustle as the girl sits up, one hand raised to shield her eyes from the light. Breathing from behind the camera, shallow and fast—excitement and anticipation.

The blue eyes are narrow now, focused; she's awake. She passes a tongue over her lips, licking blood, assessing damage.

A beat of silence.

Then, unexpectedly, she smiles—a triangular, humorless smile, but a smile nonetheless. The expression on her face is feline, dangerous. She tosses her hair back, drawing her legs under herself and smoothing out her brief skirt. And when she speaks, her voice is flat. It has no trace of fear in it, a fact that's almost as remarkable as what she says before the sound cuts out and the screen goes black.

"You are in *really* big trouble."

Part One

It is strange with how little notice: good, bad or indifferent, a man may live and die in London . . . There is a numerous class of people in this metropolis who seem not to possess a single friend, and whom nobody appears to care for.

Charles Dickens, *Sketches by Boz*

Chapter One

Wednesday

Maeve

If anyone had asked me, I'd have lied and said that being a detective was like any other job—a lot of routine and a bit of excitement now and then. The truth was, in fact, that it was like no other job in the world, except that there were good days and bad days. But the bad days were really, truly, epically bad. The bad days were spent standing too close to a decomposing body, trying not to gag. The bad days were random acts of violence on empty streets late at night with no witnesses. The bad days were domestic punch-ups that had got out of hand, dead drug addicts in dingy bedsits, elderly shut-ins whose neighbors only cared enough to call the police when the smell was too revolting to bear. I didn't care to count up how many days were bad ones; I suspected I wouldn't like the answer. But I could deal with it. I could cope.

I wasn't sure, however, that I could cope with my new case. More specifically, I wasn't sure that I could cope with my new boss. I wasn't at all sure I could stand it if all the days were bad, if every minute was another minute closer to breaking my spirit. I stared out of the car window as I half-listened to the driver beside me and wished I were somewhere else, with someone else.

It wasn't like me to be so unenthusiastic but nothing about my current situation was good. I was on my way to a crime scene I didn't want to face, accompanied by Detective Inspector Josh Derwent, one of two new additions to the team at that level. He and the other new DI, Keith Bryce, had worked with Godley before. That was about all they seemed to have in common. Bryce was quietly melancholy, and his face was as rumpled as his suits. Derwent was younger and had a reputation for being obsessively hard-working and infinitely aggressive. As far as I could tell, he liked fast driving, soft rock, and the sound of his own voice. Rumor had it he didn't like junior detectives to answer back. Handle with care was the advice circulating in the office, and I watched him covertly as he drove, heavy on the accelerator, heavy on the brake, swearing and spinning the wheel one-handed as if he were in a games arcade rather than pushing to make time on traffic-clogged London streets. Magic FM blared from the car radio, middle-of-the-road music at its most blandly inoffensive. Derwent sang along occasionally, unself-conscious even though he didn't know me at all. Not that I was likely to make anyone feel on edge, least of all him. I was the most junior of detective constables and he was an inspector, fifteen years in the job.

I had been prepared to give him the benefit of the doubt. I had suffered enough from misplaced gossip, from the assumptions made about me based on my looks, my height, my youth, my name. So when Superintendent Godley summoned me to his office and I found Derwent there already, leaning up against the glass wall that separated the boss from the rest of us, I didn't expect trouble. I should have known better. Even someone as inexperienced as me knew that when the superintendent didn't meet your eyes, it was time to get nervous.

"Maeve, you haven't met Josh Derwent yet, have you? He's taking the lead on a new job we've picked up in Brixton—a double murder, of sorts."

Derwent acknowledged me with a fleeting look, no smile. He was of average height but thick through the neck and shoulders, muscled like a bulldog. He was too rugged to be called handsome but his close-cropped hair, strong jaw and broken nose, and the tan he'd earned while training for marathons, made him distinctive. You'd certainly think twice before getting into a fight with him. The marathon running was a hobby that had raised eyebrows among my colleagues, most of whom counted a short jog to the vending machine as exercise. According to them, long-distance running was public masochism and a further sign that Derwent wasn't to be trusted. For my part, I couldn't work out how he found the time to train, but otherwise I didn't care. And he was certainly in great shape. It was really only the fact that he was standing in the same room with Superintendent Godley that made him look ordinary, but then there were comparatively few men who could measure up to the boss. Tall, with hair that had turned silver-white when he was still a young man, Godley was startlingly attractive. He must have been aware of the effect he had on people, but he seemed to be utterly without vanity. No one would dare to underestimate him because of his appearance; it was impossible to mistake what lay behind his brilliant blue eyes for anything but a sharp, focused intelligence.

But today, for some reason, the focus was off. Godley looked strained and sounded distracted, fumbling among his papers for the notes on the new case and not finding what he was looking for.

"I don't have the details to hand, but we've got two men, both tortured to death, bodies found within a mile of each other in the last twenty-four hours. Josh, I know you want to get going, so tell DC Kerrigan what we know so far while you're on the way."

It wasn't like Godley to be vague. One of the things that made him an outstanding boss was his command of each twist and turn in every case his team worked. I hesitated for a second before following Derwent out of the room. It wasn't my place to ask the superintendent if he was okay. Besides, I had problems of my own. Derwent could have looked more thrilled at the prospect of working with me. Maybe he had heard something about me from someone else on the team. Maybe I had made a bad first impression. Maybe he was just in a bad mood. Sitting next to him in the squad car, it was difficult to tell.

"Earth to DC Kerrigan. Come in, DC Kerrigan."

I jumped. "Sorry. I was miles away."

Derwent had interrupted his monologue about other motorists' short-comings to ask me a question, and I'd missed it. He was looking at me impatiently, tapping his fingers on the edge of the steering wheel as the lights in front of us stubbornly stayed red.

"I asked you what you made of Godley's briefing. I thought you might have some insight to share." The sarcasm was biting and I managed not to wince. Just.

"The boss didn't say much. Only that there were two similar deaths in the same area."

"And that didn't make you think? Didn't make you wonder what's going on?"

"I don't know enough about either case yet to make any assumptions," I said levelly. "I don't want to jump to conclusions without knowing the facts." *The facts you were supposed to share with me . . .*

"That's fair." Derwent was nodding as if I'd passed a test I didn't know I was taking. "Let's talk through the facts. Yesterday evening, Mrs. Claudia Tremlett called her local police station to report her husband missing. Ivan Tremlett was a self-employed software designer who lived in Clapham, just off the Common. He rented office space down the road in Brixton because he had three small children and they made too much noise for him to be able to work from home. He had two rooms above a laundrette and it was his habit to lock himself in. He was extremely security conscious, not least because he had quite a lot of expensive computer equipment. He didn't see clients at his office so he wasn't set up to receive visitors. Mrs. Tremlett became concerned when he failed to return home by six o'clock, because he always followed the same routine—out in the morning by half past eight, back by half past five. She had tried to raise him by phone, but got no reply from the mobile or landline. Mrs. Tremlett was extremely distressed on the phone and worried about her husband's safety. She convinced the sergeant to dispatch a unit to check that all was well."

"And it wasn't," I said knowing the answer.

"It was not. Mr. Tremlett was in the office, all right, with his computers, but neither they nor he were in what you might call a viable condition. Mr. Tremlett's injuries were not compatible with life."

It was typical police understatement: the phrase generally meant someone who was so very dead it was hard to recognize them as having been human in the first place. "Who took the case? Lambeth CID?"

"They did the initial work. Didn't take it too far—they just took statements from the people working in the laundrette, and Mrs. Tremlett, and secured the scene. In fairness, they didn't have much of a chance to get stuck in, because this came in at lunchtime."

"This" was the crime scene that was our eventual destination, if the traffic ever released us. But Derwent hadn't finished with the software designer yet.

"The last time anyone heard from Tremlett was around two yesterday afternoon when he spoke to his wife. The computers had been smashed to bits, but we might be able to raise something off a hard disk to tell us when he last used them—that could give us a better idea of when he was attacked, but let's say it was between two and five yesterday afternoon."

"No witnesses?"

"Not so far. No one in the laundrette heard or saw anything. It's a noisy place, apparently—machines on the go all the time, people in and out. Besides, no one really knew Ivan Tremlett was there. He kept to himself, and his office had a separate entrance, so they wouldn't have seen him or anyone else coming and going." The car in front of us braked and Derwent's face lit up with a demonic glow. He grinned at me. "Here's where it gets interesting."

I smiled politely in response. Interesting was never good, in my limited experience.

"Around one o'clock this afternoon, the control room received a nine-nine-nine call from the address of a forty-three-year-old male, an unemployed gentleman by the name of Barry Palmer. He lived alone in a two-bedroom house. His sister had become concerned about him, not having heard from him for a couple of days, and had gone around to see if he was all right. She had a key to his front door, so she let herself in. The house had been ransacked. She found her brother in the front room."

"And he was dead."

"Very much so."

"Did he die before Ivan Tremlett or after?"

"Good question. I don't know the answer, as it happens, but Dr. Hanshaw is meeting us there. He'll be able to tell us more."

"Why are you linking the two murders?"

"There were similarities between the two crime scenes—obvious similarities, as you'll see when you have a look yourself. I take your point about not making assumptions, but take it from me, we're looking for the same killer or killers."

"So what do Ivan Tremlett and Barry Palmer have in common? Who would want to kill them? Did they know each other?"

"Gold star to DC Kerrigan. Those are exactly the right questions to ask."

I felt patronized rather than encouraged, but at least the inspector seemed pleased. I was beginning to feel a mild, fragile sense of optimism. Maybe the new DI wasn't so bad. He would have to be something special to be worse than his predecessor, the rat-faced Tom Judd, a charmless manipulator who had taken a totally undeserved promotion and was now leading a robbery team in the East End. The team had held a massive leaving party to celebrate. We hadn't made the mistake of inviting Judd himself.

"I don't know if they knew one another, but I can tell you one thing Tremlett and Palmer share. They both have criminal records. And there's no shortage of people who might want to see them dead." Derwent paused to let that sink in. I waited patiently for the explanation. "Tremlett pleaded guilty to downloading child pornography three years ago. He was working for a small company in Kent and they found it on his computer. He did nine months. Lost his job, not surprisingly, so he set up on his own once the dust had settled. It explains why he kept himself to himself."

"And the security he had on his office." I frowned. "So they've got kids, and he's a convicted sex offender, but Mrs. Tremlett was happy to have him in the family home?"

"Apparently so. We can ask her about that. Wouldn't be the first wife to be in denial about what she'd married."

"If this all happened in Kent, did anyone in the local area know about his conviction?"

"Something else to ask her about, but Lambeth CID say not. He was on the register. No record of anyone making inquiries about him, though."

The sex-offenders' register wasn't open to general access, though a recent law made it possible for members of the public to check whether individuals were listed on it, and for what. But they had to be suspicious to begin with. The ordinary punter in the street didn't seem to realize that, for the most part, the sex offenders who were really dangerous were the ones you would never, ever suspect.

"What about Mr. Palmer?"

"Mr. Palmer is different. He was a known pedophile. Last October he was released from prison after serving a seven-year stretch for raping two little girls. Against the advice of his probation officer, he went back to Brixton, to the house where he had lived when the abuse took place. Not unexpectedly, the local community didn't put out a welcome mat for him. He reported a campaign of harassment ranging from name-calling to a paper bag full of dog shit that was dropped through his letterbox. They'd set fire to it first, so when he went to put out the flames by stamping on it, he got it all over himself."

"That old trick."

"He should have known better," Derwent agreed. "He had trouble with graffiti—scum out, kiddyfiddler lives here, that kind of thing—and the locals wouldn't speak to him or serve him in shops."

"Why did he want to come back?"

"I spoke to his probation officer just before we left the nick. The house was his mother's. She died while he was inside, so it was vacant when he got out. He needed somewhere to stay and a rent-free home was appealing. His sister wouldn't have him living with her. She's got kids herself. Palmer swore he was innocent and the sister says she believed him, but you wouldn't take the chance, would you?"

"Not if there was any alternative." Nothing that I'd heard so far sounded like good news. "So there are a million suspects and when we ask around, no one is going to have seen or heard anything."

"That's about right."

"Brilliant." I looked at him, curious. "This is shaping up to be a nightmare case. You don't seem too worried."

"It's win-win, isn't it? If I solve it, I get the credit for clearing up a double-murder. If I don't . . ." He shrugged. "No one much cares about the victims, do they? No one is going to be demanding pedophiles should be better protected."

"Cynical."

"Realistic. Anyway, don't worry about it, sweetheart. We'll work it out together. I'll make sure you're not left out at the prize-giving."

I restrained myself from rolling my eyes. Fantastic. Another copper who was going to talk down to me just because I was female. *Sweetheart, my arse.*

Derwent was still talking, oblivious. "According to the boss, this is an important case and needs sensitive handling. That's why he assigned you to work on it with me, which makes some sort of sense. The last thing I need is one of those hairy-arsed DCs from the team clumping around offending the families by saying the wrong thing."

"I'll do my best to avoid that," I said stiffly.

"That's the thing. You don't have to say anything at all. Just stand back, look pretty, and let me do all the work." Derwent squinted out through the windscreen and I was glad that he didn't look in my direction, because the expression on my face was nothing short of murderous. "This should be an easy gig for you. Just stay out of my way so you can watch and learn."

Just like that my enthusiasm for the new case, and my new colleague, slipped all the way down to zero.

And things were only going to get worse.

Barry Palmer had lived and died in a two-up, two-down redbrick cottage at the end of a long terrace of similar houses, the last survivors from rows of Victorian workers' cottages that had been obliterated during the Blitz. Derwent found a parking space a little bit further up the street and I got out before he'd switched the engine off, desperate for even a few seconds of respite from the new DI's company. On the pretext of checking out the area, I wandered away from him, scanning the surroundings. Industrial units and high-rise council flats flanked the houses on the streets on both sides, looming over the rooftops. Palmer's house was on the corner and shared a wall with a large, noisy pub of surpassing grimness named the Seven Bells. I risked poking my head in and found an old Victorian pub that had lost all of its character in a series of refits, none recent. It now had too-bright lighting, filthy carpets and faux-leather seats. The music was played at headache-inducing volume and banks of games machines churned out electronic beeps and pings as the customers fed them pound coins. The pub fronted on to a busy road that thundered with buses and lorries. It was the worst sort of location for finding witnesses to a murder, even without considering whether anyone would want to help us find Palmer's killer. No one would have heard anything strange, I was willing to bet. Even if he had screamed.

The house itself was cordoned off with blue-and-white-striped police tape looped around a pair of lampposts to create a rectangle where no one but those on official police business could go. On the other pavement, a group of neighbors were standing, watching. None of them even looked particularly shocked by what had happened. Certainly no one looked as if they were in mourning.

A uniformed PC, square in his luminous jacket, stood by the front door of Palmer's house. He looked more bored than I would have thought possible. They had already put up a blue plastic tent around the door to limit how much the onlookers saw. The windows hadn't yet been covered. They were gray with dirt, but I could make out brownish net curtains that had a floral pattern woven into the lace and looked like they had hung there, unwashed, for decades. Behind them, movement, and the occasional flare of a camera flash told me the SOCOs were already working.

A black van stencilled with the word AMBULANCE was parked right outside the house, ready to take the body away once Dr. Hanshaw had finished his preliminary examination at the scene and Derwent had given permission for it to be removed to the mortuary. The mortuary vans always gave me the creeps. I went past quickly, holding my breath in case I caught a whiff of decay. I knew that they were kept scrupulously clean but I couldn't forget what they routinely carried, or what was waiting for us inside the house. I shouldn't really have been so squeamish; I was just as much a part of the death business as any undertaker. But at least I didn't have to be hands-on.

I took one last look around, then headed toward Derwent who was waiting for me, a sardonic expression on his face. He was holding the police tape over his shoulder so I could duck underneath, a simple courtesy that made me uncomfortable. I didn't need his help, but turning it down would have seemed churlish. Then again, telling him to back off might have put a stop to the sweethearts and darlings.

"Ready to join me in the house? Or do you want to have another look round first?"

"Just getting a feel for the place," I said, not allowing myself to sound ruffled.

"I'd have thought you'd be keen to get in there. See the body." He sniffed. "Probably won't be stinking yet even though the weather's been warm. But the house looks pretty filthy from here. I bet it's ripe in there."

I sent up a small silent prayer of gratitude that I had grown up with an older brother who liked to torment me. Presumably I was supposed to respond with girlish horror. Derwent could try all day and he'd never manage to get a reaction like that from me. I smiled instead, as if the DI had made a witty, brilliant joke, and followed him to the blue tent. It was more than my life was worth to kick up a fuss about putting on a paper boiler suit over my clothes and paper booties on my feet, but I was aware that I looked ridiculous and it was no consolation that everyone else did too.

Someone had pushed the front door so that it was almost shut and I looked at it closely, imagining it as it would have looked to a passerby on an ordinary day. The paint on the door was dark brown and peeling away. Just above the letterbox, someone had scraped the word "Nonce" into the door, getting right down to the wood. The letters were thick and straggling, but easy to read. It must have taken them a while to do it. I wondered what it would have been like to stand in the hallway of the house and listen to someone carve the five jagged letters that spelled out what he was. He would have been afraid to stop them. He would have been afraid all the time.

With good reason, it seemed, because stepping into the hallway was like stepping into a nightmare. The overhead light was on, a harsh incandescent bulb in a dusty lace shade that was incongruously delicate, and the glare picked up the detail of what had taken place there. The walls were papered with a stylized pattern of flowers in tones of pale brown and cream, décor that had to date from the 1970s. The bottom foot or so was gray with rising damp. Here and there the paper bubbled away from the wall, puffed out with moisture. Apart from that, and a scuffmark or two, it had survived reasonably well. At least it had until someone had dragged something bloodstained the length of the hallway, a reddish-brown smear halfway up the wall that was feathered around the edges. Hair produced that effect when it was soaked in blood, I happened to know. The bloodstains told a sorry story to anyone who could read them. He had answered the door—God knows why—and the first thing they had done was to beat him until he bled. And that was just for starters.

I followed the trail past a malodorous sheepskin coat hanging on the end of the stairs, down to a doorway on the left side of the hall. It led into the front room, a small space made smaller by the clutter stacked on all sides and the number of people standing in it. The white suits made everyone anonymous but I picked out Dr. Hanshaw immediately. He was taller and thinner than anyone else in the room, for starters. He was also leaning at a perilous angle to get a better view of what lay on the floor. I couldn't bring myself to look down—not yet, anyway. The room stank of blood, of human waste, of full ashtrays and dirty clothes and damp. It was hot and the windows were tightly closed. There was no air in the room, and no escape from the smell.

Palmer had lived in something approaching squalor and it was hard to tell what had been moved by the intruders and what was part of his normal surroundings, but his sister had said the place had been ransacked. It looked as if he had moved none of his mother's belongings after she died, just overlaid them with his own detritus. Small, ugly ornaments and arrangements of dried flowers fought for space with empty beer cans and mugs stained brown from tannin. The gas fire dated from the same period as the wallpaper, which was probably the last time it had been serviced. Out-of-date TV listings magazines, a brimming ashtray and dirty plates were stacked on either side of a red armchair that occupied prime position in the room. The rubbed, greasy patches on the back and the arms of the chair suggested it was his favorite place to sit. He had a large collection of videos—not even DVDs—and the boxes were thrown everywhere, the cassettes fractured, the tape spilling out in shiny brown-black coils. DI Derwent pushed past me and started turning over the boxes with gloved hands. I turned away, searching for something to distract me from what lay on the floor.

And found it in the signs of violence that jumped out at me once I started looking. Fractured glass was starry in the picture frames that still hung on the wall, lighter patches on the paper showing where others had hung. Blood spatter had dried dark on the biscuit-colored tiles surrounding the fire. The drawers were pulled out of the sideboard, their contents scattered on the floor. Broken glass was mixed in with the tangle of cutlery and napkins and the stopper from a cheap decanter lay in the middle of it all. The carpet was violently patterned with brown, cream and red swirls and it was only when I looked closely that I could see where the blood had soaked into it, spreading out from the body, the meager pile drying in tufts. Unwillingly, I followed the blood back to its source.

The body lay in front of the armchair, as if he had been sitting in it and pitched forward at the moment of his death. He was naked from the waist down, the skin blanched. Blood obeys gravity when it is no longer pumped around the body by a beating heart; the front of Palmer's body would be patched with livid purple when Dr. Hanshaw turned him over. His only clothing was an undershirt, yellowing with age, pulled up above his waist. His sparse hair was rusty-red from the blood that had soaked into it; it was impossible to tell what color it should have been. One hand lay beside his head, his arm curved around as if he had been trying to shield himself from something or someone. I looked at the hand for too long, trying to work out what was odd about it. The shape was wrong, somehow.

"They took three."

I jumped, startled. Derwent was standing beside me, watching Dr. Hanshaw's careful examination of the corpse. The pathologist had just taken the internal temperature, a procedure that always made me feel embarrassed for the dead person. The public indignity of death was profound. Personally, I hoped for a quiet passing, no post-mortem required. "Sorry?"

"Three fingers. Two from the right hand. One from the left." He pointed and I realized that there was a stump where the forefinger should be on each hand, and the middle finger was missing on the right side, dried blood crusted around the wound. "They weren't messing around."

"I'm going to turn him," Dr. Hanshaw said, looking up. "Give me a hand."

To give Derwent his credit, he bent immediately and took a firm hold of the corpse's legs, something that I wouldn't have wanted to do even with gloves on. On the pathologist's command, they rolled Palmer on to his back. A hiss of shock went through the room.

"Significant damage to the genitals." Dr. Hanshaw bent for a closer look. "He was castrated. After a fashion."

Even Derwent was looking pale. He rallied enough to ask, "What did they use?"

"Possibly the same thing they used on his hands. Heavy cutting equipment—garden shears, secateurs, that kind of tool."

"Might have been something they brought with them." Sean Cottrell was the senior SOCO who was managing the crime scene. "We haven't found anything like that, and there's no garden as such—just a concrete yard behind the house. Nothing to cut with garden shears."

"Wouldn't surprise me if they came equipped," Derwent said. "Whoever did this knew what they wanted to do here. They were straight into him as soon as he opened the door."

"But what did they want?" I was pleased to hear how matter-of-fact I sounded. No one would have guessed I was struggling to keep my composure.

"It doesn't look as if he had anything worth stealing. And he served a reasonably long sentence for the child abuse. It's not as if he was out after a few months and someone felt justice hadn't been done."

"Vigilantes?" Derwent suggested. "Maybe they thought prison wasn't enough punishment. Or they wanted to get rid of him and discourage anyone with a similar background from moving in."

"Why now? He'd been living here for almost a year. Plenty of harassment—the neighbors certainly didn't want him here—but nothing like this." I made myself look again at the body, confirming what I had already thought. "I'm not saying they didn't enjoy doing it, but this looks like it had a purpose. They tortured him for a reason."

Derwent raised his eyebrows. "You'd certainly hope it wasn't for fun."

Dr. Hanshaw had been ignoring our back-and-forth, concentrating on what he was doing. "His face is badly swollen—some of that is postmortem, but it's fairly clear he was beaten severely. Whoever attacked him took their time over it." He probed the skull and gave a little grunt. "There was a significant blow to the head that caused a massive skull fracture. I'll have a better idea when I look at his brain during the PM, but I'm fairly sure I'll find this was the fatal injury."

The victim's face was a gargoyle mask, his tongue protruding from his mouth, one cloudy eye staring at the ceiling while the other was swollen shut. I made myself stare at it without flinching. Whatever they had wanted from him, they had made sure he suffered. And they had made sure he died once they were finished with him. I wondered if he had told them what they wanted to hear, in the end. I wondered if they had cared. The level of violence was extreme—it was overkill. And they had enjoyed it.

Judging that I'd spent long enough staring at the body to prove to anyone who cared that I was tougher than I looked, I turned to Derwent. "Mind if I have a look around the rest of the place?"

"Good idea. Check it out." He sounded distracted, still focused on the body. I had found it hard to warm to the new DI, but that didn't mean he was bad at his job. I might yet come to respect him, even if liking him seemed a long way off.

Threading a careful path through the forensic team, I made it to the kitchen and wished I hadn't. Every surface was thick with months' old grease and the windowsill was sprinkled with dead insects. The kitchen units were old, a white laminate that had peeled badly here and there, and the doors hung off the cupboards. Again, it was hard to tell what was recent damage and what state the room had been in before Palmer's nightmarish visitors had arrived, but the drawers upended on the floor and the tins rolling everywhere suggested that the intruders had been in the kitchen too. An officer was painstakingly examining the tiles for footprints. Someone had opened the back door and I edged toward it on the pretext of looking at the yard outside, but really so I could get some air. The tiny concrete space smelled of wholesome exhaust fumes and stale beer from the pub, better than an alpine meadow as far as I was concerned after the ungodly stench in the house. I inhaled deeply and enthusiastically, staring up at a sky that was a cloudless clear blue stitched with vapor trails.

There was a limit to how long anyone could stare at a six-foot-by-eight yard, and I forced myself to go back through the kitchen, spilled sugar crunching under my feet, and into the hall, where I bumped into Sean Cottrell.

"Mind if I go upstairs?"

"Nope. Just watch where you walk—stay on the areas we've marked. And don't run any water in the bathroom. We think they cleaned up in there before they left."

"I won't touch anything." I headed up the narrow stairs. They were covered in thin brown carpet that was worn on the treads and I took it slowly, wary of slipping, careful not to brush against the handrail though it was already black with fingerprint dust.

Cottrell's advice was unnecessary; I wouldn't have been tempted to touch anything in the bathroom. It looked as if it had last been cleaned around the same time as the kitchen—in other words, months ago, if not years. The seat was up on the loo and I pulled a face at the brown streaks running down the sides of the bowl, the stagnant water a murky gray-brown that hinted at unspeakable things lurking below the surface. It would be some poor bastard's job to sieve out anything that had been left in the bowl in case it helped to identify the killers, but not mine, thank God, not mine. The bath was grimy but suspiciously unused compared to the sink, which once had been white but was now dark gray. A reddish-brown tidemark around the plug hole looked like dried blood and I could see why Sean was keen to preserve the room for examination. There was no soap or shower gel in the bathroom, as far as I could see. An ancient toothbrush lay on the sink, the bristles discolored and warped, but there was no toothpaste. Personal hygiene did not appear to have been one of Barry Palmer's priorities, any more than housekeeping.

The two bedrooms were bleak, small and cold. One had a stripped single bed in it and very little else. The stains on the mattress made my stomach heave, which surprised me given that I had seen worse—much worse—in that very house. Maybe it was just that I had reached my daily limit on disgusting things. I gave the other bedroom a cursory glance, taking in the rumpled sheets and blankets, the curtains hanging off their rail at the window, the clothes piled up on a chair in the corner. The room smelled of unwashed flesh and stale air. The mattress hung off the bed, as if someone had lifted it to check what lay underneath, and I had a sudden vision of the killers hurrying through the house after cleaning themselves up, searching it damp-handed for God knows what while Palmer breathed his last in the miserable sitting room below.

I retraced my steps and came down the stairs to find Derwent deep in conversation with Dr. Hanshaw. Judging that he wouldn't want to be interrupted, I slipped out of the front door and took off my paper suit with some relief. The smell of the house clung to my hair and skin and I was conscious of it as I went across the street to the small knot of neighbors who still stood there, arms folded. They were a fairly representative sample of the area's diverse population; Brixton was a proper melting pot and this street was no different. The group seemed, as one, to regard me with suspicion as I walked up to them, but I gave them a smile anyway and introduced myself.

"As you may know, we're investigating a suspicious death at the address behind me. Did any of you see anything strange in the last couple of days? Anyone who didn't belong in this area hanging around? Did you hear anything out of the ordinary?"

A plump black woman shook her head. "Sorry. I don't think we're going to be much help. None of us saw anything, did we, Brian?"

Brian was small and thin with a leathery complexion. He had a foul-smelling cigarette hidden in his fist, held between his forefinger and thumb, and took a long drag on it before answering. "Don't believe we did, no."

I looked around the small circle, seven of them, seeing the same expression repeated on every face. No one was going to break ranks—not in front of their neighbors, anyway. "Right. Names and addresses."

It was like switching on a light in a cellar and seeing rats scurry for cover. The little group broke apart, Brian murmuring something about needing to get to work. I raised my voice.

"It's not a request, ladies and gentlemen. Names and addresses. Now."

There's a certain tone of voice that you learn to use during your years of street policing. Authoritative without being hectoring, it's strangely effective on even the most recalcitrant members of the public. Meekly, the neighbors returned and dictated their details to me. We would be knocking on doors up and down the street anyway, but the ones who were particularly curious—the ones who would stand on the street for hours watching nothing in particular going on—they were the ones I wanted to talk to. They were the ones who would notice anything out of the ordinary. And behind closed doors, they might just not be able to resist telling us what they'd seen.

Once I had finished with the possible witnesses, I turned to find DI Derwent behind me. He did not look pleased.

"Decided you'd had enough, did you?"

"Just collecting some details."

"Is that what I asked you to do?"

"No, but—"

"No." He leaned in, a flush of color in his cheeks, his voice hard. "Let's get one thing straight, okay? I don't like initiative. I don't like people thinking for themselves. I don't like having to search for a junior officer who's taken it upon herself to wander off."

"I didn't want to interrupt your conversation with Dr. Hanshaw."

"Right. And you couldn't wait for me to be finished at the crime scene."

"I didn't think there was any harm in it."

"Well, your first mistake was thinking. You're not here to think."

I opened my mouth to argue and closed it again. What was the point? Derwent gave a short, sharp nod, as if he was satisfied at having put me in my place. I wondered if he had really been annoyed, or if he had engineered the little scene deliberately.

"Fine. Let's get out of here, then." He checked his watch. "We've got another crime scene to visit but I want to see the sister first. She's expecting us. She doesn't want us there too late because we might disturb her precious kids."

"Where does she live?"

"Chislehurst." It was a long way east of Brixton and Derwent said what I was thinking. "It'll take us a while to get there with the traffic like this."

I trailed after him to the car, feeling dismal. Stand back and look pretty, he'd said.

It was going to be a long afternoon.

Chapter Two

I was reluctant to admit that anyone could be having a worse day than me, but Barry Palmer's sister Vera Gordon had a strong claim to it. Small and wiry, she looked far older than thirty-eight, though it was hardly fair to judge her on her current appearance. Her skin was coarse and reddened from hours of crying and her hair hung around her face in lank strands. She sat with her arms wrapped around herself, shivering uncontrollably, a mug of tea untouched on the coffee table in front of her. The sitting room was small but spotless, in contrast with her brother's home, and although the furniture was worn it was carefully chosen. One corner was piled with crates of toys, all neat and organized. It was a warm room, a family room, a place meant for being together. There was an array of family photographs on the windowsill and I leaned over to scan them.

"He's not there." Her voice was strained and hoarse. "I took down the picture of him when he went to prison. Didn't want people asking about him."

Derwent was sitting beside Vera and now he leaned forward.

"Mrs. Gordon, I know you must be very distressed about what happened to your brother."

"Just . . . finding him like that. And the house. My mother would be so upset about the house." Tears began to well up along her lashes and she dug in the sleeve of her woolly gray cardigan for a tissue. "Why did they have to do that? Why did they have to make him suffer?"

"That's what we're trying to find out."

A childish voice was suddenly raised in outrage somewhere toward the back of the house and Vera's head snapped around so she could listen. The voice subsided to a murmur and she turned back to us with a watery smile. "My little boy. He's always fighting with his big sister."

"How many have you got?" Derwent knew the answer already but it was clever to get her talking about her family. We wanted her to be calm, not hysterical. And we wanted her to trust us.

"Just the two."

"One of each, though. Which is easier, boys or girls?"

"I couldn't say. They both have their moments."

"I bet they do. I bet they do." Derwent gave her a grin, too wide to be sincere, but she seemed reassured by it.

"Mrs. Gordon, I know it's difficult, but can you tell us about Barry? All we know is that he was convicted of abusing two young girls," Derwent said.

"That was all rubbish." She sat up a little straighter, twin patches of red high on her cheekbones. "The girls were liars. They were just looking for attention."

"What sort of a person was Barry? He wasn't married, was he? Did he ever have a girlfriend?"

"No. But that didn't mean anything. He was just shy, that's all. He kept himself to himself. He was well, I suppose you'd call him a bit strange, but he wasn't dangerous or anything. Growing up, he wasn't interested in girls, and none of them would give him the time of day anyway. He lived in his own world, a lot of the time. He loved the cinema—he'd have gone every day if he could. He spent most of his time watching videos on his own."

"Did he ever work?"

"No, except for a Saturday job in the local shop when he was a teenager. He found it hard to get on with people. Didn't like taking orders much. I don't know what he might have done with his life if he'd had the right kind of encouragement, but as it was, our dad just made him feel totally worthless. He didn't have the confidence to try anything new. He just survived, really, living at home—living off Mum. Graham, my husband, thought he could have done something to keep himself busy. Stacked shelves or worked in a petrol station—something that wouldn't be difficult. He thought a job would give him some self-respect, some independence too. He couldn't understand how Barry could be happy doing nothing. But it was easier for him to stay at home. Less risky. Barry was afraid of failing so he got out of the habit of trying to do anything. And then . . . those girls . . ."

She broke off, sobbing again, as Derwent flicked a look in my direction. *Do something.* Apparently he'd found a use for me at last.

I moved from my chair to the edge of the sofa, putting my hand on her arm. "Mrs. Gordon, I know this is difficult. If there was any way we could leave this conversation until some time had passed, we would, but time is the one thing we haven't got. We want to find the men who did this to your brother, and I know you do too."

She nodded, wiping her cheeks roughly. "I do. I want to help, really, but I can't help thinking about what happened to him." She looked up, red-rimmed eyes fixed on mine. "You'll tell me the truth. What happened to him? I know they beat him, but what else did they do?"

My throat closed up in horror at the thought of what had happened to him, at the thought of telling someone who had known him and loved him how he had suffered before he died. The look on my face must have told her enough, because she dissolved again.

I sat back into my chair, afraid to look in Derwent's direction. After a couple of minutes, Vera sniffed and tossed her hair back.

"Maybe it's better that I don't know the details." Neither of us said anything, and she nodded. "I can see you think that. I won't ask again. But I do want you to know what my brother was really like."

We sat and listened as she told us about their childhood, about small triumphs and minor setbacks, about the two of them supporting one another against an unsympathetic father, about a devoted mother who had never wavered in her loyalty to her son, no matter what.

"My dad—I wouldn't have said he cared at all about either of us. But I was wrong. The day Barry was convicted, Dad collapsed. He died about three weeks later—as if we didn't have enough to worry about." She sounded bitter. Two sets of feet ran up the stairs, double-quick time, and Vera waited until her children were far enough away to be out of earshot before she went on. "The doctor said it was his heart. That was the biggest joke of all. It was the first proof we'd seen that he even had one. But it wasn't that he was sad for Barry. He was sad for himself. He couldn't stand the fact that his son was in prison. Barry had always been a disappointment to him because Dad wanted a son like himself, a drinker, a football fanatic, some-one he could take to the pub. And Barry wasn't that."

"Mrs. Gordon, you said that Barry's accusers were looking for attention. What did you mean?"

The venom in her voice surprised me. "They were dirty little cows, the pair of them. Got together and made up a story about Barry. They thought it was funny, if you ask me. He was a bit of a joke around the local area, people say-ing he was weird, and up to no good, and watch out when he's about." She sniffed again, rubbing her hands over her knees as if she was trying to warm herself. "They got off school to see counselors and the police—that's probably why they did it. The two of them were little bitches, you could see when they gave evidence. It was all done by video link so they didn't have to be in court, and they were cheeky to the lawyers and the judge, as if it was all a big game. It was lies, and everyone knew it was lies, but the jury still convicted him. One of them was eleven and the other was ten, and they knew everything there was to know about sex—described it in detail. And you could tell they'd actually done it, more than once. But not with my brother." The anger seemed to drain out of her and she sighed. "No one wanted to believe that girls that young would have lost their innocence. But Barry was more innocent than them, for all that he was three times their age."

"He served out his sentence, though. He didn't appeal."

"He couldn't face going back to court. It made him ill. Besides, his barrister said there were no grounds for an appeal. The fact that he was innocent wasn't enough, apparently." She ripped a couple of shreds off the edge of the tissue she was holding. "Seven years, he did. Never complained. Just thanked us when we visited and asked how we were. He never said anything about what it was like for him, in jail. He just said our lives were more interesting and he didn't want to talk about his."

Derwent spoke gently, choosing his words with more delicacy than I would have expected from him. "Barry's probation officer had warned him about his personal safety, returning to your family home, because he was known in the local area as a sex offender. You seem to be certain that he was wrongly convicted, yet you didn't ask him to live here."

She was shaking her head before he'd finished. "No. I did. I did. He wouldn't. Barry knew Graham was worried about it—not about the kids, but about the neighbors. If they'd found out, we would have had to move. We were worried enough about anyone finding out we were related to him. I didn't visit him half as much as I wanted to in case anyone noticed where I was going and why. Graham liked Barry. He didn't want him to come to any harm, and he agreed he should stay with us, at least for a while, just until he got on his feet. But Barry wouldn't hear of it."

"Did he know he was in danger? Did he ever tell you about threats?"

"He never talked about it. He didn't know who was threatening him— that was all he said. It could have been anyone." She gave a little laugh that had no humor in it. "Sad, isn't it? So many people could have wanted my brother dead. And he would never dream of harming a soul."

"So you don't know of anyone in particular?"

"No. Barry—he was brave. You probably think he was stupid, but he never gave in. He went where he needed to go and he kept himself to himself and he didn't want to cause anyone any trouble and now he's dead . . ." She was crying again.

"Do you know anyone named Ivan Tremlett, Mrs. Gordon?"

She shook her head, obviously bewildered by the question.

Derwent put his pen into his jacket pocket with an air of finality and closed his folder. "Right. Thanks very much, Mrs. Gordon." He flicked a card onto the coffee table and got to his feet. "If you think of anything else, give us a call."

I doubted she had heard, but as the inspector was leaving the room, I thought I'd better do the same. I muttered some condolences, putting my own card down beside Derwent's with a little bit more ceremony than he had managed. I found him in the kitchen, talking to Graham Gordon, who was washing up dirty cups slowly and carefully. He was tall and balding, and had the hangdog look of the habitually morose. In happier times it would probably have been for humorous effect, but there was little enough to smile about just then.

Derwent had obviously decided that Gordon didn't need gentle handling.

"Who do you know who would have wanted to torture and kill your brother-in-law?"

He shrugged. "No one."

The sitting-room door closed and I heard Vera's footsteps on the stairs, heading up to where thumps and bumps announced the children were playing.

"That's not what your wife says. She says there were lots of people who wanted him gone."

"Might have been. But I don't know them. You asked me if I knew anyone, and I don't."

"Literal-minded," Derwent commented with a thin smile. "I can see I'm going to have to choose my words carefully with you."

"You can choose what you like. I don't know anything and neither does Vera. Barry wasn't the most forthcoming of individuals. If he'd been being threatened, he wouldn't have wanted Vera to know because she'd have worried. And he barely talked to me." He fished around in the water, coming up with a handful of teaspoons that he slotted into the rack.

"I thought the two of you got on."

"We did. But he was always quiet. Only spoke when he had something to say." He pulled the plug out of the sink. It made loud choking sounds as the water drained out. From the look on Gordon's face, he had approved of his brother-in-law's reserve. Derwent stepped closer, making Gordon move back until he came up against the cooker and couldn't retreat any further.

"You can't have trusted him though. Given what he was. Did you really want him living here or was that just something you said to keep the peace with the missus?"

"I'd have been all right with it."

"All right with it? All right with leaving him alone with your daughter? Or even your son? People change in prison, Graham. They try out different things. Barry might have developed a taste for young boys. Would you really have been happy to turn your back on him?"

"I didn't mind Barry." The man's voice was toneless, his face stony. He picked up a tea towel and dried his hands, not hurrying. "I've known him for a long time—before all of this happened. I was there at the trial, when I could be. I heard the evidence. You didn't."

Derwent stayed where he was for a second, eyes narrowed, considering what Gordon had said. Then he rocked back on his heels with a laugh. "Just pushing your buttons, mate. Just trying to see what you really thought of him."

"Well, now you know." Gordon flipped the tea towel onto his shoulder. "You also know where the front door is. I'll let you see yourselves out."

Derwent made as if to leave, then turned back. "Seriously, though—did your kids see much of Uncle Barry?"

Gordon's nostrils flared and his face became suffused with blood. "You're not talking to my kids. No fucking way."

"I'll take that as a no, then. Don't feel bad, mate. I wouldn't have wanted them spending time with him either, if I'd been in your shoes."

I thought Gordon was going to lash out at Derwent. Despite my very real desire to see the inspector knocked into the middle of next week, I didn't want to have to arrest Vera's husband for assault on a police officer the day her brother's murder was discovered. I stepped forward smartly.

"Thank you for your time, Mr. Gordon. Sir, you wanted to visit that other location before our next interview. I don't think we'll have time unless we go now."

I sounded apologetic and looked meek, and Derwent had the sense to take the opportunity to leave with his face intact. Graham Gordon followed us out of the kitchen but headed upstairs instead of coming to the front door. I could hear voices as I reached in to close the front door behind us: a brief question from his wife that received an even briefer answer. I didn't have to wonder if he would tell her what had happened in the kitchen. He would protect her from it, just as he'd allowed her to think that he didn't mind her brother being around the children. Because part of his problem with Derwent's questions was that they had hit a nerve. He had been relieved that Barry had refused to come and live with them. Maybe he hadn't pressed the point with him. Maybe he'd backed him up against Vera, drowning out her objections. Anything for a quiet life. And now he had to be regretting it.

Grief was hard to bear. Grief overlaid with shame was harder still.

I waited until we were in the car before I tackled Derwent. "What was the point in that?

"What—pissing him off? Nothing, really. Just wondering what made him tick."

"Why? He's not a suspect."

"You never know."

"Well, we do in this case. Vera Gordon said they didn't know Ivan Tremlett. They'd have no reason to want him dead, even if they wanted to get rid of Barry—and it doesn't actually sound like they had much to do with him anyway. He didn't come around; he didn't bother them."

"Mm." Derwent sounded distracted as he moved off, still poking at the sat nav mounted on the dashboard. "Don't discount the fact that they've got the house now. Clean it up, sell it off—nice little lump sum for them. Bit of financial stability never hurt anyone."

"You can't think that they killed Barry so they could get their hands on the house."

"As it happens, I don't." He jammed his hand on the horn, blaring a warning to a Renault that was thinking about pulling out in front of us. "But you never know what you might shake loose by being a bit firm with people. That softly-softly-pretty-please approach might work for you now, but it won't when you get a bit older and lose your looks."

"I'll try to remember that."

"You're not angry?" He sounded surprised—maybe a shade disappointed too.

"Should I be?" The truthful answer to that was yes. Having tasted blood in his encounter with Graham Gordon he seemed to be determined to provoke me and I was equally determined not to let him.

"I don't suppose so. I'm glad you've got a sense of humor, anyway. Godley didn't mention that when he told me about you."

I wanted more than anything to ask what the boss had said—if he'd mentioned that I'd nearly got myself killed the previous year, or if he'd concentrated on whether I was a good police officer. I looked out of the window, saying nothing.

"Don't you want to know the details?"

And if I had asked, Derwent would have taken pleasure in telling me the conversation was confidential. I shrugged. "I can't imagine he had much to say. I haven't worked for him for very long."

"Long enough for a guy like Godley to draw some fairly sharp conclusions about you."

"That sounds positive." I spoke lightly, but I was shrinking in my seat. There was a lot to criticize, after all. The most he'd had to do with me was on a case where I had ended up in hospital by blundering into the wrong place at the wrong time. Then I had been completely wrongheaded about a suspect and nearly missed catching the real murderer as a result. Not my finest hour.

"He said you were intuitive and brave. He said you'd go to the ends of the earth to catch someone who needed locking up." Derwent looked at me, trying to see if I was embarrassed. "He said you were getting an award for something that happened last year. You saved another officer's life."

"Only by chance. That was nothing to be proud of."

"Yeah, he said you'd say that."

"Did he?"

"I think he wanted me to understand why he'd put you on this case."

"And why is that?"

"These aren't the most attractive victims, are they? Convicted criminals. And not just any criminals—the lowest of the low. Perverts. There are plenty of coppers who wouldn't bother their arses trying to find whoever's killing nonces. They'd be more likely to celebrate the fact that someone's cleaning house in this neighborhood. You've got too much empathy to be like that. I saw you in Palmer's house. You were upset by what happened to him."

"Wasn't everyone?"

"In a basic I'm-glad-that-wasn't-me kind of way. You were imagining what his life was like and how he felt when he was being attacked. You care."

He sneered the last two words like an insult and despite myself the color came into my cheeks. Having got a reaction, Derwent seemed to relax.

"I'm just taking the piss. It's a good thing to be able to imagine yourself in the place of the victim, even if the victim is a forty-something freak with child abuse convictions."

"Let's get one thing straight, okay? I'm not that different from other coppers. I'm not a fan of pedophiles. But from what his sister said, Palmer could have been somewhere on the autistic spectrum even if he was never formally diagnosed. He was vulnerable to being accused of all sorts of deviant behavior. That sort of allegation is difficult to face down even if you are articulate and able to cope with life, which, according to his sister, he wasn't."

"Yeah. Poor bloke didn't have much of a chance."

"Vera was pretty convinced he was innocent, but he was found guilty. You know more about him than I do. What was the truth of it?"

He grunted. "I spoke to the officer in the case earlier, before we left the nick. The whole thing was bullshit. Fair enough, Palmer got convicted, but the trial was during a massive scare about pedophiles, just after a little girl got raped and murdered by a neighbor in Lancashire. Juries were convicting everyone who was on trial for sex crimes, no matter how flimsy the evidence was, and the sentences they were getting . . . well, none of the judges wanted to be on the front page of the *Daily Mail* for letting them off lightly. They threw the book at them."

"If the case was bullshit, what was he doing in court in the first place?"

"The CPS were scared to drop it. It was all political—no one wanted to make the judgment that the alleged victims were lying so they passed it along the line all the way to the Crown Court. The two kids had totally different stories, although the abuse was supposed to have happened to them when they were together. They kept changing their accounts, even when they were giving evidence in court. The prosecution barrister had to do some fancy footwork to make it look as if what they'd said matched up with what he'd promised in his opening speech."

"And they wouldn't have been given a hard time by Palmer's brief."

"No. Too young for a tough cross-examination and the jury would have hated it anyway. You heard what Vera said—it was video-link testimony. Ever been in court when kids are giving evidence about abuse? No? It's embarrassing. Wigs off. Gowns off. The barristers and judge cooing, all gentle and understanding. Everyone pretending like there's nothing strange going on, nothing to worry about. Give me strength."

"Don't tell me you're on the side of the defendant." I'd met more unicorns than coppers who had tears to shed for the man or woman in the dock.

Derwent laughed. "I wouldn't go that far. But I hate those cases where you've got a witness who's obviously spinning a tale and no one challenges them on it. I'd rather not take a shit case to court, even if I was pretty sure of a win. I've seen barristers lose cases they should have won because the jury ignored the evidence, and I've seen them win when they shouldn't have, and I don't like either one, to be honest with you. I like to play fair."

I filed it away as an interesting insight into Derwent's character. I'd have said he was the type to want to win at all costs. It was going to be important to get the measure of him, if we were going to have to work long hours together. I needed to be careful not to make assumptions about him just because he was an awkward sod. Godley had brought him on to the team for a reason. I just needed to work out what that reason was, because it would make my working life a lot easier.

"Well, innocent or guilty, going to prison was probably the best thing for Palmer. At least he was protected there. He seemed to have survived prison intact only to get targeted on the outside." Child abusers were the least popular members of the prison population but were generally kept away from other prisoners. It was when he had come out and attempted to start his life again that things had spiraled all the way through bullying and intimidation to murder. "It sounds as if he was a victim of other people's prejudices long before he was murdered, so yeah, I do feel sorry for him. And anyway, regardless of what he had or hadn't done, no one deserves to die that way."

We were stopped at a junction, waiting to turn right, so Derwent was able to indulge himself in a slow handclap. "Well said. If policing doesn't work out for you, maybe you could consider a career in the law. That sort of thing would have a judge sobbing into his wig."

"You sound like my mother. She always wanted me to become a lawyer."

"Not happy that her darling girl became a policewoman?"

I shook my head. "She'd have liked to be able to boast about me if I was a solicitor or a barrister. But she'd have been just as happy if I'd become a doctor or a vet."

"Is she Irish?"

"Yes. Dad too. But I was born in London."

"I noticed the accent. Or lack of one. Not that you could pretend to be anything other than Irish with a name like that." Another glance across the car. "Besides, you look Irish. A fine Irish colleen."

If there was one thing I hated, it was being called a colleen. There was a world of difference between it and the phrase that had sounded like music through my childhood, *cailín alainn*, used by both of my parents as a term of endearment, *my lovely girl*. In their mouths it was loving—in Derwent's, pure condescension. Eight hundred years of unwanted attention echoed through those two syllables.

More than anything, I regretted the fact that I didn't speak Irish myself. I knew a few phrases but I didn't have that understanding that came from thinking in a language, knowing a culture from the inside out. And it didn't help that my cousins in Ireland whined about having to learn the language in school, hated every second they were made to speak it, and devoted as much energy to forgetting it as they ever had to committing it to memory in the first place. They still had it, and I didn't. The fact was, I was Irish to English people and English to Irish people and I never truly felt I belonged in either society, but that wouldn't stop someone like Derwent categorizing me based on his own preconceptions. And he was absolutely the sort to find Irish jokes funny. He might not have made any yet, but I was steeling myself for them; he'd make them, in time.

I settled for responding with, "I'm not exactly the typical Irish girl. I don't have red hair and freckles."

"Those gray eyes are like the Irish Sea on a cloudy day. You couldn't be anything else."

"How poetic." My voice was pure acid.

"That's me." He began humming tunelessly under his breath and I slowly realized it was intended to be "Molly Malone."

"She was from Dublin. My parents are from the country."

"Don't know any other Irish songs. Sorry."

"My loss, I'm sure."

"Just wait until you hear my version of 'My Way.' I'll take you out some-time. We can have a few beers and you can hold my coat while I take on the karaoke machine."

It would be a cold day in hell before I socialized with Josh Derwent. "I don't think that's going to happen."

"What is it—jealous boyfriend? He wouldn't like you going out for drinks with another man?"

"Hardly."

"Don't tell me a girl like you is single."

I hesitated, not sure how to answer that one. Technically, yes. Emotionally, no. And it certainly wasn't something I wanted to discuss with the inspector. "Let's just say it's complicated. And not relevant."

"Oh, so there's a story." Another sidelong glance, this time accompanied by a wide grin that showed lots of white teeth. It was like a dog's smile. "You don't have to talk to me about it, but be warned, I'll find out."

"There's nothing to find out. It's just not clear-cut, that's all. And it's not the reason why we won't be going out, sir."

Eyebrows raised. "Sir? Are we back to being formal? You can call me Josh."

I was beginning to think Derwent had misunderstood the concept of a charm offensive. "I'd rather not . . . boss. No offense. I'd just rather keep things professional. I like to keep work about work. I don't socialize very often with colleagues." *Apart from the one I occasionally sleep with, obviously.*

"I get it. You're serious about your job. I should take you seriously."

"That would be nice."

"That's the other thing Godley said about you, actually. That I shouldn't underestimate you." He glanced at me sardonically. "He's a big fan."

"So that's why he's put me on the case from hell."

"You and me both."

"That's a point. You've told me why I've got this one. Why did he put you on it too?"

"Because I'm new to the team and no one else would have wanted it." A beat. "And because I'm really, really good at my job. Godley trusts me to get this guy, so that's what I'm going to do."

"I admire your confidence."

"It's justified. I will catch him." He sounded certain. "I might hold off until he's crossed another few pedos off his list, though. Because Barry Palmer may have been innocent, but Ivan Tremlett pleaded guilty, and he's no loss to anyone."

That grin again, and I felt increasingly uneasy. It wasn't a dog's smile at all.

It was a wolf's.

Chapter Three

"Welcome to Sidley Street, home of the Kwik Kleen Laundrette and Ivan Tremlett's office, and roughly four-fifths of a mile from Barry Palmer's house. And we'll be lucky if we can get parked in this borough, let alone near the crime scene."

Derwent was only slightly exaggerating. The road was too narrow to allow for parking beside both curbs so there were cars on one side of the street only and spaces were hard to come by. He crawled along looking for gaps in the bumper-to-bumper chain of cars, finding only double-yellow lines and loading bays. A hundred yards ahead of us a van pulled out and Derwent stamped on the accelerator to get there before anyone else could steal the spot. I decided not to complain about whiplash, judging that he wouldn't be sympathetic. As he parked, I looked across the street. By chance we had stopped almost opposite the laundrette. It occupied a central site in a parade of down-at-heel shops with flats and offices on the floors above them. The buildings were redbrick Victorian originally, but a 1980s refurbishment had distinguished the laundrette with blue plastic signing decorated with bubbles. The big plate-glass window was steamed up and I could hardly make out the shapes of the machines from where I was sitting. I could see how those inside might not have noticed anything strange taking place on the street, or in the offices above them. Even if they'd been looking.

My eyes tracked upward to the three windows on the first floor. Behind them lay the rooms where Ivan Tremlett had been tortured to death, but from the outside they were blandly anonymous. It was only with a second glance that the signs of an active police investigation became apparent. The windows were covered with makeshift paper blinds and the door was tied off with Police Do No Enter tape. The SOCOs had finished with it, though, and all was quiet. There was no sign of any police presence, apart from the two of us. Nor was there any sign of anyone showing any interest in the building, or what had happened there. Tremlett had lived and died in almost total obscurity, and I wondered what had brought his killers to the narrow, dusty door that led to his offices.

We got out of the car and Derwent led the way across the road. Before we reached the pavement, a tall black man stepped out of the café next door to the laundrette, shrugging on a jacket. "DI Derwent? Henry Cowell, Brixton CID."

"Sorry for keeping you." Derwent shook his hand. "We got held up in traffic."

"Don't worry. Sounds like you're having a busy day. I'm glad it's your job now, not mine."

"Yeah, you must be happy to have palmed this off on us."

I leaned around Derwent, who was obviously not planning to introduce me. "Maeve Kerrigan."

"Nice to meet you." There was more genuine warmth in the polite smile he gave me than I'd had from Derwent all day. We were about the same age as well as the same rank, but Cowell seemed relaxed at the prospect of briefing two strange officers, one of them an inspector. I doubted I would have been as confident. "Sorry it's just me. My skipper was planning to be here but he got held up."

"As long as you've got a key, we'll be all right."

"Not just one key." He held up a bunch. "Wait until you see this."

The door to the street didn't present too much of an obstacle. One simple Yale lock was all that had stood between Ivan Tremlett's building and the world outside. I followed Derwent and Cowell up the narrow, dingy stairs to the first floor and stopped on the small landing outside Tremlett's rooms. "There are offices on the top floor, but they're vacant," Cowell explained, as he sorted through the bunch of keys he held.

"This is more like it," Derwent said.

"Yeah, these are serious locks with security keys, not standard ones. There are bolts on the other side of the door. The landlord fitted the front-door lock, but Ivan Tremlett took care of this lot."

"Everything but a barricade," I commented. There was no sign on the door, no company branding. It was entirely anonymous and discreet, apart from the CCTV camera mounted above the door and the shiny polished locks at regularly spaced intervals. No letterbox. No peephole. No communication with the outside world.

"You get the feeling Tremlett spent a lot of time looking over his shoulder," Derwent said.

"Understandably." I pointed at the camera. "I take it that wasn't any use."

Cowell looked up to where I was pointing. "It's a live feed that goes to a website, not a TV. Tremlett had it up on one of his computers so he could see what was happening outside his door if he heard any strange noises. The signal is encrypted so only Tremlett could see it—not even the people who run the website had access to the images and they were real-time only. Nothing was recorded. We weren't able to recover anything."

"And we don't have the least idea how the killer persuaded him to bypass his own security to let him in. Speaking of which . . ." Derwent shouldered past Cowell as the door swung open, keen to get inside. Amused rather than offended, Cowell tilted his head at me, standing back to let me follow the inspector. I rolled my eyes while Derwent was safely preoccupied and Cowell had to turn a snort of amusement into a not wholly convincing cough.

Going through the door myself, I went slowly, wary of stepping somewhere I shouldn't after the frankly hazardous situation in Barry Palmer's home. Here at least the room had been clean to start with. There was nothing but the slightest taint of blood in the air. My nose wrinkled anyway. There were times when I could have wished for a less sensitive sense of smell.

The first room was a small reception area with one window to the street. It was almost unfurnished, with just an armchair in the corner. He wouldn't have needed a reception desk when there were no visitors, but it looked strange all the same. The armchair was old, the upholstery rubbed and faded. It was altogether too domestic for the setting, which was bland in the extreme. The floor was carpeted with cheap, flimsy dark-gray tiles. Forensics had lifted a handful of them for further examination. Underneath, a patch of floorboards made of unvarnished pine had absorbed blood, long trails of it that had dripped between the carpet tiles in a geometric pattern. Ivan Tremlett's blood.

"We think he was beaten here," Cowell said. "The blood's from relatively minor injuries. That's why there's not a lot of it."

"The floor's been photographed and the blood should be dry." Derwent was watching me with a sardonic expression. "Don't worry about it."

"Better safe than sorry." There was no way on earth I was walking on the stains if I could avoid it, even if they had dried out. The thought made my stomach heave again.

"This is where he took his breaks—ate, drank, catnapped in the chair.

His wife said he was fanatical about keeping food and liquids out of his office because of the potential damage a spill could do to the computers." With one sweep of a long arm, Cowell drew our attention to a bin in the corner, behind the chair. "We found an empty paper cup, some used paper napkins and a bag from the coffee shop down the street. It seems that it was Tremlett's routine to buy a bacon roll and a coffee every morning, and a sandwich for his lunch. He usually didn't leave again until the end of the day. Looks as if he'd had both meals when he was killed."

"The PM will confirm it," Derwent said.

"Do we know when that will be?" I asked.

"Sometime today." He looked at his watch. "Might have happened already. Godley wanted Glen Hanshaw to do it as well as Palmer's so we're waiting for him to get round to it."

I didn't know how Dr. Hanshaw managed to keep on top of his job. There was always another body, another crime scene to attend, another post-mortem with its attendant report, another conference with the officers in the case, another appearance as an expert witness in court. He was scalpel-sharp, completely in command of his material, and rarely wrong. With all of that, it didn't matter much that he wasn't actually likable, at least as far as I was concerned. Godley got on well with him, though. And he, like me, would have been annoyed to hear Derwent speak of the pathologist in such an offhand manner, especially in front of two junior officers. I didn't quite have the nerve to tell him off, settling instead for saying, "He's reliable. And quick."

Derwent grunted. "Needs to be." He patted the back of the armchair. "So this was Tremlett's canteen. Lovely."

I pulled a face. "This is pretty bleak."

"It sure is. And loud."

Below us, the machines from the laundrette churned, a reassuring sound in other circumstances. The street was busy with a car or a van passing every few seconds. The narrow carriageway didn't help as drivers had to wait to drive forward, their engines running noisily. An occasional road-rage spat with raised voices and beeping horns added a touch of variety.

"You'd tune out most of that," I said. "You'd get used to it. They're regular sounds, mostly."

"He had air-conditioning on as well." Cowell flipped on the light switch for the room next door and a low hum started up, a fan set to come on automatically with the lights. "Everything's climate-controlled."

Derwent nodded. "It's good for the computers, but I'd say Ivan Tremlett liked control anyway. Let's have a look at where he chose to spend his days."

Cowell pushed open the door to the computer room. I braced myself, expecting to see horror. In fact, it was not as gut-wrenching as I had imagined. The room had been dismantled in large part, the crime-scene technicians having taken the computers that had sat on the narrow, custom-made table that ran around the edge of the room, leaving only dusty marks to show where they had once been. The table itself was cloudy with black fingerprint powder. Aside from that, most of the surfaces were smeared with brownish swirls of dried blood. The middle of the small room was empty apart from another great wavering bloodstain in the middle of the floor.

"I'm surprised it didn't leak through to the ceiling below."

"I've seen that before. Down through the light-fittings and drip-drip-drip, someone gets a nasty shock." Derwent laughed. "That's why I'd never live anywhere but the top floor if I had to live in a flat."

"It never occurred to me to worry about that."

My new flat was on the ground floor. It was annoying enough to have to keep the windows closed and locked all the time. Cascading body fluids would be a new low, even for me, and I had lived in some ropey places.

"There was a chair here—on castors, so he could move around his work station. He was tied to it when the uniforms broke in."

"What was he tied with?"

"Plastic ties."

Unbreakable and untraceable, they were the restraint of choice for professional criminals, and bad news for us. No fibers to compare, no ends of rope to analyze, no sticky tape to capture a partial print, a hair, a dab of DNA. Criminals weren't all stupid, unfortunately.

Cowell gestured around him. "The killer or killers started off with the computers, by the looks of things. Smashed them up, pulled out their innards."

"Standard stuff to intimidate your subject."

"And take away his livelihood," I pointed out. "These are the tools of his trade. Without them, he can't earn anything."

That was the sort of thing that would put a man under pressure. Especially if, like Ivan Tremlett, he had built up an income out of nothing. Not a small income, either, Derwent had said.

"It was top-of-the-range technology. Expensive vandalism. Once they'd worked through that, they started on him."

I winced. "I'm almost afraid to ask."

"Bruises. A few teeth knocked out. Broken fingers and toes."

I looked across at Derwent. "That sounds like a lower level of violence than Palmer. Broken bones are a definite step down from amputations."

Derwent shrugged. "Maybe he told the killer whatever he wanted to know a bit quicker than Palmer did. I'd have talked, God knows."

I didn't know what I would have done and I hoped never to find out, but I suspected I would have given in at the first hint of violence. At my school the library had a vast collection of lurid religious comics retelling the lives of the saints, the gorier the better as far as the nuns were concerned. I was brought up on illustrated tales of women martyred for their faith—St. Agnes, beheaded at thirteen in order to remain chaste; St. Catherine, bound to a spiked wheel and tortured. I had been uneasily aware at the time that I wasn't cut out for sainthood. And sex had never seemed like such a terrible fate if the alternative was beheading. "How did he die?"

"His throat was cut."

"That explains all the blood."

Derwent was roaming the small space, poking at things with a gloved finger. "You've forgotten one detail, haven't you? DI Lawlor told me about his eyes."

"What happened to his eyes?"

Cowell looked at me apologetically. "They were gouged out."

"Like St. Lucy," I murmured, distracted by the long-suppressed memory of a particularly graphic and literal illustration of bloody eyeballs rolling around on a silver plate. She had never been my favorite.

"What?" Derwent swung round, staring at me uncomprehendingly.

"Nothing." I gathered my straying thoughts. "Before or after he died?"

Cowell shrugged. "Sorry, I don't know."

"Does it matter?" Derwent demanded.

"I don't know. Well, actually, yes I do know. If it was when he was alive, it was a way of punishing him. If he was dead, it was meant as a message for someone else. A warning for other pedophiles, maybe."

"I'd prefer it if you didn't refer to my husband by that word." The voice was pure ice and came from the outer room. I jumped, shocked, and Derwent spun around fast.

The woman who'd spoken came forward to stand in the doorway. Her eyes were fixed on the bloodstained floor, and her face was pale. Claudia Tremlett, the victim's wife, tall and lovely as an arum lily.

"Mrs. Tremlett. I'm DI Derwent and this is my colleague, DC Kerrigan. We're investigating your husband's murder." Derwent's tone was considerably more solicitous than it had been when he was dealing with the Gordons, but then Claudia Tremlett was a cut above, socially. She was attractive too, and I was learning that Derwent was susceptible to that, if not to issues of class. She was unusually tall, about the same height as me. Fair, with high cheekbones, she would have looked ravishing if she'd had some color in her face other than the raw redness around her eyes. Like Vera Gordon, she had evidently been crying that day, but that was where the resemblance ended. Vera's thin London accent with its mangled consonants didn't bear comparison to Claudia's well-modulated tones and even in her youth Vera wouldn't have been more than faintly pretty.

DI Derwent hadn't finished groveling. "I'm sorry if you were offended by DC Kerrigan's choice of words."

That was big of him. I glared. *I can make my own apologies, thanks.*

"I just don't want you to see Ivan as that. He wasn't that. He was so much more," she replied softly.

"I'm sure he was." *There, there.* "We were going to come and see you once we'd finished here."

"Yes, I thought someone might come. I'm glad I met you here instead. I wouldn't have liked to talk to you about it in the house. It's my home. *Our* home. I want to keep it as a place of refuge, not somewhere I can't stay because of the bad memories. I'm sorry to say that a police interview would count as a bad memory."

I could understand what she meant—I might have felt the same way myself. But there would have to be a search at some stage so that we could look through Ivan Tremlett's belongings. It was intrusive, a sort of official burglary, and I hoped we could persuade her to leave the house for the duration. We were experts at putting things back where we'd found them; she need never know how thorough we'd been.

Claudia looked past Derwent, craning her neck to take in every detail of the room, just as we had. "I wanted to see where he died. I was just going to drive past, but then I saw the light was on."

"Did you visit your husband here often?"

"I've never been here before." She must have seen the look of surprise on my face. "Ivan kept his two worlds totally separate. He didn't work at home. He didn't have anything from home in his office. That included me and the children."

"How many children?"

"Three. All boys. Four, seven and nine." Her face crumpled. "They keep asking me when Daddy will be home."

"That must be very difficult," I said quietly, knowing that nothing we could say would be of comfort to her.

"Just give me a minute." She turned away, dropping her face into her hands. It was a pose that would have looked melodramatic had it not seemed so natural to her. I wondered if she'd ever been a model. There was a studied grace to her movements, but she was too tall to have been a dancer.

While Claudia Tremlett was distracted, DC Cowell seized the opportunity to flee. "That's all I know, basically. If there's anything else . . ."

"We'll be in touch," Derwent finished for him. Cowell handed him the keys and nodded to me before slipping through the door, and I listened with pure, uncomplicated envy as he ran down the stairs and slammed the door behind him. Escape was a good idea. There was nothing like speaking to grieving relatives to make you feel grimy in your soul. Especially when the questions you had to ask were far from easy.

With a sniff and a shake of her shoulder-length hair, Mrs. Tremlett announced herself as ready to be interviewed. Derwent surprised me by showing a degree of sensitivity as he steered her out of the ransacked office and through the dismal reception area.

"Let's talk out here in the hall, if you don't mind."

She looked around, at a loss. "There's nowhere to sit."

There was nowhere in her husband's office either apart from his greasy old armchair, but I had enough tact not to point that out.

"You could sit on the windowsill. I'll be okay here." As I spoke, I perched on the third-from-bottom step of the stairs that led to the second floor.

"And I'm happy to stand." Derwent shoved his hands in his pockets and leaned against the wall, the picture of barely tempered masculinity. I was meanly pleased that she hardly glanced at him as she brushed dust off the ledge, meticulous even in her distress. She was wearing pale gray jeans and a denim shirt that occasionally slid off one narrow shoulder. It was carelessly sexy in an unforced, unconscious way and I wondered what Ivan Tremlett had been like in life—how charismatic he would have to have been to marry and keep the aristocratic lovely in front of me, even without the criminal conviction.

Derwent must have been wondering the same thing. "Did you love your husband, Mrs. Tremlett?"

If he'd been hoping to wrongfoot her, he failed. She met his gaze unwaveringly. "Yes. Of course I did."

"You never thought twice about your marriage? Even with the fact that he pleaded guilty to downloading illegal images of child abuse?"

"I didn't say that." She drew in a breath and let it out slowly; I recognized it as a trick she had probably learned from a therapist, a means of easing tension and focusing her thoughts. Derwent was going to find it hard to shake her if she insisted on taking her time before answering his questions. "I had a difficult time when Ivan was being investigated. Of course I did. But we talked about it, and we had counseling, and our marriage was stronger afterward."

"After he came out of prison."

"Yes."

"How did he find it?"

"It wasn't a holiday. But he was well treated. He was able to teach computer skills to some of the long-term inmates, so they respected him. He was worried, of course, that he would be a target for abuse because of his conviction, but they left him alone. They believed that he hadn't done it, as did I."

"That was my next question. How did you convince yourself he was innocent when he pleaded guilty?"

"He was advised to plead guilty because it looked, on the face of it, as if he'd downloaded hundreds of images to his work account. But it was a set-up. One of his subordinates wanted his job and framed him. She had access to his password because she used to do bits and pieces for him when he was out of the office. She logged in as him—pretended to be him in chat rooms and forums that were about child abuse. She left a trail all over the Internet. It was easy for the police to follow it once they were tipped off. Ivan said that if it had been him, he would at least have made a token effort to cover his tracks, but no one listened—not the company, not the police, not the CPS. And that bitch got his job when he was kicked out, so she was happy." Claudia was flushed now, her eyes glittering as she spat out the last sentence.

"Presumably you couldn't prove any of this." Derwent sounded dubious.

"She was too careful, Ivan couldn't get anything on her. And the managing director flatly refused to believe she had been responsible. I found it hard too. I'd met her a couple of times—she'd come to dinner in our house. She even rang me after the conviction to tell me how sorry she was for me.

As if I wanted her pity." She shook her head. "Ivan trusted her and so did I. That was the only mistake we made and it's cost us everything."

"Why didn't your husband fight the case?" he asked.

"Our solicitor was totally incompetent. She told Ivan the evidence was damning and his explanation wouldn't hold up in court. She said that if he pleaded guilty at the first opportunity he'd get a reduced sentence—maybe even a suspended sentence. She said there wouldn't be any long-term consequences if we got it all over with quickly. So Ivan pleaded guilty and got eighteen months, although he served only half of it. Then he got out and no one was interested in employing him. No one would return his calls. His career was dead. But Ivan never gave up. My father lent him the money to set up on his own and he worked tirelessly to pay it back. Gradually, he made something of this." She gestured at the door that hid her husband's office from view. "It doesn't look like much, but he was doing well. He was clever. Too clever to work for other people, actually. He was better off on his own."

It sounded to me as if he had been a difficult employee. It also sounded as if he had been guilty. The story about his subordinate didn't ring true to me any more than it had to his managing director, and I didn't even know the girl. People did tend to assume they were invisible on the Internet. Even the technologically sophisticated like Ivan Tremlett could underestimate how easy it was to trace them, to follow their progress into the dark places where horrors were shared and sold, and to prove it in court. And thank God they did make that mistake, because it made our job that much easier.

"He was quite devoted to his routine, by all accounts." I kept my voice gentle, a counterpoint to Derwent's head-on approach. "Was that why you became concerned yesterday evening?"

"He was like clockwork. You could plan your day around him. I did, actually." She gave a little laugh. "The boys had their tea when he came home. We both thought it was important for them to spend time with us, so we would sit at the table with them and talk while they ate."

"Was he good with them?"

She was on her guard immediately, staring at Derwent with hostile eyes. "What's that supposed to mean?"

"Just that he had this place so he could get away from the boys, didn't he? Did he find them annoying?"

"From time to time. When he was trying to concentrate." Her body slackened, the tension leaving it slowly. But I thought she knew, as I did, that Derwent's question about Ivan Tremlett's relationship with his sons had been a pointed one. I wondered if she had trusted him enough to leave him alone with them, and the next thing she said answered that question neatly.

"My mother lives with us. There's a granny flat in the basement. She moved in when Ivan was arrested and she's never left."

"What does your father make of that?"

She looked uncomprehending. "Why should he care? Oh—I see. You couldn't have known. They're divorced. They split when I was eight. Both of them married again, then both of them got divorced again. Dad's on wife number three but Mum never bothered with meeting anyone else. She said two failed marriages were enough."

"Are you an only child?" I asked.

"Sort of. I have four half-siblings from Dad's other marriages, but I was Mum's only child."

"The two of you must be close."

"We are. Very." Her face softened. "It's wonderful for me and the boys, having her so close. They adore her."

"What did your husband think of the arrangement? It's not every man who'd be pleased to find his mother-in-law had moved into his house while his back was turned." Derwent again, characteristically direct.

"He didn't complain." That didn't mean he'd liked it, and Claudia didn't go so far as to pretend he had. "The flat is self-contained. She doesn't impose on us. Ivan had enough sense to know that it was a good thing, having her there. She minds the boys when I can't, so it took the pressure off him."

There was no way to ask it delicately, so Derwent didn't even try. "Did your mother think he was guilty?"

She stiffened. "We never discussed it."

"Strange, isn't it? Not to talk about it? Was that because you didn't want to hear what she thought?"

Instead of taking offense, Claudia tilted her head to one side, considering it. Another benefit of counseling, I presumed. She analyzed the idea he had presented to her rather than responding emotionally. "It might have been because I didn't want to argue with her. Or it might have been because she didn't think he was to blame, and she knew I didn't think he was guilty, so there was no point in talking about it when we both felt the same way."

"First option's more likely, isn't it? If you were determined to keep him as your husband, the best she could do was make sure he wasn't left alone with the children."

Tears filled the blue eyes, but they didn't waver from Derwent's face. "You could put that interpretation on it, I suppose. But that's not how I saw it."

"Didn't you ever think he might be guilty? Even for a minute?"

Once again, she was startlingly honest in her response. "I didn't allow myself to think he might be guilty. I didn't want him to be and he said he wasn't, so I never considered the alternative. I loved my husband very much. I mean, he gave me three beautiful sons, and they're the most important things in my life. I didn't want our marriage to end because I didn't want them to have to struggle as I had when I was a child. The best thing I could offer them was the stability of having Mummy and Daddy there, for as much of the time as we could manage. We never argued. We never even raised our voices to one another. Everything was so civilized." She bit her lip. "Maybe too civilized. Maybe we should have been more confrontational with one another. Then I could tell you that we'd argued, that I'd wanted him to leave, but he'd convinced me he was innocent, and you'd believe me."

"It doesn't really matter what we believe," I said gently. I'd never been in that situation. I couldn't judge her for what she'd done, but I was glad beyond words that her mother had taken on the role of unofficial bodyguard for their sons. "What matters is that it looks to us as if someone else thought he was guilty and punished him for it. We obviously need to find out who killed him and why, and we're working on the theory that it was someone who'd identified him as having a conviction for child sex crimes."

"Was there any other reason that you can think why someone would have wanted to harm your husband?" Derwent asked.

"No."

"Did he keep secrets from you, do you think?"

"I don't think he had any. He worked, or he was at home. He didn't go out without me, apart from coming here. And I know he was working while he was here because I organize his accounts. He kept a log of work done that accounted for every fifteen minutes of his day. He was meticulous about keeping it, and the invoices always matched up. His clients wouldn't have paid him for work he hadn't done, so I assumed he was here when he said he was, and he was working when he was here." She must have seen the matching expressions on our faces because her chin went up. "I did check it. I wanted to be sure that he was making a go of the business, for Dad's sake.

I wanted to trust him but I couldn't quite, after what happened. I hadn't been able to up to now, anyway. My therapist has been working with me on having faith in others, and I really have been trying. But it's hard."

It wasn't remotely surprising that Claudia Tremlett found it hard to take people at their word. The fact that she thought that was *her* problem, for which she required therapy, confirmed for me that her poise and beauty masked rampant insecurity.

"Did anyone know about Ivan's conviction?" Derwent asked. "I presume your friends and family would have been aware of it."

"We didn't exactly mention it in our Christmas cards," Claudia said spikily, but then relented. "Most people thought he'd had a nervous break-down. I just said that he'd gone away for a while—that he'd left his job in stressful circumstances, and that I was worried about him, but I hoped he'd be back to his usual self soon. The family knew, but I'm not close to my half-siblings. They're all a lot younger than me. I doubt they would have cared to talk about it."

"Did any of your neighbors seem aware of it? Anyone look at you oddly—keep their children away from yours, that kind of thing?"

She smiled slightly. "This is London, DI Derwent. No one knows any-one. The boys go to a private prep school a couple of miles away rather than the local primary, so they don't really interact with our neighbors' children. I haven't noticed anyone being especially odd, but they're not what I'd call friendly. But that's just how people are around here. I don't think we were singled out because of Ivan."

"Did Ivan seem particularly preoccupied in the last while? Was he sleep-ing okay, do you know? Did he seem concerned about his personal safety?"

"There was nothing different about him." She gestured to the door. "He was always concerned about his security, but he was more bothered about the business than about himself."

"So as far as you're aware, he had no warning."

"Nothing." She gave a long, quavering sigh. "I thought things were get-ting back to normal. But things will never be normal now. I've already had a couple of phone calls from reporters asking about Ivan, about his past. Everyone will know. We'll have to move again. And I don't know what I'm going to tell the boys."

This time, she didn't cry. I had a slight suspicion that life would be easier without her husband around. Maybe Claudia was coming to that conclu-sion too. She stood up and brushed off the seat of her jeans. It wasn't too fanciful to see it as wiping away all traces of the office building. I hoped she could walk away and not look back. She deserved to leave her husband's mistakes behind her. And if she could think about him without bitterness— well, so much the better for her. It was beyond me, but I'd worked on child pornography cases; I'd seen it for myself. I didn't need to imagine the kind of images Ivan Tremlett had downloaded. Nor did I need to imagine what kind of person would be titillated by them. It was a crime for a reason. There was a certain satisfaction in knowing how thoroughly he had been punished.

Damn. That was worryingly close to how the killer seemed to feel. It had been too long a day, I thought, as I said good-bye to Claudia Tremlett and watched Derwent lock up after us. It was time to go home.

The inspector, naturally, had other ideas. "Get a move on, Kerrigan. The traffic is going to be shite all the way back into town. We need to get going."

I fell into step behind him. My feet were aching, my neck hurt and I could barely think straight, but I didn't dare opt out. "Where are we headed?"

"Back to the nick. I want to brief Superintendent Godley before the close of business. You might as well come too. Someone has to read through the files on Palmer and Tremlett and it's not going to be me."

The files would be dense, the material contained in them would be up-setting, and it wasn't really fair of Derwent to palm the lot off on me. But that wasn't why I went down the stairs slowly, painfully, as if my shoes were soled with lead. Bad though spending the day with Derwent had been and grim the things I'd seen and heard, I would happily have done another twelve hours of it rather than spend any time at all in the office. There was unfinished business there—business I didn't want to finish. Business I didn't even want to think about.

But then, maybe I would be lucky. Maybe I wouldn't have to deal with it today. It was getting late. Most people would have gone home already. I made the most of a tiny burst of energy generated by wishful thinking and hurried across the road after Derwent. I couldn't help thinking that maybe everything was going to be all right.

I really should have known better.

Chapter Four

As it turned out, we needn't have rushed back. The superintendent was in a meeting that dragged on into the evening, a meeting that involved several senior officers and DI Bryce at Godley's side. The other officers were so senior that I had never seen them in person before, just in pictures on the Met website. Something big was going on and, whatever it was, Godley wasn't pleased about it. On the rare occasions when the door to his office was open, I had a grandstand view of him from my desk. His expression was that of a man under intense strain, with lines entrenched across his forehead and around his mouth. I had never seen him look like that, even at the height of the hunt for an active serial killer. The media had turned on him like dogs running wild and still I hadn't ever seen him look upset. Tired, yes. But not hunted, as he was now.

On the bright side, the delay meant I had plenty of time to get very familiar indeed with the details of the murdered men's files. The transcripts of the interviews with the two girls in Palmer's case showed that their evidence was contradictory and confused, as Derwent and Vera Gordon had said. It was hard, though, to fault the CPS for proceeding. Children were not usually good witnesses, especially about something as traumatic as sexual abuse. They were likely to blur the outlines of the truth, to agree too readily with suggestions from those interviewing them, to forget key details from one interview to the next. So you could spin it both ways. Either they were lying deliberately, or they were too upset to remember accurately. If they were lying, there was something depressingly plausible about the details of their accounts; the conclusion was inescapable that they had done the things they described, even if it wasn't with Barry Palmer. That lent them credibility even though their stories were weak in places. They didn't have to be accurate for them to be telling the truth, and the jury had believed them. I tried to shake off the creeping gloom that was starting to affect me. It wasn't up to me to retry the case following the death of the defendant, I reminded myself. Guilty or not, he had been singled out as a child molester and that had probably sealed his fate. But whether or not he was obviously, rampantly guilty, wasn't the issue here. What I thought of him mattered not at all. He had been murdered, and it was up to us to find out who did it.

A whiff of bullshit permeated the statements from Ivan Tremlett; without surprise, I found myself on the side of law and order. Tremlett had constructed an elaborate conspiracy to explain the images in his files, but the investigating officer had been meticulous, compiling spreadsheets to prove that the images had been downloaded at times that Ivan Tremlett had been working. The time stamps showed that he had sometimes gone looking for images between writing e-mails, as if he had needed a break, or felt he deserved a treat. He had over a thousand images squirrelled away in various corners, password-protected and disguised as innocent, personal files. That hadn't happened by accident. And I found it hard to believe it had been the work of his junior colleague, a young woman who gave a warm statement in support of him *after* he had accused her of tampering with his files. If she was trying to manipulate his employers to turn against him, as Claudia had suggested, she was playing a very long game indeed.

Halfway through the Tremlett file, Derwent walked past me and whistled to attract my attention as he threw an envelope onto my desk. "Hanshaw's autopsy reports. Thought you might want to look at them." He walked backward for a couple of paces, the better to see my face when he added, "I haven't looked at them, so just give me the main points when you get the chance."

Autopsy reports were probably my least favorite form of reading; I skimmed through them trying not to think about what I was supposed to be taking in. The sheer scale of the violence floored me. The injuries Dr. Hanshaw had listed for the two men ran into three figures—some of them very minor, some of them catastrophic. Torn muscles, broken bones, bruises and cuts, stab wounds, amputations and rough excisions—the words brought back the images I had tried to suppress from Barry Palmer's house, and conjured up images I never wanted to see from Ivan Tremlett's office. I put the files to one side and stared across the office at Godley's door, wishing dully that he would wrap up his meeting so that I could go home.

"So this is what you're up to. Watching the remake of *Twelve Angry Men*. Shame they had to slash the budget. *Five Angry Men* doesn't have quite the same ring to it."

In spite of everything, my first reaction at hearing Rob's voice was pleasure. "Hey, watch it. You're behind the times. In the modern-day Metropolitan Police Service, it would be *Five Angry Individuals*. You can't exclude the possibility that a woman *could* have a role."

"I'm not sure we'd get away with calling them angry, either. *Five Individuals with Different but Equally Valid Opinions*."

"That sounds about right." I leaned back in my chair to look up at him. He was unusually tidy in a dark suit. "What are you doing here so late?"

"Cleaning up a mess."

"What kind of mess?"

He shook his head. "I'll tell you another time."

Too many people around, I presumed. Someone had cocked up and it had fallen to Rob to sort it out. DC Rob Langton was that sort of police officer, diplomatic when he needed to be, clever without needing to shout about it, tough enough when that was called for. The mess—whatever it was—wouldn't harm his career. He had the useful knack of walking away from disastrous situations with his reputation not only intact, but enhanced. I wished I had some of his skill and more of his luck.

"What's this?" He was looking at the stack of files on my desk.

"My latest dream job." I lowered my voice. "Have you had any dealings with Derwent?"

"No. What's he like?"

"I'll tell you another time," I said, echoing him deliberately.

"I'll look forward to it." He started to walk toward his own desk but stopped and turned back, leaning down so no one could overhear. "Since we have so much to say to one another, do you want to get something to eat later?"

"Do you think that's a good idea?"

"I'm suggesting we have dinner, Maeve. I haven't seen much of you for a couple of months but I presume you still eat."

"There's no need to be sarcastic." I started reorganizing the things on my desk so I didn't have to look at him. "It's just that it's late and I don't know when I'm going to be free." *And, as you've reminded me, I've been avoiding you for two months for a reason.*

"I'll wait."

"You don't have to."

"I know."

Impasse. "Look, I can't go out anyway. Dec is coming over with the last of my stuff."

"The poor bugger. He spends his life shifting boxes of your belongings from house to house. How long did you stay in the last place? Six weeks?"

"Nine. And if you're trying to imply I have commitment issues, think again," I said, unruffled. "I only moved because the plumbing went disastrously wrong. I liked that flat until raw sewage started bubbling up through the bath drain."

"That would tend to change your mind about a place. Still, seems hard on your brother to have to do this every couple of months."

"Declan doesn't mind. Well, strictly speaking he does, but Mum makes him do it anyway."

"How is your mum?"

"How long have you got?"

"All evening." It was neatly done, I acknowledged. Rob pressed home his advantage. "We don't have to go out. We can eat at yours."

"I'm not cooking."

"No, you are not." He shuddered. "Never again."

"I never said I was good at it." I had only once cooked a meal for Rob. Vegetable lasagne. The sauce was watery, the vegetables unrecognizable slime. The pasta had the consistency of roofing felt. The cheese had blackened in the oven and set like tarmac. We had abandoned the attempt at eating it halfway through—in favor of doing something that I *was* good at, I recalled, at roughly the same time that Rob remembered too. A slow smile lit up his face and I couldn't help laughing at him, because however much I wished we had kept things between us simple and professional, there had been times when the complications were so worthwhile.

"Anyway, so we're clear on who's doing what, you're supplying the venue. I'll sort out the food."

"I'm not altogether sure that the venue has adequate facilities, by which I mean I don't know if I've got plates. Or cutlery, if it comes to that."

"Then we can have sandwiches." He shook his head. "I can't wait to hear what excuse you come up with next."

"For the record, I still don't think it's a good idea."

"Just because you can't trust yourself to be alone with me."

"I am quite capable of resisting your charms."

"Prove it."

"Nine o'clock. Dec should have been and gone by then." I blushed when I heard how that sounded. "Not because I want us to be alone. Just because I don't want him to tell Mum about you."

"Understood."

"You are not going to be able to believe how much I can resist you, by the way. You're invited for food. That means you eat and leave."

"I expected nothing more."

"Right. Well. I'll see you at nine."

"On the dot." He walked away and I looked around the office with a carefully contrived neutral expression on my face, checking that no one had noticed the little scene. The only person who was looking in our direction was Liv Bowen, the newest detective on the team and the only other female. She blew her fringe out of her eyes and gave me a meaningless smile, which I returned.

Somehow, I hadn't got around to having a conversation with DC Bowen yet. She was quite beautiful, with flawless skin and a delicate oval face. She wore her hair long, but kept it knotted at the nape of her neck. She had a dancer's body, graceful but strong, and looked like anything but a police officer. If I struggled to be taken seriously, it had to be ten times worse for her. She had come to the team from an intelligence job in Special Branch, and there was plenty of speculation about whether she'd be able to cope with the work on a serious crimes squad that specialized in murder. There were also, I happened to know, more than a few rumors about her private life. I could guess the team had said much the same about me when I joined, but I didn't know the details and I would never make the mistake of asking. My height would have made it hard for me to fade into the background even if I'd wanted to, but I tried not to draw too much attention to myself. I wore shapeless suits to work and rarely bothered with more than the bare minimum of makeup. Liv Bowen didn't seem to wear any makeup at all, but then she didn't need it. And she didn't need my support if she was going to make her way in Godley's team, I told myself.

As I was thinking that, she stood up and went over to where Rob was sitting, showing him a piece of paper. As she leaned over him, she said something that made him laugh. I swallowed. They were working together on whatever case Rob was dealing with; they had to talk, whether I liked it or not. And I did not like it, I admitted to myself. I did not like it at all.

The door to Godley's office opened and the three senior officers filed out, followed by Bryce who was looking even more gloomy than usual. The superintendent stayed at his desk, writing something on a sheet of paper. That in itself was unusual; I couldn't recall the last time he had let a visitor to his room make their own way to the door. His manners were impeccable, as a rule, and I wondered what had made him forget himself to the extent that he didn't bother making an effort with the three men who had the most potential to influence his career.

"Give him five minutes and then we'll go in, okay?" Derwent, leaning over the back of my seat, hot breath in my ear as he spoke. I resisted the urge to push back my chair at speed, settling for imagining the impact, the choking cough from behind me, the inspector lying on the floor, clutching his bits, moaning softly . . . which reminded me of Barry Palmer. Amusement seeped away, leaving shame and a little irritation in its place. But then, I couldn't be good all the time. And I would be using up my quota of goodness—and more—during my evening with Rob. It wasn't going to be easy to be on my best behavior.

Rob's back was turned to me and while I was waiting to be summoned, I allowed myself the luxury of a minute spent studying the line of his shoulders, the fingers of one hand drumming a rhythm on his thigh as he worked, the neat shape of his dark head. What had been between us before Christmas hadn't disappeared in the gray light of January, when I had called a halt. The feelings were still there, if I chose to indulge them.

But I would be strong. Head over heart. I had made the right decision and there was no going back. I shifted in my chair, suddenly fidgety, and forced myself to look away. In doing so, I met Liv Bowen's gaze again. This time, I was the one who tried a smile, and earned a long, cool look in return that made the color rise in my cheeks.

"We're up." Derwent headed into Godley's office without waiting for me and I scrambled to collect my papers and follow him. The DI was making a habit of leaving me behind.

I stepped into Godley's office in time to hear him snap, "Just make it quick, all right? I've got to go."

Derwent nodded, looking unruffled, but I had never heard the superintendent speak that way before and I was glad that Derwent took the lead, explaining where we were with the investigation. The boss listened with his head turned slightly away and his eyes focused on the floor. When Derwent had finished, Godley looked up.

"So what's your gut instinct on this one, Josh? Are there going to be more bodies?"

"I'd assume so. Without knowing what our killer wants we can't be sure why he's killing, but I don't see any reason for him to stop at two. If it's someone who fancies themselves as a vigilante, cleaning up the streets, he's got a way to go before he gets rid of every known child abuser in South London. The same goes if it's someone who gets a kick out of killing pedos—maybe an ex-con who wanted to deal with them inside but couldn't get close enough."

"Were Barry Palmer and Ivan Tremlett ever in custody in the same prison?"

I could answer that one. "No. Tremlett did his time on Sheppey." It was a small, somewhat bleak island connected to the Kent coast by bridge—the perfect place to site three prisons, according to the powers-that-be. "Palmer was bounced around the place a bit. He didn't have family so he was easy to shift to another prison when the facility he was in got overcrowded. He spent a fair bit of his sentence in the Midlands, a chunk of it in Yorkshire and the last bit in Portsmouth."

"Difficult to find out if anyone had been in prison with both men," Godley commented.

"Impossible, I'd have said. Not with the way Palmer was shuffled around over his sentence. You'd have to get a list of everyone that was in Tremlett's prison over the course of his time in custody and find out where else they'd been, and where they are now, and even then you'd never prove they'd actually met the victims." Derwent shook his head. "I'm as much a fan of hard work as you are, but I don't think we'll find the killer that way."

"Well, what can we rule out? Is he doing this for fun?"

"No." The two men looked at me, waiting for me to justify what I'd said. My "no" had been instinctive and unequivocal and I took a second to organize my thoughts. An idea was beginning to develop from the confusion of facts swirling in my brain. "The violence in these two murders is extreme, but it's focused. The men have injuries consistent with being interrogated—their autopsy reports read like an Amnesty International briefing document on torture. I think our killer wants to know something, very badly, and he didn't find it out from Barry Palmer. He might have heard more from Tremlett, but then again he might not—we won't know for a day or two at least."

"Until we find another body, I presume." Godley's expression was grim.

Derwent shook his head. "No torture manual that I've ever read includes cutting off someone's wedding tackle. He would have been useless for information after that, I'd bet. Unconscious from pain, probably."

"Yeah, I don't actually think that was part of the torture," I said tentatively.

"Do you think the killer is sadistic?" Godley asked.

"No. Although I do think he's getting a certain satisfaction from the violence, I don't see it as a sexual kink. I think it's punishment. He's tailoring it to fit their crimes." I flipped through the autopsy reports. "Ivan Tremlett's eyes were gouged out. At first, I thought that was because he needed them to work, so blinding him was the physical equivalent of smashing his computers—a fairly drastic final step, but relating to his life now rather than what he did. But then I started to think about his crime. He was a watcher, not a doer. He downloaded images of other people abusing kids—as far as we know, he didn't abuse any himself. He liked to look at children being molested because it excited him, and he was punished for that."

"And Barry Palmer?"

"The girls alleged that his assaults on them had begun with fondling, then escalated to full sex. They were quite specific about what was done to them, although they did change their stories on some of the details like places and times. The killer seems to have known the details of their testimony because he cut off the parts of Barry Palmer that touched the girls, according to their evidence." I held up my hands, forefinger and middle finger extended on the right, forefinger on the left. "These fingers are mentioned specifically in their statements."

"But for him to know that, he has to have access to the police files." There was a short silence after the superintendent had spoken. The implications of that were not appealing. I was fairly sure that everyone in the room had already thought of the possibility that we could be hunting a police officer. There were enough of them who had lost faith in the criminal justice system. There would only need to be one who'd decided to do something about it. And all they would need was a strong stomach. It was Derwent, in the end, who put it into words.

"So our killer's got access to the information we've got. He's got someone on the inside. Or the killer himself is on the inside. He's a copper or maybe a civilian clerical worker. A prison officer who lives locally. A probation officer who is fed up with looking after that sort of client."

"He'd need access to the CRIS reports to get the kind of details Maeve mentioned—the specific allegations that were made against Palmer, for example. That's got to narrow it down." CRIS was the snappy acronym for the Met's Crime Reporting and Incident System, the online archive for crimes committed in the Metropolitan area.

"That would cover police officers and some civilian workers. But don't forget, the killer doesn't have to be one of us. He just has to have access to someone who can search those files," Derwent pointed out.

Godley looked at Derwent and for the first time since I'd walked into the room he seemed fully engaged with the task at hand. "Right. Get on to IT. I want to find out who has requested the file on Barry Palmer since it was created. Ivan Tremlett committed his crime in Kent so the details would be with the local police there, not on CRIS."

"But in Tremlett's case, all the killer needed to know was what he was convicted for. There were no live victims to give evidence because he was just downloading images someone else had created," I pointed out. "He could have got the information he needed from the sex-offenders' register. If he has access to CRIS, he must be able to look at the register, or someone else is doing it on his behalf."

"Or he's relying on local knowledge. It could be someone in one of the police stations in the borough. They'd need to know about pedophiles on their patch, just to keep an eye on them. They'd be aware of Ivan Tremlett's past." Derwent dug in his pocket for chewing gum, offering it around before popping two tablets of it into his mouth. I could smell the mint from where I was sitting on the other side of the room.

Godley turned to me. "Maeve, have a look at the register and see who else is on it. Then we can start thinking about how to warn likely targets."

"Do you really want to draw this to the public's attention?" Derwent asked. "We'll cause a panic. Not because people will be worried about a killer working in their community, but because people will realize they're living cheek by jowl with pedos. We'll have mob justice running riot. Innocent people will be targeted and we'll have a nightmare on our hands. And the local force will be inundated with pointless requests for information now that the Sarah's Law campaigners have got it to apply to this area."

"If you are referring to the Child Sex Offender Disclosure Scheme, it's only available to parents of children who come into regular contact with specific individuals. Interested parties won't be able to use it for a blanket search of the area and the local force should be able to reject most of the requests, if they are indeed pointless," Godley said stiffly.

Derwent looked disgusted. "Don't tell me you think the scheme is a good idea. It's a classic example of wishful thinking. Inviting members of the public to point the finger at random people, on the off-chance they might hit a child molester. If it was that easy to pick out pedophiles, we could just round them up and put them all on an island that has a limited supply of fresh water and a healthy population of visiting sharks."

"The scheme has its limitations, yes. But it makes people feel safer and it may help protect some children." Godley was back to looking tired. He took a second to rub his eyes before he went on. "We do need to control the flow of information on this case, not least because of the possible public reaction. That's why we're going to target individuals who need to be protected. We'll encourage them to leave the area temporarily so that we don't have to worry about protecting them. Anyway, there's a limit to how much we can do. No borough commander is going to lend me people to sit around waiting for a pedophile to be attacked. It would be a waste of manpower and seriously unpopular if it ever came out in the media. Besides, I doubt the potential victims would welcome the attention. The warnings will have to be kept confidential or we'll run the risk of identifying these people as convicted sex offenders, and I want you two to handle it because there's a good chance the leak is local to the borough. We don't want the killer being tipped off about what we're doing."

Derwent stood up and went over to the vast map of London that hung on one wall of Godley's office. "We're going to need to establish what area we're covering. We've currently got two locations roughly a mile apart. We need a third to get some idea of the killer's territory. These two murders . . . the fact that they're so close together geographically might not mean anything at all except that he knew where to find the victims."

Godley winced. "I don't like waiting for another death, Josh. I don't want to feel that someone died because we didn't act quickly enough."

"We don't have a lot of choice. We can't call in help from the locals because we don't trust them. The potential victims don't want us to find them either. They just want to be invisible. And that's not going to assist us. We're looking in the same places as the killer, lifting the same rocks to see what creepy-crawlies scurry away when the light hits them. The only difference is that we don't want to squash them when we find them."

"Picturesque." Godley's face twisted into a smile, almost against his will.

I cleared my throat, feeling slightly awkward at interrupting their love-in. "We need to find out why the killer chose to start with Palmer and Tremlett too. Their crimes were very different and they didn't have much else in common. If we can get a handle on why he picked them, we might be able to work out who's next."

"Good. I like that. Something else to keep in mind."

"That'll be a lot easier if we get another victim," Derwent said, grinning widely as he chomped on his gum. Godley frowned.

"Get on with it, Josh, all right? Stop trying to provoke a reaction and get out of my office." But there was no heat in his voice; he sounded amused, not irritated.

The DI went over to the door and held it open for me. "Come on. Let the boss get on with his evening."

Godley put out a hand. "No. Wait. I want a word with you, Maeve." He looked up. "Thanks, Josh. You can head home. We'll talk tomorrow."

Derwent nodded, his face expressionless, and shut the door behind him. The superintendent and I watched him walk across the office, grab his coat as he passed his desk, and swing out through the double-doors at the end of the room without breaking his stride.

"How are you finding it?"

I looked at Godley, unsure how to answer him. "The case? It's not easy. But it's okay."

"It's a bad case. I know you'll do a good job, though. You're thorough, and that's what this one needs. I wanted you to work on it because I think you'll complement DI Derwent's strengths."

I nodded, trying to hide the doubt I was feeling. Godley narrowed his eyes.

"You're not convinced about him, are you? He's not easy to get to know. But he's decent. I worked with him a few years ago when he was just a DC. When the opening came up in the team after Tom left, he was the first person who came to mind. Keith Bryce was the second. I managed to persuade the bosses to let me have both."

"I'm sure DI Derwent's very good. I'm looking forward to seeing him in action." I couldn't bring myself to say anything nicer about him, but I was beginning to think that was my problem, not anyone else's. Godley had an almost witchlike ability to read minds and rarely made a mistake about people—if he thought that Derwent was worth having around, I'd just have to find a way to get on with him. Besides, if I was finding the inspector hard to manage, I certainly wasn't going to admit it to the boss. Not only would it reflect badly on me, but if Derwent found out I'd complained, he would make my life a living hell.

"He's got a few rough edges. He likes to make people uncomfortable. If he thinks he's managed to annoy you, he'll never leave it alone."

I raised my eyebrows. "Is that a warning?"

"Of sorts. Not that I think you really needed it. I'm sure you know better than I do how to deal with him. I just want you to be aware that you shouldn't take what Josh says at face value, necessarily. He can come across as a boorish thug, but a lot of it is put on to get a reaction."

"I'll put the sexual harassment case on hold, then." I smiled. "Really, I'm not bothered by it. I'm sure we'll get on fine."

"You are very different. You'll put the work in. Josh is more of a big-picture type. Don't let him intimidate you, but don't discount what he says either. He broke a few big jobs over at Central Task Force. He has an uncanny ability to be in the right place at the right time, and he knows his stuff." There was a note of finality in Godley's voice, as if that was the last word to be said about the DI. He stood up. "It's late. You should get home."

I looked at my watch and couldn't suppress a squeak of horror. "Oh my God. I was supposed to be in Crouch End ten minutes ago. My brother will murder me."

"Oh well. At least it'll be an easy one to solve. That sort of case is a bit thin on the ground at the moment." He smiled. "Go. Run. I'm sure he'll forgive you."

I was halfway out the door already. I ransacked my desk, cramming my notes into my bag on the off-chance I got to look at them later, grabbing my phone and texting a rapid, illiterate apology as I hurried out of the office. I had one arm in the sleeve of my raincoat while the other sleeve flapped against my side; I didn't have time to stop and put it on properly. The evening timetable was way off. I had to get home, placate Dec, get rid of Dec, tidy myself up, clean the kitchen, clean the bathroom, tidy the flat and be ready to welcome Rob by nine. No chance. I went through the list of tasks in my head, jettisoning the inessentials as I tip-tapped rapidly down the corridor, the sound of my heels echoing. I didn't really need to clean the bathroom but I should do something about the kitchen sink. The rest of the flat would be untidy anyway because of the unpacked boxes of stuff everywhere—no point in worrying about that. I would have to make time to change the sheets on the bed. And I really, definitely needed to shave my legs.

As I shouldered through the door at the end of the corridor and swung into the stairwell, I was smiling. Focused on where I was going, the need to get there quickly, and hopelessly distracted by my thoughts, the only warning I had was a faint tang of mint in the air that I had barely registered before my arm was caught, and held. Momentum spun me around so I found myself face to face with Derwent before I could do so much as draw breath. Shocked into immobility, I stared into his eyes for an uncomprehending second before my brain started working again. With awareness came a warm jolt of pure anger. I dragged my arm out of his grasp and put one hand to my chest, where my heart was doing its best to batter its way out of my rib cage.

"You scared the *shit* out of me."

"Sorry about that." He didn't sound it. "What were you talking to the boss about?"

No point in prevaricating; he knew as well as I did that he had been the subject of our conversation. He was a senior officer but he wasn't behaving like one and I replied in kind. "Godley wanted to let me know that I shouldn't think you were a total twat, even if you acted like one. I'm paraphrasing," I added.

"Was that all?"

"He said you were a good copper." I waited for a few seconds, taking the opportunity to put my coat on properly. I tied the belt in a knot, pulling it tight. "Now that we both know what the boss thinks of us, can I go? I'm late."

"Yeah." He stepped out of my way and I started to move past him. "Before you go . . . if you have any more bright ideas about this case, I'd like you to share them with me before we go into briefings, instead of making me look unprepared."

"You were unprepared. You hadn't read the files," I pointed out. "But that's my job. You're supposed to be handling the big picture, according to Godley, while I take care of the details. So don't worry about what he thought of you. Anyway, I hadn't put it all together until we sat down and started talking about it. I'd have told you in advance if I'd thought of it then. I'm not interested in playing games—I just want to do a good job and help catch this murderer."

"Very laudable." Derwent was looking amused. If anything, I found it more unsettling than when he was angry. "I like you, Kerrigan. You don't back down."

"Not often. Not when I'm right." I sidestepped him and started down the stairs. A tingle between my shoulder blades told me he was watching. He couldn't see that my heart was still pounding, or that the hand I had stuck in my coat pocket was trembling with leftover adrenaline. I kept my head high and my shoulders squared, and forced myself to take my time. I still expected him to call me back or grab hold of me again, and I found myself holding my breath until I had turned the corner and stepped out of sight.

I was late leaving work and Dec would be waiting. It was a reason to hurry. But in truth, that wasn't why I ran the rest of the way to my car.

Chapter Five

I feared the worst when I got back to the shabby double-fronted Edwardian house that was my new home. No Declan sitting on the dirty granite steps that led up to the front door. No Declan reading the paper moodily in the driver's seat of his van, which was parked almost outside the house. No Declan in the hall when I opened the front door, although the stacks of cardboard boxes outside my door were incontrovertible proof that he had been there, and recently. I stood and looked at them, thinking extremely unenthusiastically about the physical effort it would take to move them from the hall into my flat, where I was going to put them once I'd got them inside, and how much time that would leave for cleaning and primping afterward—not much, was the depressing answer. Not enough.

My flat was on one side of the ground floor. The dark and dusty hall currently filled with my junk was otherwise empty apart from a large, ornate staircase that gave a clue to the house's more dignified past. It was a distant grandeur; its sad decline into multiple occupancy hadn't happened today or yesterday or even ten years ago. High in the roof, a stained skylight allowed a grayish glimmer of daylight to penetrate, but late on a March evening it was already dark and the hall was correspondingly gloomy. The only other feature of note was the row of mailboxes nailed to the wall near my door.

On the other side of the hall there was a door that led to the flat opposite mine. It was white-painted, anonymous, and slightly ajar. The chatter of electronic gunfire floated out through the gap, the familiar sound of a computer game being played, and I wasn't totally surprised to hear Dec's voice providing a thoroughly overexcited running commentary.

There was no answer to my knock and I pushed the door open, following the sounds of shooting to the sitting room. The flat turned out to be a mirror image of my own, although it didn't have the enormous bay window that had made me fall in love with mine. I had overlooked some fairly serious shortcomings in my new accommodation so I could live with that window. The view was of a small park with iron railings around it, and at this time of year the bare branches were dressing themselves with fresh green growth. I could have spent hours staring out at it, and fully intended to, once I got some time to myself—if that ever happened. I'd never had a view before and it lifted my heart every morning when I looked out at it. My neighbor had two narrow windows that would have had the same outlook, but heavy curtains blocked it out along with extra light that might have cast a glare on the screen. This was a home where the computer game was king, I could tell immediately. Various gaming systems littered the floor, their wires miraculously untangled but trailing everywhere. Shelves of games filled one wall. I couldn't see a single book.

On the floor, two gaming chairs were positioned in front of the vast widescreen TV, where an animation of a man in uniform was currently addressing the viewer earnestly about the mission they were about to undertake.

"I fecking hate these bits," came from the chair on the left, where my brother was sitting with a handheld controller on his lap.

"Me too. Just get on with the shooting and stop talking."

"Who cares about the plot? It's all rubbish anyway. Blast anyone in gray who shouts at you or points a gun in your direction, and try not to die. That's all you need to know."

Let me not to the marriage of true minds admit impediments.

"Sorry to interrupt, guys . . ."

The two of them twisted around, Dec with a sardonic expression on his face, my neighbor with a smile. He stood up quickly and held out his hand, revealing himself to be a couple of inches shorter than me, with shaggy fair hair, a ragged goatee beard and small, steel-rimmed glasses that kept sliding down his nose. He had a shy, lopsided grin that was immediately appealing.

"I'm Chris. Chris Swain. Sorry for distracting your brother."

"Not at all. Thank you for entertaining him." I looked down at where Dec was sitting, his tongue protruding from the side of his mouth, concentrating as he switched modes on his submachine gun. "How's it going, Dec? Sorry, I got held up at work."

No answer. I turned back to my neighbor. "Your problem now is to get rid of him. This is his dream environment. He's basically moved in already."

"I just want to finish this level," floated up from the floor, where my brother had shed fifteen years and the recollection that he was a married father of two in order to devote himself more thoroughly to murdering everything that moved on-screen. "Chris does this for a living."

I raised my eyebrows and Chris smiled, looking a shade embarrassed. "I review games and technology for a couple of magazines. I've got a blog that's pretty popular so I get sent all the new stuff anyway. It's not very grown-up but it's fun and it just about keeps the wolf from the door."

"Sounds like the ideal job." I didn't tell him what I did for a living. I never mentioned it to strangers. You never knew how people would react. Even perfectly law-abiding folk tended to get twitchy once they knew you had powers of arrest. "I'm sorry to have interrupted your evening. And to have broken into your flat without being invited."

"No, no. I've seen you around and I was hoping for a chance to get to know you." He ran one hand through his hair, looking awkward. "I mean—God, that sounded a bit keen. I just meant that it's nice to know your neighbors and it's hard to get to know people. Especially in London."

"Where are you from?"

"I'm from Suffolk. Not that far from London, but it's another world. Everyone knows everyone else's business."

"Sounds like a good reason to leave."

"You might be right." He laughed a little bit too heartily. Still recovering from his earlier embarrassment, I diagnosed, and I found myself smiling a little, wanting to set him at his ease. "What about you?" he asked.

"Oh, I grew up in the suburbs. I'm used to the London way of ignoring people."

"I'm glad he didn't ignore me," Dec said, putting down the controller as the screen turned red. Game over, you're dead. He stood up and I moved back, conscious that we were both towering over Chris. Dec was six foot four and broad with it, so he took up a fair amount of space.

"Where were you until now?" Dec was using his special older-brother tone of voice and I reacted accordingly, defensive from the off.

"I told you, I got held up. Can you help me move the boxes into the flat before you go? It'll take me a million years to do it on my own."

"Why do you think I was hanging around?" He stretched. "Mum made me promise to see them inside your door. Apparently she's given you some of her most precious possessions."

"Oh, great." I didn't bother trying to sound pleased. Lately, Mum had been spending a lot of time clearing out the attic. Horrified at how little I had managed to accumulate in the previous twenty-eight years, and having given up on the thought that I might get married anytime soon, she had decided to start handing over the things she'd been keeping for me. There was no way to refuse to take them without causing offense.

"There's china in there. I know that much. She made me promise to be careful with it."

"Well, at least that'll be useful. I've been surviving with paper plates." I turned to Chris. "Sorry again. We'll leave you to enjoy your evening."

He shoved his hands in his pockets and turned his feet so he was standing on their outer edges in what was almost a parody of shyness. "I could help. I mean, I'm good at carrying boxes."

I hesitated, not sure I wanted to invite my new neighbor into my flat but reluctant to turn down any offer of assistance. It felt a bit like taking advantage, though, and we'd done enough of that for one evening, I thought.

"Brilliant." Dec clearly had no such scruples. "The more the merrier. We'll get it done in half the time."

"Okay. Where do you want to start?"

I led the two of them into the hall where we stared at the boxes with varying degrees of enthusiasm, ranging from Dec (none) to Chris (puppy-ish). I was somewhere in the middle with moderate curiosity about what they contained. "Right, lads. If you carry them in, I'll tell you where to put them."

Dec narrowed his eyes. "So let me get this straight. We carry the boxes and you stand and point. Is that it?"

"More or less," I admitted.

"That sounds fine." Chris was clearly determined to keep the peace. I let him heft the first box and Dec took the second with a grunt.

"These'll be the lead weights you wanted, Maeve."

I ignored him as I opened the door, flicking on the main light and doing a swift recce to make sure I hadn't left anything embarrassing in plain sight. It was actually reasonably tidy in the flat, for once. I was impressed with myself. "Leave the boxes along this wall, if you can. Anything with kitchen stuff in it should go over here. That's about it, really."

"And that's all you're going to do?" Dec let the box he was carrying fall from waist height to the floor. It gave an ominous clank as it hit the ground. "Oops."

"Don't make me tell Mum on you," I said sharply. "Anyway, I'm supervising."

Chris set his box down and looked at us. "How old are you two again?"

"Some things never change." Dec patted me on the arm as he headed out to pick up another load.

"We do regress when we're together." I pulled a face. "I feel I should be apologizing again."

"Don't. It's entertaining to watch you bicker."

"In that case, make some popcorn and pull up a chair. That's pretty much all we do."

Dec stacked another box on top of the first one. "Are you just going to stand there or did you want to help, mate?" He was conveniently overlooking the fact that Chris had volunteered, and I opened my mouth to tell him off for it but Chris answered him before I could say anything.

"Sorry. I—got distracted." He looked back at me again for a fraction of a second too long, then followed Dec into the hall. There was no mistaking what I'd seen in his eyes and I hurried away into the bedroom, catching sight of myself in the mirror as I entered the room. Drab suit. Wrinkled shirt. Hair that was, as usual, borderline insane at the end of a long and exhausting day. Nothing, as far as I could see, that would make a man look once, let alone twice.

"Fuck it," I said to my reflection, and got on with trying to make the best of what I had for the sake of the one man I definitely shouldn't be trying to impress.

I will freely admit that I lurked in my room until I was fairly sure they had finished moving things around. I had shed the suit and replaced it with jeans—to indicate that I wasn't trying too hard—and a soft, clinging ash-colored jumper that brought out the gray in my eyes. I had done what I could with my hair, and put on enough mascara to make me look vaguely awake without getting into panda territory. I had a flutter of anticipation in my stomach that wouldn't go away—something like that feeling before you go out when you know you're going to get drunk and misbehave and have a good time, even if you really shouldn't.

And in half an hour Rob would be there.

I came out to find Dec lying on the sofa with his hands behind his head.

"Is your little buddy gone?"

"More like *your* little buddy. He was asking me about you. What kind of films you liked, what sort of work you did, that sort of thing. But don't worry, I didn't say anything about your job. He wanted to know whether you had a boyfriend."

"And what did you tell him?"

"That I didn't like to think about your love life and it was a total mystery to me, which, I might add, it is. I'm happy to keep it that way."

"And here I was hoping we could sit down and have a really good chat about it." I sat down on the arm of the sofa. "What's up? I'd have thought you'd be dashing off home as soon as you could get away."

He moved his head from side to side irritably, as if he couldn't get comfortable. "Nothing. Have you talked to Mum lately?"

I didn't need to be a trained detective to spot the connection. I poked him in the chest. "Dead giveaway. You're worried that Mum has told me something. That means there's something to know."

"There's no getting anything past you, Maeve. Especially with those hips."

"Ha ha," I said serenely. "Back to you. What's going on? You look like shit now that I see you up close." His face was puffy, as if he hadn't been eating well or sleeping properly, and he looked pale.

"Thanks a bunch." He rubbed his jaw, rasping stubble that was halfway to being a beard. "I've been having a bit of trouble with Abby, but I don't want to talk about it. And if Mum says anything to you, just cut her off. She got the wrong end of the stick and now she won't drop it."

It would have been easier to persuade a pit bull to let go, as I knew well, but that was a conversation for another time. I was still reeling from the news that Declan and Abby were having problems. "Give me the short version if you can't face the details. Who's in trouble?"

"Both of us." He dragged his hands down his face with a groan, pulling his skin so his lower eyelids sagged. I recoiled slightly at the red gleam of flesh. It was too reminiscent of the autopsy notes on Ivan Tremlett for comfort. "Basically, things aren't going too well and we're talking about a separation. Mum's not impressed with us. She says we made a commitment and if we don't care about it, or about her, we should stop and think of the kids."

"Hold on. Why do you need to care about Mum if you and Abby are separating?"

"Imagine the phone calls, Maeve. Telling people. The family back home. What would they make of it?"

It was a perfect imitation and I couldn't help laughing. "You've got to love her perspective on life. It's not as if she and Dad have the perfect marriage. It seems to be based on mutual incomprehension and the healing distraction of Sky Sports."

"They don't believe in divorce," Dec said flatly. "That means they'll be together forever. They don't even know if they're happy. That's not what's important. What's important is staying together in case anyone thinks less of you for admitting you made a mistake."

"Why would anyone else care?"

"Mum spends her time judging other people, even if she barely knows them—she thinks her pals are the same way. As if anyone in the family or out of it gives a crap about what me and Abby do."

"And what are you going to do?" I didn't want to hear that they were getting a divorce, but if that was what he'd decided, I'd support him and I hoped he knew it.

He sat up, swinging his legs off the sofa, and put his head in his hands. "Honest to God, I don't know. Ask me another one, Maeve, because I can't tell you. It's up to Abby as much as me, and she's not talking to me much at the moment."

"What happened?"

"Look, I don't want to go into the details. But Mum is gunning for Abby, so if she phones you, just don't listen to what she says about her. She's starting from the point of view that her son couldn't be at fault, so she's not the most impartial judge of what's been happening."

"Okay."

"Is that it? No follow-up questions?"

I shrugged. "You don't want to talk about it so you don't have to. I'm not going to pry. It's none of my business."

"That's right. It isn't." He'd been braced for a fight, and I could see his shoulders sag as he relaxed. "It's not as if you know much about relationships anyway."

"I know more than you." I thumped him. "At least I've had more than one in my entire life."

"One-night stands don't count."

"I've never had a one-night stand!" *A short-lived fling here and there, maybe . . .*

"You know what I mean." He waggled his fingers dismissively. "You haven't ever been serious about anyone. You haven't made a proper commitment. You run away from that sort of thing."

"I'd rather be a free agent," I said, keeping my tone light although I was stung by what he said.

"That much is completely clear. No one gets to make a claim on you, do they? Not a boyfriend, not me, not Mum and Dad."

"Not this shit again," I snapped, seriously nettled now. It was an old conversation that we had never finished.

"Sorry. I forgot you don't like to talk about how you ignore your obligations."

"I don't ignore my obligations. I just don't seek them out. I'm not married, I don't have kids, I don't run around after Mum and Dad because I don't live near them and I don't get to see much of them because I work irregular hours. You are the complete opposite, but that's your life, not mine. Don't blame me because you resent the choices you've made. And how did this turn into a conversation about me? We were supposed to be talking about you and your marriage."

"There's nothing to say." With Dec, there always came a point when I'd pushed him too far. He stood up, a big bear of a man, and like a bear, most dangerous when he was wounded. "The trouble with you is you think you know it all. You don't have the first idea, Maeve. You can't run away from reality forever. One of these days, you're going to have to think about settling down."

"Because it's worked so well for you."

"Because it's what people do. They take a chance on being happy with someone else, and they hope it works out. You can't live life in the expectation that it will turn out badly, or you'll end up miserable and alone."

"Dec, that's all I see, every day. People who thought things were going to be all right and ended up dead."

"Those are extreme examples."

"Well, okay, let's take you. You aren't exactly selling the alternative to the single life, are you? You look like hell, you're exhausted and you're fed up. Not appealing."

"At least I tried. You can't even say that." He folded his arms. "Why are you all dressed up, anyway? Are you going out?"

"No. Rob's coming over."

His eyebrows rose slowly. "Rob as in the guy you were sort of almost seeing a couple of months ago?"

"Rob as in my colleague."

"And you've got the goods in the window because he's your colleague."

I tweaked the neckline of my jumper, aware that it was on the low side and suddenly self-conscious about it. "He's coming over because we need to sort things out. It's not going anywhere."

"Does he know that?"

"He should."

"Because you've told him, presumably. And then you open the door looking like that? You can't mess around with other people's feelings, Maeve. You can't have what you want and never mind what anyone else thinks. Rob's a good bloke. Better than you deserve, I'd say."

As he spoke, the phone rang. I leaned over to pick it up, knowing as I did so that I was probably making a mistake, wincing as the familiar voice rang from the receiver.

"Maeve, is that you?"

"Mum." I tried to make myself sound cheerful. Dec and I looked at one another, silently declaring a truce. Against a common enemy, we had to be united. "How are things?"

"Have you spoken to your brother? Have you heard the latest? They're splitting up, did he tell you that?"

Dec probably couldn't hear what she was saying, but the tone was clear enough. He got to his feet, picked up his jacket and backed away in the direction of the door.

I covered the mouthpiece. "Where are you going?"

"Home."

"Don't leave me to this."

In my ear, Mum said, "They should never have got married in the first place."

"I can't help you." He opened the door. "Just don't take her seriously. She doesn't know what she's talking about."

"I'll be in touch." I waved.

"I could have told him she would have an affair."

"Sorry?" I said into the phone, suddenly interested as Dec closed the door behind him.

"Your sister-in-law. Did he not say? She's been seeing someone else. For quite some time too."

"Who?" It was too much to hope I'd get a straight answer to that one.

"Of course he'll never say she was at fault but that's just your brother being protective. He can't see her for what she is. That little hussy."

"Mum, start at the beginning. I'm completely confused."

"If you'd been listening, you'd know. She's having an affair with a married man—a parent from the girls' school, if you don't mind. And your poor brother is mortified. Not that he's not at fault. The situation doesn't reflect well on him either."

"I don't see how it's his fault if Abby decided to have an affair," I said weakly.

"A marriage takes two, Maeve. Not that you would be aware of that."

"I am familiar with the concept of marriage, Mum."

She came back at me like a striking cobra. "Well, you wouldn't know it from the way you behave."

"Right." I took a deep breath. *Give me patience.* "This isn't about me, Mum. Abby had an affair. You think that Dec is somehow to blame. So does he, for what it's worth."

"Did he say that? The poor fellow. He's very upset."

Not least by the fact that his mother can't decide which side she's on. I looked at my watch and winced. I'd have to hope Rob was running late.

"Look, Mum, tell me what's been going on. I really want to know, and Dec wasn't very forthcoming."

It was the only invitation she needed. For the next fifteen minutes, my contribution to the conversation was limited to "Oh dear," "Oh no" and "Really?" while Mum gave me a highly prejudiced and doubtless inaccurate account of a sadly predictable tale. Dec, working late a lot, trying to get his business on track in the face of looming recession. Abby, feeling neglected, stuck at home with two little girls. Except when they were at school, when she was free to meet and mingle with other mothers—and one stay-at-home dad, who was feeling a bit neglected himself. Neither of them thought it would do any harm. Neither of them thought they would get caught. Nor did they. It was Abby who, in a fit of conscience, broke it off and told Dec what she'd done, clearly expecting him to forgive her immediately. Things hadn't quite worked out that way. It was typical of my brother to blame himself for not being able to forget what his wife had done, and typical of him to feel responsible for driving her away in the first place.

In all honesty, I didn't concentrate too hard on the details. I was still thinking about what Dec had said to me about running away from commitment. I did want to find the right person and settle down, even if the thought of turning into my mum was exceedingly unappealing. But I also needed to concentrate on getting my career off the ground. A serious relationship with Rob was unthinkable. Not only would it be a massive distraction, it ran the risk of getting one or both of us thrown off Godley's team. There was a rule about no relationships between team members—not difficult to keep to when the team was entirely composed of heterosexual men, as it had been until I joined. And I didn't want to fulfill the stereotype of the keen young female detective who slept her way around the office.

There was Rob to think about too. I had taken the view that we were both grown-ups—that as long as we were honest with one another, we could do what we liked and get away unscathed. It didn't seem to be working out that way. I didn't want to get hurt, and I didn't want to hurt Rob, either. The tight, low-cut jumper was looking more and more like a bad idea. I went into my room and hunted for something less flashy while Mum moved seamlessly from, "I knew Abby was a bad choice—he should never have married her" to "at least one of you got married. People are always asking me about you."

"Well, you don't need to tell them anything. There's nothing to say." I held up a long, black, crew-necked jumper with a hole in the sleeve, the kind of thing you put on when you've got flu and feel like death and need to wear something that matches your mood. Perfect. A nun's habit would have been more alluring. "Look, I've got to go, Mum. I've got someone coming over for dinner."

"A man?"

"Just a friend." I crossed my fingers, then uncrossed them. That was exactly what Rob was, after all. "A colleague. No one you know." If she knew it was Rob, she would get unreasonably excited. Weirdly, although he fulfilled none of the many criteria she had for potential husbands, she utterly adored him.

"It would have to be someone from work. You have no life outside of that job."

I rolled my eyes. "You're right, Mum. Can I call you tomorrow?"

A short, wounded pause. "Yes. Make sure you do."

"I will." The promise sounded hollow even to my ears. I might call her, though. If I was in a masochistic mood.

I put down the phone, but before I could change, there was a knock on the door. With a muttered curse I went to answer it and found Rob standing in the hall, burdened with three bags of shopping. "How did you get into the house?"

"One of your neighbors took pity on me." I took a moment to wonder who—Chris?—and he put down the bags. "Is this as far as I'm getting? Should I make plans to cook out here?"

"Sorry. Come in." He gathered up his things and strode past me as I reflected I needn't have worried about changing my clothes—he had barely glanced at me. I waited until he was inside to ask, "Which neighbor?"

"A female. Eastern European, if I had to guess. Nice smile."

"That'll be Szuszanna. She's Hungarian—works as a nanny, according to my landlord. I haven't met her yet. All I can tell you is that she has a heavy tread and likes music from West End shows. It was the soundtrack from *Carousel* last night."

"Interesting choice."

"You haven't lived until you've heard 'You'll Never Walk Alone' on repeat at three in the morning."

"Maybe she's a Liverpool fan."

"That is always a possibility." I watched Rob walk around the living room, inspecting the furnishings, and found myself glad that it hadn't been Chris who had let him in. In any comparison, Chris came off worse. Rob was lean and fit, a physical match for me in every way, where Chris was slight and wiry. Rob had confidence to burn while Chris was like an everhopeful but much-kicked dog. Beneath the easy manner, Rob was pure steel. Chris, on the evidence of his behavior around my brother, was not. I felt sorry for Chris, sorry that he seemed to like me, sorry that I couldn't imagine feeling the same way. And sorry for myself that I couldn't and shouldn't think that way about Rob. *Friends. We are just friends.* What I had been thinking, I assured myself, meant nothing, except that I was capable of appreciating him, in a purely aesthetic way. All of which went to prove that the road from self-awareness to comforting denial was a short and frequently traveled one for me.

Rob, oblivious to my emotional confusion, had finished looking around. "This is all right. Where's the kitchen?"

"Behind you." I pointed. It was little more than a cubbyhole off the sitting room, big enough for a basic cooker, fridge and sink and not much else.

"If I unpack the shopping, there won't be room to prepare the food." He looked at me accusingly. "Only someone who hated cooking would have rented this place."

"Brilliant deduction. What's your next trick?"

"I'm glad you asked. I'm going to make your inhibitions disappear." He didn't wait to see how I reacted, just carried one bag into the kitchen and started rummaging in it. Tuneful whistling floated out into the hall: Rob was in a good mood.

I sat down on the edge of the sofa to try to recover some composure. I was suddenly aware that I was way out of my depth. It was nice that everyone—including me—had been so concerned about Rob's romantic well-being. I was beginning to realize I should be a lot more worried about my own.

Chapter Six

"For God's sake, Maeve. I thought I'd bought everything you could possibly need. Who doesn't have a wooden spoon?"

"Me. But try the boxes."

Rob gave me a very unenthusiastic look before addressing himself to the pile in the hall. Cooking had come to a premature halt when he opened a drawer and discovered the shortcomings of the kitchen extended beyond its size and the constantly dripping tap. It was, it seemed, impossible to cook spaghetti Bolognese from scratch without a wooden spoon. Who knew?

I leaned against the wall and watched him methodically work through the boxes.

"You could help."

"You're doing fine."

"This doesn't count as cooking, so you don't get a free pass on it." A box landed at my feet. "Get hunting."

The box contained sheets, I discovered, and towels. I had never seen any of them before. "Try again."

"I think I've struck gold." Rob crouched down beside the last box in the pile and lifted out a stack of saucepans. "Here we go. A wooden spoon. I knew you'd have one somewhere."

"Mum must have put it in. What else is in that box?"

"A sieve, baking tins—cooking stuff. And cutlery. No plates."

"They must be somewhere else," I said, distracted. "I've never owned a sieve."

"Well, you do now." He twirled it by the handle. "I love your mum. She's thought of everything."

"Oh yeah, she's great." My voice was loaded with sarcasm. "Everything in that box is designed to make me feel bad for not being remotely domestic."

"It is useful," Rob said carefully, "to be able to feed yourself without having to resort to the takeaways section of the Yellow Pages."

"There's always toast."

"You frighten me. How all your teeth haven't fallen out from vitamin deficiency, I'll never know."

I grinned at him to prove I still had a full set. "Toast with Marmite. Toast with jam. Cheese on toast. Beans on toast. All the major food groups. It's the perfect food."

"Well, you're not having toast tonight."

"I am actually looking forward to a proper meal," I admitted, trailing him back to the kitchen where he got on with scraping chopped onion into one of the saucepans. "So you were more than a little mysterious about your case. What's the mess you're clearing up?"

"Remember that domestic in Chiswick a couple of weeks ago? Morty arrested the husband? The victim was Andrea Tancredi. Strangled with the electrical cord of her hairdryer."

I did remember. DS Mortimer had spent a long time telling everyone how easy the case had been to clear up. Art Mortimer was a large, bearded, untidy man and spent most days wandering the office like the last lonely mastodon on a perpetual quest for a primeval forest to call his own. Godley kept him on the team because he had years of experience and a gift for getting confessions from people, but he was not the most dynamic of police officers.

"Ray Tancredi, the husband, was having financial trouble. His property business was seriously in the shit. The house was burgled on the day of the murder—or at least, that was what we were supposed to think. Broken window, safe hanging open, money and jewelry missing—oh, and Mrs. Tancredi's rapidly cooling body in the master bedroom. The SOCOs found blood on the window that matched Tancredi, and there was a fresh cut on his right forearm. It didn't take a huge leap of logic to have a look for the jewelry that was missing in places where he had been, and Morty found it in Tancredi's locker at his golf club. He'd been golfing with his best friend that afternoon—that was his alibi for the murder."

"So he definitely staged the burglary."

"Definitely." Rob paused in the middle of chopping a mushroom. "All of this talking is making me thirsty."

"Do you want a glass of wine?"

"Thought you'd never ask."

I levered the cork out of a bottle of ruby-colored South African Shiraz and poured the wine into two mismatched glasses.

"Go back to Ray Tancredi. What happened next?"

"He was arrested, interviewed and charged with murder. He admitted staging the burglary, but denied the murder. And in fairness, he did seem pretty shocked about his wife's death."

"That means nothing," I said, hitching myself up onto the work surface beside the cooker. "Remorse."

"That is a remarkably inconvenient place for you to sit, by the way."

"There's nowhere else." There really wasn't.

"I can't believe you're willing to put up with this kitchen."

I shrugged. "Converted flats always mean compromises. I like old houses. I like the living room and the bedroom. Plus the rent is cheap for a furnished flat. I can live with the crappy kitchen and the bathroom."

"The living room is nice," Rob agreed. In addition to the bay window, it was big, with a high ceiling and wide wooden floorboards. The original fireplace was still there, even if it had been coated in a thick layer of white emulsion. I had had visions of myself curled up on the big gray sofa, drinking tea, looking out at the trees blowing in the breeze. Maybe while someone else was cooking dinner, I found myself thinking, watching Rob move deftly around the tiny space.

He looked at me, eyebrows raised, and I realized I'd missed something. "Huh?"

"What's wrong with the bathroom?"

"It's just a little bit tired, that's all." That was the landlord's euphemism for a permanent limescale mark that scarred the bath, and a loo with a chipped cistern lid. The shower was no great shakes either. "Look, I'm not going to be staying here forever. It's good enough for a few months."

"Mm." A smile he couldn't hide was turning the corners of his mouth up.

"What are you laughing at?"

"Classic Kerrigan. This'll do for the time being even though you could probably have found something nicer if you'd bothered. As long as it's not a permanent commitment, you're happy with good enough."

I looked at him warily. "Are you still talking about the flat?"

"Mostly."

I chose not to pursue it. "How did you get involved in clearing up a mess? So far you've got Ray Tancredi in prison. That seems fair enough."

"It did indeed. The only trouble was, he didn't do it."

"You shock me."

"I was shocked myself. I was only involved because I got stuck with doing Morty's donkeywork for the investigation into Tancredi's financial difficulties, because they wanted to prove he was after Andrea's life insurance. I was supposed to be chasing up the Production Orders we'd sent his bank. The CPS wanted a full record of his affairs for the last couple of years and the bank was, as usual, completely ignoring the request. Morty was off doing something more glamorous so I took the call when a Mrs. Penny Quentin rang up and asked if a detective could come to see her to discuss information she had relating to the Tancredi case."

"Mrs. Penny Quentin being?"

"Mrs. Penny Quentin being a total fox, even though she's not as young as she used to be—knock-out figure, blond hair, high heels, the works. In addition, Mrs. Penny Quentin was Andrea Tancredi's friend—or at least, she was supposed to be. Penny is also married to Eric Quentin, who was Ray Tancredi's best mate and golfing companion on the afternoon in question."

I looked at him with mock severity. "Don't tell me you flirted with the lady."

"I didn't have to. She told me everything she knew almost as soon as I walked in. And what she knew—and could prove—was that her husband had arranged the whole thing. He'd got in touch with some lads who were prepared to do the job for ten grand each. She had e-mails, phone records, a bank statement that showed a one-off cash withdrawal of twenty thousand before the murder—the works. He had no idea that she knew all of his passwords, or that she was watching what he was doing so closely."

"Where did he find the lads?"

"Eric grew up in a rough bit of Basildon. Even though he'd gone up in the world, he found it useful to stay in touch with a few old friends. A couple of phone calls set him up with two goons who were happy to commit murder as long as they got paid for it. He didn't want to get his hands dirty, understandably. He knew Ray was having money troubles so he encouraged him to stage the burglary and make an insurance claim for the jewelry. Eric knew a man who knew a jeweler who would buy the stuff that had been stolen without asking too many questions about where it had come from. Ray was desperate for cash to keep his business afloat, so he went along with it. He left work at lunchtime, dashed home, broke the window and took the jewelry. Andrea was usually at the gym at that time of day. We found her car in the garage—he wouldn't have known she'd never left the house."

"Didn't he see the body?"

Rob shook his head. "Everything that was stolen came from the safe in the study, downstairs. He was in a hurry—he just grabbed and ran. He must have got the shock of his life when he found out she had been there all along. Eric couldn't have known he would make such a balls-up of the burglary, but Ray played into his hands. And then Eric took him off for a round of golf, just a bit too late to be a convincing alibi for murder."

"Why did Eric want to have Andrea killed?"

"Eric and Andrea were having an affair. From what Penny said, Andrea was a total bitch. Eric had told her he was planning to leave Penny and get a divorce, but not so he could settle down with Andrea. Eric has been knocking off his secretary, Saskia, who is twenty-six to Eric's forty-five, in case you were wondering. Penny said it was a classic mid-life crisis, right on cue. Saskia is one of your high-maintenance types and she wants a ring on her finger. Eric is head over heels, according to Penny, and is prepared to do whatever she asks."

"She must be some secretary."

"She's got a double-barrelled surname and lives in Parsons Green. Reading between the lines, Eric sees her as his ticket to social acceptability. But that's going to be a lot harder to achieve when he's got a conviction for murder."

"Hold on. Why did Eric have to have his lover killed? I'd have thought Penny was the one who needed to be got out of the picture."

"Andrea was fed up because Eric was planning to marry Saskia, not her. Eric is considerably better off than Ray—Penny thinks that he was Andrea's exit strategy from her marriage and a chance at a much more comfortable life. When he told her he was going to have to break it off with her, she threatened to tell Penny *and* Saskia about their relationship. And Eric had the sense to know Saskia was going to flip her lid, even though she'd been happy to help him cheat on his wife for the past eighteen months. She's not the sort to put up with infidelity, or so Penny says, and she's made it her business to get to know Saskia. Keep your enemies close, and all that. There's a big difference between being the mistress and being the one who's betrayed."

"But Penny was happy to put up with it."

"She thought he'd come back to her eventually. And when she realized he wasn't going to, she decided he wasn't worth worrying about. No, Eric knew Penny wasn't going to make any trouble. Because she's been married to him for such a long time, she's entitled to a huge amount of money if she opts for a reasonably amicable divorce settlement. Penny," Rob said, stirring the sauce, "is a pragmatist."

"So what happens now?"

"Ray is going to court in the morning. The CPS are offering no evidence against him on the murder, and they've got to decide what to do about the jewelry theft. He didn't get a chance to make the insurance claim, so he never actually got around to committing fraud, and since he stole it from himself . . ." Rob shrugged. "I doubt anyone's told him yet that he's going to be a free man tomorrow, so that'll be a nice surprise. Essex Police are picking up the two thugs, with any luck, and Liv and I are going after Eric."

I felt a prickle of hostility at the mention of his pretty new colleague. "Should be easy enough. Penny's handed it to you on a plate."

"There's still a fair amount of legwork to be done checking facts, re-interviewing witnesses, and going over the evidence in the case again to make it incriminate Eric Quentin. It's not exactly the fun bit of the job." He tested the spaghetti. "Not long now."

"It smells gorgeous." I slid off the counter. "I'll go and lay the table."

"See if you can find a couple of plates in Cardboard City."

There was a small table in the bay window with an upright chair on either side. I put out knives and forks and found a candle-stub in a holder on a windowsill, presumably left by a previous tenant. It looked like the ultimate in sophistication when I had put it in the middle of the table and lit it. Three matching ghost flames danced against the darkness of the window, reflected on the glass. I had decided not to risk lowering the ancient white cotton blinds that were rolled up above the window frame. One of them had fallen down the first time I'd tried, and replacing them was on my short list of things to do in the flat. Quite far up the list in fact, I thought, as Chris Swain jogged past slowly, staring in at me. He raised a hand as he went up the stairs that led to the front door and I gave a quick wave in return.

"Who was that?" Rob had come out of the kitchen carrying our glasses.

"The guy who lives across the hall. He helped Dec and me with some of the boxes."

"Oh, right," Rob said, his face and voice blank, but I happened to know him quite well.

"Come off it. You can't be jealous."

"What gave you that idea?" Before I could answer, he changed the subject. "Did you find plates? Or bowls. Bowls would be better."

"They might be in that one." I pointed. "Dec said it was heavy."

Rob started moving boxes out of the way. I went to help, but he snapped, "I can manage."

"Don't be shitty." I hunkered down beside him. "You obviously didn't get a good look at him. He looks like a student—you know, beard and glasses."

"Oh, an intellectual."

"A nerd," I countered. "He doesn't look as if he gets out much."

"Okay." He looked sideways at me. "I wasn't jealous."

"Course not." I folded back the top of the box and lifted out a stack of plates. "Here we go. Straight from the nineteen seventies to your table."

Mum had given me the dinner set she had bought when she got married, blue-green glazed earthenware with a stylized pattern raised around the edge. I ran a finger over the pattern. "We should really be eating gammon with a slice of pineapple on top of it. And then sherry trifle to follow."

"Sorry. That's not in my repertoire."

We were almost nose to nose when I turned to smile at him and for a second I thought he was going to take the opportunity to kiss me. I waited, not moving. Instead, abruptly, he stood up. "I'll sort out the food."

I knew my face was burning red as I went and took refuge in my wine glass. By the time he came back, I had recovered what passed for composure. "This looks great. Thanks for cooking."

"Anytime." He pulled out his chair and looked at the magazine that was lying on the seat. I'd forgotten to move it. "What's this? 'Twenty Ways to Please Your Man Tonight.' Looking for tips?"

I leaned over and retrieved it, back to crimson again. "Absolutely not. It was the article about unreported rape that interested me."

"Oh, I'm sure. 'Your Happiness Plan,'" Rob read as I put the magazine on the floor. "'How to Get What You Want. What Your Style Says About You.' Do women actually believe that crap?"

"Some do. Not me." I picked up my fork and dug in. "What do you think of Liv?"

He looked up, his eyes very blue in the candlelight. "What do you mean?"

"Just what I said."

"She's all right. Bit quiet."

"She's very pretty."

"I hadn't noticed." I raised my eyebrows skeptically. "She's okay. But you know I only have eyes for you."

"Hmm." However severe I tried to look, I couldn't hide the fact that I was pleased. "Is she any good? She hasn't got much experience, from what I've heard."

"She was Special Branch—before it got eaten by the Anti-Terrorist Branch." The high-ups had decided to merge the two and create one Counter-Terrorism Command. Special Branch had come off worse, shedding support staff and officers.

"If she was worth having around, they'd have wanted to keep her. How come she didn't want to stay?"

"You're not that naive. Special Branch was dead. I wouldn't have wanted to stick around to see who made it into the new command and who got dumped. Besides, Liv said it was a good opportunity to work in a different role—she'd got too comfortable and it was time for a change. She seems fairly switched on, if you ask me. And Godley wouldn't have recruited her just because she's pretty."

I nodded, concentrating very hard on winding spaghetti around my fork.

"Wish you were working with me on the Tancredi case instead of her?"

"No." I drank the last of the wine in my glass in one long swallow, then admitted, "Okay, a little."

He shook his head. "I've got a nasty little domestic that's gone wrong once. You've got a far bigger case to handle. A potential serial killer."

"Yeah, and look how well the last one worked out for me."

"You're not exactly to this killer's tastes from what I've heard. You should be okay. Besides, I don't have to worry about you this time. You've got DI Derwent to protect you."

I rolled my eyes.

"That bad?"

I spent the rest of the meal giving Rob a rundown on Derwent's behavior during the day. It didn't work out quite as I'd hoped. Instead of leaping to my defense, he shrugged dismissively.

"You can't let him get to you. Not if he's that sort of person anyway."

"He scared me." It sounded ridiculous when I said it out loud.

"How?" Rob had been playing with his knife, but now his fingers stilled.

"He waited for me, on the stairs. He wanted to tell me off for surprising him in our meeting with Godley."

"He's a control freak. You said as much."

"I know."

"What did he actually do that scared you?"

I frowned, trying to remember. "I came through the doors and he grabbed me, as if he wanted to start off by intimidating me physically. Then he shouted at me for going behind his back. Then he told me he liked me for not backing down."

"Sounds as if you're well on the way to winning him over."

"I doubt that." I sighed. "I just don't get him. I don't have a clue what he's thinking or what he's going to do next. I think he's capable of pretty much anything. And he's impossible to work with."

"No. He's not. He's awkward and belligerent, but you're used to dealing with difficult people. Godley basically told you what to expect and how to handle him. It's up to you to deal with it." He nodded to the magazine on the floor. "Better read the article on how to get what you want and see if you can pick up any tips on diplomacy."

"I've been doing much better with that lately. Hardly anyone has complained about me." I glared at him. "I can't believe you're not on my side."

"To the death, my darling, but there's nothing you can do about this one. You're just going to have to get on with it and make the most of working on this case. This is your thing, isn't it? High-profile cases?"

"I don't seek them out." In spite of myself, I shivered. "It's not a good one, Rob. Those men—they were tortured. Horribly, mercilessly, for hours. I don't care who you are or what you've done, you shouldn't have to die like that."

"Don't think about how they died. Think about why."

It was easier said than done. I poured some more wine into his glass. "You deserve a drink after that meal. Where did you learn to cook?"

He leaned back. "You can't be that impressed by spag bol."

"Seriously. I couldn't do that."

"You couldn't be bothered to do it. That's different." He stretched. "I don't know, really. I used to watch my parents cooking. They're quite into food, so that helps."

"My dad can boil eggs. That's it. And Mum specializes in chops, fry-ups and stews."

"Good plain food."

"The most experimental they get is fish and chips on a Friday." I shook my head. "I've never seen the point in cooking. All that work and it just disappears, if you've done it well. You just get left with the washing-up."

"Yeah, I've been meaning to say, I'm not doing the washing-up as well as cooking."

"Don't worry about it. I'll take care of it. But not straightaway."

His jaw tightened. "It's not going to get any better if you leave it."

"You can't stand it, can you?" I leaned across the table. "The saucepan is in there, drying out even as we sit here. The food's just caked on. By the time I get around to washing it, I'll never be able to scrape it off. I'll probably end up throwing it out."

"I know what you're doing and I'm not going to fall for it."

"Damn," I said softly and laughed. "You know me too well."

"I sometimes think I don't know you at all."

I stared at him, wrong-footed by the change of mood, and was ridiculously relieved when he started to talk about cooking again, a nice safe subject for both of us. I stopped listening properly after a while and just watched him as I sipped my wine, noticing little things—the way the skin around his eyes creased when he smiled, the shape of his mouth, his beautiful hands . . .

There is a limit to how much anyone can say about food, no matter how enthusiastic they may be. When Rob stopped talking, I picked up my glass and stood up.

"Let's move to the sofa."

He carried the wine bottle over as well as his glass. "Have some more?"

"Are you trying to get me drunk?"

"No. I don't need to."

"Confident, aren't you?"

"Reasonably." He put the bottle down beside the sofa. "If I shouldn't be, I'll leave."

"Don't leave." I didn't even think before I said it. When it came down to it, I didn't want him to go. But whatever I'd been expecting would happen next, didn't. Rob changed the subject.

"Who else lives here, apart from weedy Chris and the delectable nanny?"

"Upstairs, opposite Szuszanna and above Chris, is Walter Green, otherwise known as my landlord. He has five properties in this street, apparently."

"He must be loaded. What's he doing living in a one-bedroom flat?"

I shrugged. "He lives on his own. Bit of an oddball, I think. I doubt he needs a lot of space." I had met him briefly before signing my lease, and might have found him unsettling if I hadn't been used to talking to strange people at work. He had frizzy graying hair, a bulbous nose and long white hands that hung down at his side limply, as if weighted. I had found myself staring at them, fascinated, and had to force myself to focus on his face instead, although I needn't have bothered. Walter was not big on eye contact. I was willing to bet he had lived with his mother until she died, and it was, he had confessed, family money that had paid for the houses—he was the last of his line, a genetic dead end. "Walter is all right. I don't think he's too strict, as landlords go. But I don't think maintenance is high on his list of priorities."

"Well, it isn't for you either, so that's all right." I could tell the mild dinginess of the flat was bothering Rob. I had caught him fiddling with the broken blind already. His own flat wasn't extraordinarily neat, but it was organized, and everything *worked*. One up to him, I thought, sipping my wine and not caring in the least.

"Top floor is an actor—Brody Lee."

"Is he famous? Would I recognize him?"

"You might. I'd never heard of him and I haven't met him yet so I can't tell you. According to Walter, Brody is filming a kids' series based on *Gawain and the Green Knight* somewhere in Eastern Europe, so he's not around much."

"Is that everyone?"

"That's your lot."

"Do they know what you do for a living?"

I shook my head. "I just skated around it when I was talking to Walter. I did say I might be coming and going at odd times because of work, but he just told me not to bang the front door. God knows what he thought my job was, but he didn't ask any more questions."

"Let's see." Rob frowned, assessing me. "Assassin. Emergency plumber. Pilot."

"Call-center worker. Fish gutter. Stripper. Drug dealer."

"All perfectly reasonable ways to make a living. And all less controversial than being a copper." He stood up. "I'm going to have a look at your tired bathroom. I can't stand the suspense."

"Down the hall, on the right."

He disappeared, whistling again. I listened to him close the bathroom door behind him and reflected that he, at any rate, seemed to feel at home. I wasn't quite comfortable yet. The sounds of the house still bothered me. The little ticks and creaks of an old building were magnified a hundred times when you were lying in bed, alone, unable to sleep. The pipes made unearthly noises in the early morning that had woken me up more than once, convinced that I'd heard a scream. Earplugs might have helped, but I didn't like to cut myself off from my surroundings. It wasn't surprising really. Being wary had probably saved my life a few months earlier. If indulging my survival instinct meant losing out on some shut-eye, I'd just have to cope without it.

When Rob came back, he sat closer to me, his thigh touching mine. The candle had burned out and the only light came from a dim lamp behind him. I couldn't see enough of his expression to know what he was thinking.

"I don't mean to be boring, but we really do need to talk."

I wriggled. "Do we? I'd rather not."

"I know. I noticed you dodging me for the last two months."

"No, I mean that I can think of things I'd rather do than talk."

"That's not what you said when we got together last year. You were the one who wanted to talk about what we were doing and whether it was a good idea."

His arm was lying along the back of the sofa behind my head and I leaned against it. "Yeah, but now I'm absolutely sure it's a bad idea, I don't want to think about it anymore."

"You can't hide forever."

It was uncomfortably close to what Dec had said earlier in the evening. I looked at him earnestly. "Do you think I'm using you?"

He moved away a few inches and laughed. "God, Maeve. Be more direct."

"It's a serious question."

"Okay, I'll give you a serious answer. No, I don't. I think you're doing your best to do the right thing by both of us but you don't have a clue what that is. I think you want this to be uncomplicated and you're terrified that it's not going to turn out that way. I think you want to be logical about it and you can't help the fact that your emotions keep getting in the way. You weren't made to be dispassionate, Maeve. Not at work. Not at home. And certainly not in bed."

I pleated the hem of my jumper, not wanting to look him in the eye. "It seems a bit unfair that everyone knows a lot more about me than I know about myself."

"That's one of the sweetest things about you. You genuinely have no idea what you're like. It makes you very unpredictable."

"But you predicted I wouldn't be able to resist you."

"Oh, that was a sure thing."

Instead of answering, I leaned over and kissed him lightly. He slid one hand up to the back of my neck and drew me toward him for a proper kiss, one that reminded me, as if I needed it, that Rob was something special.

When we broke apart, he grinned at me. "Unless you've changed a lot, I doubt you want to go any further while we're sitting in such a public place. And I noticed the bed has sheets and pillows and a duvet on it already."

"I have some standards." I stood up, taking his hand and pulling him to his feet. "Come on."

Once we had moved into the hall, out of the goldfish bowl that was my living room, Rob pulled me back toward him and kissed me again, hard. I hadn't forgotten what being with him was like—I had thought about it often enough—but he had a single-mindedness that was new, an urgency that took me by surprise. It was as if he had something to prove, to me or to himself. It was altogether too serious for me and I leaned away from him so I could look into his eyes, laughing a little.

"Wow. Take it easy." He bent his head again and I dodged. "Just a second."

"What's wrong?"

"Nothing. But there's no rush, is there?"

He took a deep breath and let it out slowly. "Right."

"From what I recall, you are very good at this. I just want to enjoy it."

That earned me a flash of the old Rob. "Let me guess—somewhere in that magazine there's a feature on ten ways to get your boyfriend in the mood for sex. Number four: flatter him by telling him he's good at it."

It was a throwaway remark but I couldn't let it go, even though I should have known better. "You're not my boyfriend."

He looked at me for a long moment, then dropped his hands from my body, burying them in his pockets as if he didn't even want to touch me by accident. The space between us suddenly felt like it stretched for miles. "You still want to have it your way, don't you? No commitment. No trust."

"No complications," I countered, suddenly angry. "Come on, Rob. Most men would prefer that."

Instead of answering, he walked away, picked up his jacket from the arm of the sofa where he'd thrown it on arrival and headed for the door.

I went after him. "Where are you going? You can't just storm off in a huff."

No answer.

The very short fuse of my temper spluttered into flame. "This is exactly why I thought a relationship was a bad idea in the first place. I warned you this would happen. We have to work together." He paid no attention. "And it would be nice if you could stop ignoring me. Sulking is very unattractive."

"So is your attitude." He turned, one hand on the door latch. "Let's recap, Maeve. You'll sleep with me but you don't want to have to talk about it.

You'll spend the evening with me as long as there are no strings attached and no one finds out."

"I said from the start that it was risky to get together. We're mates first and foremost—that counts for a lot. I don't want to screw things up."

"Bit late to be worrying about that." He shook his head. "I can't do this again, Maeve. I can't chase after you and think I've got you, then end up back at the start. I want to know where I stand. I don't think that's too much to ask."

"You are such a hypocrite. You were the one who didn't want to discuss that kind of thing the first time we slept together. You were far more interested in getting me into bed than in our long-term future, and if you'd thought about it for five minutes, you'd have known it was doomed."

"I thought we'd sort it out later. I thought I could get you to trust me if I let you get used to the idea of us being together."

"Do you want to know my rule about relationships? It has to be the right person, at the right time. Now, one of those things isn't working with you." I looked at him coldly. "I just can't decide which one it is."

"I'm so *fucking* tired of this." He opened the door and slammed it back against the wall, and one part of me was detached enough to note that I'd never seen him properly angry before. I followed him, standing in the doorway while he put his jacket on without looking in my direction. The communal hallway was shadowy, the stairs stretching up into darkness. There was a light switch somewhere, but I couldn't recall where. The lamplight escaping through my open door caught the curlicues of plasterwork that still clung to the ceiling and glinted on the brass stair-rods that pinned the threadbare carpet in place. The house was silent, but it was the tense silence of someone holding their breath.

As quickly as it had flared, my anger burned itself out. "Rob, please. Don't leave it like this."

Without turning, he said, "You know, Maeve, I think you're right. This is a bad idea."

I felt a thud of disappointment in my chest. "That's not a reason to leave."

"I'd have said it was a pretty good reason, actually." He looked at me. "For someone who doesn't want to screw things up, you have quite a talent for it."

"Go fuck yourself," I snapped, back to angry in a split second.

"I suppose I'll have to." He shook his head, slowly, sarcastically, and I thought he was going to say something else, but instead he punched the wall beside my door, quite hard.

It was a physical expression of his frustration, not an attack on me—I understood that straightaway—but I still jumped about a mile. It had sounded incredibly loud in the quiet house, and violent too. "Rob, for God's sake, get a grip."

He didn't answer. He was too busy flexing his hand, examining it to make sure he hadn't broken anything. In the silence we both heard the noise—a shuffle that might have been someone moving from one foot to another. Rob turned and peered up the stairs. He was in a better position than me to see a movement in the shadows and what he saw sent him bounding up the stairs three at a time.

"What are you looking at?" he said.

"Nothing. I—nothing." I recognized the voice with a sinking feeling. Terror made Walter skip a few paces sideways so I could see him, his face contorted with anxiety. "I don't want any trouble." He tried to sound firm. "I'll call the police."

"I am the police." Rob flipped his warrant card out of his back pocket and flashed it to prove it. "But don't worry. I'm leaving."

"It's okay, Walter. Really." I walked into the hall, showing him that I was in one piece. "Everything's fine."

He nodded, a shade uncertainly. I couldn't blame him. Across the hall, a creak announced that Chris's door was opening and I guessed he had been standing behind it the entire time. And when I looked up, Szuszanna was hanging over the banisters on the other side, a burly man beside her, frank curiosity on their faces.

"Show's over, folks." I gave a general smile, medium wattage, and waited until they had all taken the hint and left us to it. "Are you okay?"

Rob came down the stairs slowly, shaking his hand as if it hurt. "I will be."

I couldn't tell if he was talking about his knuckles or his emotional state, and I didn't get the chance to find out. He went straight past me and out the front door on a gust of cool night air, pulling it closed behind him. I shut my own door and went over to the window. It commanded a view of the whole street, but by the time I got there he was gone.

Chapter Seven

Thursday

It was my good luck that I didn't have to go into the office the following morning, or meet up with Derwent. I had a hearing to attend at the Old Bailey, a shooting that was on its way to trial. It was beyond restful to sit in Court 18 and stare at the oak paneling while the hearing dragged on, the barristers playing a polite game of one-upmanship. I had nothing to do. Chris Pettifer was more than happy to handle any queries that the prosecution had, and since he was a DS, he was entitled to.

It was my bad luck that I had forgotten Rob would be at the Central Criminal Court too that morning, dealing with his messed-up murder. I was standing on the concourse outside the court chatting with Pettifer when I felt that tingle at the base of the skull that tells you you're being watched. Somehow, it wasn't a surprise when I looked around and saw Rob on the opposite side of the concourse, Liv Bowen at his side. I stared across at him, not able to look away, trying to read the expression on his face.

"Is everything okay?" Pettifer was frowning when I looked back at him and I realized I had broken off mid-sentence.

"Fine. It's just—I hadn't seen that Rob was here." *Think fast.* "I have a message for him. From the boss."

"Better go and pass it on, then."

It took all of the nerve I had at my disposal to walk toward Rob, especially since he looked less and less encouraging the closer I got. Liv melted away with a nod to me and I had time to admire her tact before I had to think of something to say. And as it turned out, I needn't have bothered, because Rob got in first.

"What are you doing here?"

"That drugs shooting in Streatham was in for mention."

"You didn't say last night."

"I meant to. I forgot." I tried to sound normal, even though I was shrinking inside. He was obviously still furious. "How are you?"

"Fine."

"How's your hand?"

"Sore."

"You should ice it."

"I did."

Instead of persevering with a conversation that was going nowhere, I looked away. I was struggling to keep myself from showing how upset I was. Sniveling would help no one.

Rob shook his head—still annoyed, but this time with himself. "Shit. Look, I was just going to get a coffee. Do you want one?"

With a huge effort, I managed to sound lighthearted. "Why not? It might be a better idea to talk in public."

"It can't go much worse than last night."

"You'd hope not." I looked sideways at him as we walked toward the lift. "I'm sorry, if it helps."

"What do you need to apologize for? I shouldn't have left like that."

"It was my fault."

"You didn't make me punch your wall, Maeve. I did that all on my own."

"You had serious provocation."

"Don't make excuses for me. There's no need." He pushed the button to call the lift. "I just overreacted. That's all."

I wasn't going to argue it out there and then. I didn't say anything else until we had got to the canteen, queued for coffee and found a table. I scanned the room, checking to see if there was anyone we knew nearby, aware that Rob was doing the same thing. No one I knew was close enough to overhear us, but there were plenty of police officers and lawyers who would have been delighted to speculate about our conversation, and I hoped we could avoid the dramatics this time.

When we sat down, I picked up where we'd left off. "It's not an overreaction to want to know where you stand. It's not unreasonable to want things to be a certain way." I couldn't look at him; I didn't want to see disappointment in his eyes, or anger, or cold disapproval. "I thought we could do this, Rob, but I really think we have to call it a day."

"This is where we were two months ago. You took a decision to call a halt. I didn't get much of a say, remember?"

"I know. That didn't work out too well."

"Maybe because you still have feelings for me."

"Certainly because of that," I admitted. I didn't want to lie to him, even though it would have been easier. "No question about it. But that's not helpful for either of us."

"Maeve—"

"No. Listen." I made myself look at him. "I'm not going to do this to you. Not anymore. This go-away-come-back thing is too hard on both of us."

"I can live with it."

"You really can't."

"What's the alternative?"

I gathered all of my resolve. "We end it. Properly. Now."

"That's it?"

Say it like you mean it. "That's it."

"That's not what I want."

"I can't help it." I took a sip of coffee and regretted it instantly as the thin, bitter liquid seared my tongue. "I really miss you, Rob. But I miss the closeness. The jokes. I miss getting to talk to you without an underlying agenda. I miss you being around all the time. I miss that feeling I get when you're there—that sense that everything's going to be all right."

"None of that is incompatible with a proper relationship. You do know that, don't you? In fact, it's a pretty good place to start." Rob at his most persuasive, the anger replaced by a tenderness that was somehow harder to bear.

"We were idiots to think we could get away with this. I don't want to lose a friendship just because we sleep together now and then."

He leaned back. "What I want to know is why you assume it will all end in tears? Why can't we be friends and have great sex and not lose anything at all?"

"Because it doesn't work that way."

"That's how it's supposed to be. That's what people spend their whole lives looking for."

"Dec is splitting up with his wife." I blurted it out because it was uppermost in my mind. Rob's forehead creased in a frown.

"I'm sorry to hear that. But that doesn't mean all relationships in the world are doomed to fail."

"Maybe not. But they were devoted to one another, they have kids, and they still couldn't keep it together."

"It's sad. But it's not a reason to walk away from this."

"You don't understand."

"I don't, as it happens. And I don't think that what you're suggesting would make either of us happy, so I don't see the point. Honestly, Maeve, you're like one of those dinosaurs that needed two brains to coordinate themselves, one in their head and one in their arse. The one in your head appears to be kaput."

I concentrated very hard on my coffee spoon, twirling it around and around.

"Maeve, look at me." I dragged my eyes up to meet his again. "What do you want? What's your version of a happy ending for us?"

"I don't know."

"Well, neither do I. But I don't want things to stay like this." The silence lengthened. I could sense the fight was going out of him and it wasn't a surprise when he said, "Maybe a clean break is for the best."

I nodded slowly.

"But if that is what we're doing, that's the end of it, okay? Not friends with benefits. Not sneaking around now and then. We're finished."

"It sounds worse when you say it," I whispered.

"That's because I won't change my mind." He waited, but I didn't say anything else. This was what I had wanted, though it was hard to remember that when I was sitting across a table from him.

"Right then. Done."

"Done," I repeated. "And I'm sorry."

"I'll survive."

"I'm sure you will." I drank another mouthful of coffee before I remembered how it tasted. I pushed the cup away. "So what do we do now?"

"Business as usual."

"Do you think things will ever go back to the way they were?"

"That's up to us, isn't it?" He was looking past me as he said it, the frown fading as he waved at someone behind me. I twisted to see Liv standing in the doorway, looking lost. She saw us a split second after I saw her, and beamed before starting toward our table.

"I'd better go. Leave you to catch up with your new pal."

"Stay where you are."

"I've got to head off, Rob."

"What's the matter with you? Just sit there and be nice."

I didn't have time to say anything else before Liv arrived. She stood with one hand on the back of an empty chair, looking tentatively at me. "Do you mind if I join you?"

"Not at all. I was actually just about to go—" I caught Rob's eye and changed horses halfway through. "But I can stay for a few more minutes."

Rob stood up. "Let me get you something. Tea? Coffee?"

"Coffee, please. White, two sugars, and no lecture about my sweet tooth if you don't mind."

"I won't say a word. Maeve?"

"I'm okay." I gave him my best shitty look, though: *how dare you leave me sitting here alone with Liv when I didn't even want to talk to her in the first place.* He knew exactly what I was thinking; the grin on his face as he turned away said it all.

"I hope I'm not interrupting." Liv was looking wary.

"Of course not."

"It's just that . . ." She hesitated. "Are you two together?"

"Absolutely not."

"Oh. Because I thought—"

"There's nothing going on between us." *Not anymore . . .*

"Right. Do you always have really intense conversations with the people you work with?"

"Invariably. Your time will come." I smiled. "Bet you can't wait."

She looked past me, to where Rob was standing at the counter, charming a smile out of the sullen woman who ran the canteen. "It seems a shame, though. Rob's a nice guy."

"Yes. Yes, he is." I was dealing with a spasm of jealousy so strong that I was struggling to breathe through it. "Rob said you've been working with him on the Tancredi case."

"It hasn't been a lot of fun. At least with Rob you can have a laugh while you're waiting to get shat on by the judge for arresting the wrong person."

"Was that what happened?"

"He wasn't impressed, put it that way. And DS Mortimer wasn't there, so we had to take the blame."

"I'd be surprised if Morty was in this postcode. He doesn't like being in trouble."

"Oh well. We took it on the chin."

There was a kind of intimacy about the "we" that made me feel sad all of a sudden, but I forced myself to laugh as Rob set a cup in front of Liv.

"Drink at your own risk."

"I was going to warn you," I said, contrite. "I gave up on mine. It tastes like something died in the pot."

"As long as there's caffeine in it, I don't really care."

Rob raised one eyebrow. "To be honest, I doubt you'll be able to taste the coffee with all that muck in it."

"I told you, no lectures," Liv snapped.

"Just saying." Rob held up his hands and backed away a step, colliding with someone who was walking behind him. "Sorry."

"It's all right. It was an accident." The young woman smiled at him forgivingly, then ran a hand through her long red hair, shaking out loose ringlets so they cascaded over her shoulders and down her back. It was like watching an outtake from a shampoo ad, but if she was hoping to jog Rob's memory, it worked.

"Rosalba Osbourne, isn't it?"

"And you're DC Langton. You have a good memory for faces."

"Sometimes."

She gave a tinkling laugh and I looked at Liv, who raised her eyebrows.

Rob rallied. "How are things in the legal world?"

"Busy. Nothing as exciting as last year, though."

"Last year was a bit too exciting for me." Rob looked down at us as if he'd forgotten we were there. "Rosalba is a solicitor. She represented Selvaggi last December."

Not my favorite case, and definitely not my favorite criminal. I frowned. "So that's why I don't remember you. I was in hospital." If Rosalba knew why I had been there, she didn't let it show. She was far too focused on Rob to think about what I'd said anyway.

"It's nice of you to suggest I was his solicitor. I just sat in on the initial interviews. I'm far too junior to have such an important client."

"You did okay, as I recall."

"I don't remember you being in the room." She wrinkled her nose, as if confused. "I'd have thought I would."

"I watched most of the interviews on the monitors." Rob glanced down at me and Liv, as if realizing we were distinctly surplus to requirements. I folded my arms. *Flirt if you want to, but I'm not going anywhere, mate.*

"I do remember seeing you in court a few times," the solicitor said slowly.

"I came along to see the show once or twice."

"You know, it's funny meeting you like this. I always wanted to hear about the arrest straight from the horse's mouth. It sounded so dramatic."

"It was eventful," Rob agreed. Only someone who knew him very well would have spotted the corner of his mouth lift in amusement. "Eventful" was the understatement of the year.

She stepped closer, moving so she was between us and Rob, and dropped her voice, but what she said was still perfectly audible. "Look, I'd really like if we could go for a drink sometime."

I waited for Rob to get rid of her.

"Sure. Why not?"

"You don't have a girlfriend or anything, do you?"

"Not currently."

"Great. Don't take it personally. I always check."

"Very sensible."

"So when do you want to go out? Are you free tomorrow?" She had taken out her mobile and was thumbing through the calendar. "We could meet somewhere around here. There's a great bar down the road, near St. Paul's. Six o'clock?"

Rob was looking very slightly nonplussed. I gathered he wasn't used to dating alpha females.

"Fine by me."

She took out one of her business cards. "Here you go. My mobile number's on there. Text me so I've got yours."

He took the card obediently and said good-bye before Ms. Osbourne wiggled off, barely keeping her balance on skyscraper heels. We all watched her go, which I suppose was the idea behind the clinging suit and teetering footwear.

As if nothing had happened, Rob pulled out his chair and sat down. Liv gave him a shrewd look.

"Fast worker."

"Isn't she, though?" He tapped on the table, fidgeting just enough so that I was sure it wasn't a coincidence that he hadn't looked at me yet.

"I was talking about you."

Rob blinked, wounded. "Were you listening to the same conversation as me? What did I do? I just knocked into her by accident. Next thing I know, she's asking me out."

"Yeah, I noticed you trying to resist her. The kicking and screaming was embarrassing."

"I didn't want to be rude."

Liv looked across the table. "Maeve, back me up. He was panting."

Before I could answer, a ringtone shrilled and the three of us reached in unison for our phones. It turned out to be mine, of course, and a sick feeling came over me as I saw the caller's name displayed on my screen. I half-turned away, jamming my free hand to my ear to block out the noise of the canteen.

"Hello?"

"Where the hell are you?"

Good morning to you too, DI Derwent. "I'm at court."

"What the fuck are you doing there?" He sounded more bad-tempered than usual. Something told me there had been another murder, even before he said it. "We've got a body. If you've quite finished farting about, maybe you'd like to do some actual policing for a change."

I gritted my teeth. "I'm here because of another case. I did tell you I was going to be in court this morning. But I'm free now, so if you'll just tell me where I need to go—"

"Don't tempt me, darling. You're making it too easy." His tone changed. "Tell me about this very important court case. Was there any need for you to be there, as a matter of interest? Or were you just making up the numbers? Because I would have thought that an active murder investigation might have been your priority, especially when we have a fresh corpse waiting for your attention."

Be reasonable, I warned myself, but I couldn't keep the irritation out of my voice completely. "Well, I didn't know that."

"You should have."

"How could I have known?" Fuck diplomacy; he had annoyed me out of being meek.

Rob was frowning at me. He pointed at the phone and mouthed, "Derwent?"

I nodded, pulling out my notebook and uncapping a pen one-handed before scrawling the address down as Derwent dictated it. "Okay. I'll see you there shortly. As soon as I can." I disconnected before the inspector could say anything else. It was a pleasure deferred, of that I had no doubt, but I couldn't bear to sit there and listen to any more of Derwent's abuse at that moment. To Rob, I said, "I've got to go. There's another body."

"Shit."

"Exactly." I started to gather my things, glad of the distraction of a new crime scene in spite of the fact that I dreaded it more than a little.

"Was he giving you a hard time?"

"That's all he does." I stood up. "Liv, it was nice to get to talk. We must do it again sometime."

"I'm free tomorrow night," she said innocently. "There's a great bar near St. Paul's."

I laughed, properly this time, and headed for the door with an unexpected spring in my step. It looked as if Rob had been right about Liv after all. Which, I reminded myself, did not mean that he had been right about anything else.

The address DI Derwent had given me over the phone took me to Flocking Street, two quiet, shabby rows of pebble-dashed maisonettes, purpose-built flats with their own meager front doors, in an unfashionable part of Brixton untouched by gentrification. Looking at the map, it would only have been about ten minutes' walk from Ivan Tremlett's office, and fifteen at most from Barry Palmer's house. The third point of the triangle gave us an area of operations that was encouragingly small, and I walked toward the crime scene with a degree of optimism. I didn't need to check the number of the flat I was looking for. The usual hum of activity was centered on an address about halfway down the street—the vans, the police cars, the officers in T-shirts or fleeces who were searching front gardens, probing drains and gutters, the neighbors looking on. The street was closed off so the media were trapped at either end, not that there were too many of them yet—a couple of cameras and a handful of journalists making notes. They seemed to be mainly interviewing each other, I thought sardonically, slipping past them unnoticed. We had got away without anyone spotting the connection between Barry Palmer and Ivan Tremlett; I had a feeling that someone bright might just put it all together now that there was a third body. And media attention was not going to help us one little bit.

I made my way through the cordons and barriers, showing my credentials when challenged, and fetched up in the poky hallway of the property at the same time as Derwent himself, who had been heading in the opposite direction. He spread his arms wide as if he was going to embrace me and I stiffened, but he stopped a couple of paces away from me. Up close, I could see that the smile on his face was not one of welcome. And if I'd needed any confirmation of his mood, his first words would have taken care of that.

"At long fucking last. You took your time."

I didn't say anything. I had actually got there in record time, hitching a lift from a copper I'd bumped into at court. He was picked up in a high-performance unmarked car and the driver had been delighted to show us what it could do, even hindered by London traffic.

"Where's the body?"

"Bedroom."

As if in response, a camera flash exploded in the room at the end of the narrow hall.

"Down there, I take it." I looked around, seeing stained carpet and floral wallpaper that was inescapably 1980s. There was a little cup mounted on the wall by the door, a sponge in the bottom. A holy water font, I realized with a slight shock, peering in to see that the sponge was soaking wet. It was in regular use.

"What's that?" Derwent nodded toward the font.

"It's there so you can bless yourself with holy water whenever you enter or leave."

"For luck? Doesn't seem to work, then. Not for this poor bugger anyway."

"It's not luck. It's religious." I spoke more sharply than I should have. I could see the glint in Derwent's eyes as he registered that he had annoyed me. But there had been a font in my grandmother's house in Ireland; I had loved the ritual of making the sign of the cross on the threshold every time I'd passed it. The cheap white plastic font hanging askew on its nail took me back, although hers had been china, with a painted cross in gold, a treasured souvenir of a parish pilgrimage to Lourdes. I remembered standing on tiptoe to reach the font. The cold water on my fingertips, on my forehead. The look of approval on her face. Part and parcel of the experience of being on holiday in Ireland, it was an innocent memory and not one that I wanted to have tainted by murder.

"Don't try to tell me religion and superstition are two different things."

"I wouldn't dream of it." Not least because theological discussions with the inspector would be neither fun nor productive. "So what happened? Who's the latest victim?"

Derwent flattened himself against the wall to let a crime-scene technician pass by and grimaced. "We're in the way. That's the kitchen through there. I'll bring you up to speed."

The kitchen was small and old-fashioned but essentially orderly. It was minimally furnished, too small for a table and chairs but with a wooden stool placed under the counter by the door where you could sit and eat in relative comfort. A gingham curtain screened the lower cupboards from view, and open shelves above held a random selection of mismatched china and glass, which made me feel at home, given my haphazard domestic arrangements. There was a small larder. A half-empty jam jar stood beside a block of butter on a saucer, and behind that there was a loaf of bread. On the shelf below there was a box of teabags and a small container of sugar. Derwent bent and tweaked open the tiny fridge, scanning the interior. There was something poignant about the pint of milk lodged in the door, the piece of cheddar wrapped in cling film, the sliced ham and tomatoes already arranged on a plate for a meal that would never be eaten, the utter lack of anything self-indulgent. A calendar hung on one wall, the picture for March a kitten climbing on curtains. Nothing was written on it and I flicked back through the months, seeing blank pages, cute baby animals, an empty life.

The only sign of anything out of place was a mug with a teabag in it standing on the countertop near to the elderly gas cooker, where a kettle had tipped sideways off its burner. It looked to me as if someone had been interrupted in the act of making a cup of tea and replaced the kettle on the hob without paying sufficient attention to setting it down properly. Water lay in puddles on the cooker and the floor.

Quite suddenly, I didn't want to know anything more about the victim, or what lay in the bedroom, down the narrow hall. I wanted to leave the dismal kitchen, the badly lit hall with its pathetic font hanging crooked on the nail. I didn't want to confront the reality that I was standing in a crime scene.

"Dead body of the day is Mr. Fintan Kinsella, aged eighty," Derwent announced, out of tune with my mood as usual. He had put the emphasis on the second syllable of the surname as English people tended to. Kin-SELL-er. "He's one of yours."

"One of my what?" I snapped.

"Irish."

"In that case, his name is pronounced KIN-sella."

He waved his hand, unmoved. "He'd been living here for nine months."

"Where was he before?"

"Hospital. He had a bad heart. Before that he was in a retirement home for priests up in Liverpool. He spent quite a bit of the nineteen seventies interfering with young boys in his parish, apparently."

I closed my eyes for a second. It had only needed that. "Convicted?"

"Eventually. No one made any complaints against him until the rest of the court cases started to hit the headlines. Then they all tried it on. Father

Fintan was not what you'd call a serious offender. He did football training with the young lads, liked to watch them in the showers afterward. Used to suggest that some of them might like to have baths in the parish house while he held the towel. No touching, by all accounts. Not pleasant, not legal, but not as bad as some of them. I get the feeling that most people didn't take it too seriously until they realized there was money in complaining."

I didn't necessarily accept Derwent's version; the publicity for other trials may have brought victims forward but not for money, necessarily. For justice.

"He was retired a few years when they came looking for him. He admitted it straightaway. That and the fact that he was in bad health got him a non-custodial sentence. The stress made him collapse—which put him in hospital. He had a major heart operation and came through okay. Then he had nowhere to go once he'd recovered. The retirement home didn't want him back as he wasn't a priest anymore. I suppose they thought he might corrupt the others."

That wolfish smile again. It made my jaw clench involuntarily. I forced it open to ask, "So how did he end up here?"

"He worked in this part of London when he was younger. The flat belongs to a family who live in this area, ex-parishioners who'd kept in touch with him. The mother lived in this place, but she died last year. They found out what had happened to Father Fintan when they got in touch to see if he could do the funeral. And when they heard he needed somewhere to stay, they offered it to him for free. Needs a bit of doing-up but he didn't care."

"You'd have thought they would have wanted him to stay well away, given his past."

"Christian charity, I suppose." He shrugged. "Maybe they didn't believe Father Fintan could have done such a terrible thing. And apparently the mother was devoted to him."

"People believe what they want to believe." I looked at him, puzzled. "How did you find out all of this?"

"With the help of Mrs. Mary Driscoll, who was sort of an unofficial housekeeper for him. She's the one who found the body at ten this morning."

Only a couple of hours earlier. "What did Dr. Hanshaw say about time of death?"

"The usual guff about not being able to be sure. But I got him to say it was probably not long before the body was discovered. This morning rather than last night."

"That should help a bit. Did Mrs. Driscoll have a key?"

"She did indeed. She lives down the street. Did the shopping for him, cleaned the house, washed his clothes and hung them out to dry. You're more than welcome to interview her later. I've had an earful already. All I asked was how she knew the victim."

"Sounds as if he was living very quietly," I commented. "He wouldn't have had many opportunities to come to people's attention if she was doing all his shopping and cleaning. Did he go out?"

"Went to Mass every day. Asking for forgiveness, probably. Other than that, nothing."

I had noticed the small gray church built of dressed stone in the nineteenth century, probably for the benefit of Irish immigrants. It was a couple of hundred yards from the ex-priest's house—not a long walk. It wouldn't have been a strenuous outing. "Was he well known in the local community?"

"Not by the younger generations. Some people remembered him working here, according to Mrs. Driscoll, but most of them didn't know about the conviction."

"And no hint of that sort of behavior while he was here—now or then?"

"She didn't say anything about it." Derwent shook his head. "Like I said, ask her. If you can. I couldn't get a word in."

"He was living in total obscurity and they found him anyway."

"Someone did, yeah."

"Our guy?"

"Looks like. Bit of a fucking coincidence if someone else is killing pedos."

"Was he tortured?"

"He sure was," Derwent said carelessly, leaning up against the wall as if we were talking about football or the weather and not lethal violence. "As soon as the room clears out a bit, I'll take you down to see the body."

"I don't need to," I said too quickly. "I mean, I'll see the autopsy reports."

"No substitute for smelling the fear, Maeve." He straightened up. "Let's go and have a look now."

"Now?" I stepped back involuntarily.

"Lost your nerve?" His eyes were glittering with pleasure.

"No." I swallowed. "But I don't want to dash in there if it's crowded. I might as well see the rest of the place first."

"Won't take you long. But come on." He was looking amused as he led the way out of the kitchen and down the hall; he knew that I didn't want to be there, that I was playing for time.

"Bathroom." He flicked on the light. Lilac tiles, forest-green bath, sink and toilet: a blindingly bad combination that should never have been attempted. A brown towel hung from a hook on the wall. Mold was blooming on the ceiling and the room smelled fusty, but it was basically clean.

"The living room is at the back." Another small room, this time with dark-brown carpet, a print of da Vinci's *Last Supper* on the wall, a gas fire, a small radio. No television. The chairs looked hard, uncomfortable, and only one wooden-framed armchair showed signs of use. A crumpled pink cushion was squashed against the back of the seat. A lonely life, I thought, looking around. A sad life. There was a small brass crucifix on a table near the window, and a missal lay on the floor by the chair. The view was onto the garden, an uninspired patch of grass.

"The back door's at the end of the hall."

I followed Derwent. He turned a key in the frosted-glass door and pushed it open with a flourish. "Voilà."

The garden was just as bleak as it had looked from inside the house, the grass surrounded by high fences belonging to the neighboring flats. Derwent looked without comment at the clothesline and bird feeders that were the only other features. The line had plastic pegs clipped along it at intervals, ready for use. The bird feeders were three-quarters full, as if they had been topped up the previous day. One of the neighbors had a tree that was in full blossom, and tiny petals drifted across the grass with every breath of wind. They collected against the fence like a wavering frill of antique lace. At first glance it looked pretty, but the petals were already shading to brown as they rotted.

He had lived quietly. He had kept himself clean and the flat tidy, with the help of Mrs. Driscoll. He had taken pleasure in looking after the little birds who visited his garden, and not much else. He had kept his faith if not his status, spending his days in prayer either at home or in the local church. He had been a nice enough man to keep the loyalty of those he'd served during his time in London, and a decent enough man to admit his guilt when challenged.

He had also been an abuser, a manipulator, a powerful man in his community who had taken advantage of his position and caused harm to innocent children. Very few people were entirely bad, or entirely good for that matter. I wasn't going to judge him either way. I didn't need to. He was the victim in this case, not a suspect, and I would work as hard to find his killer as anyone else's.

And to do that, I needed to see where he'd died. I turned back to Derwent. "Let's see the bedroom."

"Follow me."

The scene-of-crime guys were finishing up when we went back to the hall and we waited as they filed out past us lugging bags and camera equipment. Bringing up the rear was one I recognized as Tony Schofield, a prematurely bald officer who lived on his nerves. To me, he had always seemed too highly strung for his job, but he had recently been promoted and was now officially a crime scene manager. He nodded to us

"Straightforward enough. We've done pictures and dabs and Dr. Hanshaw's released the body. I'll send in the mortuary men when you're finished."

"Anything we should avoid?"

"Try not to get human tissue on your clothes, I suppose. It's hell to get out." He saw the look on my face. "Sorry. Bad joke."

Derwent clapped him on the shoulder. "Don't give up the day job for a life in comedy, mate."

"Probably not a good idea." Schofield laughed nervously, then reverted to serious. "No, the room's clear. Obviously take the usual precautions."

The inspector looked at me. "Waiting for something?"

I was waiting for a miracle that might mean I didn't have to open the door, but Father Fintan hadn't got one so why should I? I snapped on thin blue latex gloves and used my elbow to push the door open, touching it as little as possible. I stepped in, moving to one side to allow Derwent to follow me. There was just enough room for us to stand side by side at the foot of the bed. The room was small, papered in navy dotted with bulbous red cabbage roses. There wasn't much in it apart from the bed, a small wardrobe and a chest of drawers that did double-duty as a bedside table. Someone had left the light on in the center of the ceiling, but it was struggling to do much about the general gloom. The only good thing you could say for the wallpaper and the overall ambience was that it hid the worst of the blood spatter.

The body was lying across the bed, fully clothed in a white shirt, a navy cardigan and black trousers, though the shirt and cardigan were unbuttoned and the trousers weren't fastened. Thick gray socks bulged over tartan slippers. His hands were laced over his stomach, silver rosary beads looped around them, as if he had been praying when he died. The hands were waxy, the nails long but well shaped, the fingers short. He had been a small man but not thin: his stomach was domed. It was hard to say much else about his appearance because his head was, to all intents and purposes, gone. Bits of bone and brain matter had exploded across the bed, coating the coverlet and headboard in blood and unidentifiable mush. What was left was not readily identifiable as human.

"Jesus."

"Yep. Being blasted in the face with a sawn-off shotgun won't do much for your complexion."

I had already noticed the holes in the bedcovers from stray pellets. "One shot, do we think?"

"Shouldn't have taken more."

"Risky, in a place like this, with neighbors all around. And not in character for our killer to be so direct."

"One shot isn't that risky. People ignore that sort of noise because they don't know what it is." Derwent stepped over to the window, peering out at the view of a blank wall. "And he did take a roundabout route to killing the not-very-good father."

"You said he was tortured. How?"

"See the rosary beads?" I nodded. "He was branded with them. Heated on the gas burner in the kitchen or the fire in the sitting room, I'd say. There was an oven glove on the floor in here. Looks as if the killer didn't want to burn his fingers."

Now that I knew what to look for I could see a chain of blisters in the shadow of the open shirt. I frowned. "That's horrible, but it sounds a bit halfhearted for our guy. It's a long way from castration and amputation."

"We don't know what else occurred. He could have knocked out teeth, broken bones in his face—that sort of thing. Plenty of tooth fragments in this room—there's just no way to tell whether they were shot out of his head or beaten out of it. It's gone now, but they recovered a heavy wooden crucifix from under the bed. It had been hanging on the wall." He pointed at a large nail near the bed and now that I looked I could see a darker patch of wallpaper where dust had settled behind the cross. "It was a big thing, two feet long. Loads of trace evidence—blood, hair, that kind of thing, as if someone had used it as a bludgeon. You could do a fair bit of damage with that."

"Mm. It's still not what you'd call an escalation. But then, Kinsella's crimes weren't as bad as those of the other two victims, arguably. If you accept that the killer is making the punishment appropriate for each of them

based on their record, it sort of makes sense that he wouldn't be as violent."
I sounded abstracted even to myself.

Derwent was studying me. "What are you thinking?"

"Maybe that he's losing interest."

He looked skeptical. "Do you really think he couldn't be bothered? Does
this look like going through the motions to you?"

"In a way. Maybe he didn't like killing a priest. We could be looking for
someone who is a Roman Catholic. Or was brought up as one."

"Could be."

I stepped around the bed, looking everywhere but at what remained of
the head. One glance had been enough.

"Presumably the body wasn't like this when it was found."

"You presume correctly. But Hanshaw didn't disturb the corpse too
much. There's rigor mortis in the hands—he didn't bother to break it. Said
he'd recover the rosary at the PM. The angle of the body is a bit off. He
wasn't as much on the bed as that. And Hanshaw did the undressing."

I looked up quickly. "Did he? So the shirt was buttoned up again after
the branding?"

Derwent nodded.

"Left him his dignity," I said, almost to myself. "He—or they, it could
have been more than one—must have decided the victim didn't know anything useful. He let Kinsella dress himself again. The killer even let him
pray, though making him use the same rosary that was used to torture him
is a sadistic twist, isn't it?"

"He was sitting on the bed," Derwent said. "When he was shot. Sitting
on the edge. Praying."

"He knew he was going to die."

"It was quick. And he was old." Derwent moved, suddenly restless.
"Finished?"

I was. I went out of the room with a definite feeling of relief that I could
leave the grim scene behind, but the details were still horribly vivid in my
mind's eye. I would never get used to looking at bodies, I thought dismally,
which argued that a change of track might not be such a bad idea. I could
leave the team—switch to financial investigation, maybe. There were very
few bodies in fraud. That might kill two birds with one stone, because if
Rob and I weren't on the same team anymore . . .

I clamped down hard on that particular train of thought. I had been
thinking about Rob in a completely unguarded way—a hopeful way. And

what a waste of time that was. It was over, I acknowledged, walking blindly down the narrow hall toward the door. He had moved on already, and so should I. There was no point in thinking about him anymore, and there was no point in considering leaving the team. Not when I still cared passionately about my job, and wanted to do well. My thoughts went to Godley and as we stepped into the open air, I turned.

"Has the boss been here? Is he coming down?"

Derwent shook his head. "Too busy."

"I wouldn't have thought he'd prioritize anything over a serial killer." Godley was as hands-on as his workload allowed and he had seemed so engaged with the case the previous night.

"Keep your voice down." He took my arm and squeezed it, hard. "Do you want to give the game away?"

I looked around. The only civilians were miles away. "Firstly, you're paranoid. There's no one near enough to hear. And secondly, do you seriously think you're going to be able to keep this under wraps for much longer?"

"Maybe not. But that doesn't mean I want it to come from you. We're going to need to manage the release of information carefully. The media aren't going to be easy to handle; don't make it any harder for us than it needs to be."

That was fair enough. And even if I didn't think I'd done anything wrong, a tactical apology might go a long way. "I'm sorry. I'll be careful. Look, I'll go and talk to the neighbors. See if they heard anything."

"No need."

"You can't have done it already." I hadn't taken that long to get to the address.

"Not me. Colin Vale. I asked the boss if we could have a bit of extra help and that's who he sent."

Colin was a good detective, beyond painstaking. I nodded. "We could do with the support."

"I thought you'd be pissed off." It was not my imagination that Derwent looked disappointed. He looked past me and I turned to see the lanky DC folding himself in two to duck under the crime-scene tape. "Here he is now. How did you get on?"

Lugubrious at the best of times, Colin was looking downright tragic now. "Not good at all." He pointed with his pen. "Next door to the left: out at work. They run the corner shop and leave the house at the crack of dawn, come back at God knows o'clock. I went along to the shop and checked with them anyway but they saw nothing, heard nothing, knew nothing. Next door to the right: the lady is deaf as a post and practically mute as well. From what I can gather, she didn't notice anything. Upstairs is empty and has been for months. Top left is being renovated and the builders were using heavy equipment all morning from about seven o'clock. They didn't notice anyone coming or going but again, not easy to get through to them because of the language barrier. They're Ukrainian."

"Top right?"

"Claire Halperin is her name. She's a nurse—works shifts. She was doing nights this week, off at seven in the morning, usually back here by eight. She ended up getting home a bit late today because she went to the supermarket on the way. Got here shortly after Mrs. Driscoll called nine-nine-nine and saw the first responders but that was her first inkling that there was anything wrong. She hadn't seen anyone hanging around over the past few days, definitely didn't notice anything out of the ordinary yesterday or this morning, and I'd say out of the lot of them she's the best possible witness. Young lady, but the sort who notices things."

"Did she know the victim?"

"She did. She looked in on him now and then. Mrs. Driscoll called her once when Mr. Kinsella took a turn and Miss Halperin checked him out, stayed with him until the paramedics arrived, that sort of thing. He was all right, she said—they didn't even keep him in overnight. But he was quite frail and she got into the habit of dropping in every couple of weeks for a chat. She liked him. Very shocked to hear he's dead." Colin looked at me morosely. "I didn't give her too much information about the circumstances."

"That's probably for the best."

Derwent was looking annoyed. "He lived in a shoebox with twenty other people practically within arm's reach; the walls are made of paper and nobody noticed a fucking thing. He was shot dead. No one saw anything suspicious. No one remembers anything useful like, say, a tall dark stranger covered in blood running down the street at nine in the morning or a car they didn't recognize with the engine running. Any chance someone remembers overhearing an altercation? A cry for help? A fucking shotgun blast?"

"Apparently not. But I haven't done the premises across the road yet." Colin gave a deep sigh. "Not much chance, I'd have said. Not with the way the maisonettes are laid out. You're basically hoping someone was in their kitchen looking out, or leaving the house, at the exact moment that your victim let their killer in. Because otherwise, you wouldn't see anything. And there's no sign of damage to the door or in the hall. It doesn't look like it was a forced entry. You're just hoping against hope that one of the neighbors was nosy enough to take notice when someone called to the door, basically, and I don't like the odds. But I'll ask them anyway."

"You might as well keep yourself busy that way as any other." Derwent paced back and forth. "Don't let me keep you."

He seemed completely absorbed in his own thoughts. With anyone else, I would have gone off and found something useful to do. But with Derwent, I didn't dare.

"What's the best thing for me to do?" He looked at me blankly and I risked a suggestion. "You mentioned talking to Mrs. Driscoll."

"Yeah. Sure. Why not. Go and talk to Mrs. Driscoll. And then get back to the nick. I'll go to the morgue. Make sure we didn't miss anything on this one. It bothers me that there isn't as much violence. It bothers me a lot."

"Not all killers escalate. They're not machines."

He didn't look at me. "Maybe the priest was better at talking to the killer. Maybe he convinced him to put him out of his misery. God knows, he was better off dead."

A fitting epitaph for a disgraced priest, but a cold one, I thought, as Derwent strode off to his car. I frowned a little. I was bothered too, but not about the violence. There were ready explanations for that; I had supplied a couple myself. What I couldn't work out to my satisfaction was why the three victims had all died in such different ways. Barry Palmer's skull was fractured, Ivan Tremlett's throat was cut, and Fintan Kinsella's head was blown off. I could understand using different means of torture, but I couldn't imagine a killer who would be at ease with three such different methods of dispatch. Beating someone to death required brute force and a certain lack of finesse. A slit throat was the ultimate in neat efficiency. Shooting the priest was certainly violent, but it maintained a degree of distance between murderer and victim, and suggested a kind of fastidiousness that didn't sit well with the other deaths. None of it made sense. It almost made me wonder if we weren't looking for a single killer, but three, which was surely ridiculous. Still, it was worth suggesting.

And I had not suggested it. The idea had occurred to me as soon as I saw Kinsella's body, but I hadn't even hinted at it. It was almost as if I were keeping it to myself, so I could discuss it with Godley at the earliest opportunity. But I would never do a thing like that. I had promised the inspector the previous evening. I'd said I wasn't interested in playing games. I'd never have *lied*. Not to him.

I watched Derwent drive away and I wasn't aware of the slightest twinge from my conscience.

Chapter Eight

Somewhat against the run of play, things started to improve as the day progressed. It probably wasn't a coincidence that DI Derwent was tied up all afternoon with the post-mortem. He would have been disappointed to realize that my interview with Mrs. Driscoll was far from a chore. In spite of the circumstances I enjoyed every minute of it.

Mrs. Driscoll lived on the other side of the road, not quite opposite the crime scene, in a ground-floor maisonette that was the mirror image of the priest's. She was small and wiry with dyed blue-black hair that looked as if it would be coarse to the touch. She was probably in her seventies but still spry, and her pale, watery eyes missed absolutely nothing. As promised, she was garrulous, but also entertainingly opinionated. Before I managed to ask her so much as a single question, I got to hear all about the ex-priest's neighbors and the Loughlins, who owned the flat where he'd lived.

Her living room was immaculately tidy, and I recognized the same take-no-prisoners attitude to dust that I'd noted in the victim's flat—every surface was polished to a mirror-like shine. A vast squashy three-piece suite covered in vibrantly floral upholstery took up most of the space in the room, and the remainder was devoted to a huge flat-screen TV. The curtains were the same material as the sofa and chairs, but were tied back with elaborately beaded tassels. The carpet was maroon, as were the skirting boards and dado-rail, and the wallpaper was gold with a maroon swirling pattern. The effect was somewhat startling but the room was comfortable—or it would have been, had it not been stiflingly hot. On a day when the spring sunshine had the uniformed officers out in their shirtsleeves, it was heated with two radiators and an open fire. I sat as far away from the hearth as I could and sipped the glass of water she had provided, rationing it as sweat beaded on my upper lip and trickled down my back.

Family photographs sat on every possible surface; I had had a good look at them while Mrs. Driscoll was getting the water. In pride of place were four large, leather-framed graduation pictures, three boys and a girl awkward in mortarboards. They were all standing in stiff poses holding scrolls, and all with identical embarrassed smiles. The hair and clothes dated the pictures to the mid-nineties. The same faces smiled out of wedding pictures that were tucked away on a low bookshelf, arranged so the spouses were more or less obscured. Poor Abby had a similar lack of prominence in my parents' front room. She would be relegated to a drawer by now, I guessed, reminded with a pang of my brother's difficulties. From the legions of babies, toddlers and children who waved and squinted pinkly in their frames, I deduced that the Driscoll children had provided grandchildren in abundance. I didn't dare ask about them, fearing that I'd never get Mrs. Driscoll back on topic. Besides, she was not the sort of witness who required coaxing to be forthcoming. She was more than ready to talk, and was loud in her defense of the dead man's reputation: "Now that he's not here to tell you himself and may perpetual light shine upon him may he rest in peace amen."

"Amen," I echoed. "So you were aware that he had been convicted of child abuse?"

"Indeed I was. Not a word of it was true. That poor man, God bless him, he was the sort who'd break his heart for you. He wasn't the man to argue. He went along with it sooner than say that the lads were lying. He used to tell me, 'Mary, it was true as far as it went. I was there when they washed in the house, but I was making sure they minded themselves and the property. There was no malice in it.'"

"But the events that were described did happen."

She waved a finger at me. "You have to realize, these were poor young fellows who had no access to hot water. No one else was looking after them. Filthy, they were, and full of nits and God knows what. Father Fintan washed their clothes and let them clean themselves to give them some self-respect. You couldn't turn your back on them or they'd rob you blind in a second. So he made sure they weren't left alone—for their own good. He was an innocent. He wouldn't have seen that there was any harm in staying in the one room with them. And indeed there was not. Didn't Christ himself wash the feet of his apostles?"

"So they say." All of this was delivered at machine-gun pace and I was struggling to keep up. "Did he do anything similar when he worked here in this parish, do you know?"

She drew herself up to her full height, which was roughly five foot nothing. "He did not. Nor did he need to. This area is respectable. This is not the sort of place where the children run wild. They may do that kind of thing up there in Liverpool, but not here. They wouldn't dare behave that way. No child would ever go into that church needing to be washed, or they'd feel the back of their mammy's hand." From the look on her face, I didn't doubt it. "Father Fintan was a lovely man. A decent man, through and through. We were happy to welcome him back when he needed somewhere to go."

"Didn't he want to return to Ireland?"

"He had no family there anymore. His sisters went to Canada, but they're both dead now. His parents were long gone, as you'd expect. His brother was a priest on the missions somewhere—Africa, maybe. Or the Philippines. I wouldn't know, frankly. They were scattered to the four winds, anyway, so he had no home to go back to. This was the closest thing he had to a home." The watery eyes blinked twice and moisture seeped into the vertical wrinkles that scored her cheeks. "Ah, sure, we'd all like to go home, but you find out what that means when you start to think about it. It's where they remember you, where you're loved. That was here, as far as he was concerned. He'd been away too long from Ireland. He didn't know it anymore, and they didn't know him. He was better off here."

Until someone brutally murdered him, I thought but didn't say. As if she had heard me, she fixed me with a beady eye.

"Robbery, was it? Were they looking for money?"

"We're not sure of the motive yet. We're keeping an open mind."

"That's what that other fellow said. That terrible eejit who came here earlier."

I beamed. "Inspector Derwent?"

"Him. He's an awful idiot, isn't he? A know-all. They're the sort who know the least."

"That's what I've always found."

"He wasn't interested in listening. Kept interrupting to ask his questions but he wasn't even paying attention to the answers. He just kept saying, 'Yep, yep, yep' when I was talking, trying to get me to hurry up. I know I can be a bit slow to get to the point, but I wanted to make sure he'd understand about Father Fintan. No one would have wanted to kill him. Not like that. God bless us and save us, when I saw what they'd done to him . . ." She closed her eyes, suddenly looking frail, and I recalled what she'd found when she opened the bedroom door. At least I had had plenty of warning.

I had been able to prepare myself. And I had still found it difficult to look at what remained of the old man.

"It must have been a terrible shock."

"Ah, well it was, you see. But I was worried anyway because he wasn't up. He was always out of bed when I got there. Usually he'd have been at Mass at seven. I didn't see him there this morning but I didn't think anything of it. I suppose I'd assumed that he wasn't well, or he'd woken up late or something of that nature. When I opened the door and called out to him and there was no reply—well, I knew *something* was wrong, but there wasn't any other sign that anything had happened. Except that his bedroom door was closed. When I saw that, I thought he was dead, but I thought he'd have died in his sleep." She sounded completely matter-of-fact about it. "I was already praying for his soul when I opened the door and found him."

"That must have been very upsetting, Mrs. Driscoll. So there was nothing out of place in the flat? Nothing that bothered you?"

She shook her head, but there was a tiny hesitation before she did so.

"In the kitchen . . ." I began.

"Oh, you saw that, did you? The kettle." She nodded, her pale eyes shining. "Now, I wondered about that, because he would make himself a cup of tea when he got up, before Mass. That was all he'd have. No breakfast or anything. Not until after, and even then it would only be a bit of bread. But he'd have the tea before he went out, around half past six, and I'd wash up the mug for him with his other things when I came in during the morning."

"Do you always visit him at the same time?"

"After Mass, but sometimes earlier, sometimes later. The odd time I'd be as late as half ten. I was nearly that late today, as it happened. Just by chance I had a phone call from an old friend and that held me up this morning. Of all the mornings to be late. Although if I'd walked in on whoever it was, I'd be lying there dead and you'd be looking at me, not talking to me."

She was probably right but I didn't want to agree too heartily. "Better not to think about what might have happened, Mrs. Driscoll. I'm glad it didn't turn out that way." I hesitated before asking her a question that was potentially committing me to spend the rest of the day in her sauna of a sitting room. "Is there anything else you think we should know about Father Fintan or what happened today? Anything we haven't asked you? Anything that's bothering you? Anything else you noticed?"

"Well, there was just one thing. It's probably nothing. But when I was getting the milk in this morning—that would have been at twenty to seven, and I'm sure of that because I had the television on in the kitchen—I saw that there was a Royal Mail van outside the flat, and a postman going up to the door with a package in brown paper. A big thing. Rectangular, about that big." She sketched out a shape that was roughly eighteen inches long and a foot wide.

"Are you sure it was Father Fintan's door?"

She nodded. "I looked to see. I was going to ask him what it was when I saw him."

"I didn't see a parcel in the flat," I said slowly, thinking about the sparsely furnished rooms I'd looked around.

"No more did I." She blinked rapidly. "I had a good look too. While I was waiting for the police. I wanted to make sure there wasn't anyone hiding behind a door, you know. I couldn't do anything for Father Fintan so I just said a few prayers for him while I was looking. No parcel at all."

"And no wrappings."

"Nothing." She sat back in her armchair, triumphant. "Not a bit of paper or anything."

"And you're sure it was his flat?"

"Positive. I saw the door open." She sounded definite, an ideal witness.

"Are you sure it was an official Royal Mail van? Did it have the company livery on the side?"

"It was red anyway." We were on shakier territory, I could tell immediately. She sounded suddenly vague. "It was the right size. I think it was. I didn't really look at it, to be honest with you. I wouldn't have known what sort of van it was, what make or whatever. I saw him get out, and I saw the color of it. He was in the uniform—the jacket and so on—so I just assumed it was a proper post van. I didn't think anything else of it."

"You didn't see the number plate." It wasn't a question.

She shook her head. "I'm sorry."

"Don't worry. This is really helpful. You did see the postman, which is more important anyway. Could you tell me what he looked like?" I was trying not to sound too excited, but my heart was doing its best imitation of a runaway horse at a full gallop.

"I was looking at the package, not at him. I didn't know he would be important." She sounded as desolate as I felt. "He was white. Brown hair, maybe?"

"Old? Young?"

"Not old. About the same age as Brian." I looked baffled and she shook her head, irritated with herself, then pointed at one of the pictures. "My middle son. He's thirty-four."

"Height?"

The best she could do was that he was neither especially tall nor particularly small. Average, in fact. And average build. She had helped to narrow it down to about a quarter of the population of London. And that was assuming she was right about the hair color, his age, and his race.

I thanked her anyway, genuinely grateful for some suggestion of a lead, and extracted myself from the flat at the cost of recounting, as briefly as I could, all I knew of both sides of my family. I only went back three generations, covering a span of years that she gave me to understand was woefully short and inadequate, but we parted on good terms nonetheless.

I collected Colin, who had managed to cover the rest of the street in the time it had taken me to do one interview, and we went back to the station together. As soon as we walked through the door, Superintendent Godley came to the door of his office.

"I gather Josh is tied up elsewhere. Come and tell me what happened this morning."

With Colin's help I filled him in, describing how the priest had been killed and what Mrs. Driscoll had seen. He listened intently, making an occasional note.

"So we're now looking at a very active serial killer."

"Or killers." I trotted out my theory about multiple murderers, feeling that it fell a little flat. Perhaps it was the dismaying realization that we had hardly any leads on one killer, let alone several. Perhaps it was the sketchiness of Mrs. Driscoll's description of our one and only suspect. Perhaps it was a general lack of enthusiasm for a serious, complicated, headline-grabbing inquiry. Any or all would have been entirely reasonable.

Godley sighed. "Right. Well, let's start with what we know. We need to trace a red van that may or may not have been an official Royal Mail vehicle. Colin, check with the local sorting office and see if there was anyone making parcel deliveries in that location around that time this morning, just so we can rule it out. Also, we'd better check with the occupants of the flats on either side of the priest's, to see if they were the recipients of the parcel. There's a chance that Mrs. Driscoll got it wrong, even if she won't admit it."

"Right. And then if it looks suspicious, I'll get on with finding the van."

"Check the area for ANPR cameras—that'll be your quickest route to finding it. Otherwise, call in local CCTV."

"There won't be anything from the street itself," I said. "It's all residential, no businesses. I didn't see any private CCTV cameras on any of the flats."

"Nor did I," Colin said. "We're not going to get the van outside the house. Best I can do is put it in the borough heading in the right direction, always assuming I can find it. We don't have a make, anything on the plate or a year of manufacture. And I guarantee you, red vans will be surprisingly popular in that neck of the woods."

"Think positive, Colin." Godley's expression lightened briefly. "If it can be identified, you're the one to do it."

The DC did not seem to be particularly cheered by the superintendent's confidence, but then I too would have been somewhat soured by the prospect of spending many hours watching CCTV of variable quality, looking for something that might never appear.

"It's obvious that this one is a major inquiry. We can expect the media to be interested from now on, so I'll let the press office know." Godley was back to looking grave. "As far as manpower goes, I'll talk to Josh about his requirements when he gets back, but in the meantime I'll allocate officers as needed. Maeve, what are you doing next?"

"Checking with IT to find out if anyone accessed the PNC records for both Kinsella and Palmer, or the sex offenders' register for the area. It's definitely worth considering that there might be someone on the inside helping the killer or killers."

"It is," Godley agreed. "That's why I asked Peter Belcott to get in touch with them as soon as he got in this morning. It was before we got word of the latest murder, so he's waiting for them to get back to him with an updated list at the moment."

I made a fair attempt at looking pleased even though I wanted to lie on the floor and whimper at the prospect of working with my least favorite colleague, the ever-irritating DC Belcott, whose presence on the team was a constant source of bemusement to me. About the only silver lining was the thought that he had had to spend the morning on the phone to the techies, a thankless task at the best of times.

Godley had moved on. "Have a chat with local CID as well. See if there's any information coming back to them from their informers about this. Have you made contact with them?"

"I met one of their DCs yesterday." It felt like a lifetime ago.

"They should be inclined to help. They'll be glad this one isn't on them." He rubbed his eyes. "Do bear in mind that if we do find someone on the force who has been helping the killer, we're going to have to tread carefully. I want to know straightaway if anything comes of that line of inquiry."

"Understood."

I took what he said to mean he didn't want to be bothered if we didn't get anywhere, and left him to his thoughts. Whatever they were, they seemed to be stopping him from sleeping at night, if the bags under his eyes were anything to go by. None of my business, I assured myself as I crossed the office, heading reluctantly for Belcott's desk. He was on the phone. I was just the right height to appreciate the brutal haircut he had had recently, so his hair was too short to obscure the weirdly squared-off shape of his skull. I stared down at his scalp gleaming through the dark bristles, the queasy white of a cave-dwelling thing that's never seen the sun, and felt my stomach turn over.

He glanced up and I rearranged my face into a smile, almost certainly not quite quickly enough. Raising one finger to tell me to wait, he returned to his conversation without seeming to be in a hurry to wind it up. As his side mostly consisted of grunts, I wasn't entirely clear on whether it was work or personal. But then, as far as I was aware, Belcott didn't actually have a personal life. I found a spare desk and sat on the edge of it, feet swinging. I could be patient if I needed to be.

Long after my patience had worn out, long after I had given up sitting and started pacing, he finally hung up and swiveled around to face me.

"Still here?"

"Obviously. What have you found out?"

Instead of replying, he stood up, pulling the waistband of his trousers up and puffing out his chest. "I think this one needs to go straight to the boss."

My interest sharpened. "Did you get a result? Really?"

"Might have done." He leaned over so he could see into Godley's office. "Might have a single name, as it happens. He doesn't look busy. Are you coming?"

I followed him, nonplussed. I hadn't really been expecting to find a trail of electronic bread crumbs that would lead to whoever had been helping the murderer—or maybe the murderer himself. It was a good idea, but nine times out of ten a good idea comes to nothing. It was something of a shock to discover that yes, there was one registered user of the PNC database who had consulted the records of all three victims in the days *before* they were murdered, and only one.

It took Belcott a very long time to explain to the superintendent, and, by extension, me, how very clever he had been in narrowing down the list that IT had supplied. I saw Godley's eyelids flicker, as if he had finally lost his grip on his patience, and his voice was sharp when he interrupted.

"Right, Peter. Can we get to the end of this sooner rather than later? I'd like to know who was responsible for this today, if possible."

"Of course." Belcott sounded surprised and not a little wounded. I didn't dare look in his direction. "The only person to have consulted those records in the past two weeks is a civilian clerical assistant in Brixton, one Caroline Banner. She's been working there for eleven years, so it's probably worth checking back to see if she's been up to no good all along. Nothing in her file to suggest it, I have to admit. She's a model employee, and her background checks have all been fine—no close relations with criminal records, no associations with known villains." He shrugged. "No accounting for who'll turn bad if they get offered enough to do it. Everyone has their price, I suppose."

"It needn't be money," I pointed out. "Not everyone is motivated by cold hard cash."

"What else would it be?"

"Intimidation, perhaps. Or, considering the victims, she might have been persuaded that what she was doing was just and proper."

"Hard to argue with that. Sounds as if the killer is doing the world a favor, if you ask me."

"Thank you, Peter." Godley was probably the only person alive who could quell Belcott completely in just three words. His repressive tone was probably also designed to discourage me from tackling Belcott myself, but I wouldn't have bothered to argue with him anyway. I was more interested in finding out what he knew.

"Did you get a list of every other search she's conducted in the last couple of weeks?"

"Amazingly enough, I did think of that." He waved a sheaf of pages at me, not giving me time to read anything that was on them. "But it's part of her job, legitimately, to access the PNC database about convicted criminals living in the local area. It's going to take me a while to separate out the ones who fit into the victim profile you've been seeing. By which I mean nonces."

Godley frowned. "You'd better list the sex offenders of all kinds—not just pedophiles. We don't know what the parameters are for our killer. Just because we have three victims with convictions of that nature, we can't expect him to stick to cats of one color."

"It's still going to take me a while."

"As soon as you've got the list, circulate it to DI Derwent, to Colin and Maeve, and to me. That's your priority."

"What's mine?" I knew what I wanted to do, but I wasn't sure if Godley would allow it. "Caroline Banner needs to be interviewed, but should I wait for DI Derwent to get back?"

"Is he still at the morgue?"

"So it seems."

Godley tapped the end of his pen on his desk, thinking. "Right. You're absolutely correct: we do need to talk to this woman, right now. I want to know what she's been saying and to whom. But I don't want to spook her either, so I'm not letting the boys from the DPS arrest her for misconduct in public office—yet. Nor do I want to have personnel breathing down my neck, telling me I can't ask her any questions because of pending disciplinary proceedings. Maeve, go and find her. Interview her, but gently. Don't tell her she's not in trouble, because she certainly will be, but play it down. Go for the sympathy angle—tell her about Ivan Tremlett's kids. We don't know why she's helping the killer, but we do know that these victims don't cause many people to shed tears. So make them real for her. We need her to want to help us. If she feels guilty, so much the better."

I nodded.

"Peter, thanks for helping on this one." There was a definite note of dismissal in the superintendent's voice and I wasn't the only one who'd noticed it.

"Don't you want me to speak to the Banner woman too?"

The answer to that was evidently no. Godley leaned back, looking indefinably authoritative all of a sudden. "There'll be more useful things for you to do here. Like working on that list."

"I'm happy to talk to her on my own," I said, and subsided at a glare from the superintendent.

"There's no question of that. You'll need someone with you because this is going to be a criminal case eventually, and you need to be protected from the defense. They'll go for you if they find out you spoke to her informally before she was arrested. What are you going to say if she suggests you said anything inappropriate?"

"But I wouldn't."

"I'm sure you wouldn't. That doesn't mean she won't claim you did." He looked past me, scanning the office and I knew what he was going to say before he said it. "Why don't you take Rob with you? He's sensible on these occasions."

Why not take Rob with me? Because it would be hellishly awkward, actually, Superintendent Godley.

"I think he's busy. He's out tying up the loose ends on the Tancredi case."

"At a guess, the ends are loose no more. He's sitting at his desk."

Of course he was. And I had run out of reasons why he shouldn't be the one to come with me. I trailed a tetchy Belcott out of the office, almost wishing that he had been told to accompany me. Almost. No matter how great the potential for embarrassment if I worked with Rob, it was still likely to be better than the short, sweaty alternative represented by Peter Belcott.

Rob being Rob, of course, he made things easy for me. He was back to his usual self-possession, that amused reserve that had deserted him so comprehensively the previous evening and had still been subdued during our conversation at the Old Bailey. In fact, if it hadn't been for the bruising across the back of his hand, I might have doubted that he had lost his temper at all. He listened courteously to my floundering explanation of where I was going and why I needed him to come too, or rather, why Godley had said he should come along when I definitely hadn't asked for him, although I was glad he was free to join me. When I had finally wound down to silence, he picked up his keys and stood up.

"As long as I get to drive, we can go where you like."

"Fine by me."

"Do we know she's definitely at work today?"

"Godley rang them. They've got her sitting in an interview room waiting for us."

"Does she know why?"

"Doubt it. Although you never know, she might have a guilty conscience. If you'd been passing confidential information to someone who shouldn't have it, you might suspect that's why you're being interviewed, I suppose."

"You might at that."

Walking out to the car with him felt more or less like the old days, although much like someone with dormant toothache, I couldn't help poking at the source of the pain to see if it was really gone, and discovered with one look at him that no, it was not. I was exceedingly aware of him sitting in the car beside me—aware too of taking care to avoid physical contact with him, of taking care to choose the right words as we talked. But from him there was no sign of awkwardness and I did my best to match his composure.

On the way to Brixton I told him about my morning's work, describing the priest's house and his body—more specifically, what remained of it after the shotgun blast that had ended his life.

"That does sound a bit odd in the context of the other murders. What did Derwent say when you suggested multiple killers?"

I let my silence answer for me and he laughed. "Like that, is it?"

"I hadn't thought it out before he left. I only put it all together before I went in to talk to the boss."

"A likely story." He glanced at me. "Seriously, Maeve, watch it. Twisting Derwent's tail is not the way to deal with him."

"You don't even know him."

"I know you. You're dangerous to yourself and others when you start playing games." He sounded nothing but matter-of-fact—distant, if anything—and when I looked he was concentrating on the road.

"I'm not playing games. I just took the opportunity to talk to the boss while Derwent was otherwise engaged. And it wasn't as if Godley was delighted to hear the idea anyway."

"That's nothing compared to how thrilled Derwent will be to hear about it secondhand. I'm not saying you were wrong to talk to Godley about it while you had the chance, but you're going to have to watch your step. Think about how you're going to approach it now, not when he's in your face demanding an explanation."

"Thanks for the career advice."

"Diplomacy is not your strong point," Rob said frankly. "I'm trying to save you from yourself."

"And I'm grateful." Not least for the fact that we had just arrived at the car park of the police station where Caroline Banner worked, bringing a neat conclusion to a conversation that was making me edgy.

With the minimum of fuss, Rob managed to insert the car into a space that I would never have attempted.

"Show-off."

"It's starting to rain and I wanted to get close to the door."

I shook my head. "You wanted to prove you're a better driver than me."

"I don't need to prove that. You've done it for me."

"How do you work that out?"

"How many times have you dinged your car this year?"

"How many points have you got on your license?" I countered.

"Six. I like fast driving." He grinned. "Your turn."

"Three dents, a broken taillight and a scrape along the side. I hate parking." I looked at the windscreen; he hadn't been lying about the rain. "We should make a run for it."

"Lead the way."

In spite of my head start, he got to the door before me and held it open. I went through without demurring, wondering why it bothered me when Derwent went out of his way to be solicitous toward me and why it didn't seem to matter when it was Rob. Perhaps it was because I knew Rob viewed me as an equal in all things except maybe driving and certainly cooking, and I had a pretty good idea that Derwent despised me. He would have been livid if he'd known where I was and what I was doing, and the thought put an extra bounce in my step as I headed for the reception desk to introduce myself and find out where Caroline Banner was waiting. Given the severity of the allegations I had assumed she would have been put in an interview room, but the thin, harassed DI who came to greet us explained that she was sitting in his office. I must have looked surprised because as he set off to show us the way, at a pace that had me struggling to keep up, he said, "It wasn't my idea. It was your boss who requested it. Said he wanted to keep things friendly for now."

"That's the brief," I acknowledged.

"I don't like it myself. If it was up to me, I'd have her out of here." He swung around to look at me. His hairline was receding almost visibly and his expanse of forehead was corrugated with wrinkles. "I was supposed to meet you yesterday. Geraint Lawlor. I had to send Henry Cowell instead."

"He was very helpful. Knows his stuff too."

The inspector grunted. "That's him. Rising star, or thinks he is." He spoke brusquely, but I thought he was genuinely proud of his junior officer.

"While I'm here, I wanted to check whether you'd heard anything about the murders from local informants."

"Whatever we find out, we'll pass it along to you immediately. So far, nothing. And we have been looking. Just because we managed to pass the buck to you, that doesn't mean we're happy about having this sort of thing on our patch."

"I'm sure you're not."

He gave me a short, sharp nod, and paused outside a door. "This is it. Are you ready?"

I nodded, feeling anything but, and followed him into a small room jammed with papers and files where a white-faced woman was sitting, kneading a balled-up tissue in her hands.

"My office," Lawlor said unnecessarily. "And this is Caroline Banner. I'll leave you to talk."

It was obvious from the hunted expression on her face that she knew why we were there, and equally obvious that she was guilty. But it became apparent very quickly that she was neither a moral crusader nor a regular associate of hardened criminals. Caroline Banner was middle-aged, gentle of manner, and absolutely terrified. I explained why we were there and she nodded.

"I knew someone would work it out. I told them I'd be found out."

"Mrs. Banner, you must understand that we need to know who you've been passing information to."

"I can't help you."

"Can't—or won't?" Rob's voice was gentle.

"I can't. I don't know them. I don't want to know them. I just want to be left alone." She sounded as if she was on her last nerve.

"You do know that's not going to happen. This is serious, Mrs. Banner. This is a breach of confidentiality that's left three men dead. Maybe more."

"Do you think I don't know that?" There were tears standing in her eyes but she was angry. "Do you think I wanted this? Any of this? As far as I know, I didn't do a thing to get myself into this situation. I love my job and I work hard. I would never have abused my position if I'd had a choice."

"Why didn't you?"

"I had to decide between looking up some information and risking my son's safety. That's not difficult, is it? If I hadn't done it, someone else would have. And I would have worried about Alan every day for the rest of my life. I didn't really have to think about it."

"Are you saying that threats were made against your family?"

She nodded.

"How was it done?"

"It was a phone call. Five days ago, in the evening. I was at home." She swallowed, remembering. "I picked up the phone and said hello, and a man asked if I was Caroline. I said yes. I didn't even think."

"Did you recognize the voice?"

"No." She sounded definite. "I've thought about it a lot, as you might imagine. I'd never heard him before. He didn't sound old, but I had the impression he wasn't very young either. And his accent was just ordinary. Middle-class. Like mine."

"A Londoner?"

"I suppose so. There wasn't anything distinctive about it."

"Would you know the voice if you heard it again?"

"Yes." The answer was immediate, unpremeditated. She looked at Rob, stricken. "But I can't help you. I won't be a witness. I wouldn't take the risk."

"What did the man say to you?" I asked.

"He told me to listen, and not to say anything. He told me that he knew I could get at records on the PNC and the sex offenders' register, and that he needed me to look up a few things for him. He asked me to look for convicted pedophiles in this area—any offenses involving children, anywhere and at any time."

Rob had been making notes. Now he looked up. "Did he use those exact words? He called it the PNC, not the police computer or database?"

"Yes."

I exchanged a look with Rob. That suggested an insider. "What were you supposed to do with the information?"

"He gave me an e-mail address to send the list to."

My interest quickened. "What was the address?"

"Gibberish," she said crisply. "Random letters and numbers. It was a free Internet account, not a proper one. And the day after I sent the list, I sent a message asking him to leave me alone from now on, but it bounced back, so I think the account had been closed."

"We'll need the details anyway."

"Of course."

"Have you got a copy of the list?"

"I didn't keep anything. Too dangerous. And I don't remember the details, honestly. I was trying to do it quickly, without thinking about it. I suppose there were ten or twelve names in total, but I can't be sure."

"You're going to have to think about it," I said, allowing an edge of authority into my voice. "You're going to have to run the search again, exactly the same way. We need to know what you passed on to the man who threatened you."

Used to obeying direct commands, Caroline Banner nodded, although she looked miserable about it. I felt a tiny bit bad about bullying her, but it was necessary. I needed the list and she needed anything at all that might make things a little less black for her.

"What did he say after he gave you the e-mail address?"

"He said he knew I was a diligent employee and I would want to say no, so he was going to make me an offer I couldn't refuse." Her mouth twisted. "I thought that was rubbish, you know. It sounded so clichéd. I was just about to hang up when he said that he'd been watching Alan. He'd seen him at football practice. He told me the position he plays, and the number on his shirt. He told me Alan had fallen that day and grazed his knee, so I knew he was telling the truth—he had been watching him, or someone had on his behalf. He told me that if I said no, or if I told anyone about the phone call, he could arrange for Alan to be taken away and I'd never see him again, dead or alive. I'd never know what had happened to him, except that I could have stopped it if I'd wanted to."

"And you believed him."

"I did," she said simply. "He wasn't lying, I could tell. He just sounded so cold. As if what he was saying was reasonable. He'd have done it, I know it. He might do it still. You have to protect us. You have to make sure Alan is safe."

"How old is Alan?" I asked.

"Eleven." The tears came then and she wiped them away with the back of her hand, the tissue having lost the power to absorb anything more. "I couldn't take the risk. You can understand that, can't you?"

I could, sort of. She had justified her decision to herself, and to us. But her actions had condemned three men to die horribly, and the saddest part was that she hadn't even bought herself peace of mind. No matter what she did or where she went once she got out of prison, she would be looking over her shoulder for the rest of her life, probably with reason. Because if there was one thing I was learning about the killer we were seeking, it was that he would stop at nothing to get what he wanted, whatever that might be.

Chapter Nine

Reluctant she undoubtedly was, but Caroline Banner came up with the goods. With a little bit more coaxing and access to a computer, she gave us a list of twelve names, the first three of which were instantly familiar to me as my victims.

Rob was frowning. "Is this the order you had them on the original list?"

"As far as I recall."

"Palmer, Tremlett, Kinsella, Merriman, Forgrave, Flanders, Johnson, Tait, Carey, Bardock, Lomax, Dyton. That's not even close to being alphabetical."

"It wasn't designed to be. That's not what he asked for." She looked from Rob to me. "Did I not say? He wanted the names of the sex offenders who lived closest to the A23."

"Why?" I said blankly, wondering why we hadn't noticed that before, when it ran through Brixton like a spine and lay right in the middle of my map of the murders.

"No idea."

I hadn't really expected her to know, but the vacant way she replied annoyed me nonetheless. She had absolved herself of all responsibility for what she had done, and seemed to have no curiosity about what the implications of her actions were. I couldn't help myself; I pointed at the top of the list.

"You do realize these men are dead, don't you, Mrs. Banner? Ivan Tremlett had three kids who are going to grow up without a father. Mr. Palmer and Mr. Kinsella lived alone, but they had people who loved them too, people who will mourn them and miss them. They were tortured before they died—tortured and mutilated—and we don't know what motivated the killer any more than we know who is responsible. So maybe you should do a bit more thinking about what you know about the man who contacted you. Make sure you share everything with us this time, instead of conveniently forgetting details that might be helpful in tracking him down."

Rob's hand came down on mine, hard, unseen by Caroline Banner. She was snuffling in her tissue again. I glared at him and got more or less the same look back.

"Leave it," he muttered.

I couldn't argue with him there, in front of her, but I could feel anger tightening in my chest. He guided her through what she'd told us once more, checking every detail with the utmost courtesy and gentleness while I simmered beside him. I had enough self-control to leave Mrs. Banner with the idea I was grateful to her for her help, and enough presence of mind to talk to the worried DI Lawlor on my way out. I wasn't really able to do much for his state of mind. There would be more interviews for Caroline Banner, and a whole lot of trouble for DI Lawlor. It had been a worthwhile interview—the first hint of a breakthrough—and Rob had been instrumental in getting Caroline Banner to trust us. All the same, I couldn't look at him. I stared out through the windscreen, waiting for him to start the car. Instead, he folded his arms.

"Go on." He sounded resigned, but there was a hint of amusement there too that made my hackles rise.

"What?"

"You'd better say it now."

"I don't have anything to say."

"You mean you're not angry with me?"

"I didn't say that." I glanced at him briefly, looking at his chin so I didn't have to meet his eyes. "I'm livid, as it happens. But I don't need to talk to you about it."

"I'd prefer it if you did."

"And I'd prefer it if you let me do my job. There was nothing wrong with how I was interviewing her. Nothing at all."

"You scared the shit out of her. You told her that the man she helped is capable of extreme violence. You basically made her aware that the threats he made are worth worrying about."

"She was worried anyway, but she was worried about herself and her family. She hadn't even thought about what her actions meant for other people. She's a selfish, stupid woman, and she wasn't even trying to be helpful, even now."

"Do you blame her?" When I didn't reply, he sighed. "Look, Maeve, she was right. If she hadn't given him the information, he would have got it from somewhere else. Those men would still be dead. Or another three men would have been top of the list, and they'd be the victims you seem to care so much about."

"Someone has to." I felt a tingle at the back of my nose and blinked furiously. I would not cry. "You didn't see Palmer and Kinsella. You didn't see how they were living. They weren't dangerous. They didn't deserve to die like that. And she didn't seem to care about what she'd done to help the killer."

"You're not going to change someone like that, though. She's never going to see it the way you do."

"Do you have to act like you're so fucking wise all the time? You're not perfect, Rob, even if you like to think you are. So stop patronizing me," I spat.

"I wasn't," he said gently, which didn't calm me down in the least.

"Apparently you know just how to deal with Josh Derwent, even though you've never had to work with him. Apparently you know just how to cope with going to the most horrendous crime scenes without giving a shit about the victims. Think about why they died, not how. That's what you said, isn't it? Well, I can't. I can't separate it out like that." I ran out of steam all of a sudden, aware that I had got sidetracked, aware that I had revealed more than I had intended.

"Is that what this is about? What I said about Derwent? I was just trying to help."

"Well, maybe you should let me worry about him. It's really none of your business."

I heard him take a breath, but instead of saying whatever he had planned to, he started the car. We left the parking space with rather less finesse than he had used to get into it, by the grace of God not quite scraping the wall or the car next to us. I didn't say anything until we were well out of Brixton, stuck in traffic as we crawled toward Vauxhall.

"I'm sorry for shouting at you. But you were being a condescending git."

"Not my intention."

"I don't suppose it was." I paused for a second. "Godley suggested I should tell her about Ivan Tremlett's kids. It wasn't just me going off on one. I'm more professional than that, I hope."

A swift, assessing glance. "I didn't mean to suggest you weren't."

"That's how it came across." I couldn't help sounding truculent, and I wasn't really surprised when Rob didn't reply. We spent the rest of the drive in silence, and when we got back to the nick I let him talk to the superintendent on his own while I looked for Peter Belcott. It was probably the only time in my life that I was pleased to have a reason to talk to Belcott, and it was fair to say the feeling wasn't entirely mutual. He looked up unenthusiastically as I approached.

"Back already?"

Instead of answering, I laid a copy of Caroline Banner's list on his desk, sitting on the edge so I could lean over to see what he'd found. "Do they match up with anything you've found so far?"

He scanned it, then flipped through the sheaf of pages that represented her searches on the PNC. "Right. Got your three victims, obviously. Merriman . . . that's Anthony Grayson Merriman, aged forty-three, convicted of abusing his stepdaughter from when she was nine until she was thirteen. Lovely."

"Have you got an address for him?"

"Talavera Road." He wrote it down beside Merriman's name and I craned my head to see, trying to recall if I'd seen the road on the map, and if it was remotely near where the other three had died.

"Stanley Flanders is on here too. Seems to have been a common-or-garden flasher, Peeping Tom, that kind of thing. Seventy-four, God bless him."

"Address?" I snapped.

"The Mayhew Estate."

I had seen that on the map and from Barry Palmer's road: the estate consisted of eight gray concrete tower blocks, stained and square. A social experiment in twelve floors, they had been designed to be the new wave of modern living in the 1960s, and they loomed over the neighboring streets threateningly.

"What about this one?" I tapped "Forgrave" with the end of my pen.

He flipped through the pages, scanning them intently. "William Forgrave. He's thirty-six, lives in Camford Mews."

I opened the *A–Z* that was on Belcott's desk and found Camford Mews in the index. It was not exactly a surprise when I found myself just outside the triangle made by the previous three victims' addresses. "Widening the search," I said, almost to myself. "What did he do?"

"Forgrave was convicted in nineteen-ninety-five of raping a fifteen-year-old girl the previous year and the attempted rape of two thirteen-year-olds in nineteen-ninety-three. He got ten years."

I was working it out. "In nineteen-ninety-five, he would have been twenty. Sounds as if he got started early. I'm surprised he didn't get life."

"Maybe they were asking for it."

I shuddered and slid off his desk as if it were suddenly red-hot. "Thanks for the help anyway."

"Just doing my job." No more than the truth.

The door at the end of the room opened and Derwent walked in, looking as if he had been hurrying to get there. He saw me straightaway and raised his eyebrows. *What's going on?*

I started toward him but before I got anywhere near, Godley put his head out of his office. "Josh, don't take your coat off. You and Maeve need to go and check on a few potential victims. Maeve, did you and Peter manage to get the contact details of the people on the list?"

"Peter's given me the first three. He's still looking for the rest."

"It's somewhere to start. Get going. Colin and Rob can work through the next few names."

Derwent was looking wary. "Do I have a few minutes? I wanted to check up on a couple of things."

"Delegate it. Harry Maitland is free. You can call him from the car and brief him that way. Just don't hang around here. If we've got a chance of preventing another murder, we need to take it or we'll be crucified by the media, and rightly so."

"I'd rather do it myself."

"I'm sure. But Harry is capable. Get on with it, Josh."

I had already grabbed my bag and jacket. I stood by the door, waiting for the DI, who walked past me as if I weren't there. I trailed after him down the corridor.

"Do you want me to drive?"

"What?" He didn't even look around.

"If you're going to be making calls on the way, it might be easier if I drive."

He swore under his breath. I didn't dare ask again, and when we got to the car, he got into the driver's seat without saying anything further about it.

"Where to?"

"Anthony Merriman is first on the list. Talavera Road." I read out the postcode and he set the sat nav, poking at it bad-temperedly, then reversed out of his parking space with a squeal from the tires. I settled back in my seat, resigned to another silent drive across town. The best I could hope for was better traffic on the way.

"Another lovely place to live," Derwent observed as we parked down the street from Camford Mews. It was a bleak back street where a developer had slotted in a small block of flats between the yard of a funeral home and a vacant industrial unit. From where we sat, we could see the front doors of the flats, four on each floor, twelve in all.

"Forgrave is in number nine." I peered. "Bet it's on the top floor."

"It's always the top floor. Go and check it out, but don't knock on his door yet. I'll be right behind you. I've just got to phone a man about a dog."

I got out of the car, feeling slightly uncomfortable. We were on a courtesy call, so we weren't tooled up with CS spray or the extendable batons known universally as Asps—a pleasingly lethal name, though it was the abbreviation for the company that made them, Armament Systems and Procedures, rather than anything more descriptive. I would have liked to be wearing a stab vest at the very least, but Derwent hadn't suggested it and I didn't like to. The breeze had picked up and this early in the year it still had an edge. It cut through my clothes, pressing my shirt against my body as I walked toward the flats. It was a reminder that I had nothing to protect me, and I put my hand in my bag, checking for my radio, scanning the street to see if there was anything out of place.

We had drawn a blank in Talavera Road, discovering that Merriman had moved away a couple of months earlier without informing the authorities. Black mark for him, but a name crossed off our list at least. The new residents were Pakistani, a young couple who had done their best to help, although they didn't have a forwarding address for Merriman. Derwent had warned them to take care as best he could. Understandably, he didn't go into details about why they might need to be wary. It wasn't the sort of thing they needed to know.

A pedestrian walked past me—a large man being walked by a very keen Labrador. He smiled breathlessly as he went by and I could hear him wheezing as he moved down the street, the dog pulling on its lead, powering onward. I went past a white BT van that was parked outside the flats, two wheels up on the pavement, but the engineer was nowhere to be seen and the vehicle was locked. A car went by at speed, making me jump; it was a metallic blue Subaru, the windows tinted so dark that I couldn't see the driver, and I noted the number plate without even thinking about it.

The door to the flats had been wedged open. So much for security. It was probably the engineer, at work in the building on someone's broadband and in too much of a hurry to remember the code for the door. It made it easy for me to get inside, but I went in with my heart thumping, my eyes wide, hyper-alert for signs of danger. The main door opened onto a hallway where concrete steps led up to the next story, and I craned my neck to see up the stairwell. No sign of life. The flats' front doors were accessible via open balconies on each floor and I looked left and right, seeing flowerpots outside one flat, a bike chained up outside another. The flats were respectable, if modest. It was noticeable that there was no graffiti on any of the surfaces, and the stairwell was spotless. The funeral home would be a reasonably quiet neighbor too, I guessed. Not such a bad place to live. Not a great place to die, though.

Still with an uneasy feeling, I started up the stairs. I went quietly, taking my time, and had got as far as the first landing when I heard the front door bang closed. DI Derwent took the stairs two at a time, his footsteps echoing through the stairwell, and I whipped around with my finger on my lips as he turned the corner and saw me.

"Anything?" He said it quietly, but I still winced, shaking my head. "Carry on, then."

So he was happy for me to go first. I should have been pleased that he was letting me take the lead but, feminist or not, I would have given a lot to be standing behind him at that moment. I couldn't help thinking about how solid muscle has a way of absorbing the worst a shotgun had to offer, for instance.

Nothing to see on the first floor. I took the next flight at a steady pace, not as quickly as I would have usually, not as slowly as the first. Derwent was close behind me, almost clipping my heels. The second floor. Flats 9 to 12, a sign informed me helpfully. Forgrave's was to the right. I stopped again and listened, hearing nothing except Derwent's breathing behind me, slow and regular. We walked together along the open corridor, moving quietly but with purpose. I was starting to relax as we got nearer to Forgrave's flat and there was no sign of anything wrong. He had no window boxes, no little personal touches to draw attention to himself. We passed flat 10 and I jumped sideways as a dog erupted into a volley of barks, high-pitched and sharp. I could hear it scrabbling at the wood as it tried to claw its way out. Derwent laughed.

"What do you think it is, a Jack Russell?"

"Something like that." My mouth was dry. I swallowed, then cleared my throat. "Good guard dog, anyway."

"Can't be much wrong if he was quiet before we got here."

I was inclined to agree. Derwent shouldered past me and rapped on Forgrave's door, waiting for a few seconds before bending down to open the letterbox. "Hello? Mr. Forgrave?"

No response. He stayed where he was, scanning the view through the narrow slot.

"See anything?"

"No." He put his mouth to the gap, pitching his voice lower so it couldn't be heard outside the flat. "Mr. Forgrave, it's the police. Can you open the door?"

We listened, the seconds ticking by. The only sound was the dog's continued scratching from next door. I used the time to take a closer look at the front of the flat, not seeing any sign of a forced entry. There was one window to the front, but Forgrave had chosen to fit frosted glass for privacy. Only the top of the window was clear. Derwent, straightening up, saw me looking at it. "Want to have a peek? I'll give you a leg up."

I put my foot in his linked hands and steadied myself on the window frame as he lifted me. I had a couple of seconds to check the room before he grunted and let me slide to the ground.

"Jesus, what do you weigh?"

"Not a huge amount, actually. I thought you were fit. That was pathetic."

"I run, I don't do weightlifting." He grinned at me with one of those changes of mood that caught me so off-guard. "See anything of interest?"

"Not a lot. It was hard to see much. It's not exactly bright in there. But everything seems to be in order."

"Right. Well, on to the next one, I suppose. Who else is on the list?" He started walking toward the stairs and I followed, hunting in my bag for the sheet of paper.

"Stanley Flanders. He lives on the Mayhew Estate."

"That's an easy one. I can see it from here."

"Yeah, we just have to find the right flat, that's all. Only about two thousand to choose from."

"We've got a number for him."

"We do, but the place is a maze."

We had reached the first floor. Derwent was whistling. He rattled down the last flight of stairs at speed, heading for the main door, pushing it open. I put my foot on the first step of the stairs and then stopped, annoyed with myself. I turned back and began to run up again, muttering, "Back in a second."

Derwent said something I didn't hear as the door banged.

"I just need to leave a card," I called over my shoulder, taking the stairs two at a time, getting back to the second floor in double-quick time. I hurried along the balcony to Forgrave's front door, scrawling a note as I went. *Please call us urgently regarding your safety.* The dog was barking again, this time perched on the windowsill. The net curtains had draped themselves around its head, making it look like a mockery of a bride. It was light brown and shaggy, not a Jack Russell after all—not anything much, by the looks of it. I stuck my tongue out at it as I passed and it fell off the windowsill in an ecstasy of rage. Moving fast, I flipped open the letterbox and shoved my card through, making sure it fell down onto the mat in case anyone saw it poking out.

I had already turned to go when I heard the noise, and at first I thought it was the bloody dog again. It was halfway to a howl, a sound that lifted up the hairs on the back of my neck, and I stopped dead.

"Kerrigan!" Derwent was standing in the street, looking up. "Get down here."

I flapped a hand at him, still listening. Deep growls from the dog interspersed with an occasional yelp. A hearse turning in the funeral home's yard, the engine low and throaty. Silence from behind the door. I had been imagining things. I stood for another second, annoyed with myself, then started to walk away.

And heard it again.

It took all of my self-control to keep walking at the same pace until I reached the stairwell, and I was already reaching into my bag for my radio when I got out of earshot of the flat. I switched to the force wide channel, cursing as I fumbled with the buttons.

"MP, MP from Hotel India six four, active message. Urgent assistance required at nine Camford Mews, Brixton. Believed intruders, possibly armed with a shotgun. I can hear noises from inside and I believe the occupant is being assaulted. Request Trojan units and ambulance."

The controller took it in her stride, smoothly contacting a Trojan Armed Response Vehicle with the address, informing ambulance control and then passing the incident to a senior officer who would manage it while there was a chance that guns might be involved. The routine was well-rehearsed.

"Trojan unit with you in four minutes."

Four minutes was a hell of a long time to wait when you were being tortured, I couldn't help thinking. But all the same, it was remarkable that just like that, the cavalry was on the way.

I went to the balcony on the first floor and leaned out, looking for Derwent. He was at the main door downstairs.

"The fucking thing's closed. Let me in."

"I heard something. Back-up's on the way," I said, as loudly as I dared.

"What?"

I leaned out a bit further. "I think there's someone in Forgrave's flat. I've called for back-up."

"The hell you have. Why didn't you tell me?" Derwent hissed.

"There wasn't time." I looked along the street, seeing a police car nose into view at the far end, sirens off thankfully. "Here they are. They're sending ARVs as well."

"You'd better be sure about this, Kerrigan."

I had a moment of sheer panic. If it was a mistake . . . if I'd imagined something, and called in the troops for no reason . . . the flat had looked empty. Derwent had neither heard nor seen anyone. But I had, I thought. I had heard a cry of pain that was like nothing I had ever heard before, and yet I had instinctively known it for what it was.

The uniformed officers had got out of their car and another patrol car was parking behind the first. Two of them headed toward the back of the building, keeping close to the wall so they wouldn't be seen out of the windows. They wore stab vests as a matter of course, but it wasn't much protection really, and I waited, cringing a little, for a shot that would tell me they'd been spotted, targeted. The other two joined Derwent and I saw them conferring. He leaned back, looking up to me.

"Come and open the door, for God's sake."

I slipped down the stairs and pressed the button that released the door lock. Derwent pushed in, closely followed by one of the uniformed officers who was, it turned out, an inspector, the shift supervisor. He had a pepper-and-salt beard and a reassuring manner.

"Paul Lancaster." I introduced myself and he smiled. "Bit of a drama, isn't it? I think we're going to need to clear the building in case things kick off when the armed units arrive."

"Shouldn't be long now." I looked at my watch, trying to remember how long it had been since I'd called it in—a couple of minutes but it felt like twenty.

Lancaster turned to Derwent. "I'll leave you to clear this floor. PC Snow will help. I'll take DC Kerrigan up to the next floor so we can check for any other occupants. We'll have to wait to deal with the top floor when the AFOs get here."

"I should go up with you. It's too much of a risk to send DC Kerrigan. She's not wearing body armor."

"And neither are you," I pointed out. "There's absolutely no need to take my place."

"Still, I'd prefer to." He raised his eyebrows. "Want me to pull rank?"

"Stop bickering and get on with it." Lancaster headed for the stairs and Derwent followed, giving me a last look as if to check I was staying where it was reasonably safe. With bad grace I went to the first flat and knocked on the door as softly as I could, while PC Snow did the same next door. It was something to do, anyway—something that might take my mind off what was happening two floors above.

We had cleared the ground floor (one occupant, an old lady who angrily refused any help from Snow and left the premises carrying her most precious possessions in a Tesco carrier bag) when a marked silver BMW pulled up, the yellow sticker in the window announcing that the first armed officers were on the scene. Lancaster and Derwent had seen them from the floor above and came down at speed for a briefing that lasted all of twenty seconds. In the meantime, another two teams had arrived along with their commander and the nine of them headed for the stairs, more like soldiers than police officers in their black helmets, blue fatigues and body armor. Six were armed with Heckler & Koch MP5 submachine guns that looked more or less like the most lethal things imaginable, while another two carried square-muzzled Glocks that weren't far off the pace. The last was hefting an Enforcer, a mini battering ram that was known in police slang as the Big Red Key because it could open pretty much any door.

Lancaster and Derwent had taken cover on the opposite side of the road and I ran to join them, squatting behind a parked car that would be about as useful as tissue paper if the submachine guns started firing in our direction.

"Not hanging about, are they?" Lancaster turned to grin at me as the armed officers fanned out along the balcony, checking the other flats for signs of life. Satisfied, they moved into position around the door of flat 9. I had the distinct impression Lancaster was enjoying himself. Derwent was chewing gum, his jaws moving rapidly, tension written on his face.

From our position down on the street, we only had a limited view, but it was easy enough to reconstruct what happened next. At a word from the commander, the officer with the Enforcer stepped forward and shouted "Police" at almost the same moment he swung it into the door. I saw the timber frame splinter with the first blow, break with the second, and give way completely with the third impact. As the officer fell back, his colleagues pushed into the flat, shouting to disorientate anyone inside who might have considered putting up a fight. My heart was pounding as if I were in there with them. I had never wanted to be a firearms officer, but I could see the attraction. There was something atavistic about charging into a confined space while armed to the teeth, backed up by eight equally well-equipped colleagues who were trained to respond to aggression with targeted, measured violence.

On this occasion, there was no aggression to respond to, it seemed. In a surprisingly short space of time, the commander came to lean over the edge of the balcony and gave us the thumbs-up before getting back on his radio. He was requesting paramedic assistance and my stomach twisted as I thought about why. Maybe this time the killer had left his victim to die alone. Maybe I should have tried to break into the flat myself instead of calling for back-up. I didn't get long to consider the maybes; Derwent was out from behind the car before I had even straightened up, and disappeared through the main door at a sprint. Lancaster and I followed, running up the stairs as sirens whooped in the distance. We caught up with him at the door of the flat, where the commander was explaining what had happened.

"We've got four males in the flat, three in custody and one awaiting paramedic assistance."

"Three?" Derwent's voice was sharp.

The commander nodded. "No names yet, but I'll leave that up to you. No ID on any of them. Two older blokes, one young. They were in the kitchen at the back of the flat when we went in."

"Were they armed?"

"We found a handgun on the floor by the cooker—a Beretta nine millimeter. Looks like one of them dropped it when they heard us coming. Better than being caught in possession, I suppose. They didn't offer much in the way of resistance. We had officers blocking the fire escape at the back and enough of us at the front to give them a fair idea there was no point in trying to fight their way out. Don't know who they are or why you want them, but I'd say they were pros from the way they reacted."

I was desperate to find out if William Forgrave was okay. "You said there was one awaiting a paramedic?"

"He's going to need treatment for burns, by the looks of things. Nasty stuff. They used a steam iron."

"He was being tortured?" Lancaster sounded shocked, and I recalled that he would have no idea why we had been at the address.

"Looks like it. I don't think he was having much fun, put it that way."

Derwent moved restlessly. "Is the flat clear? Are we okay to go in?"

"It's all yours."

I followed Derwent inside, past the shattered door that had been propped up against the wall. The living room on the right—the one I had peered into—was full of men: four of the armed officers and three suspects who were sitting down, hands cuffed in front of them. Two of them were sitting on the sofa while the third, a thin middle-aged man with a deep tan, was leaning back in an armchair with his eyes closed. Derwent barely paused and I only had time for a quick glance before we moved on past the flat's one bedroom to the kitchen at the back. A couple of officers were in there, giving fairly rudimentary first aid to a man who lay on the floor, his limbs vibrating as if he were wired to the mains. William Forgrave, I presumed. He was short and paunchy, as if he rarely took any exercise beyond climbing the stairs to his flat. He was wearing a pair of jeans and nothing else, all the better to show off the angry triangular burns that patched his torso. The soles of his feet were dotted with tiny blisters. It would be a long time before he could walk without pain, and a long time before he looked into the mirror and recognized what he saw, because his face was a mess behind his heavy black beard. It had swollen badly already, but I could tell that his nose was broken. His front teeth were chipped and his mouth hung open as if his jaw might have been damaged too. The kitchen floor was spotted here and there with droplets of blood. A steam iron stood on the table, turned away from me. It was still plugged in, I noticed. The air in the kitchen was warm and humid, close to stifling when you thought about why that might be, and the windows had misted up.

Derwent had determined with a glance that the victim was in no state to talk to us, and had turned his attention to the kitchen counter.

"Where did these come from?"

One of the officers stood up. "Personal effects from the gentlemen in the living room, sir. We thought we'd let you have a look. That was everything they had on them. Obviously, some of it is evidence."

They had been arranged in three separate piles, one for each of them. My attention was caught by a brass knuckleduster, a wicked-looking thing with blood spattered across it. That would explain Forgrave's facial injuries. Derwent sorted through the piles with the end of a pen, examining each item without touching them. There was one mobile phone between the three of them, a small, cheap Samsung model. I was willing to bet it was a pay-as-you-go one, probably bought that morning. It had taken a while to filter through to the criminal world that carrying a personal phone was as good as having a permanent location beacon—the phone companies could and would supply the police with information about where they had been and when, and who they had been calling. The professionals took steps to avoid it by using phones they could dump after each job. I was starting to see why the commander had thought he was dealing with proper criminals.

The knuckleduster's owner was a smoker: a silver Zippo lighter stood beside it, along with a pack of Benson & Hedges cigarettes. He had also been carrying a sheaf of cable-ties held together with a rubber band.

"That looks promising. Ivan Tremlett was restrained with ties like those."

Derwent made a noise in his throat that was probably agreement. He was looking at the third pile, at a money clip in the shape of a bear. It was in silvery metal with shiny clear stones for the eyes and claws, and its paws were clamped down on something approaching a thousand pounds from the thickness of the roll.

"Are those diamonds?"

I was being flippant, but Derwent nodded. "Set in platinum. What would that set you back?"

"More than I've got in my savings." Not that I would have wanted it anyway. "Flash, isn't it?"

"Oh yes. Like the man who owns it."

My interest sharpened. "Do you know who that is?"

"I have a fair idea."

"Tell me."

"You'll find out." He took out his own phone and dialed a number.

I shook my head, frustrated. "I don't know what's going on. Why would three professional criminals be engaged in a campaign of torture and murder? None of the victims had a connection with organized crime."

"Weird, isn't it?" Whoever Derwent was calling picked up then. I worked out it was Godley from listening to the DI's end of the conversation. When he hung up, he said, "The boss'll be here in a couple of minutes."

"By helicopter, presumably?"

"He was out and about. At a meeting. He's not far away and he was in the car already when I rang."

"Is he pleased?"

"What do you think? Course he is."

And are you? I almost added, but didn't quite dare. There was something I couldn't read in Derwent's manner, something he was suppressing that seemed to me to be excitement.

He had moved on to the second pile and was examining a small folding knife, dull black in color, with a blade that couldn't have been longer than three inches. It was wickedly sharp.

"That's one for forensics." He looked up and grinned at me. "Not bad. And I was going to let you walk away."

"You were out on the street. We almost missed it completely. We would have if I hadn't gone back to drop in my card."

"Yeah, well, everyone gets lucky now and then."

Including William Forgrave, though he probably didn't see it like that. A couple of paramedics had arrived, competent in green overalls, and had taken over from the officers. They were preparing to transfer him to a stretcher and I nudged Derwent.

"We should get out of the way. Besides, don't you want to meet the three suspects?"

"Yeah. Why not?" He sounded as if he was trying not to laugh. "Wait until the boss gets here. He's not going to believe this."

I followed him down the hall feeling increasingly out of my depth. The DI stopped in the doorway of the living room and I almost collided with him. The three suspects looked up with varying degrees of interest. The two on the sofa were muscle, pure and simple: one was young with close-cropped fair hair and a sprinkling of spots on his chin and neck, while the other could have been his dad. He was twice the width and what remained of his hair was gray. He had the battered nose and cauliflower ears of the habitual fighter. He was wearing the uniform of a BT engineer, down to the ID swinging from a chain around his neck. The young lad had a purplish scar running up one arm that looked like a souvenir from a knife fight. Not the sort you want to tangle with. Neither looked particularly worried about their situation, as if being arrested was all in a day's work.

I turned my attention to the man in the armchair just as Derwent said, "Well, look who we have here. Hello, John. Nice to see you again. What brings you back to these parts?"

"None of your business." His heavy eyelids didn't even flicker; he didn't look surprised to be addressed by name. I stared at him, at the tan that spoke of life in a hot country, at the thick, ash-colored hair that curled over his collar, at the heavy ring he wore on one hand and the Rolex watch that didn't quite go with the steel handcuffs he was sporting. He had a long nose, full lips and a square jaw, and his skin was so smooth that I found myself wondering if he'd had Botox. His white shirt had a smear of blood on the shoulder, drying to brown. The overall impression I got was of a coolness that bordered on the psychopathic, and I knew I had seen his face before, but I couldn't place it.

"What you do *is* my business, you know that. Must be something big, if you're here yourself. I thought we'd seen the last of you." Derwent had his hands in his pockets and was rocking back and forth on the balls of his feet. He had moved closer to the suspect, looming over the man he was addressing. I slipped into the room and stood beside one of the firearms officers who was cradling his MP5 like a baby.

"No comment." The tanned man was having to lean back with his head at an awkward angle to maintain eye contact with Derwent. It seemed it was too much trouble. He pulled a face and looked away with an air of finality, as if he was bored with the conversation.

"Come on, John. Talk to me." He lowered his voice so I could only just catch what he said. "You don't want me to make you talk, do you? Only I've learned quite a bit from you and your lads, over the years. Very inventive, some of the things you come up with."

"But not legal."

"A couple of minutes is all I'd need, wouldn't you say? I'm sure I can get a couple of minutes alone with you."

The man didn't look remotely impressed. "Keep talking, sonny, because I ain't."

There was a sound of footsteps outside the flat. Shadows crossed the window, the frosted glass making the silhouettes unidentifiable. I caught a rumble of conversation in the hall and heard Godley's voice.

Derwent had noticed too. "If you won't talk to me, maybe you'd like to have a word with an old friend."

The man looked up, suddenly interested, as Godley appeared in the doorway. They locked eyes immediately. I looked from the arrested man back to Godley and flinched at the expression on the superintendent's face. Never usually easy to read, his demeanor was openly hostile—murderous, I would have said, had it been anyone else. He sounded calm, though, when he spoke.

"John Skinner. This is a surprise. It's been a long time."

I jumped, wondering if I had misheard. I looked at Derwent, who was watching me, waiting for my reaction. I got it now. I understood why he had been so excited, even if I didn't understand anything else. John Skinner was a notorious murderer, armed robber and kidnapper, a violent thug and career criminal who had fled to the Costa del Sol to fight extradition on a whole collection of outstanding warrants. Now he was sitting in the living room of a convicted pedophile in a back street of Brixton, and I couldn't begin to imagine why.

Skinner smiled thinly. "Inspector Godley. Sorry—it's Superintendent now, isn't it? I find it hard to keep up."

"Understandable." Godley's eyes were watchful. "I never thought you'd leave sunny Spain again."

"I had my reasons."

"So I've heard."

It was Skinner's turn to let his mask drop. Strain twitched a muscle in his cheek. "You've got to let me go, Godley. I've got business."

"No chance."

Skinner's upper lip lifted, showing his canines in what might have been a smile if it hadn't been so clearly a snarl. "You haven't changed. I'd have thought you'd be sympathetic. You got a daughter, don't you? Isabel. Lovely girl. Takes after her mother. And how is Serena anyway?"

Godley shook his head. "This isn't about me."

"On the contrary. If you stop me from doing what I need to do, it's all about you." Skinner paused a moment, then said: "It's Moorcroft Road, isn't it? Number forty-seven, Moorcroft Road, NW3—"

He broke off as Godley moved, lunging across the room, completely oblivious to the shouted warning from the armed officer as he crossed in front of him. The room turned to chaos in an instant. The older man pushed off the sofa and grabbed for the machine gun while the young one fought the other officer for control of his Glock, only mildly hampered by the cuffs. I had time to see that Godley had pulled Skinner off his chair and was systematically punching the living daylights out of him before Derwent cannoned into me, pushing me to the ground. I fell awkwardly, whacking my face against the edge of the TV table, and saw stars.

"Stay down!" Derwent ordered, going past the armed officers to try to separate Godley from Skinner. Dazed, I wondered why he didn't bother with the others, but then again, Skinner was the important one. And then one of the armed officers stepped back onto my hand and I was too busy trying not to pass out to pay much attention to anything else. I was only dimly aware of reinforcements arriving, of the younger man being hit with a Taser just as he got hold of the handgun and turned to wave it at the officers who were coming in. The big man got a dose of CS spray that put him on the floor, rolling from side to side. He had an unexpectedly high-pitched voice and he bleated, "My eyes! My eyes!" until someone took pity on him and led him outside. Skinner went too, with blood dripping from his mouth and nose, attended by a paramedic on one side and an escort of armed officers.

Hands took hold of my arms and dragged me to standing. I put up as much resistance as a rag doll; I was feeling about as robust.

"Are you okay?" Derwent's voice. I nodded, speechless. "Better get your head looked at. It's bleeding."

It was the least of my worries. I looked past him to where Godley was sitting, head bent, his phone jammed against his ear. He was leaning his head on one hand and his knuckles were red-raw from the fight. He looked defeated, as if he and not Skinner was the one who had been beaten. His voice sounded unlike I'd ever heard it before, close to panic, and what he was saying over and over again explained why.

"He knew my address, Bill. How did he know my address? How the hell did he know my address?"

Chapter Ten

As was becoming depressingly normal after a big arrest, I ended up in hospital. The only thing to be said for this particular occasion was that I was walking wounded rather than flat-out unconscious, and I was only there for a check-up. One of the paramedics had taken a look at me at the scene and declared that I probably wasn't concussed, probably didn't need stitches and probably hadn't broken any bones in my hand, but all Godley heard was "probably" and ordered me to do as I was told and go to A&E. Which was fine, except that it drew attention to the non-heroic role I'd played in John Skinner's escape attempt and meant I missed out on celebrating Skinner's arrest with the rest of the team. The really annoying part was the three-hour wait nursing my bruises, watching more seriously damaged people jump the queue. My only distraction was a magazine someone had left behind. It was the kind that featured lurid true-life stories so they could use eye-catching headlines on the cover. Mostly, the headlines turned out to be bollocks when you got down to it. Nonetheless, I spun it out, reading every word of "I Gave Birth to My Grandfather's BABY" and "I Lost FIFTEEN Stone by Eating BURGERS." The alternative was a poster about malaria. Needs must.

I got as far as the horoscopes and was so annoyed by mine—"You don't like taking advice, but it's time to listen to someone close to you. On this occasion, they're right and you're wrong!"—that I couldn't stand to read another word. I tossed it onto the chair beside me and looked up to see Godley standing in the doorway scanning the room, tall and grave, his iron-clad composure back in a big way. Surprised, I put my hand up and waved until he spotted me. His face lightened. He half-turned and said something over his shoulder and I felt even more unsettled as Derwent appeared beside him. As they made their way across the crowded waiting room, I forced a smile. I didn't like being seen at a disadvantage, by either of them. I wanted

Godley to see me as a reliable member of his team, not a liability, and I wanted Derwent to see me as little as possible. Whatever weakness he noticed, he would use against me, and I was on my guard at once.

"To what do I owe the pleasure?" I asked as soon as they were within earshot. "Don't you have somewhere better to be?"

"We're at the end of a long queue of people who want to talk to John Skinner. The earliest we're going to get to talk to him is tomorrow morning. And we wanted to make sure you were all right." Derwent was doing his sincere face, his forehead crinkling with concern. "Has anyone seen you yet?"

"Just a nurse to see if I needed urgent attention. And I don't," I added quickly. "In fact, I could probably go home."

"Stay where you are." Godley sat down on the chair opposite me with a blink-and-you'd-miss-it wince.

"Are *you* okay?"

"A few bruises from earlier. Nothing serious," he said shortly, and I instantly regretted drawing attention to it. After a couple of seconds, he cleared his throat, as close to awkward as I had ever seen him. "About what happened. I wanted to apologize."

"To me? There's no need."

"There's every need. I should apologize for my unprofessional behavior to every police officer who was at the scene. It put everyone at risk. But I do want to apologize particularly to you, since you were injured."

"Injured is putting it a bit high," I began but he held up a hand to stop me.

"You have a gash on your forehead, a bruised hand and possible concussion, and you had a serious head injury last year, Maeve, so don't make light of this, please. It's my fault and I'm going to take responsibility for it, whatever you say."

"Actually, it's not your fault. It was Inspector Derwent who pushed me. If anyone should apologize, it's him." I spoke lightly, hoping to God Derwent had a sense of humor.

"Forget it. I'm not going to apologize. It was for your own good." He smiled at me, then glanced at Godley and I saw concern on his face. The superintendent was looking shattered, and it was more than simple fatigue. I leaned forward impulsively.

"Sir, you mustn't be too hard on yourself for what you did. It's completely understandable, given what he was saying."

"I doubt that, Maeve, but thank you." A short, painful pause. "I take it you've worked out what Mr. Skinner was getting at."

I was reluctant to put it into words, but the superintendent waited me out. "He was saying that he knows where you live. And he knows all about your family. I sort of guessed that he was threatening them."

"He was. And I didn't help the situation by attacking him. It was hardly calculated to get him on my side."

Derwent laughed. "Seriously, boss, you have no chance of managing that unless you've got a time machine."

"Why is that?" I looked from one of them to the other. "What happened?"

Instead of answering, Godley stood up. "I'm going to get a coffee. How about you?"

"Thanks, boss. White, no sugar."

"I'd love a cup of tea," I said hopefully, but he shook his head.

"Better not have caffeine before you see the doctor."

"Tea won't do me any harm," I protested halfheartedly. I knew it was a lost cause, and all I got from Godley was a reproving glower before he stalked out of the room. He turned heads as he usually did. I doubted that he was aware of it. He certainly wouldn't have cared.

Derwent had been watching me watch Godley. "Don't take it personally that the boss didn't want to stick around. We've been telling this story all afternoon. He can't stand to hear it again."

"What's going on? Did he arrest Skinner back in the day or something? I wouldn't have thought that would make him hold a grudge. From what I know of Skinner, he's been arrested by every London copper over a certain age." It had been sort of a rite of passage, until Skinner spoiled everyone's fun by moving to Spain.

"Don't believe a word of it. Everyone likes to boast about catching John Skinner, but there aren't that many who actually have. Godley is one of them, but that's not why Skinner hates him. Being arrested is part of the game for him." He leaned closer to me and lowered his voice so no one else could hear what he was saying. The waiting room was not an ideal place for confidential discussions. "You know Bryce and I used to work with the boss on the Central Task Force? He was our inspector when I was a DC and Bryce was a sergeant. At the time, John Skinner was single-handedly skewing the crime stats. He was making us look really bad—pretty much every serious crime that was committed in East London came back to him, but we couldn't get anyone to give evidence officially. It didn't even get as far as witness tampering; no one would risk annoying him by talking about him on the record. The bosses were screaming for us to do something, but we needed to catch him in the act of committing a crime. Godley got assigned to run an undercover operation targeting Skinner."

"And arrested him."

Derwent shook his head. "Not a chance. Skinner behaved like a choirboy. He went about his business and the bodies kept piling up. He had such a strong hold on his gang that he didn't need to tell them what to do. They could keep things ticking over the way he wanted even if he was banged up in solitary. We watched him for weeks and then the bosses decided they'd spent enough time and pulled us off it. You can imagine what it was costing. Twenty-four-hour surveillance doesn't come cheap."

"I'm not seeing how this pissed off John Skinner."

"Give me a chance. Godley was a bit annoyed that he hadn't got anything on Skinner. He decided the best thing to do was to put pressure on him some other way. We'd seen Skinner's father driving a stolen car during the surveillance. It was enough to arrest him, and we were lucky with the judge. Dean Skinner was deemed a flight risk and not allowed bail. His son was furious."

"Well, that was the idea."

"Yeah. But it turned out not to be the best idea Charlie ever had." Derwent looked around ultra-casually, checking to see Godley wasn't on his way back yet. "Mr. Skinner died on remand. He had a massive stroke the night after the hearing where he was refused bail. He was still alive when they found him, but in a coma, and he never came round. John was distraught. He knew his father was only in that situation because of him, but he blamed the boss, not himself."

"Naturally." I was wondering how Godley himself had felt about what had happened. From what I knew of him, he would have been as unforgiving to himself as Skinner had been.

"Skinner has something of a gift for vengeance—he's left a trail of bodies behind him since he was a teenager. Never forgives, never forgets. He went after Godley in a big way. His family have had to move house twice and they've got alarm systems like you wouldn't believe—panic buttons, CCTV, the works. Godley's daughter changed schools a few times. She couldn't have any friends back to the house, couldn't tell anyone anything about her dad or his work. She even had to change her surname so there was nothing to make a connection with the boss. As you can imagine, his missus was not happy with all the upheaval, not to mention the effect it had on Isabel. Godley went to pieces for a while. He almost left the job. Gradually, he came to terms with it and managed to settle things with Serena, but I don't think it was easy, then or now."

"Is that why he doesn't have any pictures of his family in his office? To keep his private life separate?"

"Got it in one. That was the agreement he reached with Serena. He never talks about her or Isabel. He's ex-directory—never gives anyone his home number, does it all off his mobile. He works long hours in the nick because he refuses to take the job home with him. And he doesn't let many people—including other coppers—know where he lives."

"Sort of a double life."

"Yeah. I don't think Serena likes him talking about work either. He doesn't have anyone to share it with now, and that has to be hard." Derwent shook his head. "The thing is, it changed him. Godley, I mean. You never met anyone as aggressive, back in the day. Gung-ho as they come and tricky with it—I mean, he didn't always toe the line. But something about this affected him, and not for the better if you ask me. He felt guilty about Dean Skinner, even though he really shouldn't have. John didn't pick it up off the street—his dad was the same. Deano was a thug through and through and he could have had his stroke anytime. Okay, he was in prison because Godley put him there, but he'd done more than enough to qualify for a spell behind bars, and it wasn't as if it was his first time."

"*You* wouldn't have let it bother you."

"No, I fucking wouldn't." He grinned at me. "But that's the sort of person I am. The boss is more sensitive."

As usual, he made it sound like an insult, and I assumed that to Derwent, it was. All that I had heard just made me think more of Godley, not less.

"Anyway. Godley started to behave himself. Do things by the book. Draw back if there was a risk of someone getting hurt. It didn't do him any harm with the bosses. He got promoted a couple of times, off the Task Force, and I lost touch with him." He sighed. "It was sort of deliberate. Me and the lads—we weren't that happy with the new version of the guv, even if everyone else thought the sun shone out of his arse. He didn't have the same passion for the job. He didn't have the same joy in it. And it made it hard to work for him, to be honest. You'd suggest something that would have been perfectly okay before the Skinner incident and it was like you'd suggested goosing Mother Theresa."

I had seen Godley's ice-blue disapproval myself, and I couldn't help smiling at Derwent's description of it. But something was puzzling me. "If you didn't like working for him, why did you join the team?"

He shrugged. "Maybe I've mellowed."

If what I had seen of Derwent so far was the mellow version, then I didn't want to see him when he was feeling edgy. But before I could point that out, Godley returned with a cardboard tray.

"Did you know the hospital has a Starbucks concession? God bless private enterprise." He handed me a cup. "Don't get too excited. It's camomile tea."

"Great," I said bleakly, not managing to sound pleased, and the two men laughed. "Sorry. That was rude of me. I'm sure it will be lovely."

"Better than nothing." Derwent popped the lid off his coffee and inhaled the steam. "Mm. Want a sniff?"

"Don't taunt her." Godley sat down again, concentrating on not spilling his own coffee as he set it down by his feet. "How far did you get?"

"Just before Skinner left the country."

"When did that happen?" I asked.

"About five years ago," Godley said. "He got himself into a bit of a mess. He'd been running a highly successful crew who specialized in bank robberies where the managers' families were held hostage to coerce them into opening the vaults."

"Tiger kidnaps," Derwent interjected, and got a glare from Godley.

"Yes, thank you, Josh. I've never liked that particular nickname."

I hid a smile. The boss was always hostile to anything that glamorized crime. Derwent made eye contact with me for a long second, his face absolutely blank, but I knew what he was trying to convey: *See what I mean?*

"The last of the kidnaps went badly wrong. A hostage tried to escape—he was the daughter's boyfriend, as far as I can remember, and not inclined to cooperate. The kidnappers panicked and shot him, which made the neighbors twig that something was up so they called nine-nine-nine. Imagine how pleased we were to discover that the kidnappers had phoned Skinner right after the shooting on a number we could trace back to him. The lad was shot in the back, seriously injured, and the kidnappers couldn't decide what to do—leave him to survive as best he could, abandon the whole job, or put him out of his misery. The other hostages heard them asking Skinner's advice and they were prepared to give evidence that he was in charge."

"I didn't think anyone ever agreed to give evidence against John Skinner."

Godley nodded. "It was unusual. The family were extremely angry and determined not to let him get away with it. The boy survived, but he was never going to walk again. I imagine that a dose of guilt played a part in their decision. Besides, we got them away to a safe house before any of Skinner's acquaintances could even think about shutting them up. We had him for the lot—kidnapping, armed robbery, murder. The only thing left for him to do was run, and that's what he did."

"On a false passport?"

"On a private yacht. He sailed off with a couple of suitcases of cash and jewelry, and an address book full of contacts. He'd already bought a villa on the Costa del Sol, in case of emergencies. He thinks ahead. That's one of the things that makes him so dangerous."

"So why come back? It looks as if he was doing nicely for himself in Spain."

Godley shifted in his seat, suddenly uncomfortable. "It's hard to blame him for this one. When he did a runner, his wife flatly refused to go too. They have a daughter, Cheyenne, and Gayle didn't want her to grow up in Spain. Skinner had to agree to leave them behind. They went out there for holidays—he didn't lose touch. He set them up in a nice house in Hertfordshire, private schooling for Cheyenne, tennis and riding lessons—everything you could want." Godley picked up his coffee from the floor and sipped it, as if he was playing for time. Derwent took over again.

"Five days ago, Cheyenne Skinner disappeared. According to her friends, she'd been invited to a private party in Brixton by someone she only knew via the Internet. It was a pop-up nightclub in an empty warehouse—one night only of dancing and debauchery, according to the invitation. She went on her own, which was stupid. And she never came home."

My mind was racing. "Was there actually a nightclub?"

Derwent nodded. "They've traced the organizers who couldn't recall seeing Cheyenne, but there were a couple of hundred people there. The event was a word-of-mouth thing—you know, they told fifty people and asked them to invite the coolest people they knew. Everyone was supposed to wear masks." He snorted. "Maybe I'm getting old, but I don't see the attraction of spending an evening in a dark, dirty warehouse getting wasted with a bunch of tossers in disguise."

"Me neither," I said automatically, thinking about what he'd told me. "So they don't know if she was actually at the event."

"She updated her Facebook status to say that she was. That was at ten to ten and it's the last that was heard from her. Local CID have been on it but they've basically got nothing—no witnesses, no trace of her belongings or her phone."

"So she disappeared in Brixton."

Derwent grinned at me. "Yeah. You've spotted it, haven't you? Skinner wasn't happy with what Gayle told him about the way the investigation was being handled. He decided to take care of things himself. First things first: draw up a list of likely suspects. Then go round and beat the crap out of them until you get tired of it and put them out of their misery."

"But he was only targeting pedophiles." My mind was working at about half-speed as I struggled to understand what I was being told. Maybe I was concussed after all. "How old is Cheyenne?"

"Fourteen," Godley said bleakly. "The same age as my daughter."

I was starting to see why Godley was so rattled. "Who's been investigating it? You said local CID?"

"It was being handled at borough level. There was no ransom note received, that we're aware of, so no kidnap squad. I'd thought it might have been something to do with Skinner—that she'd been taken to put pressure on him for some reason, or to get back at him for a past grudge—but then he wouldn't have been wasting his time trying to scare up a lead from the local sex-crimes brigade."

"Even without the Skinner connection, given her age she's surely a high-risk MISPER. I'd have thought it merited a bit more than local CID."

"Me too," Godley said, his mouth thinning to a line. "I spent a lot of this week trying to persuade the high-ups to let the team take over the investigation. But for reasons known only to themselves, they decided not to bother."

"Cheyenne's a bit of a bad girl, by all accounts. Takes after the old man. I think they probably thought she could look after herself, fourteen or not." Derwent glanced at Godley before continuing. "And to be fair, the bosses probably wanted to keep you out of it if they could. Given your history."

"I think they were aware I would have been completely professional, Josh," Godley replied stiffly.

"Yeah, but anything that brings you to his attention is bad, isn't it? Because of what happened before."

"He has his own idea of fair play. I think if we'd been able to find his daughter, he might have been willing to let the old grudge drop."

Derwent snorted. "Do you believe in the tooth fairy as well? For Skinner, there's no such thing as fair play. And he meant what he said. He'll never forgive you for what happened to his dad."

Godley winced and didn't respond. I thought that Derwent had been sailing a little too close to the wind. I found it strangely reassuring to see that he didn't limit his insensitive comments to his dealings with me. In the meantime, diplomacy called for a change of subject.

"So what happens now?"

"We'll interview Skinner tomorrow. He'll be charged with the murders you and Josh have been investigating, of course, and with false imprisonment, GBH and whatever else we can think of in relation to William Forgrave. The other two have been interviewed once already, but they weren't feeling very cooperative. We'll have another bash at them."

"And Cheyenne?"

"I'm going to take over the investigation." Godley sounded completely determined. "She may be streetwise, but she's vulnerable. And as of this moment, no one has the least idea where she may be. You don't have to be John Skinner to turn into a homicidal maniac in those circumstances."

"Making excuses for him?" Derwent asked.

"If you'd told me I'd have something in common with John Skinner, I'd have laughed at you, but if it was my daughter who had gone missing, I might have done the same myself." The look on Godley's face told me he meant it.

"It bothers you, doesn't it? The fact that the girls are the same age." Derwent was staring at Godley with a strange expression on his face, part pity, part curiosity. "Is it because you can imagine yourself in the same situation? Or is it because you're afraid he will take it out on you and yours if anything's happened to the girl?"

I was surprised once again by Derwent's frankness, and even more surprised that Godley didn't cut him off with a glare.

"A bit of both, I suppose. I'm worried about Cheyenne. I don't like that no one's heard from her. I don't get a good feeling about it. And of course I'm concerned about Skinner. If any harm comes to Isabel because of John Skinner—"

"You'll never be able to live with the guilt," Derwent finished for him.

"Probably, but that wasn't what I was going to say." Godley smiled at Derwent pleasantly, but his eyes were as ice-cold as his tone of voice. "If he does anything, anything at all to upset her or Serena, I'm going to teach him a lesson about vengeance that he'll never forget."

Derwent didn't look particularly surprised, but I couldn't say the same of myself. I had the impression Godley had forgotten I was there, that what he was saying was unguarded and honest, and that somehow made it all the more shocking.

"Maeve Kerrigan?"

I looked up to see that a nurse had emerged from the casualty area and was scanning the waiting room. *At last.* I abandoned the tea and the conversation with some relief, saying a quick good-bye to Godley and Derwent as I went. "Thanks for coming to check on me. I'll see you tomorrow."

"Not too early," Godley called after me. "Take things easy. That's an order."

I smiled back at him, but I had no intention of obeying.

It took a while to work through the list of medical professionals who needed to see me and confirm that I wasn't concussed or badly injured, and I was utterly exhausted by the time I was given permission to go home, sporting a large white bandage on my forehead. I wasn't expecting anyone to be waiting for me when I came out. If things had been different, Rob might have turned up to see if I was okay, but that didn't seem likely. He would know what had happened by now. Everyone would. Skinner's arrest, and the circumstances of it, would be the only talking point in the office, and I squirmed at the thought of what people—Peter Belcott, specifically—would be saying about me. Nothing to my credit, that was for sure.

I was right. Rob wasn't in the waiting room, but there was someone I knew. Derwent was still sitting where I'd left him, his arms folded and his knees wide apart in the ball-airing pose so beloved of self-consciously macho men. I walked over.

"Comfy?"

"You must be joking." He stood up and stretched. "All okay?"

"According to the doctor, there's nothing wrong with me that an aspirin and a good night's sleep won't cure."

"Well, let's make sure you get home in one piece. Come on." He jangled his car keys at me as if I were a dog being taken for a walk.

"Let me get this straight. You're offering to drive me home?"

"Would you prefer to get the bus? You know people are going to stare."

I did, as it happened. They were staring already.

He grinned. "I promised the boss I'd take you home. It was the only way I could get him to leave. Besides, I do feel a little bit bad about knocking you over. This is the least I can do."

My first instinct was to refuse. Earlier that day I would have gone to great lengths to avoid a car journey with DI Derwent, but I was tired and it was too good an offer to turn down. And besides, in a weird sort of way he was starting to grow on me.

"All right. But no music. I do have a headache. And it really is your fault."

He was on his best behavior all the way back, chatting about nothing much and staying away from anything to do with work, anything personal, anything that was likely to make me squirm. So he was capable of being pleasant, I mused—he just chose to be a twat.

As he pulled up outside the house, he whistled. "Very grand."

"You're kidding, aren't you? It's practically falling down. Besides, I only have a tiny bit of it."

"Which is your flat?"

I pointed. "Ground floor. I've got the bay window."

"Thief magnet," Derwent observed. "Never rent on the ground floor. Especially if you're a woman on your own. Too dangerous."

"Thanks for the advice." I got out of the car and slammed the door as hard as I could. I hoped it would make his ears ring. I heard his window whine down as I walked toward the front door and braced myself for the comeback.

"Look after yourself, Maeve."

I turned, suspicious. "Are you being *nice*?"

"I'm just worried you'll sue me if you have any long-term damage."

"For everything you've got and then some." I waved as he drove away, tires squealing. Derwent was not what you could call understated. I walked up the steps and let myself into the house, planning a long soak in the bath to get rid of the hospital grime. A night in front of the TV sounded like a good plan.

A good plan it may have been, but it wasn't meant to be. Chris Swain was standing in the hall talking to a jaw-droppingly handsome fair-haired man—on the short side, but green eyes and a dazzling smile made up for the lack of height. Chris was somehow diminished by him, even though he was a shade taller. Then again, he was the sort of person who would never stand out in a crowd of two. The pair of them turned and stared at me.

"Jesus, Maeve. What happened to you?" Chris's hands clenched into fists. "It wasn't your boyfriend, was it?"

"Oh no. *No.* Definitely not. And he's not my boyfriend anyway." I floundered, not having thought of a reason for my injury. "It was just an accident at work. Nothing serious."

"What sort of an accident?" Mr. Beautiful had a great voice too, resonant and mellow. "Oh God, did you fall off the pole?"

"It's the height, isn't it? You must think I'm a pole-vaulter because I'm so tall. Because I know you're not suggesting I'm a stripper." I was trying not to laugh. His timing was impeccable; I had a feeling I was looking at my neighbor the actor, and his next words confirmed it.

"Brody." He held out his hand. "We haven't met, but I've heard all about you. Maeve, isn't it? What is it you do for a living that's so dangerous?"

Half-speed thinking let me down again. I found myself telling him the truth. "I'm a detective constable with the Metropolitan Police."

"Are you serious?" Chris was looking stunned.

"Absolutely."

He shook his head and said, for no apparent reason, "Well, I'll be damned."

"I'm off duty," I said dryly. "There's no need to panic. Unless you've been breaking the law, of course."

He laughed, but he didn't look pleased. It was the same old shit, the same wariness for no apparent reason, the same us-and-them knee-jerk response and I couldn't be bothered to deal with it. I turned to let myself into my flat.

"Where are you going?" Brody draped himself over the wall beside my door, one arm up so he could lean his head against it in a typical poster-boy pose. "Why don't you come upstairs for a drink?"

"Because I'm tired and I need a bath," I snapped. He was cute, but I wasn't in the market for flirting. As if he realized I was out of patience, he straightened up and dropped the smarm.

"Come for one drink. Chris is coming too. He's got the gin and I've got the tonic. If you have any ice, you'll have earned your place at the table."

A tray of cubes was the only thing in my freezer compartment. I wavered. "I do, actually."

"Then you can't leave us hanging." He gave me a pleading look. "Just one drink. You look as if you need it after the day you've had. And I definitely do. Do you know how hard it is to get a decent G and T in Romania?"

"Is that where you've been?"

"For months. And now I've finally been written out."

"Killed off?"

"Not quite. Married, which in kids' TV is the same thing. My story is over." He bowed deeply. When he straightened up, he was laughing. "Christ, it'll take a while to lose the medieval courtliness. I hope I don't get an audition for *EastEnders* until I've got it out of my system."

Agreeing seemed to be my only way out of this conversation. I was struggling to keep pace with it as it was. "You're on the top floor, aren't you? I'll come up with the ice in a few minutes."

"I knew you wouldn't be able to resist the prospect of a drink with the Vladimir and Estragon of Northcliffe Road. Walter, of course, is Godot. Szuszanna is noises off." He lowered his voice. "Have you heard her and Gyorgy going at it? The music is supposed to drown it out, you know, but they still sound like foxes fucking. I haven't the heart to tell her."

I looked at Chris. "Do you understand half of what he says?"

"Not even that much." He shrugged. "Come on, Brody."

The two men started up the stairs, Brody taking them two at a time, holding his hand out as if he were clutching a sword. Chris trudged after him with his head bent, watching his feet as he climbed, not an ounce of showmanship in him.

"This is how I stormed the castle," floated back down to me. I unlocked my door, shaking my head in wonder. I had had some strange housemates in my time, but Brody Lee was in a category of his own. In spite of myself, I was rather looking forward to getting to know him better. Besides, I needed distracting. I wanted noise and conversation and not to think about work, or the look on Godley's face when he said he would teach Skinner a lesson, or the fact that a fourteen-year-old girl was missing and every passing second made it less likely we would find her at all, alive or dead. Not thinking about all of that seemed like the best idea I'd had all day.

Chapter Eleven

I wasn't what you would call a slow mover, but it took me a while to get myself ready for socializing. I had wanted a bath—I had dreamed of a bath—but I settled for a shower, peeling off my crumpled clothes with relief and dropping them in a pile on the bathroom floor. If I never wore them again, I wouldn't be heartbroken.

I stood under the shower with my eyes closed for several long minutes, letting go of the day before I spent time with civilians. It was hard to explain the things I did and saw as part of my job and I hoped against hope that I could put Brody off if he asked about it. He did seem like the kind of person who would be happy to talk about himself all evening. On the other hand, he had a quality I would have liked to possess, the ability to put a question in such a direct way that the person on the receiving end finds themselves answering whether they want to or not. I was regretting already that my cover was blown. Not that it mattered. I hadn't been looking for reasons to arrest my new housemates. I was more than happy to give them their privacy, assuming they were prepared to give me mine.

I could have stayed in the shower for longer, but I couldn't ignore the fact that the water was stinging on my skin. After I had dried off, I stood in front of the long mirror in my bedroom to take stock, discovering an elbow raw with carpet burn and a bluish shadow down my left thigh, the promise of a really lovely bruise that ran more or less hip to knee. I had fallen with a clatter, taken by surprise. It wasn't remarkable that I had souvenirs. Annoyed by the enormous square bandage, I unpeeled the tape, gambling that what was underneath would be less eye-catching. It was not a pretty sight—a bluish-red bump with a puncture at the center where the edge of the TV table had broken the skin.

"Survivable," I said to my reflection, not allowing myself to meet my own eyes in the mirror. I got dressed briskly, pretending it was business as usual, but I felt somehow fragile. I had not allowed myself to slow down after the attack that put me in hospital some months earlier, as if admitting I had been properly hurt would make my recovery harder. This was nothing in comparison, yet I wasn't able to shrug it off. It made me feel vulnerable, and I hated that.

I brushed my hair in Brody's honor but that was the extent of the prettying up; I was too tired and battered to try to look good. Anyway, I didn't care enough to bother. I had identified Brody as a flirt, the kind who charmed women just to keep his hand in, and although he was easy on the eye, he didn't do it for me.

His flat, however, most definitely did appeal. When he opened the door, I gasped, and not just because I was still out of breath from climbing the stairs.

"Wow."

"I get that reaction a lot. You look pretty wow yourself, if it comes to that. Nice top."

"I was talking about this room." I walked past him, turning in a circle to take it in.

"My last girlfriend did it. She was an interior designer. Very keen on paint." He rolled his eyes. "You can imagine how interesting."

I was barely listening. The flat took up the whole attic of the house, and practically all of it was one open-plan space. The ceiling was steeply pitched but that added character, even if it would have irritated the hell out of me to live with it. Brody, being pocket-sized, probably didn't bang his head as much as I would have. The whole thing was painted white—floorboards, ceiling, walls. There wasn't much in the way of furniture, though it was an appealing mixture of contemporary and vintage pieces in tones of beige and cream. It was cynical to wonder if that was because the colors went so well with his hair, but then I was cynical by nature. I dodged under a chrome floor lamp that arched over ten feet, ending in a big paper lantern. It cast a pool of light over the coffee table, which was made of wine crates glued together. This was clearly the height of hipster chic rather than cheap student-style improvisation. Three glasses were already sitting on the table, fizzing gently. Chris was leaning back in a scruffy, tan leather armchair, one foot crossed over the other knee. He waved at me awkwardly and it was a gesture so unstudied in comparison to Brody's careful elegance that I felt a rush of affection for him. If it was mixed with pity, he didn't need to know that. I waved back.

"I've poured already," Brody said.

"So I see." I handed him the bowl of ice. "Do the honors."

He dropped three cubes into each drink as I sat down in the chair next to Chris, and handed me a glass. "Get it down you. You're one behind. We couldn't wait until you got here."

"Desperate for a drink?" I wasn't surprised; I had smelled it on his breath as soon as he opened the door. It explained Chris's flushed cheeks and glittering eyes.

"Darling, you can't imagine." He looked at the table. "Shit. I forgot the nibbles. Can't have drinks without nibbles."

"Don't worry on my account," I began, but he was gone. I heard him rummaging in the tiny kitchen, opening cupboards and clanking bowls.

I turned to find Chris leaning toward me.

"Ignore most of it. He always takes a while to settle down when he's been away. He's not always such a luvvie."

"I'll keep that in mind." I took a sip and the burn from the gin almost drowned out the sweetness of the tonic. "Bloody hell."

"Yeah, he knows how to make a proper drink."

"Don't tell anyone, but I used to be a barman. And I might be again if I don't get another gig." Brody put a bowl of cashews down between us. "Fair warning—these are a few months out of date."

Chris peered at them. "You know, I have a phobia of dying in a stupid way. Being poisoned by a dodgy nut would be on the list. Are you sure they're okay?"

"Nope." He leaned over and took a handful. "It's like Russian roulette, isn't it? Come on, Chris. Live a little."

I took advantage of the bickering to set my glass down on the table. The ice would melt and dilute my drink a little if I left it for a while. I wasn't a big drinker and I didn't like getting drunk with people I barely knew. Too many victim statements began with that scenario. And that pretty much summed up why cops weren't like normal people.

As if Brody had read my mind, he turned to me. "So, Maeve, we've been speculating like mad on what you actually do. What sort of thing do you detect?"

"Serious crime." I left it at that, hoping that a bald answer would deter Brody from asking anything more. His eyes narrowed.

"What counts as serious? Murder? Rape? Child abuse?"

"That sort of thing."

He paused, his drink halfway to his mouth. "You're shitting me, aren't you? You don't investigate murders."

"Quite often, actually." I looked at Chris, who was still leaning back, a cryptic half-smile on his face. The only sign that he wasn't completely relaxed was that his foot was tapping restlessly. "Is that so hard to believe?"

"Yes," Brody said instantly. "You're too pretty. You'd never get cast on a cop show. Not as the heroine, anyway. You might make a good job of being the hero's girlfriend." He raised his eyebrows at me as if inviting me to suggest he'd be an ideal person to play the hero.

"I'll stick to real life, then." I picked up my drink and took another minuscule sip for the sake of having something to do. The raw alcohol almost made me choke.

"What are you working on at the moment?"

I couldn't face telling him about the murders. "We're looking for a teenager who's gone missing."

"Don't they do that sort of thing all the time?" Brody sounded completely uninterested.

"Some do. We just want to trace this girl to make sure she's okay."

Chris was nodding, earnest as ever. "What's her name?"

"Cheyenne."

"Classy." Brody popped another nut into his mouth. "What happened to your face? Did you get punched?"

"It was an accident."

"Come on, give us the details." He looked at Chris. "Cagey, isn't she?"

"Maybe she doesn't want to talk about it, Brody." Chris's voice was quiet but firm.

"I think our Maeve was being brave. I think she threw herself in front of someone to protect them from being hurt and she caught the punch instead. Am I right?"

"Completely," I said, nodding slowly. "You couldn't be more right."

"Thought so. It's like a gift. And I bet I'm right in saying that you like living dangerously."

"Not particularly."

"Oh, come on. I've heard all about your boyfriend. Sorry—your not-boyfriend. I gather he's all dark and threatening." He shot a look at Chris, making it quite clear who had told him what he knew. "He's a copper too, isn't he? Do you work with him?"

I smiled, unmoved. "He's one of my colleagues. Not all that threatening when you get to know him, either."

"Walter didn't like him. But then Walter isn't that keen on the old Bill. They don't tend to approve of his little habits." Brody pinched his forefinger and thumb together and inhaled deeply from an imaginary joint.

"Brody! Shut up, all right? She is a police officer, you know. And it is illegal. Are you trying to get Walter into trouble?"

"I didn't hear the details," I said quickly. "In one ear and out the other."

Brody laughed. "That's lucky. What else should I confess to while you're in a forgiving mood?" He stared at Chris. "What have you got to hide, Swain? What's making your toes curl with fear?"

"Nothing, obviously." Chris shifted in his seat, clearly uncomfortable. "But I don't like you talking about Walter behind his back. Leave him out of it."

Perhaps realizing he'd gone too far, Brody shrugged. He turned his glass upside down and shook a single drop onto the floor. "All gone. Who's for a refill?"

"Slow down, mate."

"Piss off." He stood up, swaying a little, and peered at Chris's glass. "Come on, *mate*, you've hardly touched yours. Make an effort."

I was quickly running out of patience with Brody. I was tired, my forehead was hurting and I wanted to go to sleep. The headache that had been bothering me earlier was back, and this time it had brought reinforcements. For the sake of neighborliness I had dragged myself up to his flat, but I was not prepared to put up with drunken scene-making. I stood up.

"You know, I'd love to stay, but I'm going to have to leave. I've got work in the morning and those serious crimes won't investigate themselves."

"What about your drink?"

"You can have it." I slid it across the table toward Brody. "Sorry, but I really shouldn't be drinking anything stronger than tea tonight anyway."

"So have tea." It was Chris who spoke. He had got to his feet as well. "Don't worry about Brody. Just ignore him. He's attention seeking."

Brody snorted. "If I wanted your attention, I could be a whole lot more drastic about how I got it, believe me."

"Stay a bit longer," Chris said, almost pleading. "I'll make you some tea. I'll make us all some tea."

"Another time." I smiled at him, privately promising myself that it would never happen.

"You *twat*, Brody. Thanks for spoiling a nice evening." Chris looked genuinely annoyed.

"By doing what exactly? Trying to enjoy myself? Excuse the fuck out of me." He threw himself back into his seat, took a slug out of my glass and coughed.

"You're excused," Chris said under his breath. "Maeve, I don't blame you for not wanting to be here. I don't want to be here either. I'll walk you down."

"There's really no need. I can find my own way to my flat."

"Well, I'm leaving too. So we can ignore each other and keep our distance, or we can walk down together." He gave me his surprisingly charming, lopsided smile. "I know which I'd prefer, but maybe you have a different view."

"Well, if you're leaving anyway, I can't object." I looked down at Brody. "Thank you for the hospitality. Sorry I couldn't stay longer."

"No, you're not. You're a pair of fuckers and I can't believe you're leaving me on my own."

"Too bad," Chris said with a toughness I wouldn't have expected from him. He raised his eyebrows at me. "Shall we?"

"You'll be back," Brody said from the depths of his armchair. "And you'll be welcome, Maeve. But you, Chris, you can forget it. You're dead to me."

Chris sighed in a martyred way but didn't respond, and neither did I. I took a long look at the room as I left it. I had a feeling I wouldn't be back anytime soon.

Once the door closed behind us, Chris's shoulders slumped. "I'm really sorry to have dragged you into that. He's not himself. I think he's depressed about being kicked off his show."

"No one likes being unemployed," I said, trying to sound understanding. It was hard to concentrate when I felt as if my bones had been replaced with damp cotton wool. "And you hardly dragged me up here. I came of my own free will."

"You came because Brody wouldn't have left you alone if you hadn't agreed to it."

"Which is nothing to do with you, so there's no need to apologize."

"Okay, then. But I still feel guilty."

Chris was staring at me with big sad-puppy eyes but I had run out of sympathy, or at least the energy to express it.

"And you promise me he's not always like that."

"He's not great when he's drinking, put it that way."

"I've never seen two and a half gins go further. He doesn't seem to have much of a head for it."

"He doesn't drink much usually. Bad for his weight and his skin, he told me. So when he does get drunk, he really goes for it." Chris shook his head disapprovingly. "Anyway, never mind him. How are you?"

I was taking my time negotiating the stairs, holding on to the banister. "Just tired, I think."

"Are you sure? You're looking quite pale."

"How can you tell in this light?" The stairwell was gloomy; I could barely see his face even though it was close to mine when I turned. "I'm fine. I got checked over at the hospital. No concussion, they promised me."

And yet I was feeling woozy. I wondered with a flicker of concern if they'd missed something, if I shouldn't have been sent home. Or maybe I was getting the flu. Chris was still peering at me.

"I'm fine, I promise you," I said again.

"You're walking like you're hurt. That bang on your head isn't the only damage, is it?"

"It's not serious."

"I've got painkillers, if you want. Ibuprofen, definitely, and I might have some codeine somewhere. I could pop over."

No more socializing. I forced a smile. "Thanks, Chris. There's no need."

"It's no trouble."

We turned onto the last flight of stairs and the "Hallelujah" chorus started up in my head at the sight of my own front door, the promise of peace and privacy. "I just want to go to bed."

Before Chris could reply, a shadow moved behind the stained-glass inlay of the front door. A second later the bell rang.

"I'll get it." Chris slipped past me and ran down the last few steps, fumbling at the door as if he was too conscious of me watching to be anything but clumsy. He pulled it open, but only a few inches, peering through the narrow gap suspiciously. Everything about his body language suggested he wanted to slam it closed again, but he didn't quite dare. He settled for saying, in a tone that was borderline rude, "What do you want?"

Curious, I leaned sideways to catch a glimpse of who was outside, and when I did, my heart jumped.

"Rob." My voice wavered as I said his name. He pushed past Chris as if there were no one barring the door and came toward me.

"Are you okay?"

I nodded, clutching at the last shreds of my composure as I wondered why it was I felt like crying. "It's nothing."

He had stopped on the step below mine. "Doesn't look like nothing. Did you put ice on it?"

"Isn't that my line?"

"It's late." I had forgotten Chris was there, but he was still standing by the door, watching us. "Maeve's tired. She was just going to bed."

Rob twisted around to stare at him, stony-faced. "Then it looks as if I turned up in the nick of time, doesn't it?"

Chris reddened, but whether it was with embarrassment or anger I couldn't tell. "You should leave."

"Not happening, pal."

Chris might as well have tried to argue with the furniture; he wasn't going to get anywhere. As if he realized that, he switched his focus to me. "Walter doesn't want him here. You could get in trouble."

"I'll talk to Walter if he's upset about it." I kept my voice very calm, reassuring him. "Look, Chris, I know you're worried about me and I do appreciate it, but I'm all right. And I'm quite capable of telling Rob to leave if I want him to."

"Better believe it." Taking his cue from me, Rob sounded more amused than hostile. "I wouldn't dare argue about it either."

Chris ignored him. His eyes were still fixed on me. "You know where I am if you need me, Maeve. Just knock on the door. Anytime."

I was trying very hard not to laugh, knowing that it was absolutely essential to allow Chris to believe I might need to call on him. I wanted to leave him with his self-respect intact, even if his dignity was long gone. "Right. Thanks again." I turned to Rob, not quite catching his eye. "We should go into my flat. Stop causing a commotion in the hall."

"You're right. Much better to cause a commotion in private." He nodded to Chris, who had gone red again. "See you later."

I unlocked the door and pushed him through it with minimal concern for either his well-being or the paintwork. I shut it firmly behind us, seeing Chris still staring at me through the narrowing gap before I did so.

"Remember, just knock on the door. Anytime." Rob was leaning against the wall, an innocent expression on his face, when I turned around. I frowned at him.

"Can I just point out that I have to live here?"

"So?"

"So stop taking the piss out of my neighbor, please."

"Come on, Maeve. You can't expect me to take him seriously. It was like being threatened by a not-very-fierce rabbit."

"Rabbits can bite," I said vaguely.

Rob looked at me quizzically. "Have you eaten?"

I shook my head.

"Typical. I should have brought something with me." He peeled himself away from the wall. "I suppose there's no point in hoping there's anything in the fridge."

"You don't have to take responsibility for feeding me." I wandered after him, standing in the door of the kitchen as he inspected the contents of the cupboards.

"So, basically, you've just got eggs. I'll do you an omelette." He glanced up at me and winced. "Let's have a proper look at you. I could see fuck all on the stairs."

I started to back away but he took me by the arms, pulling me into the kitchen so he could see me clearly.

"It was just a stupid accident." I could feel myself starting to blush at his close scrutiny.

"I heard you got pushed over."

"Yeah, by Derwent. He put me on the ground. For my own good, apparently."

"Is that so?" Rob was frowning. "Why don't you tell me about it while I do the cooking?"

I levered myself up onto the counter and swung my legs, knocking my heels against the cupboard doors as I filled him in on the events of the day. It reminded me a little too much of the last time he had been in my flat, and I resolved not to pick a fight with him this time. He made no comment on what Derwent had done in Forgrave's flat, but he was interested in God-ley's reaction to Skinner's taunts, and how he had been at the hospital.

"Sounds as if the boss was pretty close to the edge."

"You're not wrong. I've never seen him like that." I shivered. "It was just rage. He's always so calm. At least outwardly."

"Yeah, I think that's the point. There's a lot more going on there than he ever shows the likes of us."

"Don't you think it's disturbing, though? That he lost control like that?"

Rob didn't answer straightaway, as if he was choosing his words carefully. "I think that if anyone threatened someone I loved, I'd find it hard to restrain myself."

"Not in those circumstances, surely."

"Absolutely in those circumstances." He looked up, his eyes steady. "If you love someone, the rules change. Reason goes out the window. You'd do anything for them. That's the point."

I was annoyed to find my heart thumping against my ribs. I couldn't look away from him. What I said in the end was slightly sharp-edged. "Remind me, why are you here?

"I was worried about you. I wanted to know you were all right."

"You should have phoned. I'd have told you how I was."

"I wouldn't have believed you." He laughed. "Come off it, Maeve. We both know you'd have said you were fine."

"Which is the truth."

"Which is total rubbish, actually. You look dreadful."

"Thanks very much."

He tipped the egg mixture into the frying pan and swirled it around. "This is how you make an omelette, by the way."

"I can see the broken eggs from here."

"Well, watch and learn."

I pointed with my toe. "You haven't noticed, but I fixed the tap too."

"I had, actually. Well done."

"I did it after you left." I had needed something to take my mind off what had happened.

"How long did it take you?"

"Hours. I had to ring Dec halfway through for advice."

"I'd have done it for you."

"I know. But I didn't want to ask you." I hesitated, then plunged in. "And I didn't want to ask you to come over tonight, but I'm really glad you're here."

"That's a relief."

I waited, but he didn't say anything else. I could see why. I was the one who had insisted on ending it before. Twice, now. The last thing he had said was that he wouldn't change his mind, that over was over, and Rob generally meant what he said. I had told him I didn't want us to be together because I was afraid of risking everything I'd worked so hard to achieve, but suddenly I was more afraid of losing him. I fought panic, knowing that I might have missed my opportunity, knowing suddenly what that would mean to me.

He had been concentrating on the pan, tilting it sideways to coax the uncooked egg to the edge. He glanced up briefly and then looked again. "What's the matter?"

I blinked unshed tears away. "Nothing."

"Let me guess. You're fine."

Something about the resignation in his voice made me lose my grip on myself. I put my hands up to my face to hide it from him as I sobbed, "I'm not fine. I'm not. And I miss you. And I know I've made a complete mess of it, but I was just trying to do the right thing." I dropped my hands and said, slightly desperately, "If you could just forget what I said before . . ."

The rest of what I was going to tell him was lost forever because he stopped me mid-sentence by pulling my face down to him and kissing me. I wrapped my legs around him, holding on to him, every nerve end singing at his touch. It was as intense as a first kiss, as shatteringly exciting, but this time the stakes were higher. Either this worked or it never would. And where once I might have run a mile from the very idea of a proper relationship, now, somehow, I didn't feel the need. Maybe it was because of the knock on the head, but everything was much clearer than it had been even that morning. There was Rob and there was me, and being together made us both happy. Nothing else really mattered, not at that moment, anyway.

In the end, it was the smell of burning that distracted us from each other. Rob swore and grabbed the smoking frying pan, dumping it in the sink. "That's one omelette ruined, and I'm not too sure the pan will recover."

"Leave it. Who cares?" I was light-headed with emotion, giddy with relief. More than anything, I wanted him to kiss me again.

"Aren't you hungry?"

"Not remotely." I blinked at him, still slightly dopey, and couldn't think of anything to tell him but the truth. "It was just an excuse to get you to stay."

"Fair enough." He came back to stand between my knees. "Where were we?"

I slid my arms around his neck. "About to do something much more fun than cooking."

"Heresy."

"No, I don't think it was that."

He moved back so there was just enough room for me to slide off the counter, then pinned me against it so he could kiss me again. His hands slipped under my top, exploring.

"Find anything you like?" I managed to say when we came up for air, and was quite proud of myself for putting a coherent sentence together.

"A couple of things." He grinned and I reflected ruefully that it was practically impossible to catch Rob out, no matter what the circumstances were. "Should I leave in a huff now, or do you think we might make it as far as your bedroom this time?"

"I'd say there's a good chance of getting into the room at least before anyone storms off."

"Well, that'd be progress." Rob followed me down the hall.

I turned at the door to apologize for the untidiness of the room and was literally swept off my feet. "Hey!"

"I'm doing masterful tonight." He undercut it immediately. "You don't mind, do you?"

"Not much." A little too late, I said, "Watch the door—ow."

"Shit. Sorry." He let me slip to the floor and rubbed the back of my head, which had clunked against the doorframe. "Are you okay?"

I was giggling helplessly. "Just stop asking me that, all right?"

"I will when you stop injuring yourself."

"Technically, you were responsible for it that time."

"Okay. We won't count it. I notice we haven't actually got through the door yet. So strictly speaking, we're still where we were last time."

"I wouldn't say that." I stepped into the bedroom and pulled him after me. "You are a total idiot, and yet I still want to sleep with you. What does that make me?"

"I'd have said sensible." He was removing clothes with single-minded efficiency; there was no one like Rob for stripping to the basics at speed. "Come on. Get them off."

"Are we back to masterful?"

He snorted. "Desperate, more like. Do you know how long it's been?"

"For me, yes. For you, I have no idea."

He pulled his shirt over his head and stopped, suddenly serious. "Just so we're clear, there's no one else, Maeve. There's only you."

"Good," I said lightly, feeling my heart flip over with happiness that took even me by surprise. "Keep it that way."

"Remind me why I should?"

"Oh, I will." He looked up at that and I smiled wickedly, enjoying the expression on his face as he crossed the room to where I was standing.

Desperate he may have been, but there was no sign of it from how he behaved in bed. He was as considerate and intuitive as ever, as completely in tune with me as he had always seemed to be. I forgot the bruises, the worries I had about work, the strange little scene with my neighbors. I pretty much forgot my own name now and then, not that anyone was asking.

Afterward, lying back in the circle of his arms, I sighed. "Why don't we do that all the time?"

He kissed the top of my head. "Remember how you were saying you were an idiot?"

"I said *you* were an idiot."

"I wasn't listening properly. Anyway, it's nothing to do with me. It's all about you being stubborn."

"Smug git." I yawned. He kissed me again.

"Go to sleep."

"Mm." I was thinking about what we had just done, how it had been the opposite of screaming, chandelier-swinging show-off sex and all the better for it. I had never felt as close to anyone as I did to him—close, but not stifled or overwhelmed. Deeply involved in the conversation in my head, I found myself mumbling, "What's wrong with being quiet anyway?"

"Nothing?" he suggested, sounding mildly baffled and I was going to explain but instead, quite suddenly, I fell asleep. It was a deep and dreamless sleep, and when I woke up some time later, I was alone. I heard the shower running and sat up, confused. The clock on the bedside table said it was a quarter past one. I couldn't think why Rob wasn't lying beside me. I checked my phone twice to see if I'd missed any calls while I slept.

When the door opened, he came in soundlessly, gathering up clothes as he moved through the dark room. I waited until he was right beside the bed.

"What are you doing?"

"Jesus, you scared the shit out of me."

I put the bedside light on. "Where's the fire?"

He started to get dressed, as if what he was doing was perfectly normal and reasonable. "No fire. It's just time to go."

"It's one o'clock in the morning."

"Yeah. Time I left."

"I don't understand," I said flatly.

He was buckling his belt. "Have you seen my T-shirt?"

"Over there somewhere." I pointed, distracted by his bare torso, the muscles moving under his skin. I made myself concentrate. "Explain, please. Where are you going?"

He turned around before he put his T-shirt on and his face was affectionate. "Look, I don't want to make a nuisance of myself. I want to leave before you think I should go."

"But I don't want you to go." I hugged the bedclothes to my chest, suddenly cold.

"Not now, you don't. But later on, you might change your mind. And I'd rather you missed me than that you were fed up with having me around."

"That's not fair," I protested.

"You've got form for it."

"People change. Maybe I've changed."

"Yeah, maybe." He was pulling his socks on. "But you'll have to prove it. Anyway, it'll make it easier to keep it quiet like you wanted."

Dimly, I recalled what I had said before I slept. "That's not what I meant, I think." I bit my lip. "Would it help to convince you to stay if I told you that at this moment, I don't care who knows about us?"

"'At this moment'? Not really." He smiled wryly. "Isn't this what you wanted? No relationship, just uncomplicated sex?"

"You know there's no such thing."

"I do. But you seem to need convincing." He leaned across and kissed me one last time. "See you tomorrow."

"Today," I said sulkily.

A quick grin. "How right you are. See you later, then."

He was gone before I could stop him, and I listened to the front door of the flat closing, then the muffled thud of the main door. A car engine started a minute later and I pictured him driving away. He was right; it was what I had wanted. I was free.

It felt an awful lot like being alone.

Chapter Twelve

Friday

At half past seven the following morning I was back in hospital, but this time as a visitor rather than a patient. But I could have done with some medical care myself; I had a headache that painkillers couldn't touch and my eyes felt gritty, as if I hadn't slept at all. I took the lift to the fifth floor, risking only a brief glance in the mirror that confirmed I was as pale and drawn as I felt.

When the lift doors opened, I hurried out and collided with Derwent, who had been pacing up and down the hall.

"Look at the state of you. Did you get run over on the way?"

"Thanks a lot. Do I have to remind you the boss said I was to take things easy this morning? I shouldn't even be here."

"If you'd wanted to stay in bed, you could have said."

"Obviously, I didn't. But you can't expect *Vogue*-standard glamor in the circumstances."

"You don't want to aim that high, love. Shoot for human and we'll all be happy."

I forbore to point out that he wasn't exactly model material himself. "Where are we going?"

"Forgrave is in room four-two-two." Derwent started to head in that direction and I fell into step beside him.

"On his own?"

"A private room. Nothing but the best for our William. Also, it makes it easier to guard him."

"Do you really think Skinner would try to get at him again?"

He shrugged. "Better safe than sorry. John Skinner being in custody doesn't make a blind bit of difference to what happens on the outside. If he wants to kill him, he'll get someone to do it for him."

"Cheery stuff."

"I won't tell Mr. Forgrave. Mind you, I don't think he'd be much of a loss."

We had arrived at room 422 and Derwent waited impatiently as the uniformed officer who was posted outside the door examined our warrant cards.

"Good to go?"

"Knock yourselves out."

I might have thought it was a chance remark if the officer's eyes hadn't been trained on the bump on my head. It was the first dig of the day, but I could guarantee it wouldn't be the only one. I followed Derwent into Forgrave's room, thinking black thoughts and not actually caring if it showed on my face.

It was hard to tell what expression William Forgrave was wearing between his beard and the bruising. His eyes were so swollen they had narrowed to slits, the skin around them the color of ripe plums. His lip was quilted with stitches and looked as if it hurt. One cheek had blown out, giving him a distinctly lopsided appearance. He was bare-chested, the dressings on his chest mercifully hiding the burns I had seen the previous day.

"All right, William?" Derwent picked up the chart from the end of the bed and flicked through it. He whistled. "I don't speak medic but this looks nasty."

"Who are you?" Forgrave's voice was hoarse.

"Police. We're the ones who saved your bacon." Derwent sat on the edge of the bed, one foot swinging. I sat on the upright chair by the bed, moving it back so I wasn't too close to Forgrave. He smelled of stale sweat and old blood, and his breath was rank. Derwent didn't seem to care, leaning forward to say, "Remember when the cavalry turned up yesterday? We called them."

Well, technically I *did*. I decided not to tout for recognition, though. It just wasn't worth it.

"Ta." Forgrave didn't sound particularly impressed.

"Is that all you've got to say?" Derwent flipped through the chart again. "Actually, it's probably all you can say considering the state of your face."

"I can manage." The words were blurry on the consonants but recognizable.

"Excellent. In that case, you can answer a few questions for us. What happened yesterday?"

"Got beaten up."

"Why?"

Forgrave rolled his head on the pillow. "Ask them."

"We will. But I want to hear your story. You're the victim here."

"No story."

"You were tortured, William. That's not normal. Did they tell you why they targeted you?"

A nod.

"So you know it's because you're a registered child abuser."

Another nod.

"Do you know what William here did, Maeve? I've been looking him up."

"I don't, actually."

"He raped a young girl."

"Technically." Forgrave's hands had bunched into fists.

"Actually. She was only fifteen."

"Almost sixteen."

Derwent shook his head. "It was illegal. She couldn't consent to it even if you convinced her it was a good idea. She was underage. That's why you got convicted."

"I made a mistake."

"You targeted her, William. You found her on the Internet, in a kids' chat room. And you thought she was younger than she actually was, didn't you? You were looking for thirteen-year-olds. That's your type."

"You're wrong."

"Don't think so. What happened in nineteen-ninety-three?"

"Nothing."

"You joined a fan club for a boy band so you could meet girls. You started writing to a thirteen-year-old in Scotland—all nice and friendly, pen pals. You groomed her. You told her you loved her. You told her you wanted to marry her. You persuaded her to lie to her parents and get a train to Manchester, where you had booked a hotel room. What you didn't know was that she was going to turn up with her best friend. Imagine your surprise when you opened the door and found two of them. You must have thought it was Christmas."

"That's not how it was."

"You tried to have sex with them, didn't you? But you couldn't get it up. And you found it too hard to control two of them anyway. You ended up losing your nerve and doing a runner."

"That's your version."

"That's what happened. The two girls were very clear about it. Plus, you left DNA all over the place." He turned to me. "The DNA database didn't exist yet but William was unlucky. The samples were kept on file and when the database was set up, the local coppers remembered to register him. They knew it was just a matter of waiting until he tried it again. People like that always do."

"No." Forgrave sounded definite. "It was different."

"You met the next one on the Internet. You persuaded her to meet you. You had sex with her. The only thing that was different was how you contacted her—and that you were able to screw this one." Derwent leaned forward. "You're a dangerous predator, William. You proved it. You got ten years. That's not a light sentence."

"I got counseling in prison. I got parole after five years. I've changed. The parole board believed me."

"People like you don't change—you just get better at hiding what you are. You probably got let out because of overcrowding."

"No."

"You're not going to impress us, William, so don't bother." Derwent paused. "Did you know Cheyenne Skinner?"

"That's what they wanted to know." Forgrave swallowed. "I'd never heard of her until yesterday."

"So you hadn't been in touch with her? You hadn't been e-mailing her?"

"No. I don't do that anymore."

"Sure?"

"I told them—I stopped. I grew out of it."

"Ever had a girlfriend? I mean, one that was old enough to be legal?"

"I find it hard to meet women."

"You have to try in the first place." Derwent jerked a thumb in my direction. "You haven't even glanced at my colleague since we've been here. Admittedly, I've seen her look better, but she's not ugly."

I could have *murdered* Derwent.

"I'm not really in the mood for flirting." Forgrave raised a hand and gestured at his face.

"Still, though. You have to admit it's strange."

"Do I?" He coughed a little, then closed his eyes. "Are you finished?"

"For now." Derwent stood up. "Come on, Kerrigan."

I didn't bother to say good-bye to Forgrave; I just headed for the door, aware that Derwent hadn't moved but not realizing why until I turned around. He was watching Forgrave, who was watching me.

"Yeah, you looked that time. I knew you would. But it's too little, too late, I'm afraid." His voice was soft. "I can always spot a liar, William. We'll find out who you've been e-mailing and what else you've been doing since you've been out of prison. Because you didn't convince Mr. Skinner that you were pure as the driven snow, and you haven't convinced us. One way or another, you're going to get your comeuppance."

"You won't find anything."

"Think not?" Derwent smiled. "Good luck with your recovery, Mr. Forgrave. Try to think happy thoughts, won't you?"

I wasn't doing that well with the happy thoughts myself. I had enough self-control to wait until we were out of earshot of the officer who was guarding Forgrave before I ripped into Derwent.

"How dare you?"

"What?"

"You asked me to come here. You told me you wanted me to help with the interview, and you didn't even ask me if I had any questions for him."

"Yeah, that wasn't the help I was looking for." He patted my shoulder. "Don't feel bad, Kerrigan. You did your bit."

"You used me."

"Oh, spare me the feminist outrage." He pressed the button to call the lift. "I told you; you need to make the most of being young and relatively attractive. Use the tools at your disposal and don't fucking whine about it."

I folded my arms. "Like the way you use your legendary charm?"

"Don't start." He jerked his thumb in the direction of Forgrave's room. "That guy reeks of wrong. I know he's been up to something."

"He does seem on the dodgy side," I agreed reluctantly. "But I'm still angry."

"All right." The lift arrived and Derwent got in, putting a hand out to stop me from following. "Work it off on the stairs. I don't want you bending my ear about it on the drive to the office. I'll see you in the car park."

I stepped back as the lift doors slid closed, speechless with rage. It would take a lot more than a few flights of stairs to make me calm down, but Derwent needn't have worried about me complaining. Silence was what he wanted, so silence was what he got, all the way to work. And if he chose to characterize it as sulking—which he did—that was fine by me.

———

The briefing room was almost full already and there were still people filing in. I pushed through the crowd to find a place to perch, swerving away from a seat near Rob in favor of sitting beside Liv Bowen. Rob nodded to me amiably enough. No one looking at us would have thought we had been together the previous evening, which I suppose was the point. I decided not to spend too much time analyzing it, and promptly began to do exactly that. It was almost a relief to be distracted by the scrutiny of my colleagues. Most of them seemed to be inordinately fascinated by my bruises. I had perfected a flinty glare to ward off the crass comments.

Liv, whom I would have expected to be more sensible than most, inspected my face as I sat down. "Come up lovely, hasn't it?"

"It'll fade."

"No doubt." She tilted her head to one side, considering it. "Bruising sort of suits you."

"Oh, thanks a lot."

At that moment Godley entered the room in the company of a middle-aged woman who had a distinctly no-nonsense air about her. She was wearing a black trouser suit that was a shade too tight and had a buff folder under one arm. Like a classroom full of badly behaved teenagers, we settled down to something approximating silence as the last of us shuffled in and sat down.

"Everyone ready? Good." Godley stood at the front of the room, his hair gleaming silver under the harsh fluorescent lights that buzzed overhead. "This is DCI Marla Redmond from Brixton CID. She's come to brief us about their ongoing investigation into the disappearance of a teenage girl on Saturday. Most of you will be aware that we have John Skinner in custody. The girl in question is his daughter."

There was a low buzz of conversation during the couple of seconds it took DCI Redmond to swap places with Godley and gather her thoughts. She looked tense, her pale face free of makeup.

"Right, we're currently searching for Cheyenne Skinner, a fourteen-year-old girl from Hoddesdon in Hertfordshire." She flipped open her folder and took out a school photograph, a girl in a blazer and white shirt. She held it up to let everyone have a look, then gave it to Liv, indicating that she should pass it around. I studied it with interest when it came to me. The first things I noted were the girl's arched, overplucked eyebrows and a lot of honey-blond hair that had been teased into tumbling curls for the photograph. Cheyenne had heavy-lidded eyes, a full mouth and a distinctly snub nose. The embroidered crest on her blazer read "Our Lady Queen of Heaven RC Girls School," which had to be less strict than the secondary school I had attended. The nuns would never have allowed me to get away with a tenth of the mascara and lip gloss that Cheyenne was wearing. You couldn't truthfully have described the girl as pretty but there was something attractive about her, a gleam of spirit in the dark-rimmed eyes. She looked a lot older than fourteen too.

"We have no sightings of Cheyenne since Saturday evening when she left home to attend a pop-up nightclub held in a warehouse off Coldharbor Lane."

"A what?" Colin Vale was looking baffled.

"It's a club set up for one night only in a building that's basically derelict. They had lighting, a sound system and a bar of sorts, all run by generators. It was illegal—they didn't have a drinks license, which the organizers have admitted. But the warehouse is in an industrial area that's not too close to any residences and no one complained about noise to us, so they weren't found out until the girl disappeared."

"How did she know about it?"

"She was invited by someone she'd met on the Internet. We don't know who this person was, although we've made strenuous efforts to trace them, as you might imagine. The account they were using seems to have been shut down and Cheyenne didn't keep much on her computer, probably because she was told not to. We only know about this individual from a message that Cheyenne forwarded to her friends to show off."

I looked across the room to where Derwent was standing and caught his eye. I mouthed, "Forgrave?"

He shrugged, but he looked concerned.

"Was she being groomed?" Colin Vale asked.

"Looks like it. I've sent the message to the Child Exploitation and Online Protection center and they confirmed it had all the hallmarks they would look for. The tone is flirtatious—comments about her appearance, her choice of clothing and so forth. And the person, who went by the name of Kyle, asked her to be sure to keep their messages secret to make it more special."

"Manipulative," Derwent commented, glancing in my direction again. It was strikingly similar to what he had found out earlier about Forgrave's crimes. If alarm bells hadn't been ringing before, they definitely were now.

"How do we know this person was the source of the invitation?" Rob asked.

"We're going by what Cheyenne told her friends. She was extremely nervous at the prospect of going to the club, because she was going to meet 'Kyle' for the first time. And we have a copy of the invitation because one of my officers thought to hit the reprint button on her printer. Luckily for us it was the last thing she printed." Marla allowed herself a small satisfied smile as she took a piece of paper out of her folder and held it out to Liv. I leaned over to look at it, seeing a pair of masked skulls at the top of the page.

"What's the logo?"

"That's the organizers, The Brothers Grim. They've done a few different events, they told me—flash mobs, pop-up shops and galleries. Very trendy. Very popular with the bright young things."

I was reading the wording of the invitation. Dancing and debauchery, as Derwent had said. "It looks as if they were planning an orgy."

DCI Redmond shrugged. "I think they would have chosen a more comfortable venue if that had been on the cards. Take it from me, the warehouse is exceptionally drafty."

"Okay, but this is definitely for adults, isn't it? This isn't aimed at teenagers."

"The organizers didn't specifically say that those who attended had to be over eighteen. They didn't need to, as they didn't have a license in the first place. They also didn't place many controls on who attended. The invitation was passed on by word of mouth and they limited the numbers on the night, making sure that there weren't more than two hundred people there at any one time. But by all accounts it was an older crowd—mid-twenties, mostly."

"Any chance of getting a list of those who attended?" Colin again.

"We've tried. We've been using social media to reach out to those who might have been there. We launched a Facebook appeal that's had a fair bit of attention and we also got on Twitter. Considering the way the invitation was circulated, we thought the best way to contact those who attended was via the Internet."

"I haven't seen anything about her in the conventional media," Belcott said.

DCI Redmond looked uneasily at Godley, who stood up. "A decision was taken—not by us, I might add—that this was an opportunity to put pressure on John Skinner to return to the UK."

"You used Cheyenne as bait. You went soft on the investigation so he would come back." I had been thinking it, but it was Liv who said it, and she sounded as disgusted as I felt.

"That's not the case. DCI Redmond has been working extremely hard to locate her. But there was a belief that if John Skinner was sufficiently worried about his daughter, he might return. Which was, in fact, what happened."

"And three men died before we worked out he was here." I didn't bother to keep the bitterness out of my voice. I felt protective of my victims, even more so because of why they had died. I was glad that I didn't have to add Forgrave to their number. I was quite comfortable with not caring for him in the least.

"They were pedophiles, though," Belcott said. "Let's not get too upset about it." I couldn't look at him.

"It wasn't our choice." Godley's voice was flat. End of discussion. I recalled the strain he had been under for the previous days and could accept that he hadn't wanted to go that route. "Besides, the media would have focused on her father, not on Cheyenne. We didn't want the complications that would have brought to the investigation."

"Are we sure that this online boyfriend isn't a front for one of Skinner's enemies?" Rob asked. "Attacking his daughter would be the ideal way to get revenge on him, and I imagine there are a fair few people who would like the chance."

"That's one of the reasons I'm glad this team is joining the investigation. We're drowning in information and I don't have time to work out what's important." Marla Redmond smiled slightly. "You're more familiar with Skinner than we are. We thought it would be worth having a look in the files to see who might be pissed off with him."

"It'd be easier to count the people who aren't." Peter Belcott folded his arms and rested them on his belly, looking smug for no reason I could think, except that smugness was his default setting.

"That's why we need your help," the DCI said patiently. "You have a better chance of spotting the genuine enemies." She looked at Liv. "You're right. Cheyenne was bait. But she's also a missing teenager. And however streetwise she may be, she is still a child. With every minute that passes, we have less chance of finding her alive. Gayle Skinner is the wife of a known criminal and she enjoys the lifestyle that's given her, but don't think that means she doesn't care about her daughter. I don't want to have to go and tell her that we've found a body and I'm damned if I'm going to do less than my best to find Cheyenne, regardless of who her father is."

I found myself liking Marla Redmond. She had clearly been fighting that particular battle for the past couple of days, and maybe that explained the strain on her face. I was sure that her priority was the girl, first and foremost.

"What about if she's just run away?" Belcott was holding the picture. "She looks a lot older than fourteen and if she's anything like her old man, I bet she's a stubborn one."

"We've considered that too. However, we can't see why she would need to. She lives with her mother in a nice big detached house on a quiet leafy street. According to Gayle, they got on very well, and according to me, she was allowed to get away with far too much. Gayle had no problem with letting her go into London overnight, for instance, although she did think Cheyenne was staying with a friend. Cheyenne and her mum do everything together, from shopping to visiting tanning salons, and I just can't see Cheyenne leaving home and not making any contact with her mother for almost a week."

"What's she wearing around her neck?" DS Bryce held up the photograph and pointed to a silver chain just visible under her shirt, weighted into a V by something that hung out of sight.

"Now that is interesting. It's a white gold oval pendant ringed with diamonds. She always wears it, apparently. The pendant has a religious image on it—a picture of the Virgin Mary, I'm told. It's double-sided; the back is set with twelve diamonds and has an M surmounted with a cross engraved on it. It's a traditional piece of jewelry for Roman Catholics but this particular pendant is unique. It was made for her, a gift to mark her confirmation."

I stifled a snort. What DCI Redmond had described was a blinged-up version of a Miraculous Medal, as worn by pious Catholics the world over. I had had one myself when I was in school, but mine had been plain silver, modest and discreet, as they tended to be. All that could be said for Cheyenne's version was that it sounded distinctive.

Godley took over. "I'll be allocating tasks to those of you who are free to work on this operation. Some of it will be file sifting, I'm afraid, but I also want to re-interview family and friends, plus our potential witnesses, and take a look at the warehouse. It's no reflection on the work done already." He glanced at Marla Redmond, who was looking pink. It couldn't be pleasant to have a senior officer take over your case just when you were out of ideas and resources. She would be feeling the pressure. I hoped like hell I never ended up in a similar position. "I want anyone who's available to give your names to DI Derwent, please. Some of you will be going over to Brixton to work with DCI Redmond's team. Please bear in mind that DCI Redmond is the lead investigator in this case and take your direction from her."

"What about Skinner?" Belcott asked.

"We're going to interview him shortly. He's been nicked for the three murders that DI Derwent was investigating." Godley scanned the room until his gaze fell on me. "Maeve, you can sit in."

I was surprised to be singled out and not a little embarrassed, especially since Belcott was glaring at me with the full force of his considerable capacity for resentment. On the other hand, it was an opportunity not to be missed. And it wasn't as if I hadn't worked for it. I had seen far too much of John Skinner's work over the previous few days not to want to look him in the eye when he explained himself.

The silence in the room was beginning to fragment around the edges, as various muttered conversations started up. Marla Redmond turned to Godley, who bent his head to listen to her. He was nodding courteously as she spoke, but I had a feeling that he had moved on already. The next challenge for him was dealing with John Skinner without letting him get the advantage as he had the previous day. Godley would be determined not to give in to his emotions this time, but it was easier said than done, and the muscle that flickered in his jaw told me he was on edge.

"Well, that worked out nicely," Liv said. "You getting to sit in on the interview, I mean."

I grinned. "Just think, I could be stuck reading the files on him."

"Don't. You know that's what I'm going to end up doing."

"At least with Skinner they make interesting reading," I offered, but she rolled her eyes, then got up and went to join the queue in front of Derwent. It looked as if he was going to be there for a while, taking names and allocating duties. I would let him take the lead on discussing Forgrave with the boss, I decided. Jumping in ahead of him would make me exceedingly unpopular, I had no doubt.

Outside the meeting room I waited diffidently while Godley said goodbye to DCI Redmond. I didn't want to move too far away in case I missed my chance to go to the interview room with him and Derwent, but I didn't want to listen in on his conversation either. I became aware that someone was standing behind me, leaning against the wall, and turned to find myself altogether too close to Peter Belcott.

"What do you want?"

"I want to know why Godley's so keen on you." He spoke softly and I felt his breath on my face, warm and stale even at that hour of the morning. I turned away a little, repulsed. "What's going on, Maeve? Do you suck him off? Is that it? Give a little head to get ahead?"

"For fuck's sake, of course not."

"Strange how you always seem to be the one who gets the good jobs, isn't it?"

"Who else wanted to work on the dead pedophiles, Peter? You? I don't remember a great deal of enthusiasm. It was a shit job and it turned out to be more exciting than anyone expected." I shrugged. "What can I tell you? Maybe I'm just lucky."

"I don't believe in luck."

"Stop looking for a conspiracy. There isn't one." I spoke flatly, knowing that Belcott was quite capable of spreading the rumor that I was involved with Godley, and that my colleagues would be delighted to believe it.

He stepped even closer, his voice so low that only I could hear it. "I just want you to know that you're only here to fulfill the diversity criteria. Godley probably wants you in the room so you can distract Skinner by flashing your tits at him."

"Get a hobby, Peter. And leave me alone." I made myself sound unconcerned although my flesh was crawling. I was loath to admit it, even to myself, but Belcott had a knack of speaking to my deepest fears—that I was only included in the team as a makeweight, that whatever interest anyone senior showed in my career was motivated by something baser than the desire to encourage a promising young officer. And it didn't help that just this morning Derwent had used me for exactly the purpose Belcott had mentioned. I would be seriously deluded if I thought that of Godley, however.

"Is everything okay?" Rob, pausing beside us, his eyebrows raised.

"Never better, mate." Belcott slipped past me and I nodded at Rob to tell him that it was all right, nothing for him to worry about, nothing to see here, move along. He didn't look totally convinced but he walked away, holding the door open for DCI Redmond and following her out. Godley had made a good choice. Rob could be trusted to liaise with the local CID without ruffling anyone's feathers, which was more than could be said for some of the team.

Godley turned and saw me. "Maeve, good. We'll go down to the interview rooms and get things set up. When Josh is finished here, he can collect John Skinner for us."

"Are you sure that's a good idea?" I asked tentatively, but I was genuinely concerned.

Godley looked surprised, turning to look at me as he went through the door and headed for the stairs. "Why?"

"Yesterday, before you arrived at William Forgrave's flat, DI Derwent was pretty hostile toward Mr. Skinner." I shrank from telling Godley the specifics, but I was fairly sure he knew what I was implying.

"Don't worry about Josh. He's a total professional. He behaved a lot better than I did yesterday."

I shook my head. "That was different. You were provoked. He was just aggressive from the get-go."

"He's that sort of person. That's one reason why I keep him around." Godley grinned and I caught a glimpse of the rule-bending copper he had once been. "Besides, I think John Skinner might benefit from a bit of a chat that's not in the presence of his legal representatives, don't you?"

"I don't know what you mean," I said sedately and he laughed.

"Keep it that way. Josh could be a very bad influence on you. Stick to doing things by the book."

I followed him down the stairs, not sure whether to be pleased or not. I wasn't one of those officers who had joined the police because it was the biggest gang around; I genuinely wanted to do the right thing, the right way. And I had thought Godley was the same—that he was faithful to the fairness that was supposed to underpin our work. I was getting a not-wholly welcome insight into what really motivated him. I wasn't sure I liked it.

What I really didn't like, though, was being told that rule breaking wasn't for me. It was one thing for me to decide to stay on the straight and narrow, and another for Godley to tell me to mind my own business. There was a hint of condescension in it that I recognized from Derwent's more strident put-downs and I wondered exactly how much he had been able to influence Godley since he had joined the team. I had always thought Godley was the sort of person who knew his own mind and couldn't be swayed by anyone else's opinion, but he had been under intense pressure recently, and it looked to me as if Derwent had taken advantage of that.

All in all, I was in a thoughtful mood as we arranged the chairs in the interview room; two for Skinner and his legal representative and two for Derwent and Godley across the table. My place was by the door, which I didn't mind at all. I didn't want to catch Skinner's eye.

As soon as we had set up, Godley dispatched me to retrieve Skinner's solicitor from reception. As it happened, he was the only person waiting there, which was fortunate because he was not what I was expecting. He was much younger, for starters—mid-thirties, I estimated. He was balding but kept his hair short to make up for it, and his features were pleasantly hawkish. Two other things completely wrong-footed me: the hole pierced in one ear, and the fact that he had been whiling away the time by playing Angry Birds on his iPhone. It just seemed altogether too human.

"Mark Whittaker." He jumped up and held out his hand. I introduced myself, noticing the extremely expensive dark suit that fitted him to perfection, the crisp white shirt, the silk tie and gold cufflinks. Clearly, representing John Skinner was a rewarding business.

"How's John this morning?" Mark had an Essex twang and the cheeky chappy charm to go with it. Again, definitely not what I had been expecting.

"I don't know, I'm afraid. I haven't seen him since yesterday."

"We had a long day." He sounded pretty relaxed given that his client had been charged with murder, among other things. "I bet he slept well. I didn't. Too much to do."

"Have you represented him for long?"

"About ten years." He must have seen me looking surprised because he grinned. "He's a friend of the family."

"Nice friend."

"John's all right."

I had three murder victims who would disagree with that but there was no point in arguing.

"I don't mean to be nosy, but what happened to you? Car accident, was it?"

"I tripped."

He whistled soundlessly. "Looks nasty. You should have taken some time off work."

"And miss this? I don't think so."

I pushed open the door and ushered him in. Godley had obviously met him before and the two of them made polite conversation while we waited for Derwent. It was all pleasant enough but I sensed a slight reserve in Godley and recognized that Whittaker's easy manner might not be the whole story. Friend of the family or not, Skinner would want a lawyer who was as tough as he was himself.

A prisoner as important as Skinner should have been moved around the nick with an escort of officers, but Derwent was alone when he came in with Skinner. He had him cuffed, though, and was walking close behind him with one hand on the bar between his wrists. Only I could see what he was doing, holding it up a couple of inches higher than what would be comfortable for Skinner. It was an easy way to ensure compliance and intimidate the subject, and Skinner's shoulders were rigid with tension. I wondered what Derwent had said to him while he was unobserved—and what else he had done. He unlocked the cuffs and took them off, slipping them into his pocket as Skinner rubbed his wrists, then skirted the table to join Godley.

Without much enthusiasm, Skinner greeted his solicitor, then glared at Godley. "It's you this time, is it?"

"Sit down, Mr. Skinner."

"What are you doing to find my daughter?" Skinner's face was pale beneath his tan and from the bags under his eyes it seemed that he had passed an uncomfortable night. His nose was swollen and his jaw looked puffy on one side where the superintendent had punched him.

"It's in hand." Godley's face was like stone. He pointed at the chair. "Please. Sit."

He stayed where he was. "I'm her father. You need to tell me what's going on. Have you found her? Has anyone heard from her?"

Mark Whittaker stood too and put a hand on his arm. "John, take a seat. Let's get through the formalities first and then talk."

"Do you know something?" He stared at his solicitor, then back at Godley, and he looked as frantic as any worried parent I'd ever seen despite his hard-man reputation. "What have you found out?"

"Nothing at all." Godley sounded more compassionate this time. "I promise you, I will tell you as soon as we know more. You're under arrest for murder, Mr. Skinner. That takes precedence at the moment. But we're talking to Gayle and going over the case in detail. If there's something that's been missed, we will find it."

"They haven't been trying." Skinner swallowed. "You know they've been fucking it up."

"Sit down, Mr. Skinner," Godley said again, with much the same effect.

Derwent had had enough. He stood up and strode around the table, grabbing the back of Skinner's chair and shoving it against him so his knees buckled. "You know the rules, John. Cooperate."

I might have expected Mark Whittaker to be outraged, but he didn't look it. He muttered something in his client's ear, and Skinner capitulated, and sat down. Godley nodded to Derwent to start the tape, then ran through the usual caution.

"We're here to ask you about three murders that were committed in the last week in the Brixton area, and an incident yesterday involving a fourth man. You've also been arrested for GBH and false imprisonment in relation to him."

Skinner shrugged, unmoved. "You know I did it. I'm going to plead guilty. Can we speed this up?"

It wasn't truly surprising that Skinner intended to plead guilty when he had been caught red-handed, but I was still unsettled by how matter-of-fact he sounded. He had to know that even if he had a sympathetic judge impressed by moving mitigation about his daughter's disappearance, he was looking at a whole-life tariff. There weren't many criminals who took that lightly, even if they were no stranger to prison.

"Mr. Skinner, why are you in the UK? You live in Spain now, don't you?"

"You know the answer to this, Godley. My little girl's missing. I came back to find her."

"How did you intend to do that?"

"By finding out who took her."

"Where did you start looking?"

"Where you should have." He rubbed a hand over his face. "Gayle told me her mates said she'd gone to meet a stranger she'd been e-mailing, a boy. I'd have thought she'd have more sense."

"Why?"

"Because you know as well as I do that it was a pedo, don't you? Some pervert who wanted to attack my daughter." His voice broke a little on the last word. "He persuaded her to meet him somewhere she thought was safe, somewhere he felt in control. It's not rocket science to work out he was local. So I got a list of the local pervs and started asking questions."

"Where did you get the list?"

"No comment." He would cooperate, but only so far, I realized. He was only giving us what we could already prove.

"We know you intimidated a civilian worker at the police station in Brixton. Who told you to contact her?"

"No comment."

"How did you decide who to target from the list she gave you?"

"No comment."

"The victims were all those who lived closest to where your daughter was last seen, weren't they?"

"I suppose so."

"The three murder victims—Barry Palmer, Ivan Tremlett and Fintan Kinsella—were tortured before they were killed."

"That's right."

"Did you torture them?"

"Are you surprised?"

"Why did you torture them?"

"To find out what they knew. They weren't inclined to be helpful. I was just making sure they had a reason to remember anything that might be of use."

"Did it occur to you that they weren't able to tell you anything because they didn't know what happened to your daughter?" Derwent asked.

"Them's the breaks." Skinner was completely impassive. "They got what they deserved."

"Ivan Tremlett had his eyes gouged out. Barry Palmer was mutilated. Why was that?"

"Got to make the punishment fit the crime, don't you?"

Godley pounced. "How did you know the details of their crimes? Who shared that with you?"

"No effing comment."

"Mr. Skinner, you were arrested yesterday afternoon at nine Camford Mews, the address of one William Forgrave. Is that correct?"

"Yes." His voice was toneless.

"You were found there in the company of two of your associates, Brandon Lennox and Howard Lennox, in the act of torturing William Forgrave."

A shrug. "We were asking him a few questions."

"Were they with you when you spoke to Barry Palmer?"

"No comment."

"What about Ivan Tremlett?"

"No comment."

"Fintan Kinsella?"

"You know the answer to this one by now." A half-smile, wholly humor-less.

Godley changed tack. "Your daughter went missing on Saturday. When did you return to the UK?"

"Monday."

"And Mr. Palmer died on Tuesday morning. I'd have thought you'd have wanted to move a bit faster."

"You can't always rush into things." He shifted his weight as if trying to get comfortable and failing. "I wanted to talk to all of the scumbags on the list as soon as I got it, but I had to take it slow. Get them at the right time. Make the arrangements. Avoid getting caught, ideally, though that didn't work out."

"Very professional," Derwent commented.

"Fuck yourself."

Godley ignored him. "You murdered Ivan Tremlett the same day, in the afternoon."

"That's right."

"And Fintan Kinsella early Thursday morning."

"Mmph." He looked away.

"What's wrong, Mr. Skinner?"

"The priest. I didn't like what happened with him. I knew he wasn't in-volved as soon as I'd spoken to him, but I couldn't leave him to talk about us. I didn't stick around to see what happened. All I know is that he was taken care of."

"He was shot in the face," Derwent said dryly.

"Well, now he's in a better place." Skinner still seemed uncomfortable and I recalled that Cheyenne was at a Catholic school. The strange half-heartedness of Fintan Kinsella's murder started to make sense.

"How did you get them to let you in?"

He showed his canines again in what passed for a smile. "Haven't you worked that out?"

"You played dress-up." I hadn't meant to draw attention to myself, but I couldn't help it.

Skinner swiveled in his seat to look at me. "Not personally, but yeah.

You're dead right. And it worked. People trust uniforms, even in this day and age. You'd be amazed how many doors open to you if you've got a clipboard and a van." He turned back to Derwent. "Are you proud of yourself? You're responsible for that little bit of handiwork."

I realized that he was talking about my face and blushed deeply, even as Derwent shook his head. "It's all down to you, John. We wouldn't have been there if you hadn't been there. I'm not taking responsibility for any of it."

That was in character, at least. Abruptly, Skinner seemed to tire of trying to provoke Derwent.

"Are we finished here? I did the lot. I'm not going to tell you who helped. I didn't find anything out, but then, neither did you lot." He leaned across the table, his eyes locked on Godley's, and the pleading in his voice was completely sincere. "For Christ's sake, have some compassion. I've never liked you, but I rate you as a copper. If you'd been looking for Cheyenne from the start, she'd be back at home now. Stop bothering with me and look for her, before it's too late."

With a rush of sympathy, I understood that he was sacrificing himself to save his daughter. That explained his solicitor's detachment, since his instructions were clearly to place as few obstructions in Godley's path as possible. It also explained Skinner's willingness to plead guilty to whatever we wanted. He had enough pride not to involve any of his associates if he could avoid it, and he still hated Godley—of that I had no doubt. But he could hate him and need him at the same time.

Godley's face was somber. "We just don't have much to go on, John. I'm sorry. I will bring her home to Gayle if I can."

"Alive, though. You do think she's alive, don't you?"

Godley couldn't quite bring himself to be reassuring. He was too honest. "I'll believe she's alive until I know anything to the contrary. And whatever happens, I'll find the person who took her and bring them to justice."

Skinner's face twisted. "Justice. What do you know about justice? You'll put him in prison for a few years, or a mental hospital. Bang him up, give him three meals a day and all his entertainment for nothing. I've seen what you do to punish people and it means fuck all. That's not justice." He spat on the floor as if he wanted to clean his mouth of the very word.

Derwent pushed his chair back and Godley snapped, "No, Josh. Leave it."

"You find him, Charlie. Find him and tell me who he is. I'll take care of the rest."

"Stop there, John," Mark Whittaker warned. "Don't say too much."

Skinner ignored him. "Just like I've been doing for the past few days. Making things right. That's real justice. Street justice."

Godley was looking at him, curious. "Is that what you thought you were doing, John? Dispensing justice? What makes you think you know better than a judge and jury?"

"Years of experience." He lowered his voice. "Don't tell me you don't want some of that power, Charlie. Don't tell me you wouldn't rub out a few people if you could have it done by lifting a finger and pointing."

"Is that what you're going to do? Have him killed, this person who's taken Cheyenne?"

"Eventually." There was a world of meaning in that single word and I shivered.

"You're not going to be in a position to do anything of the kind." Derwent's voice was silky. "What do you think you're going to be able to achieve from prison?"

"More than you." Skinner slammed his hands down on the table with a suddenness that made me jump. "You find him for me, Charlie, and when you do, there'll be a proper reckoning. None of your law, your human rights bullshit. He's going to pay for what he's done to my girl. Even if you find her alive and well, I want him punished for taking her in the first place, and I want him punished my way. Nothing you can do will stop me."

At that moment, someone tapped on the door, inches from my head. I stood and opened it at a brusque nod from Godley, slipping out to find Keith Bryce waiting in the corridor, struggling to catch his breath. He always looked miserable, but there was something desperate about him at that moment.

"Is the boss free?"

"Not unless it's life or death."

"Better get him, then."

I edged back around the door and caught Godley's eye. I didn't need to tell him he was wanted; he was already standing up.

"Interview suspended at oh-nine-forty-three. Superintendent Godley leaving the room."

The door closed behind him and I sat down, feeling highly conspicuous as the three men looked at the uninformative wood of the door by my right shoulder, waiting for Godley's return. After a couple of minutes that seemed to last for years, he opened the door again and came in. His eyes went straight to Skinner, and his face told the story before he could say a word.

"John, I'm so sorry."

And at that, Skinner—the Met's most-wanted criminal, the scourge of society, the brutal, unfeeling thug who had personally ordered the violent murders of three men that week alone—began to weep.

Part Two

"Will you walk into my parlour?" said the Spider to the Fly,
"'Tis the prettiest little parlour that ever you did spy;
The way into my parlour is up a winding stair,
And I've many curious things to shew when you are there."
"Oh no, no," said the little Fly, "to ask me is in vain,
For who goes up your winding stair can ne'er come down again."

Mary Howitt

Chapter Thirteen

Friday

Maeve

I followed Godley through a gate that led into a bleak yard, hurrying to keep up, Derwent just behind me. The yard had been the car park and loading dock for the business that once occupied the warehouse. It was long gone, whatever it had been, and the painted markings on the ground had worn away, faded to ghosts. Weeds had taken hold where the concrete was cracked. They swayed in the light breeze that caught at the hem of my skirt and blew my hair across my mouth. I tucked a lock of it behind my ear and looked up at the warehouse building itself. It glowered back. The brickwork was stained and had split apart in several places, the mortar crumbling away like dust. Most of the windows were shattered, even those on the ground floor that were still protected by close-set iron bars. The loading bay's shutter was so heavily rusted I doubted there was any need for the chain and padlock looped through the catch; it would never move again. There were other doors, though, other ways in, for us and for the pigeons that cooed and rustled on the high window ledges, and doubtless for the rats and spiders and beetles too.

In the shadow that fell across the far corner of the yard, a small knot of dark figures stood huddled together like mourners. Godley headed toward them and as we approached, they turned one by one to watch us. I might have felt self-conscious if I hadn't known that everyone there was focused on the superintendent, not me or Derwent. He was still walking a pace or two behind me and I resisted the temptation to look around, to check out how he felt about the latest development. Neither he nor Godley had spoken in the car on the way over. It had felt like a long drive, though we had made good time.

There were four members of the team in the group in front of us, and they had collected together like oil coagulating in water. It was a tacit demonstration that they were with the others but not of them. The other five stood around exhibiting varying degrees of discomfort and hostility. Right in the middle, on her own, stood DCI Redmond, and my first thought was that in the two hours that had passed since I had seen her, she had aged years. Her face had fallen in on itself, the skin dragged down by disappointment and the slackening of tension that had in itself been almost unendurable.

"Well?" Godley's tone was not reassuring and I saw her wince before she gathered herself to respond.

"I wanted to take your team on a field trip so they could get a feel for the location where Cheyenne disappeared. That's what we agreed—cover the ground again and see if anything new comes up."

Godley nodded and she passed her tongue over her lips as if they were dry.

"We got here about forty-five minutes ago. I walked them around the site. We didn't go into all of the buildings because some of them are too dangerous."

"But they'd been searched before," Godley said, not quite making it a question.

"Of course. The SOCOs went through the entire location, room by room."

"When?"

"Last Sunday."

"Pictures?"

"Yes. We can compare them—see what's changed, if anything."

"Quite." The tiniest hint of impatience had crept into the superintendent's demeanor—something about his stance, the angle of his head. Marla Redmond had noticed it too because her chin went up.

"We fanned out to look around the main open space." She pointed. "That's it behind you. There's nothing in it but some old pallets and bits of furniture. I think it's used as a doss house occasionally by the local tramps, but like I said, it's a bit too drafty for comfort."

"Is that where the nightclub was?"

She turned the other way. "It was in this part of the premises. These were offices. That was the canteen, on the second floor, and that's where they set up the club. The ceiling is low enough to be able to fit lights, apparently, and there's a serving area they used as a bar."

There was tinfoil stuck to the windows she indicated. "Did they do that? Cover up the windows?"

She looked past Godley to where I was standing and nodded. "For privacy, and to block out the street lights, I think. It was just on this side, where the windows can be seen from the street. The other side of the room looks out on a blank wall."

"Did you go up there today?" the superintendent asked. *Back to what you don't want to talk about, Marla . . .*

"We were just about to." She swallowed. "There's a staircase that leads up from the warehouse floor to the office space in this part of the building. It's got a window about halfway up, but not to the outside. It was the only source of natural light for the break room used by the warehouse workers. It's practically the only unbroken window in the whole place, but it's filthy with cobwebs and dust—you can hardly see through it."

"But someone did."

"Right. Yes. One of your team looked through and saw a body."

"On the floor? On a chair?"

"She's on a sofa. Wrapped up in a rug." Marla's face crumpled for a second, but she regained command of herself so quickly that I almost thought I had imagined it. "I'll take you through to see her now."

"Not yet. I'll wait for Glen." He spoke shortly, making it clear the subject wasn't open for discussion. The chief inspector nodded as if she understood. Perhaps, like me, she could sense Godley's reluctance.

"Was the break room covered in the original search? Are you sure the body wasn't there all along?" Derwent demanded.

"The room was searched. She wasn't there. Not on Sunday, anyway."

The superintendent turned on the spot, eyeing the gappy chain-link fence and broken doors.

"Am I right in thinking this place was wide open? Anyone could have walked in at any hour of the day or night?"

She was instantly on the defensive. "We had done the forensic work and released the site. I don't have enough pull to request the manpower that would be needed to keep it secure around the clock, and the owner is a bank that repossessed it about six years ago. They don't care what happens to the premises. They're just waiting for the land to be rezoned for residential housing and then they'll sell up to a developer. In the meantime, the buildings can take care of themselves."

"Yes, but you do see the problem, don't you? Now we have no idea when the body was dumped here, or by whom." I shivered at the cold disapproval Godley wasn't attempting to hide, glad it wasn't aimed at me.

"I appreciate that, but—"

"Do you also appreciate that we have no idea where the girl was in the meantime? We already knew she had been here, and that her abductor had access to the buildings too. The body being found here tells us nothing. And we had nothing to go on already."

"Then we're no worse off than we were before."

I could have told her answering back was a bad idea. Godley didn't raise his voice, but he didn't have to. Pure rage was in every word, and at that moment, it was all focused on Marla Redmond.

"Except that we have a dead body and we are no closer to finding the person or persons responsible. Except that I have just had to tell a father that his only child is dead. Except that we are now looking at a murder and hoping to God it's a one-off."

"What else could I do? You know my hands were tied. You of all people should understand that this was completely outside my control."

He didn't answer her directly but the fact that he turned away made me feel he did understand, that his frustration was not totally with Marla Redmond but with the bosses who had let them both down.

"Can you give Glen a call? Find out when he's likely to get here?"

Derwent took out his phone and scrolled through the contacts. Godley stared into the middle distance and DCI Redmond whirled around, marching up a ramp that led into the building with her heels stabbing the crumbling concrete at every step. I felt sorry for her but I also knew that Godley was fundamentally fair. At some stage, he would calm down enough to acknowledge that she had done her best, even if her best had been catastrophically far from good enough.

I drifted over to the lads from the team. "Well, that was fun."

"You should have been here when Colin spotted the body," Harry Maitland said lugubriously. "The shit properly hit the fan. *She* started screaming about why none of *them* had noticed it, as if that mattered." He was pointing at the group from Brixton CID subtly with his thumb, not that any of them missed it. I nodded to Henry Cowell who waved at me. I would go and talk to him in a minute, I thought, wondering where Rob was. He had left with Marla Redmond; he should have been with the others. I edged around to Colin's side. He was not emotionally literate enough to be suspicious if I asked, whereas Harry Maitland would have twigged that something was up immediately.

"Is Rob around?"

"In there." Colin pointed toward the building where the body lay.

Getting a head start, I assumed. I thanked him and crossed the un-bridgeable gap between the Serious Crimes team and the local CID by exchanging pleasantries with Cowell, much to the irritation of our colleagues on both sides. He was as unconcerned as ever, inclined to shrug about the long odds of the body turning up where it had, and totally unmoved by the looks he was getting from my lot.

Dr. Hanshaw hadn't been far behind us, as it turned out, and he and his assistant Ali appeared before Cowell and I had exhausted the very small number of things we had to talk about. They walked across to Godley who had gone to meet them, and the three of them stood in the middle of the desolate yard, the wind lifting Hanshaw's sparse hair and fluttering the folds of his raincoat. The pathologist listened as Godley explained the little we knew, his shoulders hunched, his head bent like a hunting heron. I found it hard to prepare myself for what I was about to see, now that he had turned up. I had secretly welcomed the superintendent's reluctance to visit the scene where Cheyenne's remains lay.

Godley walked back to us. "We're ready. I want to limit the numbers of onlookers. If you've seen the body already or if you have no reason to be there, find something else to do."

Everyone who had been there before us seemed to have taken the opportunity to have a good look and there wasn't a rush to join Godley, Dr. Hanshaw and his assistant as they walked up the ramp toward the door Marla Redmond had used. I hesitated, not sure that I could justify adding myself to the party, but Derwent gave me a tiny shove as he passed.

"Stop standing around staring into space, Kerrigan. Are you going to come along or what?"

"I didn't want to assume—"

"Yeah, yeah." He pushed open the door and I hurried past him into a dank white-tiled stairwell that smelled of damp and pigeon shit and the sweet foul mustiness of dried piss.

I could hear footsteps echoing in the distance and turned in that direction, hurrying to catch up.

"This is nice, isn't it?" Derwent said conversationally, right behind me. "We get to go to all the fun places." He reached out and grabbed my arm, pulling me sideways with some violence. "Watch it."

I looked down stupidly, seeing broken glass on the ground where I had been about to step. "Thanks."

"All in a day's work."

I rubbed my arm where his fingers had gripped me. "Next time you save me from hurting myself, can you try not to be so sadistic?"

"The end justifies the means."

"I rarely find that's true."

Instead of replying, he favored me with his big bad wolf grin. I took more care to look where I was putting my feet as we trailed the echoing footsteps around two more corners until we came up behind the others. Godley opened one side of a pair of double doors and we filed through, finding ourselves in a long dark corridor with closed doors on either side. It was disturbingly reminiscent of a scene from a nightmare. Derwent reached out and flipped the wall switches, but the fluorescent lights stayed off.

"No power."

"They used generators for the club," I reminded him.

At the far end, a door was propped open and some dim daylight filtered through, throwing a pale gray square against the wall. It darkened momentarily and a figure I recognized as Marla Redmond's moved into the hall, looking down in our direction. She raised her hand.

"Go carefully," Godley cautioned. "I don't want anyone ending up with a broken ankle."

"I'll go first," Derwent volunteered.

Dr. Hanshaw opened his bag and took out a torch. "This should help."

We went in single file down the center of the corridor. As my eyes got used to the lack of light I could pick out bits of rubbish littering the tiles, and old notices stuck haphazardly to the walls, abandoned along with the building. There was something unsettling about it, the building's past life echoing through its current dingy reality.

"You found us," the inspector said unnecessarily as we reached her. She pointed. "This is the break room."

It was big and shadowy and infinitely unwelcoming. Dr. Hanshaw, focused on what lay inside, slipped past DCI Redmond without acknowledging her. I hung back, allowing the others to go in before me. I never got used to this moment, the first shock of seeing violent death in all its reality, and the day I didn't find it shocking was the day I would quit.

The pathologist had reclaimed his torch and was bending over the stained orange sofa that stood against the wall, inspecting what lay there before he did anything else. I stood beside Derwent and looked across to where Rob was standing. His face was grave. He was staring down at the girl's body like an avenging angel.

"You stayed with her," Godley said to him, his voice low so as not to distract Hanshaw or his assistant from their work.

"I didn't want to leave the scene unattended." Almost to himself, he added, "And I didn't want her to be alone."

I felt rather than heard Derwent react to that, stiffening to attention like a dog seeing a rabbit. "Nice of you, but I don't think she's likely to mind either way, mate. She's dead."

Godley turned to glower at him but Rob didn't need anyone else to stand up for him.

"You're right. She is. And I'm going with DCI Redmond to meet her mother in about half an hour to tell her the news. I'd like to be able to tell her that we treated her daughter with respect—that we looked after her as best we could, even though we were too late to save her life. I like to think that it might be some consolation for her, at some point in the future, to think about that."

"Very caring of you. That's the modern police force, isn't it?" Derwent corrected himself. "Police *service*. We can't use the word 'force' in case people think we might be aggressive."

"There was a reason I never let you inform relatives about their loved ones' deaths, Josh," Godley said heavily. "I see you haven't changed."

Derwent didn't look remotely abashed. "Not much."

I moved sideways to get a better view of what Hanshaw was doing. He was still playing the torch over the body, peering closely, inch by inch. The point of light was startlingly bright, picking out details like chipped varnish on a fingernail, a gleam of eyeball between tangled lashes, an earring glinting in a dirt-smudged lobe. The rest of her disappeared into the darkness until I blinked, made myself look away from the dancing light, and looked again.

Bare feet stuck out from the bottom of a wool blanket that was wrapped around the body. The blanket looked old, scratchy, the material worn and dappled with faded stains that were not recent enough to be relevant to what had happened to Cheyenne. It was tied around the middle with a stretchy bungee cord, the kind used to keep belongings attached to a bike rack. I stopped looking at the blanket to look at what made the shape beneath it instead. The feet. The feet were small, a little plump. The toes were stubby, the nails painted with something that sparkled in the wavering light. It was hard to see the soles of her feet but they looked darker than the shadow would have made them; I thought they were dirty and wondered if she had been made to walk through the corridors behind me, if she had stepped on grit and broken glass and cast feathers and rat droppings before she died, if she had been hunted through the dark rooms, the endless hallways, the bricks-and-mortar nightmare of the derelict warehouse. I wondered if she had ever left the building at all, despite Marla's confident assertion that it had been searched, every inch of it. Godley wondered the same thing, I guessed, glancing at his stern profile. That was why he had reacted so angrily in the yard. A job half-done; a girl very dead.

At the other end of the blanket, I could see her head and her hands poking out. Her hands were loosely wrapped around each other, the fingers curled in. I made myself look further, seeing honey-colored hair that straggled limply, rat-tails instead of curls. Her face, bloodless, grotesquely white against the harsh orange of the sofa. The features were recognizably Cheyenne's; she wasn't bruised or bloated by decay. There was no need to lie to her parents in saying she looked peaceful, because she did. Bundled in a blanket, disheveled, dirty and dead, but at peace.

Hanshaw gave the torch to Ali, who stood holding it up high to cast as much light as possible, angled so the beam went over the pathologist's shoulder.

"We can get lights in here," Godley said, and without turning around Hanshaw raised a hand in acknowledgment.

"No need at present. I can work like this. When the body's removed, you might want a better view of the scene, but I'm not going to do much here. A quick examination and we'll wrap her up."

He started to peel back the blanket, his gloved hands working slowly.

"Her forearms are tied with another bungee," he announced to the room over his shoulder. "Legs are not tied. She's naked. Some bruising to the ribs and neck. Finger marks on the inner thighs and knees." He bent closer, probing. "Probable sexual assault. I'll do a rape kit, obviously."

Derwent leaned sideways to see for himself, then turned away quickly. I watched him stumble out of the room, cannoning off the doorframe as if he hadn't seen it. Not so tough after all, maybe. Godley was as still as if he had been carved out of marble, and looked equally cold, equally remote.

Hanshaw was getting on with his job, shooting a quick set of pictures, putting bags around Cheyenne's hands and feet to preserve trace evidence, taking samples of her blood and other body fluids. He was swift without rushing, careful but confident, and I knew that if there was anything the body could tell us, he would find it.

Feeling that I had seen enough, I retreated to the back of the room. Aside from the sofa, it was almost empty. A coffee table was upside down in the corner, three legs pointing to the ceiling while the fourth was gone forever. Someone had wheeled in an office chair that sagged drunkenly to one side, the seat teetering on the brink of falling from its base. It reminded me of Ivan Tremlett and I felt revulsion knot my stomach. So much blood had been spilled for nothing. John Skinner had achieved as little as any of us. He would find that just as hard to endure as the loss of his child.

A voice in my ear said, "Are you okay?"

I jumped. "You scared me." I looked reproachfully at Rob, trusting my expression to show my annoyance when I couldn't raise my voice above a thread of a whisper.

"Sorry. I was trying to be quiet."

"And succeeding." The scene in front of us was like a painting: the light and dark, the supine figure of the girl with her shadowy attendants. A Rembrandt, I thought, half-recalling something similar with a dissected body as the centerpiece that had featured in my art history textbook in school. I hadn't liked to look at it, even then. I hadn't known it would be my livelihood one day.

"Creepy, isn't it?" Rob looked around the room much as I had done, eyeing the décor that was the last word in post-apocalyptic chic. "What happened to Derwent?"

"Got the collywobbles." I saw his face twist into a grin and couldn't stop myself from matching it despite the circumstances. It was just perfect that Derwent of all people had failed to keep it together. "He's in the corridor, I think."

"Must go and ask him how forceful he's feeling." He made as if to do so and I grabbed his arm.

"For God's sake, don't provoke him. You warned me about that."

"Yeah, but I didn't mean it should apply to me." The smile faded. "This is a turn-up, isn't it?"

"It's what we were expecting. She'd been gone too long."

"Mm. But I don't think she's been lying there all that time. It's cool enough in here but there'd be some deterioration, wouldn't there?"

"I couldn't say. Hanshaw will know."

"Ghoul," Rob said.

It was what I had often thought myself, but I felt it was a little unfair. "He's just doing his job."

"Speaking of yours, how was Skinner?"

"Before or after he heard Cheyenne had been found?"

"After?"

I shook my head. "Not good. Broken. He'd already coughed to the murders. Not that he had much choice."

"Did he say how he knew who to target? And what they'd done?"

"Nothing so helpful. He told us the bare minimum. Wouldn't implicate anyone else, no matter how the boss approached it."

"Well, he wouldn't, would he? You know the rules as well as I do. Never plead guilty to conspiracy because it dumps your co-conspirators in the shit, and never point the finger at anyone else to try to save yourself."

"It's a moral code of sorts."

"It's a coward's best hope of surviving prison unscathed."

"I don't think John Skinner is afraid of doing time. He seems to have it all worked out."

"No doubt." Rob looked distant for a second, and grim with it. For once I could guess why.

"Not looking forward to seeing Mrs. Skinner?"

His eyebrows lifted a millimeter, which for him counted as surprise. "Got it in one. I can't think it's going to be pleasant."

"You won't have to do the talking." We both looked at Marla Redmond who was chewing her lower lip mindlessly.

"Right." Hanshaw straightened up, his gloved hands hanging from his wrists as if they didn't quite belong to him. "That's all I'm prepared to do here."

"Can you tell us when she died?"

"You know better than that." Hanshaw never liked to hazard a guess about anything, particularly time of death. He would give an estimate once the autopsy was over, not before.

"Any idea why her arms were tied?"

"None. Looks to have been post-mortem. There's no bruising and the cord was tight."

Godley frowned. "Important for the display, do you think?"

"Maybe. The body looks as if it was carefully positioned. Showing the head is interesting. The killer wasn't trying to hide what he'd done. On the other hand, I can think of more accessible places to leave a body if you want it to be found and admired." Hanshaw shrugged. "Maybe he knew you'd be back."

"Or maybe he knew leaving her here would tell us nothing about where he took her."

"Plenty of trace evidence on the blanket and her skin," the pathologist said. "Lots to keep the forensics boys busy. You'll get something from her."

"Hope so." Godley turned. "Right. I'll get my SOCOs to do this room and a sweep of the whole warehouse so we can be sure we haven't missed anything." The words *this time* hung in the air, unspoken. "Kev Cox will manage the crime scene. I'll get him to liaise with your guys so they can compare notes."

DCI Redmond nodded. "I was going to go up to Hoddesden to talk to Gayle Skinner."

"I think that's a good idea."

She looked wary and I understood immediately that she was afraid to encroach on Godley's territory. This was very definitely his case now. "Did you want to do it?"

"Break the news? Not on your life." He smiled thinly. "I've done that once today. That was enough. Anyway, she knows you."

She nodded and made for the door, pausing beside Rob. "I'm going now. If you still want to come, you're welcome to join me."

"Definitely." He waited for her to leave, then looked down at me. "I have to go."

"I'll see you later, then." I said it quietly, so no one else would hear, and he responded in the same low tone.

"Probably not tonight."

I wondered why not but there was no way I was going to ask, and he said good-bye without further discussion.

"Where's Josh?" Godley was looking around as if Derwent could have concealed himself somewhere in the desolate room.

"He went outside. I'm not sure why."

"He's not as unfeeling as he pretends to be. He has known John Skinner for a long time."

"They're hardly friends," I pointed out.

"Sometimes that makes it worse. He's not used to feeling anything as benign as pity for him."

"Cheyenne doesn't look much like Skinner."

"She's the image of her mother." Godley winced. "I should probably have gone up to Hertfordshire with them."

"I'm sure DCI Redmond will do a good job."

"Are you?" There was an awkward silence before he relented. "She's not the worst. And I do think she's managed Gayle well enough."

"Faint praise."

"Sorry. I can't pretend to be impressed."

I wasn't going to defend her for the sake of it, but I couldn't resist asking, "What would you have done differently?"

"Honestly? Everything." He turned back and looked at the body. "But I don't know if it would have changed the outcome."

"Probably best not to wonder about that."

"Probably. But do you think that will stop me?"

Before I had to answer, a rattle from the hallway announced the arrival of the mortuary men wheeling a trolley with a folded body bag on it. I backed away a step, fetching up against the wall. I must have been looking green.

"You don't have to stay for this bit. In fact, you don't have to stay at all." Godley took out his phone and scrolled through the address book. "I've got somewhere more useful for you to be."

The person he was calling picked up before I got the chance to find out more.

"Marla, have you left yet? Good. Is there room in the car for another of my officers?"

I could hardly believe my luck.

Godley disconnected. "They're waiting for you in the yard."

"Is there anything in particular you want me to do while I'm there?" *Because I feel as if you're just getting rid of me . . .*

"Find out what Cheyenne was really like. I don't think her dad has the first idea—then again, fathers never do. But you were a teenage girl once. You should have some insight into her character."

I pulled a face. "I haven't been a teenager for a while, boss."

"Even so."

There was no point in arguing; he had made up his mind. I followed the twisting corridor back to the yard, hurrying as best I could in the half-light of the deserted building. I emerged blinking into daylight and saw a car with its engine running at the main gate, waiting for me. I lifted a finger—*give me one second*—and hared across to where Godley had parked. Derwent was leaning against the car, on his phone. He covered it with one hand.

"Where are you going?"

"Hertfordshire." I picked up my bag from the backseat and swung it onto my shoulder. "Are you all right?"

The look he gave me made me wish I hadn't bothered to ask. I didn't hang around waiting for a big farewell. It was safe to assume he was embarrassed about his quick exit from the break room. I wondered what had happened, but I didn't quite dare to ask. It was enough, frankly, to know that Derwent wasn't so tough after all. It made up for a lot, one way or another.

Chapter Fourteen

There were four of us making the pilgrimage to break the bad news to Gayle Skinner: me, Rob, DCI Redmond, and a short, seedy detective sergeant named Ray Small. Two from the old team, two from the new. Arguably, it wouldn't take four of us to tell her Cheyenne was dead, but Marla didn't volunteer to leave Ray Small behind. Besides, he was driving. I felt that my presence there was unnecessary and I didn't like it any more than I liked to think Godley had wanted me somewhere else, for reasons known only to himself, and Hertfordshire was the first place that sprang to mind. It looked almost as if I had asked to go, I was uncomfortably aware, and Rob didn't seem completely at ease as the car nosed through the big factory gates and into the afternoon traffic.

Fortunately, perhaps, I didn't have to make much in the way of conversation. Rob was in the front with DS Small, Marla Redmond having commandeered the backseat so she could sleep. I apologized slightly awkwardly for spoiling her plans, but she shook her head.

"I can sleep sitting up. It's just more comfortable back here. You can stretch out." She demonstrated, propping her feet up and leaning back against the headrest. Her eyelids closed almost instantly, and before we had reached the main road, she was fast asleep.

Either because he was wary of waking her or because he was that way inclined, Small was monosyllabic to the point of rudeness. Rob settled into silence almost immediately and I sat behind him, listening to the engine's soothing hum and staring out of the window at North London as it slid by.

The journey didn't take too long once we were free of the clogging traffic in the city center. Hoddesdon was well within commuter territory and easily accessible by fast road. It was a prosperous little town, and Cheyenne had lived in one of the nicer parts, on a wide leafy road with large detached houses set well back, mostly behind security gates.

Small broke his silence. "We're nearly there, boss."

Marla Redmond straightened up, going from dead to the world to wide-awake in an instant. Leaning over to see herself in the rear-view mirror, she finger-combed her hair into something like order, and then dug in her bag for lipstick. Armor, essentially. She hadn't needed it to face a team of hard-edged police officers, but for Gayle, it was an essential.

Small turned into the driveway that led to the Skinners' house and leaned out to poke the intercom as if he had done it many times before. While we waited for someone to answer the bell and let us in, I leaned over to peer at the building. It was of recent construction in pale yellow brick with a giant, pillared porch and big square windows. They had gone all the way to the edge of the plot at the sides, using every inch of space to loom over the more modest houses on either side. The front garden had been paved over, the better to display the family's collection of cars. A silver Range Rover was parked on one side of the front door alongside a black Audi TT, and the boot of a Porsche 911 poked out behind it. When the gate swung open, Small drove forward and stopped behind a top-of-the-range Mercedes, blocking it in.

"That's not one of Gayle's cars." DCI Redmond was also leaning forward so she could see. "I don't recognize it."

"It's probably the cleaner's." Small had made an actual joke, I realized with some surprise. He shrugged. "Around here, anything's possible."

"Right." The inspector was back in take-charge mode. "Obviously, I'll do the talking. If either of you two want to ask any questions, feel free, but I'd appreciate it if you'd wait until we've given Gayle a little time to get used to the news."

"We won't rush her," Rob promised. I wasn't going to make a fuss about him speaking for me, but I hoped he wasn't going to make a habit of it. I got enough of that from Derwent.

"Gayle's not the easiest person to deal with." Marla Redmond hesitated, then decided against trying to explain what she meant. "You'll see what I mean, I suppose."

The front door had opened and a thin middle-aged woman with iron-gray hair was peering out.

"We've been spotted."

Small looked in the same direction as me. "Oh, that's Lydia. She's the housekeeper. Don't ask me why Gayle needs staff. She's not exactly pushed for time."

"Status," DCI Redmond said briefly. "She wants what the neighbors have got. If she can't fit in, she can at least keep up with them. Mind you, Lydia's been around for years. I got the impression from talking to her that she pretty much did all the hard work with the girl. Gayle's not much of a one for discipline or domestic chores." She opened her door and got out, giving the housekeeper a brief wave. "Back again," she said unnecessarily.

"Any news?" The woman's voice cracked, as if she hadn't spoken for a while.

Instead of replying, DCI Redmond walked quickly across the neat brick pavers toward her. I let Small follow her before Rob and I took up the rear. The sergeant was wearing a tweed sports coat and black slacks, neither of which looked the better for the car journey, and he had a strange, scuttling walk that took him on an indirect route to the front door. I realized he was checking out the Merc as he slid past it.

Having reached the shelter of the porch, DCI Redmond spoke in a low voice so it wouldn't carry into the house. "Lydia, there is some news, but it's not good. Where's Gayle?"

"In the sunroom." The housekeeper made the sign of the cross, her lips moving silently as she did so. Her face was sheet-white.

"Does she have anyone with her? A friend?"

"She has someone. A visitor." Lydia looked vague. "I think he's Mr. Skinner's friend."

Marla Redmond was too well-trained to react in any obvious way, but I could feel curiosity vibrating in the air around her as she stepped into the hall, the two of us following behind her and Small. The hall was square and tiled in cream marble. The doors were pale oak like the staircase that wound up to the first floor with a wholly unnecessary flourish. There were no pictures on the cream-painted walls, but a bronze sculpture of a leaping deer had pride of place on the table in the middle. "We'll just go through and see them, then. Thank you, Lydia."

The housekeeper didn't move. "What happened to my darling girl? Is she dead?"

Marla didn't reply but her face must have revealed the truth, because the woman twisted away, a muffled cry forcing itself out of her body. I recognized the hopeless urge to run and hide from bad news.

"Lydia, I'm sorry." The inspector patted her shoulder. "I can't tell you the details now, but we found her body this morning."

"Where?"

"I need to talk to Gayle first. I'm so sorry," she said again.

"Of course. Of course." Lydia turned back. Her expression was that of a sleepwalker waking up on the edge of a long drop. "Down the hall and through the sitting room. It's on your left."

"We'll find it."

"I should really show you."

"There's no need."

Small cut in. "Why don't you go and make a few cups of tea, there's a love. Hot and lots of sugar. Drink a bit yourself—get yourself settled. Nothing like a cup of tea to help with a shock."

"Mrs. Skinner doesn't drink tea." Her voice was still hoarse, but it was lifeless, her eyes vacant. "She doesn't take anything with caffeine in it."

"Doesn't matter. She might change her mind, see, when she's heard. Better to have it ready just in case." He steered her toward the back of the hall and ushered her into what I presumed was the kitchen.

"Thanks, Ray."

"Pleasure." He jerked his head to indicate a door on the other side of the hall. "In here?"

"Absolutely."

The sitting room was a symphony in cream—sofas, carpets, curtains, the lot. A huge room, it was as blank as the screen of the huge television that hung on one wall. It reminded me of a hotel more than a private house. There was no trace of the people who lived there, no sign of a personality in the choice of furniture or fabrics. It was the essence of luxury, though, and I couldn't help checking the soles of my shoes to make sure I didn't mark the carpet, smiling as I noticed Rob doing the same. Small had no such qualms. He wore heavy lace-ups with rugged soles that left a distinct pattern tufted in the heavy pile as he trekked across to the double doors at the end of the room. They were glass and he took a wary look through, standing to one side so he couldn't be seen. He frowned, then nodded.

"This way, boss."

Marla Redmond inhaled deeply, checked her face in the gilt-framed mirror over the fireplace and went to join him.

I didn't even see Gayle Skinner herself when I first walked into the sun-room. The sunlight was dazzling—almost blinding. As my eyes got used to it, I could see I was standing in an octagonal room that was composed mainly of glass, including the roof. The windows were firmly shut; there wasn't a breath of air. The temperature had to be in the thirties and I felt my throat dry immediately. Eventually, by dint of squinting, I made out Mrs. Skinner sitting on a wicker sofa on one side of the room. She was wearing a white dress that was too fitted to come across as virginal, and a pair of sunglasses that hid most of her face. She didn't seem to be much older than me, though it was hard to tell under the makeup and glasses. It made sense that she had been young when she got married. Skinner was the sort to want a much younger wife. Easier to control, for one thing.

DCI Redmond went across to her, her hand outstretched.

"Gayle. Sorry to interrupt you."

"Oh God." It was a drawl. "You just keep coming back, don't you?"

"When there's any news." Marla managed to keep her voice even and her manner friendly in spite of Gayle's rudeness.

"This is the woman who's been investigating Cheyenne's disappearance." Gayle waved a languid hand in the direction of the narrow-faced man who was sitting near her. He was leaning back in his chair, completely relaxed. His hair was a shade of black that was too dark, too uniform to be the result of anything but dye. "DCI Redmond, this is Kenneth Goldsworthy. Kenny's a friend of John's."

"Why does that surprise me?" From her tone, Marla Redmond had evidently heard of him; we all had. Bedfordshire and Hertfordshire were Ken Goldsworthy's own personal fiefdom. He was the main importer of drugs to both counties, the main recipient of the proceeds from the brothels of Luton and Stevenage, the main launderer of dirty money through a range of legitimate businesses, and the main target for the policing efforts of at least two forces. He was a slippery individual who could afford excellent lawyers and had never spent as much as a night behind bars, something he was very proud of indeed.

And he was, by reputation, no friend of John Skinner's. Quite the opposite. They had spent the nineties engaged in a turf war that had been bloody, violent and ultimately resolved by Goldsworthy retreating from the areas of London he had infiltrated and selling up his businesses in Surrey, Sussex and Kent. Intelligence suggested they had agreed to keep to their own areas, with Skinner getting the lion's share. For the last decade they had operated independently of each other, pretending the other one wasn't there, but that didn't mean Goldsworthy was happy about seeing Skinner's empire grow and prosper. What he was doing looking comfortable and at home in Gayle Skinner's sunroom, white shirt open to the third button and fat Rolex gleaming in the sunshine, I couldn't begin to guess.

The four of us were still standing and it slowly became apparent that Gayle was not going to invite us to sit down. She shook out expensively layered hair that was the same color as her daughter's, dragging long white-tipped nails through it.

"Was there something you wanted?"

Marla looked from her to Goldsworthy and back. "I wanted to speak to you in private, actually."

"There's nothing you can say to me that I wouldn't want Kenny to hear." She gestured grandly as she said it, ice cubes clinking in her glass, and I suddenly twigged that she was absolutely hammered.

"It's about Cheyenne. It's not good news, Gayle." I would give Marla points for persistence if nothing else.

Behind the sunglasses, Gayle's face went still. "What do you mean?"

"I mean that we found her body this morning."

A tiny pause.

"Are you saying she's dead or something?"

Marla's voice was gentle. "That's exactly what I'm saying."

"Fuck off." She stood up, staggering a little, and pointed at us. "Fuck off, the lot of you. You're wrong."

"I'm so sorry. I know this is hard to take in. I'm sure you'll have questions for me, but just take your time."

"Don't patronize me," Gayle Skinner spat. "I don't want you here."

She set her drink down and stepped out from behind the coffee table, unsteady on heels that were skyscraper high, then shoved Marla with enough force to send her staggering back a couple of paces. Rob reached out and steadied her, a courtesy that she acknowledged with an irritable nod. She was not having a great day as far as keeping her dignity went.

Ken Goldsworthy had uncoiled himself from his chair slowly, like a heat-dazed lizard. "Now, Gayle. Come and sit down. You've had a shock."

"Filth. Get out of my house. Fucking pigs. If John was here, you wouldn't dare."

"I'm not here to make trouble, Gayle. I just needed to tell you about Cheyenne."

"Does John know?" Her chin was quivering and two tears slid out from behind the dark lenses. "Did you tell him too?"

"One of my colleagues told him."

"Oh my God. He'll be going mental." She put one hand to her head. "I can't think. What did you say? You found her this morning?"

"Yes. At the warehouse where the nightclub was held."

"You mean she was there all along?" Gayle pushed her glasses up onto her head, giving me a proper look at her for the first time. Her eyes were the same shape as her daughter's but the rest of her face was finer, built on a different scale. Her nose was suspiciously neat, the end delicately contoured, and I was fairly sure I was looking at the upgrade, while poor Cheyenne had inherited the original. "You mean you just missed her?"

"We don't think so." Marla launched into a long, wordy explanation of how they couldn't have failed to notice the body; how it looked like it had been left there recently but we wouldn't know for a while; how really there wasn't much else she could tell her except that she was desperately sorry not to have better news and that the investigation was being handled by a different team from this point on, and that Rob and I were representing the team.

I took my cue to introduce myself, then Rob, with a distinct feeling we were stepping into the firing line. Gayle shook my hand distractedly. "I was wondering who you were. I knew I hadn't seen you before." She looked past me to Marla. "Who's taking over? Why did they get rid of you?"

"It's a bigger case, now. It needs someone more senior to head it up." She sounded bitter. "The person taking over is Superintendent Charles Godley. He's in charge of the murder squad."

It didn't seem to mean anything to Gayle, but Ken Goldsworthy smothered a laugh, turning it into a totally unconvincing cough. "John must be delighted."

"He just wants to make sure his daughter's murderer is brought to justice." The inspector sounded prim.

"I'm sure that's the case, yeah."

A rattle of cups announced the arrival of Lydia. She put down the tray and then flung herself at Gayle with a howl, hanging around her neck.

"Our poor darling. What are we going to do without her?"

It was enough to shatter Gayle's fragile self-possession. For the first time she allowed herself to break down properly, sobbing and clinging to the housekeeper.

"I think that's my cue to leave," Ken Goldsworthy muttered to no one in particular.

Rob was two steps behind him as he slid into the sitting room, and I was another step after that. The sitting room was blissfully cool and dim. Goldsworthy stopped to take off his sunglasses and I shut the double doors behind me, more or less in DS Small's face. I looked through the glass with my best eff-off expression. It wasn't his case anymore and he knew it, but he wasn't pleased.

"Mr. Goldsworthy, before you go, can I trouble you for a word?" Rob said pleasantly.

"Don't think I have anything to say." He fished his car keys out of his pocket. Up close he was showing his age, with wrinkles fanning around his eyes and a looseness to the skin around his neck. "Give Charlie my best. How's he keeping?"

"I'll tell him you were asking after him. Does John Skinner know you're here?"

"Not unless he's got the place wired for sound. He's banged up, I hear." A smile. "Poor old John. Not got the luck, has he?"

"You could say that." Rob took a step closer. "It does interest me—you being here. You're not exactly mates, are you? Why would you be here with Mrs. Skinner?"

"To offer her my sympathy. I had heard her daughter was missing."

"You hear a lot, don't you?"

"I keep myself in the loop. Knowledge is power, as a great man once said." He sniffed. "Don't know who, if it comes to that. But he was right, whoever he was."

"You wouldn't happen to have heard anything about who took Cheyenne, would you?" It was a long shot, but I thought it was worth a try.

He shook his head. "Not a word. If I do hear anything, you'll be the first to know."

"Very helpful of you."

"I do my best."

"Only we do have to consider that it was one of John's enemies. You know, someone who has a reason to want to get back at him." Rob was frowning as he spoke, mock earnest. "Remind me, who won when the two of you had your little spat in the nineties? It was John who got the bulk of the territory, wasn't it? You got left with Beds and Herts. Not what you'd call a gold mine."

"You're looking in the wrong place if you're looking at me." His voice was flat. "I don't go after people's kids. Don't get me wrong: I don't love John

Skinner. I'm very happy he's in trouble. But I didn't have anything to do with the girl going missing."

"Why should I believe you? You're up to something." Rob moved forward again, deliberately crowding him. He was taller and broader than Goldsworthy, who had foolishly come out without backup. There was a time and a place for physical intimidation, and I was glad Rob was there to provide it. "Why are you here, Kenny?"

"From what I hear, John's not coming out anytime soon." He jangled his keys. "Leaves a vacancy, doesn't it?"

"And it would piss him off if you slept with his wife."

The smile widened. "I'll tell you something. It would piss him off a whole lot more if he had to get divorced so she could marry me."

"That's the plan?"

"Is it hard to believe? She's a very attractive woman."

And you're not exactly a prize. "She's stayed loyal to her husband for a long time, even though he's been abroad," I said. "What makes you think things will be different now?"

"Prison's a lot different from sunny Spain." He popped a tiny breath mint into his mouth. "Not half as much fun to go and visit, is it? And with poor Cheyenne gone, what do they have to keep them together?"

"No one knew she was dead until this morning."

"Nor did I," he said quickly. "I was just thinking when I heard that it would be hard for Gayle. Being on her own, I mean."

"Cold," I commented.

"Spare me the disapproval. John Skinner wouldn't behave any different if it was the other way round. You show weakness, you have to expect to come to grief."

"How is it weak to be in prison because you were trying to find your daughter's kidnapper?"

Goldsworthy shook his head. "He should have kept out of it. That's his trouble, you see. He can't delegate. Can't trust his men. You never get your hands dirty—that's the rule."

"And you're managing to keep to that, are you?" Rob asked.

He held up his hands and turned them so we could see the front and back, then headed for the door. "Spotless. You won't get anything on me, sonny. Many have tried. Better men than you." Over his shoulder, he threw, "Ask Charlie Godley about it when you get the chance. He'll tell you."

I would do that, I thought. There were lots of things I wanted to know about Godley's past life as the scourge of organized crime. Goldsworthy would be a good place to start.

Back in the sunroom, Marla had made it into a chair. Small was standing but with his backside propped up against a window ledge. He had shed the jacket, I noticed. Gayle and Lydia were still on the sofa, but sitting apart now, each clutching a mug. Gayle looked up at us through spiky wet lashes. She looked tiny, hunched over like a child in trouble.

"Oh, it's you." She peered up at Rob. "What did you say your name was again?"

"DC Rob Langton." He put his card on the table along with Godley's. "Superintendent Godley sends his regards. He'll be coming to see you tomorrow himself. He didn't want to bother you today."

"That's nice of him." I couldn't tell if she was being sarcastic or not. She gave a sniff, then blew her nose on a tissue the housekeeper supplied. "So what happens now?"

"We're reinvestigating the case from the start." The side of my face felt hot where Marla Redmond was burning holes in it by glaring at me. "In the light of what's happened, we need to review the evidence that's been collected so far by DCI Redmond's team. It changes our perspective on the case."

"So it's not that they did a crap job."

"Certainly not." *Probably not.*

"What do you want from me?" She sounded listless, as if she had no energy left. I wondered how much of the brittle drawl had been put on for Goldsworthy's benefit.

"Now? Nothing. Except your permission to have a look at Cheyenne's bedroom."

"Whatever you want." She took another sip from her mug and pulled a face. "This is disgusting."

"Keep drinking it," Small ordered. "It'll do you good."

"I know I'm being weird. I just don't seem to be able to take it in. It doesn't seem real. I keep expecting her to walk through that door."

"Shock," Rob said. "It'll take a while."

"Why did this have to happen?" She started to cry again, rubbing at her eyes with the balled-up tissue. "I just don't understand why this had to happen."

"I'll show you Cheyenne's room." The housekeeper stood up. "I want to do something to help."

The other two looked as if they wished they had thought of that as a way of getting out of the room. The sound of Gayle's sobs was disturbing, especially when there was so little you could offer as comfort. I felt I had to say something.

"I'm so sorry, Mrs. Skinner. I wish we had been able to find her for you."

"I know you do. But you didn't."

"No. We didn't. Is there anyone we can call for you? Someone you'd like to stay with you?"

"Lydia's here." She sniffed. "I'm used to being on my own. Even Cheyenne was never around. I never knew where she was, to be honest with you, and there's no need to look at me like that. I'm not proud of it, but I didn't want to fence her in. My parents were hell on me and it made me a rebel. I got married when I was eighteen, just to get away from them. Eighteen. I didn't have a clue."

I was quietly patting myself on the back for having guessed correctly. She looked younger than thirty-two without her sunglasses, though she had the unnaturally smooth skin of the high-maintenance Botox addict, like her husband.

"You mustn't blame yourself, Mrs. Skinner," Rob murmured.

"Who else is there?" Her eyes welled up again.

"The person who took her," I suggested. *Or possibly your husband for getting her involved in his dirty world.*

"You will find him, won't you?"

"It's a promise." Now that the urgency had passed, the entire might of the Metropolitan Police was at our disposal. I hoped she hadn't noticed the irony.

The housekeeper was waiting by the door and we followed her out, into the hall and up the spiraling oak staircase. Cream carpet stretched as far as the eye could see.

"I bet this is fun to keep clean," Rob said.

"Not my problem. The cleaner comes twice a week. I do everything else—cooking, ironing, looking after Cheyenne. And Gayle, if it comes to that." She threw open a door. "This is Cheyenne's room."

It was more of a suite. A little hallway led into a sitting room with a computer desk and television, a big sofa and two beanbag chairs. It was a typical teenage girl's room in that there were random posters on the walls for bands I'd never heard of, and pictures of young and pretty actors, borderline androgynous with their long eyelashes and pouting lips, safe and unthreatening. I looked for a couple of minutes at the collage of pictures she had framed: her friends posing, wearing bizarre outfits at fancy-dress parties, leaping off a diving board into a sparkling blue pool. In the background and not quite in focus, a man in a polo shirt and shorts looked on. I thought I recognized John Skinner, which made sense. The same two girls appeared with Cheyenne again and again.

"Who are these two?"

Lydia came into the room far enough to see where I was pointing. "Cheyenne's best friends. That's Katie Harper and that's Lily Flynn."

Katie was the dark-haired one, Lily, the wistful blonde. Katie had a brace on her teeth in most of the pictures, a mouth full of metal that didn't stop her from smiling broadly. They were both shorter and thinner than Cheyenne and I lingered over the photo that showed the three of them together, Cheyenne in the middle with her arms tight around the other girls' necks, pushing them down. She looked overexcited, her face pink, her eyes wild.

Cheyenne had collected little bits and pieces of rubbish—scraps of paper, stickers, a chocolate wrapper—and pinned them to her noticeboard. A collection of concert-ticket stubs and wristbands hung down the right-hand side; she had been to Glastonbury the previous year, and Latitude. Aged thirteen. I wondered if her mother had gone with her, or if she'd been unaccompanied there too.

The room was immaculate otherwise. Pale pink cushions stood on point along the sofa, and a big fluffy rug the same color was draped over the back. Gauzy curtains hung at the window and around the archway that led to her bedroom.

"Did she keep it like this?"

"Not her. She was a messy madam." Lydia was standing in the hallway, hanging back. I could understand her not wanting to enter the room, and I could understand that she wanted to keep an eye on us. I caught sight of myself in the mirror with Rob behind me looking very tall and out of place, his suit extra-dark as if it were drawing the light into it, my face severe and hard. We looked sinister, appropriately enough. We had come with the news of Cheyenne's death, and if she had lived, we wouldn't have been there.

"Was her computer here?" I pointed at the desk.

"She had a laptop. A white one. Your lot took it away."

Which meant we would be receiving it sometime later that day, along with the other evidence the other team had managed to collect.

"Bedroom through here?"

"And bathroom. And wardrobe."

I understood why she'd mentioned the wardrobe when I saw it. It occupied a space about the same size as my own bedroom, with floor-to-ceiling shelves and hanging rails that were loaded with clothes. I checked a few labels.

"High-street stuff."

"She didn't have expensive tastes, for all that Gayle would give her anything. She liked to shop with her friends and they shop at Topshop or Jane Norman or Oasis."

I was rattling through the racks. "Size twelve. Size ten. What was she?"

The housekeeper rolled her eyes. "Whatever she could fit into. She wore things tight. Spilling out of them, she was. Refused to try on a fourteen, which is what she was. I bought her underwear but I had to cut out the labels before she saw the size."

"Do you know what she was wearing at the club? It would help us to be able to describe her to the other people who were there."

"No." Lydia scanned the rail. "Something new, probably. I don't see that anything's missing. Apart from her jacket. It was dark green, a blazer sort of thing. Wool."

"Did you find any labels or receipts in her bin?"

"No." She didn't sound certain, and I waited. "There was something by her bed. A Topshop tag. I don't know what it was."

"Did you keep it? Throw it away?"

She frowned. "I think I threw it away."

Dead end. "Okay." A kilt and blazer swung from hangers at the end of the wardrobe. "School uniform?"

"Yes. I washed it. For when she came back."

The kilt was about twice as long as any of the other skirts. "Quite a contrast from her usual style."

"Oh, she hated it, but she looked lovely in it. Just lovely. Much nicer than in any of this tat." She glared at the rest of the clothes, disapproval all over her face.

Somewhat inevitably Cheyenne had slept in a four-poster bed, the canopy draped in gauzy hangings that matched the curtains. Soft toys filled the window seat and a pink elephant sat on the pillow, legs splayed, a melancholy look in its black button eyes. Row upon row of bottles of nail varnish, perfume, hair products and makeup of all kinds filled the top of the dressing table, jostling framed pictures of her parents out of sight behind the mirror. Rob nudged open a drawer to reveal a few inhalers rattling around inside it. He picked one up and checked the canister.

"Ventolin. She was asthmatic?"

"Not badly. She used to get wheezy when she was stressed or after she did exercise. I couldn't get her to take her inhaler with her when she went out but I put one in her schoolbag every day, just in case."

The drawer next to it contained a curling iron, straighteners and a hair dryer, all neatly put away with their cords wound around them.

"She always left them plugged in." Lydia went to stand beside him, looking down into the drawer. "I used to come up and check before I drove her to school. The number of times she'd left the straighteners on. Look."

She lifted the cloth that covered the table to show me a series of brown scorch marks on the painted surface.

"You looked after her," Rob said.

She snorted. "I stopped her from burning the house down."

"That too."

"I did my best." She looked away, and her voice was muffled when she spoke again. "Didn't always approve of her mother's ideas, but what could I do? She needed discipline but Gayle didn't know how to do that. She only knew how to love her. That was what she never had herself, you see. It was the other way round. Lots of rules and no love."

"You seem to know her very well." I had moved around so I could see her face.

"I've worked for her since Cheyenne was six months old. They're my family." She straightened a brush and comb, her fingers lingering on them for a second longer than was necessary. "I'll stay as long as she needs me."

"How do you think Gayle will manage?"

"She doesn't know what's hit her at the moment, what with John being arrested." She shook her head. "God knows. I think she'll fall apart. She loved her, like I said. Wanted to be her friend. That was the problem."

"Speaking of friends, do you have contact details for Katie and Lily?"

"Have you got a pen?"

Rob produced one and I had my notebook to hand. She wrote their mobile numbers down from memory, along with addresses for both of them.

"They both live over toward Hatfield. I used to pick her up from their houses all the time. She couldn't wait to be able to drive so she could come and go as she liked. Always wanted to be independent, you see." She gave a long, quivering sigh. "You just think to yourself, what could I have done different? What could I have said to her that would have stopped her from going to meet a stranger? Why didn't she have more sense?"

They were unanswerable questions. I looked around at the room, seeing a girl caught between childhood and the grown-up world that she longed to join. She had only seen the promise of freedom, not the dangers that went with it. Useless to tell the housekeeper that she had done her best, that there was no point in regretting things unsaid. She knew as well as I did that it was all too late.

I bullied DCI Redmond and DS Small into driving me over to Hatfield so I could meet the friends, accompanied by their mothers. To give them their due, they didn't complain much, even though it took them out of their way. It would be a couple of hours until the girls were home from school and I settled down in a café to wait, alone. Rob, looking unaccountably embarrassed, had made his apologies and returned to London with the other two officers. He had somewhere else to be, he had said. Which was fine, of course. I read through another witless magazine without taking in a word of it and drank three cups of tea, and just as I was about to leave I remembered: it was Friday. Of course Rob had somewhere to be. He had a hot date.

I tackled Katie Harper first. In person, she was blossoming from the braces-wearing giggler of the photographs to a self-possessed young lady with a winner of a smile. She was wearing a lot of smudgy eye makeup but with jeans and a hoodie so it didn't look as if she was trying too hard to be grown-up, unlike her best friend.

There wasn't much sign of the smile once I broke the news that Cheyenne's body had been found. I explained that because it was a new investigation I needed to ask the same questions all over again and Katie nodded, fully prepared to cooperate, but there was little she could add to what I knew already. Cheyenne had told her about Kyle and how she'd been contacted by him through Facebook.

"Aren't you supposed to be over sixteen to have a Facebook account?" her mother asked.

"Thirteen, actually. But Cheyenne changed her birth date to pretend she was nineteen. They don't check up." Katie's mother was not looking impressed, and her daughter rushed on. "It was just Cheyenne. She said people would think she was a baby if she used her real age."

"What people? People who didn't know her?" I asked.

She nodded. "She used to chat to people all over the world. She got a guy in Australia to help with a geography project once."

"So this wasn't the first time she'd met someone over the Internet."

"It was the first time she went to meet them in person. But no, she had loads of friends online." Katie turned to her mother. "You don't have to worry. I would never do something like that. I just use it for keeping in touch with people. You've got to be on there or you miss out. You know I don't have any friends on the Internet I don't know in real life."

"That was the rule," Mrs. Harper explained.

"Very sensible." I didn't say that a similar rule would have saved Cheyenne, but I can't have been the only one who thought it.

"Why did he get in touch with her?"

Katie shrugged. "He saw her pictures, I think. Liked the look of her. She kept her profile open so anyone could see it. She liked the attention."

"Did she get a lot of it?"

A blush. "Her pictures were quite. . . ."

"Grown-up?" I suggested.

"Mm."

"In what way?"

Katie wriggled. "Well . . . she was in her underwear. Or posing like this . . ." She pulled her hoodie off her shoulder and struck a glamor model pose.

"What?" Mrs. Harper was looking appalled. Her daughter bit her lip. Someone was going to have to do a lot of talking to be allowed to keep her Facebook profile.

"Did you see any messages from Kyle?"

"Just the one Cheyenne sent us. I showed it to the other police lady." She meant Marla Redmond.

And that was that. I didn't get anything new out of Katie. Lily, who was already aware Cheyenne was dead when we got there thanks to a text from her friend, was a little bit more helpful, though I had to wait while her mother persuaded her to come out of the bathroom.

"Lily has got a very vivid imagination," Mrs. Flynn whispered. "She's been having awful nightmares, thinking about what happened to her friend. I don't know if it's better or worse to know."

"Always better to know," I said.

"Do you think so?" She played with her necklace, looking nervy enough herself. "If she asks, don't give her too many details, will you?"

"We don't really have that many, to be honest with you. But I'll watch what I say."

It was a very wan teenager who trailed into the living room eventually. She was quiet, her answers brief but not intentionally unhelpful.

I was true to my word and took care with how I phrased questions, not wanting Mrs. Flynn to pull the plug on the interview before I was finished with my list.

"Do you know what Cheyenne wore to the club?"

A nod. *Praise be.*

"Can you describe it to me?"

"It was a white minidress. It went over one shoulder and had a fitted bodice. It was really light material, almost see-through, and the skirt was pleated. And she had gold strappy sandals and a pale pink mask. She had little flowers and sparkles for her hair."

"Wow. You have all the details."

"I like fashion," she said quietly. "Cheyenne tried it on for me before she went. She wanted to look amazing."

"Did she go on the train dressed like that?" Her mother sounded frankly incredulous.

"No, she was going to get changed in McDonald's. She had everything with her in a plastic bag."

"What was she going to do with the clothes she was wearing for the train?" I asked.

"She was going to hide them. She didn't care what happened to them, though. She didn't mind the idea of coming back the next day in her dress. Cheyenne liked the attention."

She had liked it a little bit too much, I thought. "Is there anything else you think I might need to know?" A shake of the head. "Do you have any questions?"

"What happened to her? How did she die?" Lily's eyes were wide, her voice so faint that I had to lean forward to hear her, but the questions were instant, urgent, as if they had been at the forefront of her mind.

"We're not exactly sure. We're finding out, though."

"Was she hurt? Before she died?"

I could see that Mrs. Flynn wanted me to say no. I settled for, "It's hard to say at the moment, Lily. But I saw her this morning and she looked as if she was asleep."

"Really?"

I nodded. "Does that help?"

She wriggled.

"Can I ask you something else?" A nod. "You and Cheyenne were very different, weren't you? How come you were friends?"

"She was fun," she whispered. "She made me laugh. And she never made me feel stupid. She stuck up for me when a girl in our year was being mean."

"What did she do?"

"She told her she'd get her dad to get someone to burn down their house. She meant it too. Their garden shed went up in flames the following night." A slight smile touched the corners of Lily's mouth. "I didn't have any trouble after that."

The trains from Hertfordshire into London were running behind schedule thanks to "a person under a train" at Liverpool Street Station. The person in question got scant sympathy from my fellow travelers; it was the height of rudeness to allow your suicide to interfere with other people's evenings out, after all. I trailed home, bone-tired, aware that while I was hacking through the public transport system, Rob was being vamped solid by the beautiful Rosalba Osbourne. It made me so cross that I almost took the front door off its hinges as I slammed it.

"Steady on, darling." Walter was halfway down the stairs.

"Sorry. Bad day." I fumbled my keys and had to sort through them again to find the right one for my door.

"I wanted a word with you, actually." Wheezing as he worked his way down to the bottom of the stairs.

"Oh?" I turned my back on my door. There was no way I was inviting him in.

"It's a little bit awkward." His eyes slid over my face and up to the cornicing. The smell of pot hung around him like a veil. I was probably getting a contact high just by standing within two feet of him. "I should have talked to you about it sooner."

I had a feeling I knew what was coming. "Go on."

"It's just that I didn't know your job when I took you on as a tenant."

"I wouldn't have expected it to be a problem."

"No, it isn't. I'm a law-abiding fellow."

"I'm sure you are," I lied.

"I don't want any trouble, that's all. My tenants are like my friends, usually."

He jerked his thumb at the door opposite. "Chris has been here for many years. Brody's the same."

I wouldn't be staying for many months, I hoped, but I wasn't going to say that. "There's no reason for there to be any trouble."

"No. But . . . people want to be able to relax, do you see what I mean? They don't want to have to toe the line in their own home."

"Mr. Green, I have no interest in causing anyone any difficulties. I have a duty to report any wrongdoing if I become aware of it, but I'm not the sort to notice things." Not when I know better than to be officious. "So if someone was, say, smoking cannabis in their own flat, behind a closed door, I wouldn't pick up on that."

"Really?"

"Not if it was for personal use."

"That's all it would be," he said quickly. "I'm sure that's all it would be."

"Dealing, on the other hand, I would have a problem with," I warned.

"Nothing like that. Nothing at all." He was sweating.

"Then everything's fine." I waited a second. "Is that all?"

"Your boyfriend."

"He won't cause any problems either."

Walter's face twisted. "That's not it. Not exactly." His tongue darted out and played at the corner of his mouth as he worked out what he wanted to say. I averted my eyes, repelled. "Look, I know it's none of my business, and I can't tell you not to have him here, but I think it would be best if you saw each other elsewhere. He must live somewhere. Go and stay with him if you want to be together."

"You're right, it is none of your business." I stared at him. "Why on earth would you say that? Is it because he frightened you the other night?"

He shook his head, flustered. "No. It's just better, that's all. Better not to have too many strangers around."

"He's not a stranger to me," I said tartly. "And I noticed Szuszanna has her boyfriend stay over more often than not."

"True, true." He started to shuffle away. "Forget it, then. I just wanted to say."

"Well, you have said."

He waved without turning. Completely perplexed, I watched him go back up the stairs. There was no way I was going to do as he asked. I had a perfect right to have visitors in my flat. There was nothing about it in the lease. And it wasn't as if we were noisy. Quite the opposite.

I collapsed on the sofa and watched mindless television for a while, trying and failing to wind down. My phone sat on the coffee table, completely silent. The hours slipped by without a call or a knock at the door. It was just me and the remote control and a phone that never rang.

When I finally gave in and went to bed, I stared into the dark, too cross to close my eyes. I told myself I was just annoyed about Walter, and what he'd said. That was certainly a part of what was keeping me awake. As I waited in vain for sleep, I came to one conclusion, which was that I would make a point of having Rob to stay over, just to prove I could, just to make it clear that I wasn't going to be told what to do.

If he ever wanted to again, obviously.

Chapter Fifteen

Saturday

After a night of tossing and turning, my hair was a sight to behold. Fortunately I woke early enough to justify the time spent on taming it into smooth waves with the straighteners I rarely had the chance to use. I sashayed into the office bright and early with my head held high. I was wearing a charcoal-gray trouser suit that fitted me extremely snugly, hugging my hips and curving at the waist and generally leaving as little to the imagination as work wear can. I usually put it back on the hanger as a result, but today I was feeling reckless. Under it I wore a black top that was very slightly sheer and very definitely low-cut, rather than the plain white shirt I would usually have chosen. The jacket buttoned to a point where the top was barely noticeable, or so I had assured myself when I had one last qualm before I left the flat. Then, of course, I had bumped into Brody in the hall and his appreciative wolf whistle nearly sent me back inside to change. I might have, had I not needed to get to work early. There was also the fact that I was basically more interested in the Cheyenne Skinner case than in what I chose to wear to work on it, even if I had felt the need to make more of an effort than normal. I was pretty sure my colleagues would feel the same way.

Sure, but wrong. The first person I met was Liv Bowen, who raised her eyebrows. "Looking good. Where are we off to today?"

"Interviews."

"That can't be for Belcott's benefit." She folded her arms and narrowed her eyes, assessing me. "Hmm. When you came in, you looked over there, didn't you? That's Rob's desk. He's not in yet."

"So I see." I dumped my bag on my seat. "If I tell you I'm impressed with the Grand Inquisitor act, will you drop it?"

"Maybe." She looked back at Rob's empty chair. "God, it'd be a shame if he missed seeing you. You've got your hair done and everything. I wonder where he is."

Wrapped around a red-haired solicitor, probably.

"I have no idea," I said evenly. "And I'm not going to find out."

"Oh, that's okay. I'll text him." Before I could stop her, she'd whipped out her mobile phone and sent a message.

"Thank you, Liv. Very helpful." I tweaked the neckline of my top so there was very definitely no cleavage on display and went to knock on Godley's door. He was sitting at his desk, looking as if he had been there for a couple of hours already.

"Maeve. Come in. I like the hair."

"Er, thanks." I was totally wrong-footed. "I was wondering where you wanted me to start today."

"Josh is spending the morning doing interviews. You should go along."

It was always Derwent, I thought with an internal sigh. I made myself look cheerful and alert. "Who are we seeing?"

"We've been appealing for people who were at the club to come forward and we've managed to trace almost a hundred—some who volunteered they were there, others who were pointed out to us by the more helpful club-goers. There are a few with criminal records. They need talking to. Josh has lined up an interview with one of them."

"What about William Forgrave?"

"What about him?"

"His MO when he was an active pedophile matches the way Cheyenne was targeted." I felt suddenly unsure of myself. "Didn't DI Derwent say?"

"He did. And I've put DS Mortimer in charge of finding out what For-grave has been up to—if anything—since his release from prison." The cutting edge as exemplified by Morty was not impressive. Something of what I was feeling must have shown on my face because the superintendent smiled. "Don't worry. Bryce is keeping a close eye on him."

"I'm sure they're doing a great job."

"Mm. Well, you concentrate on your bit and I'll let you know what happens with Forgrave." Godley paused. "You didn't like him, did you?"

"He unnerved me."

"Josh said the same."

"Did he? He didn't seem to be unnerved."

"He hides it well. And speaking of hiding things, the first thing on the list is to swing by the offices of the nightclub's organizers."

"The Brothers Grim. I can hardly wait."

"I want to get a copy of their mailing list. It's not in the material Marla Redmond sent over yesterday evening. I haven't been able to get hold of her this morning, but I suspect that means they didn't get it. I imagine the organizers want to keep it out of our hands, but I'm not inclined to give them a choice about it."

"Okay. I'll be persuasive."

"Even demanding, if need be." He raised one eyebrow.

"I might leave that up to DI Derwent."

"Very wise. He likes that sort of thing. When you get the list, e-mail it to Colin Vale. He's going to convince their ISPs into giving us bricks-and-mortar addresses. I'm tired of waiting for people to volunteer to help us out. I want to know who was there and what they saw, and if we have to track them down and sit on them until they cooperate, that's fine by me."

"Now you're talking. So where do the Brothers Grim work? Are they brothers in real life?"

"Drew and Lee Bancroft, aged twenty-seven and twenty-nine. They don't have an office as such. Lee has a flat in Hampstead and they work out of the spare bedroom. Josh has the address."

"I'll go and find him." I stood up.

"He's on his way in. He's not such an early riser as you."

"Oh, he gets up early enough," I said seriously. "It just takes him ages to do his makeup."

Godley laughed. "I won't tell him you said that."

"I don't think I would survive the day if you did."

I closed the door behind me carefully as the superintendent reached out for his phone, his mind already on the next job on his list. I turned to find Liv Bowen standing in front of me, holding her mobile up so she could read what was on the screen.

"'Hung-over. Just getting in shower. Pity me.'" She blinked twice, all innocence. "Sounds as if he had a good time, doesn't it?"

I couldn't stop myself. "You know he was meeting that lawyer last night, don't you? Is getting drunk on a first date a good sign or a bad one?"

"Bit of both, probably. You're not annoyed, are you? Given that you were never really together? According to you?"

The door opened behind her and Derwent swung into the squad room in a somewhat ill-advised, brown leather bomber jacket. For once I was truly pleased to see him. My face must have shown something of what I was feeling because Liv twisted to see where I was looking.

"Oh." There was doubt in her eyes when she turned back. "You must be getting on better with him."

"Well, we could hardly have been getting on worse." She clearly thought I had abandoned Rob in order to make a move on Derwent and, revolting though that thought was, I decided not to enlighten her. Instead, I gave the inspector a dazzling smile as he came toward us and Liv trotted away to allow us our privacy. Derwent looked singularly unimpressed but that wasn't really the point.

"Me and you again, Kerrigan. Saddle up."

"By which you mean get my stuff."

"By which I mean stop standing around posing and get a move on. You don't seem to think what we have to do is important but this is a murder investigation." He walked away toward the door, shaking his head as if he couldn't believe my attitude.

"I'm aware of that. Going to Hoddesdon was not my idea." I grabbed my bag and went after him, taking long strides to catch up. "Besides, what happened to you yesterday? Did you come over all faint in the break room?"

"I don't know what you're talking about." He slammed through the door.

"You ran out of there like you were going to lose your breakfast. You're not pregnant, are you?"

"Don't try to be funny, Kerrigan. Women aren't funny."

"That's a bit of a sweeping statement, isn't it? It's like me saying all men are shits."

Derwent rattled down the stairs. "Yeah, but you'd be right."

"Really?"

"All men are shits because all women have unrealistic standards. We all get called that at one time or another, no matter what we're like. I would always assume that someone you thought was a shit would turn out to be a good bloke."

"Charming."

He shrugged. "That's how it is. I'm just being honest."

"And unpleasant." I looked sideways at him as we marched across the car park. "Seriously, what is it with you? Do I bring out the worst in you or something?"

"You said it, not me."

"All right, that's it." I stopped. "I am not getting into that car until we resolve this. You seem to have a massive problem with me, apparently because I'm younger than you and female. You haven't stopped putting me down since we started working together and I'm not really sure why that is, but I am sure that if you'll let me, I'll prove I'm a good copper, first and foremost."

"You don't have to prove anything to me, darling. I told you. You just have to look pretty and stay out of the way. Full marks on the first part, by the way. I like the new hairdo."

"Look, I don't need protecting. I don't need patronizing. I can be just as useful to you as any other DC. And I am never going to react to your baiting by getting upset and storming off, so I suggest you just drop it."

Derwent was leaning his elbows on the roof of the car, listening with a wry expression. "All right."

"All right what?"

"All right, I'll drop it. As far as I'm concerned, from now on you're just one of the blokes."

"Does that mean I get to drive?"

He grinned. "Not in this lifetime."

Well, I couldn't expect miracles. I got into the passenger seat and hooked out the *A–Z* from the seat pocket behind me.

"Where are we off to?"

"No need for the map or sat nav. I can find my own way to Hampstead High Street from here."

"Ooh, swanky."

"The street is. Not so sure about the flat. It's above a mobile phone shop, apparently. On the third floor."

"Let me guess. After never living on the ground floor, Derwent's second rule of flat-renting is never live above retail premises."

"Got it in one." He pulled out of the car park. "You never know who's going to move in there. You could end up above a sex shop."

"Yeah, in your dreams. Think how convenient that would be."

"You've got me wrong, darling. I don't like kinks. Vanilla is good enough for me."

"Just as a matter of interest, is this the way you talk to other blokes?"

"Of course."

"Well, that explains a lot."

"Something tells me I'm not going to hear what your sexual preferences are."

"You're so right." I judged it was time to move the conversation on. "I'm dying to know, though, what are your other flat-renting rules?"

"Never move in with a new girlfriend. You just can't be sure what they're hiding."

"Rule four?"

"Never let a new girlfriend move in with you. They're harder to shift than rising damp."

"Rule five?"

"Don't move in with anyone you've been seeing for longer than six months."

"That doesn't leave you much of a window."

"If you haven't moved in by then, the only reason to do so is to demonstrate you're capable of making a commitment. Next thing you know, you're looking in jewelers' windows, calculating how much of your salary you can spare while she's pointing out the rings of her dreams. And all you wanted was to save money on the rent." He shook his head. "It's a slippery slope. Don't start on it in the first place."

"You're not married, are you?"

"Nope."

"Live with anyone?"

"Still looking for Miss Right."

"But you're such a catch," I murmured.

"I get plenty of pussy. I'm just picky, that's all."

"You know, I think I'd rather go back to how things were." I put my hands over my ears. "Stop thinking of me as one of the blokes. I don't want to hear another word about your love life. I've heard about as much as I can take."

"There's no going back, Kerrigan. And I'm in a chatty mood."

We couldn't arrive in Hampstead soon enough as far as I was concerned. Mercifully, traffic was light, and once we found the address Derwent was all business.

"Remember, they've been interviewed before. They'll have some idea what to expect. Don't be afraid to ask them questions out of left field. Shake them up a bit."

"Got it. What did the Brixton lot say about them?"

"Not much. They were pretty cooperative, apparently. Smooth talkers, though. 'Terrible to think something like that happened at our event, if there's any way we can help, blah, blah, blah.'"

He rang the buzzer and waited by the intercom. A disembodied voice said, "Yes?"

"DI Derwent." The door clicked and Derwent pushed it open. "Very welcoming, I don't think."

"They probably didn't want you announcing your business in the middle of the High Street," I whispered, following him up the stairs. "Not everyone likes to advertise that they've got the police around."

"It's probably on Twitter already."

The third floor seemed an awfully long way, and I was gasping like a freshly landed flounder by the time we reached it.

"You need to work on your cardio," Derwent said, knocking on the door. "That's terrible."

"I know." I was trying to get my breathing under some kind of control. It was warm in the stairwell and I was bitterly regretting not wearing a shirt, since I couldn't exactly undo my jacket. *Hi, I'm here to interview you about the murder of a teenager, and have you seen my norks?*

I forgot all about that as soon as the door opened. It was as if everything had snapped into focus. I was there to do a job, and do it well, and that job was finding out what the man in front of me knew about the night Cheyenne Skinner met her killer. He was barefoot, wearing board shorts and a Superdry T-shirt that was tight on his chest and around his extremely well-developed biceps. He had light-brown curly hair that was long enough to spiral in corkscrews, and a surfer's tan. It was all most unexpected considering we were in the middle of North London, and particularly considering I had been anticipating someone more like Chris Swain. The Brothers Grim were supposed to be Internet geeks—social-networking nerds, not athletes.

"Come in. Welcome." His voice was deep.

Derwent strode into the hall, making up in self-confidence what he lacked in height, but it had to annoy him that he needed to tilt his head back to look up at the guy. "I'm DI Derwent, and this is DC Kerrigan. Which Bancroft are you?"

"Lee." He stepped back so we could move into the living room of the flat, where another man was standing by the sofa, his hands jammed in his jeans pockets. "This is Drew."

They were strikingly similar, but as I came closer to Drew, I started to see the differences between them. He was a shade shorter and slighter than his brother, with a narrower jaw and a longer face. They had the same mouth and nose, but Drew's eyes were set closer together. He looked friendly, though, and exactly as fit as his brother even if he wasn't quite as massive; his arms were ropey with muscle. They had the same hair too.

Derwent was rotating, admiring the room. "Which one of you lives here?"

"Me." Lee was a man of few words, it seemed.

"Not bad. You've got a nice view down the street. And it's big, isn't it?" He looked around. "Two sofas and a dining table but it's not cramped."

"That's why I chose it." It was a brusque enough answer but not intended to be rude, I felt; he was just stating the facts.

"Not everyone wants to live above a shop but there are compensations." Drew's voice wasn't as gravelly as his brother's—a tenor rather than a bass— and he was more polished. I guessed that the "smooth talker" comment had referred to him and him alone.

"I must remember that." Derwent sat down on one of the sofas without being invited to.

Lee turned to me. "Please. Take a seat."

They waited until I had sat down beside Derwent before they sat too. It was a slightly old-fashioned courtesy, but I appreciated it nonetheless.

Derwent had adopted an offhand tone, as if he was bored with the inter- view already. "I know you've already spoken to our colleagues, but this is a new investigation. The missing girl's body has been found, so we are now treating it as murder."

"I'm sorry to hear that." Drew frowned. "That's really terrible. Poor girl."

"Where was the body?" Lee asked.

"I'll come to that." Derwent yawned. "Sorry. Late night."

He hadn't been sleepy in the car, and I happened to know for a fact that he had worked until the evening with Godley, so he hadn't been out drink- ing. The tiredness was a trick to make them think he wasn't really listening. He turned to me. "Do you want to start, Kerrigan?"

"Sure. Of course." I smiled at the brothers but my mind was running away from the questions I wanted to ask in favor of second-guessing my boss. I knew enough about Derwent's penchant for mind games to recog- nize that letting me take the lead was another way of reassuring the broth- ers. I was, after all, the junior officer. I was the younger one, the one who lacked experience, the one who was being allowed to try her luck on an interview that fundamentally didn't need to be done. It was clever of him to make them think that. I just needed to quiet the nagging doubt at the back of my mind that he felt the same way himself.

I cleared my throat. "I'd just like to ask a few questions about you to begin with. Can I take your date of birth?"

"The fourth of June, nineteen-eighty-four. Lee's is the ninth of November, nineteen-eighty-two," Drew added with a wide white smile.

"Do you both live here?"

"No. I live in Archway." Drew raised his eyebrows. "Not as plush but I like it."

"I'm going to need your address." I passed him my notebook and he wrote it down. His handwriting was untidy, the letters lazily formed, and it sloped in both directions. The graphologists would probably make something of that; all it suggested to me was that he didn't do a lot of writing by hand.

"Have either of you ever been in trouble with the police? Any convictions?"

"No. Nothing at all. We've been good."

"Not even a licensing offense? I hear you got done for not having one for the nightclub."

Drew looked at his brother for a split second, then laughed. "You know, we tried to cut a few corners with the admin. It didn't work out too well. We were more interested in making it a really great event than in filling in forms and making applications to the council. Our mistake."

"Have you run that sort of pop-up nightclub before?"

"No comment. I don't want to get us in trouble again."

"Assume that we're not interested in breaches of licensing law," Derwent drawled from beside me.

"Okay, then. Not exactly the same. But we did run a speakeasy in a basement off Brick Lane for a week. The punters dressed up as Prohibition-era lushes—suits and hats and seamed stockings, you know the thing—and we staged a raid every night for fun." Drew turned to his brother. "Hey, we could have saved money on hiring the actors if we'd known the police would have done it for free."

Lee mustered a half-smile. He was more watchful than his brother, more wary, and I had a feeling he hadn't been taken in by Derwent's laid-back approach. He was chewing on his thumbnail and when he took it out of his mouth to smile, I saw that the nail was damaged, twisted and warped as if it wouldn't grow properly.

"What made you decide to run a pop-up nightclub in a derelict warehouse?"

"It didn't cost us anything to rent," Drew said candidly. "And clubs are easy. Loud music, booze, low lighting, enough of a dance space that people can get their groove on. You make it feel exclusive by having passwords and complicated directions and all that shit."

"People buy into exclusivity," Lee explained. I tried to control my sense of wonder that he was able to manage a full sentence with a verb and everything.

"Nothing exclusive about a rat-infested pigeon graveyard that's halfway to falling down, if you ask me."

Lee looked at Derwent assessingly. "You're not our target demographic. Too old."

Drew cut in before Derwent could recover himself to respond. "We're too old too. Don't feel bad. We're aiming at the student crowd, pushing up into the recently employed—nineteen to twenty five, basically. They've got time on their hands and they want to find interesting ways to entertain themselves. The ones who are working have money; the students make us look good by dressing up and really going for it. Everyone's a winner."

"How did you find the warehouse?"

"The Internet. There are a few websites about derelict buildings—everyone's interested in something, am I right? It was featured on one as easily accessible, no security. We're always looking for interesting spaces—new challenges. An industrial space was perfect for this party. We liked the contrast between the dereliction and the glamorous people. That's where we got the theme. *The Beautiful and the Damned*. Everyone who came was supposed to be one or the other, but preferably both."

"F. Scott Fitzgerald," I said. "Have you read the book?"

"No." Drew laughed. "Does that shock you? We're not that thorough. Besides, there's no need to read it if you're just borrowing the title. I don't think our night was what he had in mind when he wrote it."

"How much do you charge?"

"Depends on the event. If it's a big one, fifteen or twenty quid will cover it. The smaller ones, like the speakeasy—they were more expensive. Up to fifty quid, but if you booked in a group of six, you got a reserved table and a bottle of champagne thrown in. Those events cost a lot to set up. But it's worth it, believe me. We don't get complaints."

"How do you spread the word about your events?"

"E-mail," Lee said.

"May we have a copy of your mailing list?"

"I'm sorry. It's commercially sensitive." Drew sounded genuinely sad not to be able to help and I had to remind myself that he was bullshitting us.

"Do you really think the Met police are planning to go into event management for teenagers?" Derwent snorted. "Do me a favor. Give us the fucking list, Drew, and stop pretending you can't."

Another glance passed between Drew and his brother before he sighed. "Right. We'll let you have it. But you must promise to keep it out of the public domain."

"Not sure I can do that." Derwent stretched. "Freedom of Information Act. It's a bugger, believe me. If anyone wants to see it—"

"—we'll find a reason to say no," I finished calmly. "Don't worry. We'll look after it."

Derwent handed over a piece of paper with Colin Vale's e-mail address on it. "Send it to that address. Now, if you don't mind."

There was a laptop open on the coffee table and Drew leaned forward to do what Derwent asked, his fingers flying over the keyboard as he typed.

"It's just a starting point, you know. The e-mail is the beginning. It's the stone in the pool. The ripples go a long way. Half the people on the list won't have considered going. But they probably passed it on to a few of their friends, and *they* passed it on to their mates, and we ended up turning people away on the door."

"Cheyenne got in. She was only fourteen. Not quite in your target demographic either."

"We weren't checking IDs." There was a tightness about Drew's mouth that I hadn't noticed before and I put it down to guilt: if they had done their job properly, Cheyenne would never have made it through the door. "I sort of remember a girl with long fair hair and a ton of makeup, but there were lots of girls there who looked like that. And it was a masked event, remember, so I couldn't see most of her face. I can't be sure if it was her."

"Who else worked the door?"

"Not Lee. He was managing the bar. We had a couple of temporary guys—freelance door staff. Bouncers to you and me."

"How did you recruit them?"

"They're friends. We got to know them at the gym. They're a bit rough and ready, but they sort out the troublemakers and no one argues with them. If they say the place is full and it's one out, one in, that's what happens."

"Rough and ready? Does that mean they might have criminal records?"

"We don't ask that kind of thing. They're just useful to us, that's all."

"I'm going to need their names and contact details. And anyone else who was working for you that night."

"Sure. We had a couple of DJs and three girls working the bar. And one of our mates helped with the lighting rig—setting it up and taking it down again."

"Was he there on the night?"

"No. He doesn't like loud music."

"What time did you get there to set up?"

"We were there from lunchtime. I drove the van over with the lighting and sound stuff and met Sam. Lee was getting the booze so he took the car. We unloaded in the yard, then hauled everything up two flights of stairs. Never again, am I right?" He grinned at Lee. "Ground-floor events only."

"Sam is the one who set up the lighting," I checked.

"Yeah. He's an electrician. But like I say, he was gone by seven." Drew pressed a button on his laptop and a printer in the corner whirred into life. "That's the staff list. Names and numbers. Matthew Dobbs and Carl Mc-Cullough were the door people."

"Any idea where we might find them?"

"Cotter's Gym." The brothers spoke in unison, then laughed at one another.

"It's in Kentish Town," Drew added. "They spend most of their time there. It's sort of a social club as well as a gym. If your idea of chitchat is talking about muscle-building supplements."

"And do you hang out there too?" I was looking at Lee.

Drew was the one who answered. "We work out there. But we don't stick around to chat. Too busy."

"Being the Brothers Grim keeps you on your toes, does it?" Derwent sounded frankly skeptical.

"It takes a lot more effort than you'd think," Drew said defensively. "We put on at least two events a month. Not always nightclubs or bars. We do exhibitions in unusual venues. During London Fashion Week we organized a shop in a vacant retail space so young designers and fashion students could sell a few pieces to the buyers that were in town. We had a model-scout working in the shop, taking Polaroids of likely looking girls. That drove a lot of business our way. Everyone wants to be a model these days. Easy money."

"I'd have said everything you do is easy money." Derwent slid an inch further down in the sofa, as if he could barely keep his eyes open. "What do your parents think? Don't they want you to get a real job?"

"Our parents aren't around anymore. It's just the two of us. And we're happy doing what we're doing."

"Are you finished?" Lee asked abruptly.

"For the time being." Derwent got to his feet slowly and winced, leaning from side to side to stretch out his back. "I'm getting stiff. Must be my age."

"I didn't mean to offend you by saying you were too old for the Brothers Grim events." Drew smiled. "We'll add you to the mailing list, if you like. You can come along. See if you fit in."

"Not sure I'd like to. We've been tracing people who were at the club—people who have convictions for violent offenses. What do you think about that?"

Drew shrugged. "I'm not comfortable with sitting in judgment on anyone, okay? I just provide the venue. I don't care about people's pasts."

Derwent shook his head, disgusted. "The two of you have no idea, do you? You created a perfect hunting environment. It was dark, it was badly supervised, it was in a building that was borderline dangerous and certainly full of places to hide. You did things on the cheap, and it shows. No booze license. No proper bouncers. Tickets sold on the door to people you didn't know, whose ID you didn't check. Cash only at the bar so we have no receipts to trace. If it wasn't for the fact that your punters are as dim-witted as the pair of you, we'd be struggling to find anyone who was there."

"You're making it sound seedy, but it isn't. You should come along to our next event." Drew was still working his charm offensive on Derwent, seemingly oblivious to the fact that he was never going to succeed. "I'll send you an invitation if you give me your e-mail."

"Don't bother. I think you were right the first time." He looked down. "What about you, Maeve?"

"Not my speed either, I think. No offense."

"None taken," Drew said lightly.

"What's your first name again?"

I looked at Lee, surprised, and Derwent replied for me. "Maeve."

"How do you spell it?"

"Mike alpha echo victor echo," Derwent said. "Not too bad, considering it's an Irish name."

"Thanks a lot." I glared at him, then smiled at the brothers. "And thank you. We do appreciate you taking the time to talk to us."

"Anything we can do to help. We're just really sorry that you didn't find her alive and well."

"Us too." I followed Derwent to the door, turning to shake hands with both of them before we left.

Derwent made it all the way down the stairs to the street before he started to take the piss. "Well, you pulled, so that's something. 'How do you spell your name?'" he mimicked.

"Maybe he was curious."

"Yeah, maybe, but why would that be?" He cocked his head to one side, waiting for an answer.

"I have no idea."

"Don't you?" He laughed all the way back to the car, where a yellow and black penalty charge notice wiped the smile off his face.

"It is a loading bay," I pointed out.

"I was on police business. I had the fucking card in the window." He flung both the card and the ticket into the backseat.

"Were you really not interested in interviewing them?" I couldn't help asking. "What was all the fake yawning?"

"Who says it was fake?" Derwent got into the car and slammed his door. I hurried to do the same on my side of the car since he was quite capable of driving off without me. "I hate hipsters. I hate all those bullshit jobs they do. You know that pair probably earn more than we do? And for doing what, exactly? Sending out e-mails and renting space so people can imagine they're cool. Do me a favor."

"You can't stop people from wasting their money."

"Shame, isn't it? And now we have to go and see these bouncers too." Derwent sighed. "Would it have killed them to make sure the people they hired were clean?"

"They don't strike me as too worried about that kind of thing."

"Me neither." He glanced across. "You might want to do up that top button on your jacket, love. I'm guessing you've never been to a real gym before. They won't know whether to throw you out or hang you on the wall if you walk in with your tits on show like that."

It killed me to do what he suggested, but looking down, I had to acknowledge that he had a point.

Cotter's Gym was a small, white-painted square building that lurked down an alleyway off Highgate Road. "No frills" didn't even begin to describe it: the place was bleakness itself, with basic equipment and rubberized flooring. A couple of large men were using the free weights, hefting dumbbells the size of bin lids. They were not Dobbs and McCullough, they conveyed by grunting. But if we wanted Dobbs and McCullough, we should go through to the back room.

The back room was the social hub of the place, by which I mean there was a kettle and a collection of chipped mugs, a few posters of naked women stuck on the walls as Derwent had predicted, and a couple of small round tables where you could sit and soak in the ambience. Five gym members were doing just that. Three of them were playing cards, while the fourth looked on. A heavyset black man looked up from his paper.

"The Old Bill, if I'm not mistaken. What can we do you for?"

"We're looking for Matthew Dobbs and Carl McCullough."

"In connection with what?"

"Murder," Derwent said baldly. It didn't have quite the sensational effect you might have expected. The card players didn't miss a beat, and the man who had spoken to us licked his finger and turned the page.

"Sounds exciting."

"Come on. I haven't got all day. Which one of you is Dobbs?"

The man who had been watching the card game raised a finger.

"McCullough?"

"That would be me." The black man folded his newspaper and laid it to one side with an air of resignation. "What murder? Who died?"

"A little girl who shouldn't have been playing with the big boys." Derwent spoke softly but that made it all the more menacing. Without knowing why, I shivered. It had something of the same effect on the two men, because Dobbs moved over to McCullough's table. The two of them were older than the Bancrofts, late thirties at least, and solid with muscle.

"Are we talking about the girl who went missing on Saturday? The one from the warehouse?" Dobbs asked.

"Cheyenne Skinner." Derwent pulled out a copy of the school photograph and showed them.

"She's dead?" McCullough shook his head. "Oh dear, dear, dear."

"Did you know she was missing?"

Dobbs said, "Drew mentioned it to me during the week. He asked us if we'd seen anything strange. We didn't, though."

"No more so than usual at one of those events." McCullough looked disapproving.

"Do you remember seeing Cheyenne at the warehouse?" I asked.

There was an infinitesimal pause before Dobbs replied. "Possibly."

"What do you mean?"

"They wore masks. But there was a girl like that. On her own."

Another pause and then McCullough shrugged. "We weren't going to let her in. Not alone. We wouldn't if she'd turned up to a proper club like that. We're professionals, you know. We just do the boys' events as a favor."

"So if you weren't going to let her in, who did?"

"One of the brothers. I can't recall which."

"He came and picked a few people out of the crowd. It's something they do to liven up the queue. She was at the front. I suppose about ten of them got in at the same time. Mainly girls."

"Drew said he couldn't remember letting her in."

"No reason why he should, if it was him. It was pretty quick. 'You and you and you and you.'" McCullough folded his arms. "We only remember because she was begging us to let her in. She said it was life or death."

"She did?" I looked at Derwent. His face was unreadable. "Did you see her later on?"

McCullough shook his head. "But there was another way out. Down the back stairs."

"You always need more than one way out for safety," Dobbs said sagely.

"Didn't you get people coming in that way if there was no one on the door?"

"They weren't too worried about that, they said. It was hard enough to find the main way in, let alone getting in through the back. That place was a rabbit warren. And Lee was keeping an eye on it anyway. It was near the bar."

"He didn't mention it."

"Maybe he didn't see her either. It was a busy night. Lots of people. And the room was dark."

"Have you been spoken to by any other police officers about this?"

"You're the first."

Score another one for Godley's team. We thanked them and headed back out to the car.

"Call the girls who worked the bar. Let's be thorough, for a change."

I got hold of all three of them, one after another, in varying stages of wakefulness and helpfulness. Yes, they had been there. No, they hadn't seen anything strange. Yes, they had been working with Lee all night. He had gone out to change over the beer barrels a few times. That had taken a couple of minutes, not more. Otherwise, he was there all along.

"Well, that gives him an alibi."

"Drew wouldn't have had a chance to slope off either. He was in plain view all night, according to the bouncers."

"They were decent enough," Derwent admitted. Any copper who had done a Saturday night town-center shift knew the worth of good door staff; they could make the difference between keeping a tricky situation under control and a full-blown riot. "I'd trust them, to be honest. You want a safe pair of hands doing that job, and they both knew their stuff."

"You should be glad we can cross a few people off the list. What do you think DCI Redmond was playing at? She didn't scratch the surface of this case," I said.

"I know you want me to say something about how you should never put a woman in charge of an investigation."

"I don't, actually."

"Well, that's what I think." He was frowning, abstracted. "Why do you think Lee didn't mention he was in charge of the way out?"

I shrugged. "Maybe because we didn't ask him."

"Mm. Let's look the Bancrofts up on the PNC when we get back. And the bouncers. Run everyone who was working there through the system and see if anything pops up. Someone isn't telling us what they know, and I'm buggered if I'm going to put up with it."

"Where next?"

"To the home of Tom Malton, proud possessor of a conviction for GBH. He actually owned up to being there. Makes me think he's trying to come across as open and honest because he's got something to hide."

"You really are a cynic, aren't you?"

"And usually proved right in the end."

"Where does he live?"

"Camberwell. Not too far to travel to the club."

"Not too convenient for us," I remarked.

"The world doesn't exist for your convenience, Kerrigan. You're starting to sound like the Bancrofts."

Something—the parking ticket, or the sheer drudgery of the morning's work—had put Derwent in a foul mood. I had enough sense to keep quiet and wait for him to vent it on the next interview, or the one after that. The explosion would come, I was fairly sure. I just didn't want it to be aimed at me.

I could have told you Tom Malton had enjoyed the privileges of a public-school education within a minute of meeting him; he had been indelibly marked by it. He had the sort of accent that turns "oh" to "eau" and since his favorite expression seemed to be "oh gosh," we heard it a lot in the course of introducing ourselves. He was wearing unfashionably baggy jeans and a rugby shirt and he had the pink-and-white complexion of a Gainsborough lady. Derwent lasted all the way to the sitting room of Malton's modern and very comfortable flat before he came out with it.

"How the hell did someone like you get a conviction for GBH?"

"Being stupid, really." Malton sat down on the edge of an armchair, his hands tapping his knees, his heels together. "I had a row with a guy at uni— I mean, we were both drunk."

"And?"

"I pushed him out of a window."

"What floor?"

"The third."

Derwent whistled. "And he didn't die?"

"Almost. He fractured his skull. He was in a coma for ten days." Malton was trying to sound matter-of-fact, but he was clearly upset about it. The pink in his face had deepened to a rich rose color. "They said he only survived because he was so drunk, he was relaxed as he fell."

"Shit."

"Yah. Absolutely."

"What happened after the coma?" I asked.

"He woke up. No idea what had happened. I couldn't even remember what the fight was about, but around ten people saw me do it, so I couldn't pretend it wasn't me. Even if I'd wanted to, which I didn't."

"Did he make a good recovery?"

"No. Not really. He dropped out. Still has memory trouble. Still walks with a limp." Malton looked as bleak as his boyish features allowed. "I keep in touch with him."

"How much time did you do?"

"Oh gosh. Three years." Malton smiled at the expressions on our faces. "Not much, is it?"

"It's more that you're here now," I said. "I wouldn't have thought you'd survive."

He laughed. "It wasn't too bad. I did my degree, but by correspondence. I got on okay with the other chaps. They didn't know what to make of me, really, and I just take everyone as I find them, so it was all right."

I still thought he was tougher than he looked. Derwent seemed to feel the same way.

"What do you know about the girl who disappeared at the nightclub in Brixton last week?"

"Nothing at all."

"Did you see her there?" Derwent showed the picture, but Malton shook his head.

"Definitely not. But I was distracted."

"Were you drunk?"

"I don't drink anymore."

"What then? Drugs?"

"Not them either." He swallowed. "My girlfriend dumped me. In the queue. It was her idea to go. It really wasn't my thing. I should have gone home—cut my losses. But I went in anyway to try to persuade her to take me back."

"Didn't work?"

"Not even a little." He smiled ruefully. "Not meant to be, I suppose."

"Do you have a computer here?"

"Just at work."

"What do you do for a living, Mr. Malton?"

"I work for my father's company." He sounded very slightly embarrassed. We knew what he was saying. Daddy had given him a new start when no one else would have hired him.

"Doing what?"

"Venture capital."

"Fancy name for gambling," Derwent observed.

"Pretty much," Malton agreed wryly.

"Ever e-mail people you don't know because you like the look of them on Facebook?"

"No." He looked appalled. "What a strange idea."

"Isn't it, though?" Derwent stood up and nodded to me. "I think we're done here."

In the car, he said, "If Little Lord Fauntleroy is guilty, he's the best actor I've ever seen."

"Agreed."

"We should still check up on him. Talk to his probation officer."

"Agreed. Hey, which do you think was worse, public school or prison?"

"School. Absolutely." It wasn't a bad impersonation and I laughed. For a fraction of a second, Derwent and I were almost getting along.

The squad room was busy; almost every desk was occupied and a low hum of conversation filled the air. Derwent ground to a halt behind Harry Maitland's chair.

"Where did you get those? Is that the nightclub?"

"Yeah." He flicked through the images he was viewing on-screen: masked faces caught by the flash against a background of bodies and dark walls. It was the slightly tawdry chaos of a dance floor late at night, where everyone is a little bit too drunk to be completely conscious of how they look. Awkward poses, unfortunate angles, smeared makeup and sweaty hair zipped by as Maitland clicked through at speed. "These are images we've collected from blogs and social-networking sites. PC Google helped. And the Brothers Grim website has a page where you can upload your pictures. That's where this lot came from."

Looking again, I saw that the images were watermarked with the skulls from their logo.

"What are you looking for?"

"The girl. We're trying to spot her in the background in any of these to give us some idea of when she disappeared. Could have been at the end of the night, for all we know. I've found her in a few already. Have a look at the ones on the printer."

Derwent headed off to check them out. I looked across the room and saw that Rob had made it into work. He was on the phone, one hand shielding his eyes. He looked pale and, without a twinge of pity, I recalled what Liv had said about him being hungover. I looked back at the screen and grabbed Maitland's shoulder.

"Stop! That's Lee." I pointed at a bare-chested man in a white mask, his halo of curls silhouetted against a light.

"What is he wearing?" Maitland leaned in closer. "Black shorts. Is that it? He looks like a stripogram."

"In fairness, if you had a body like that, you'd wear little shorts all the time."

"I've worked bloody hard to get this body, thanks." He patted his belly lovingly. "Many pints of Guinness and more than a few kebabs."

"Your self-discipline does you credit."

Derwent came back with a sheaf of printouts and peered at the screen. "Which one of them is that?"

"Lee."

"How can you tell?"

"They look different."

"Not a lot."

"No, not a lot."

"It figures that you can tell them apart." Derwent turned to Maitland. "Kerrigan was drooling all over one of them."

"No, I wasn't."

"Okay, he was drooling all over her."

"Sounds messy," Maitland commented, keeping his eyes on the screen, which was wise.

"We need to know where Lee and Drew were as well. Can you look for them too?"

Maitland groaned. "Don't tell me I've got to start again, Kerrigan."

"Yes, you do." Derwent weighed in on my side for a change. "Look for him, and look for a guy who's exactly like him."

"Same clothes? How will I tell them apart?"

"Drew was wearing an earpiece." I watched the next few images slide by. "That's Drew. He's wearing a black mask. That should make things easier."

"Okay. White mask, black shorts: Lee. Black mask and shorts: Drew. Got it. Are they suspects?"

Derwent leaned in. "Look at this picture, Harry. Everyone in it—everyone—is a suspect. And the next one. Everyone. And the one after that. Do you get the idea? We don't have a fucking clue who took Cheyenne, so in the absence of anything you might call a lead, let's just work out where they were and when they were there so we can rule them out or keep them on the board."

"Don't get your knob in a knot," Harry said calmly. "I'll do my best."

"That's my boy." Derwent slapped him on the back, then looked at me. "What about those PNC searches?"

"I'll do them now."

I sat down at my computer, unfolding the list the Bancrofts had given us while Derwent dragged up a chair and pushed it next to mine. He was a little bit closer than I would have liked, but I had nowhere to go; I was jammed up against the desk as it was.

"Start off with the bouncers, just to make sure," he ordered, and I was about to but I didn't get the chance.

"Josh. Just the person I wanted to see." Godley was standing in the doorway, his face oddly blank. "I've got Glen's postmortem report on Cheyenne."

"And?" Derwent said.

"And you're not going to believe this."

Chapter Sixteen

It was unlike Godley to make such a dramatic statement and it turned heads around the room. Derwent pushed back from my desk, rolling his chair over to where the superintendent was standing. Curious about what was in the report, I stood up and moved a few paces in the same direction, aware that I wasn't the only one. We gathered around Godley in a loose circle. If we weren't supposed to eavesdrop on what he had to say, we'd be told soon enough.

"What do you mean?" Derwent asked. "What's the big deal?"

"How she died."

Derwent clenched his hands. "What did he do to her?"

"Absolutely nothing."

"What?"

"She died of natural causes."

"That's impossible," Derwent said flatly.

"It's not impossible. She asphyxiated, according to Glen, but it was brought on by a severe asthma attack."

"She had asthma." Rob's voice came from close behind me and I resisted the urge to turn around. "From what the housekeeper said, it wasn't serious enough for her to remember to carry her inhaler."

"So she went out without it, got an unexpected attack, died, disappeared for a week and then wrapped herself up in a blanket before lying down stark naked on a sofa in an abandoned warehouse with her hands tied. Yeah, that makes sense."

"Dial down the sarcasm, Josh. No one is suggesting that the cause of death means there was no foul play. Obviously something bad happened to her. Just as obviously, she was missing for the six days between her disappearance and the discovery of her body, and no one has come forward to say they were looking after her. The only thing the cause of death suggests to me is that she wasn't supposed to die when she did."

"When did she die?" Everyone turned to look at me. "During the six days. At what point did she die?"

"Between twenty-four and thirty-six hours before she was discovered. Glen says he can't narrow it down any more than that. It was cold in the warehouse. Her body was well preserved."

"Was she sexually assaulted?" Derwent asked.

"Yes."

It wasn't a surprise, but I could feel everyone around me react to that one word—a tiny shift in the atmosphere in the room. The faces I could see were grave.

"Repeatedly?"

"So it would seem. Glen found bruising and abrasions at different stages of healing that had clearly been inflicted over several days."

"Given that she died of natural causes, is there any possibility that it was consensual? Rough sex that went wrong?" Maitland looked around as a ripple of disapproval ran through the circle. "Sorry, but it's worth asking. Just because she was underage and it was illegal, it doesn't mean she wasn't a keen participant."

"It is worth asking, but I don't think it's likely. She hadn't eaten anything in the days before her death. There was nothing in her stomach but some brownish liquid."

"Sounds as if he was withholding food to keep her weak and make her biddable," Derwent said. "What does Hanshaw think?"

"He thinks the asthma attack was brought on by stress. Fear, pain—that sort of thing would do it. Her symptoms could have worsened over time if she was panicking about not being able to breathe properly, so it needn't have happened in front of her kidnapper. It's possible that her kidnapper didn't know or care that she was ill and was surprised by her death."

"You go to all that trouble to kidnap a girl and then they go and die on you."

"Shut up, Peter." Godley looked irritated and Derwent turned around to glare at Belcott.

"I'm just trying to lighten the mood." He didn't seem to be particularly abashed.

"When you're in a hole, stop digging," Maitland advised.

"If I can interrupt, I'd like to bring your attention back to the report."

Godley's voice was cold. "The cause of death is not the only unusual thing. Glen swabbed Cheyenne's hands and nails. There was a large amount of another individual's saliva present on the swabs. When they were run through the DNA database, they got a match, but it was to a woman."

"So he's working with a partner," Belcott suggested. "A Hindley and Brady for the twenty-first century."

"Who's the woman?"

"That's where it gets interesting. Patricia Farinelli is twenty-nine. She was arrested for taking part in an illegal demonstration against animal testing in Cambridgeshire in two-thousand-three. Her DNA was recorded on the database, but in fact she was released without charge."

"An animal rights nut," Maitland said. "Doesn't mean she's not cruel to kids."

"She worked as the manager of a nursery until eighteen months ago, when she didn't turn up for work one day. She hasn't been seen since."

For a moment, there was silence. I broke it with, "She's a missing person?"

"It wasn't his first kidnap," Derwent said softly.

"So it seems. Patricia lived in Stoke Newington. She was very close to her parents, so when she didn't get in touch with them for a couple of days, they raised the alarm. There was an investigation, but it didn't get very far. The officer in the case, a DS Rai, is working today but he wasn't in the nick when I called. Without talking to him I can't be sure, but I don't get the impression it was a priority. Miss Farinelli wasn't viewed as high risk." He leaned over and handed me a sheet of paper. "Maeve, can you try and track the OIC down? Find out what happened?"

"Will do."

"Wait a second. She disappeared eighteen months ago, hasn't been heard from since, and her saliva is all over a dead teenager's hands. What the hell?" Derwent shook his head, frustrated. "Nothing about this case makes sense."

"Not at the moment." Godley gave a small, grim smile. "I did say you wouldn't believe it. And there's something else you might like to know. Rob?"

"We met Ken Goldsworthy at Mrs. Skinner's home yesterday."

"What the fuck was he doing there?" Derwent sounded genuinely shocked.

"Making a pass at Gayle. While John's away, Ken thinks she should play."

"Bloody hell."

"Who's Ken Goldsworthy?" Liv sounded plaintive.

"He's a John Skinner wannabe," Rob said.

Derwent sucked air through his teeth. "You wouldn't want him to hear you say that. He's not as successful as Skinner, but he's a very bad lad indeed."

"They don't get on," Godley explained, in the understatement of the century. "They had a dispute over territory a few years ago. It was . . . unpleasant."

Derwent laughed suddenly. "Do you remember Goldsworthy's granny?" He looked around. "Anyone not know the story?"

"Me," Liv said promptly, and there were other shaking heads.

"It's a good one. John and Ken had been knocking lumps out of each other for a while—nicking drugs, getting in first to do jobs the other one had been setting up, throwing their weight around. Things hadn't got serious yet, by which I mean no one had died. That came later. But one of John's boys got beaten up by a few of Ken's lot, and he ended up in a coma in intensive care. John was furious. He wanted to send Ken a message, to get him to back off. And he happened to know Ken's granny had just died a month before. So he dug her up."

"Oh my God." Liv put her hand to her mouth.

"He didn't stop there. He broke into Ken's house and tucked the corpse up in his bed. Remote control in one hand, unlit fag in the other, propped up watching a porno film with the electric blanket on high. He said he only regretted not being there to see Ken's face when he found his nan waiting for him."

There was a ripple of laughter around the room.

"What I say is, if you're going to have a feud, make sure it's with someone who's got a sense of humor."

"Unfortunately, Ken doesn't." Godley's face was somber. "Things went downhill from that point on. I don't imagine Ken would dream of forgiving him for that, even if they got over their territorial difficulties. So turning up at his house—"

"—is pretty much an act of war," Derwent finished.

"So that's where we are." Godley scanned the room. "Those of you who are working on tracing and interviewing potential witnesses from the warehouse, please carry on. Josh, can you concentrate on finding out what Ken's up to? I find it hard to believe he's involved in Cheyenne's death but I can't be sure yet, and I really don't want to miss something obvious. It's also worth warning the county forces and the Task Force if this row is going to kick off again. Now that John is looking at a serious sentence, you have to assume Ken thinks there's nothing between him and a take-over."

"I don't actually know what John would resent more—losing his missus or his empire."

"What about both?" Rob suggested.

The little group that had gathered around the superintendent began to dissolve. I went back to my desk to make a start on finding out more about Patricia, pleasantly aware that I would be free of Derwent for a while now that he had something more interesting to do.

"Rob, do you want to fill me in on what Ken said yesterday?" Derwent asked.

"No problem." The two of them headed for the small meeting room and Derwent closed the door firmly behind them. I wished them the joy of each other's company. As far as I could tell, Rob hadn't even looked at me.

Glad to have something to occupy me, I rang the police station in Stoke Newington and asked for DS Rai.

"He's just walked in the door." A tiny pause. I imagined DS Rai glowering at the woman I was speaking to. When she spoke again, she sounded as if she was trying not to laugh. "Can I get him to give you a call back?"

I agreed and left my name and number, adding that I was ringing about Patricia Farinelli's disappearance and that it was quite urgent. I would give him fifteen minutes, I thought, poking my computer into life. Fifteen minutes was long enough to take off your coat and get a coffee, or whatever it was Rai needed to kick-start his shift.

I filled in the time by looking up the Bancroft brothers on the PNC. Nothing came up on either of them. Purely as a formality, I rang the DVLA to check that the date of birth Drew had given me matched their names.

"No match to either one," said the pleasant Welsh voice on the other end of the line.

"Really?" I wondered if I should add driving without a license to the brothers' tally of offenses. "Drew might be short for Andrew."

"I've got an Andrew Bancroft but the DOB is wrong. Four, six, eighty-three." He read out the address and it was the one Drew had given me.

"Lying about his age. Tut tut." I wrote it down. "What about Lee Bancroft?" I gave the address of the Hampstead flat and his date of birth.

"I've got an Alexander Bancroft." I would have taken a million years to realize Lee was an abbreviation of Alexander. "The year is wrong, though. Eighty-one."

"Naughty boys, telling porkies about their ages." It fitted in with the cult of youth they were devoted to, and their disdain for authority. I shouldn't have been surprised. "Thanks for that."

As soon as I replaced the receiver, my phone rang.

"DS Rai, Stoke Newington. You were looking for me."

He sounded bored and a touch hostile. I poured as much honey into my voice as I could. "Thanks so much for calling me back. It's just in connection with Patricia Farinelli's disappearance." I explained why I was asking about her.

"I don't think I can help you much. I didn't spend that much time on the case, to be honest." The boredom had cranked up a notch, if anything. I tried to control my irritation.

"Why was that?"

"Because there was nothing to investigate. She was a grown woman, single, and she had nothing to keep her in London. Her parents threw a fit because she went away without telling them. They assumed she'd been kidnapped and murdered. I think she just did a runner. We looked at her flat. Her passport was gone, and a suitcase, and a whole lot of clothes. Nothing strange about deciding to start a new life somewhere else."

"It's a bit drastic, though, isn't it? Leaving work and never formally resigning? Never even saying good-bye even though you know your family will be worried about you?"

The shrug traveled down the line. "Depends on what you're leaving behind. Maybe she didn't care."

"Did you find anything to suggest where she might have been going? E-mails or Internet contacts?"

"She took her laptop."

"Holiday brochures?" I was getting desperate.

"Nothing like that. But it wasn't a big mystery. She emptied her current account over the next few days—took out the maximum each time until it was all gone. So she had enough cash to see her on her way, and enough sense not to leave us any clues about where she'd gone so she couldn't be traced. I know you're excited about it because her DNA was found on your victim, but it could be a false result for all you know. There's nothing to say it connects."

"Yes, it could be a false result. Or, which seems more likely, it could be that Patricia was kidnapped by the person who took Cheyenne. We've got two missing females, after all. That looks like a pattern."

"Might be." He sounded dubious.

"Now that her DNA has popped up again, do you want to revisit the case?"

There was a pause; I could practically hear his brain ticking over. "It sounds as if you've got it covered."

"I'm going to need to talk to the Farinellis."

"You'll have to do it over the phone. They live in Tuscany now."

"Are they actually Italian?"

"Born and bred. Patricia was born here, though. She's their only child," Rai said casually, not seeming to appreciate how much worse that made her disappearance. "I'll give you contact details for the parents. I'm sure they'd appreciate a call."

"I'm sure they would," I said thinly, dropping the sweetness as it was patently having zero effect. I wrote down a couple of telephone numbers for the Farinellis, mobile and landline, hoping that they had decent enough English to be able to understand what I would need to ask them. "Have you got any paperwork you could send over?"

"I'll have a look." *If I can be bothered.*

I put the phone down with a sigh and braced myself to call Patricia's parents. I wasn't sure what was worse—giving them hope that she might still be alive, or letting them know their worst fears for her might be true.

"What's the matter?"

I was leaning on the work surface in the dingy office kitchen, my head in my hands. I looked up to see Liv in the doorway.

"I was looking for something to kick and I ended up in here." I put my head back down, knowing that my eyes had been red and that she'd noticed.

"Find anything?"

"I made that dent in the fridge." Her shoes tapped on the tiles as she went to look.

"Wow. Toes hurt much?"

"Much."

"Can I ask why you needed to kick the fridge?"

"It was standing in for smug, supercilious wankers who think a woman's life isn't worth worrying about."

"Uh-oh." Liv picked up the kettle and filled it. "I'm going to need a cup of tea for this one."

"Can you make two?" I straightened up and tried to sort out my hair, which was not the better for having my fingers knotted in it. "Although I think I really need something a bit stronger than tea, and I wouldn't usually say that."

"I take it you're upset about Patricia Farinelli."

"I'm upset about the waste of skin in Stoke Newington who decided there was no need to investigate her disappearance in spite of the fact her parents were absolutely sure something bad had happened to her. But of course DS Rai knew better than the people who loved her. He looked into his crystal ball and decided she was perfectly safe and well, so he didn't need to do any work at all. He could just close the file and get on with forgetting she'd ever existed."

"So he wasn't able to help."

"No. Not me, and not the Farinellis." I handed Liv two teabags and watched her drop them into mugs. "When I rang up, I got Patricia's mum. She burst into tears as soon as I said who I was. She assumed I was ringing to say we'd found Patricia's body. And then, once I said we hadn't, she thought we'd found her. She went from despair to delight and straight back again in a couple of minutes."

"It's always tough on the families when there's a disappearance."

"Especially when they're left completely uninformed, assuming that someone is trying to find their beloved daughter when actually no one has bothered to lift a finger."

"What was his excuse for not taking their worries seriously?"

"The fact that they came across as 'clingy,' mainly, and the fact that she was an adult capable of making her own decisions. But there were a few other things that muddied the water." I told Liv what DS Rai had told me about the missing woman's belongings. She looked thoughtful.

"I'm not trying to defend Rai, but that sounds pretty reasonable to me. I mean, if there were things gone from her flat and her bank account was cleared out, it does sort of suggest she decided to leave and just went about it in a messy way. I'm not sure I could justify spending a lot of police time on trying to find a grown woman who doesn't seem to want to be found."

"First of all, she wasn't the sort of person to walk out on her job without saying anything. She ran the nursery and had a good relationship with the owners, so there was no work stress to run away from. She got on well with her colleagues. Very well, in fact—she was a bridesmaid for one of them, and godmother to another one's kids. She adored children, according to her dad. She used to talk about her job constantly—lots of cute stories about what the little ones had done and said."

"Okay, that doesn't sound too bad," Liv said cautiously.

"It certainly doesn't sound like the sort of job you'd walk away from without as much as a phone call. And Patricia was the only member of staff who had the keys to the nursery. If she'd been planning to leave and never return, you'd have thought she'd have left the keys behind, either in the building or in her flat."

"But she took them?"

"So it seems. They were never found. And that wasn't the only strange thing about her packing. Mrs. Farinelli told DS Rai she was worried because Patricia had left her contact lens case and formula behind. That didn't make any sense—she'd been wearing the lenses the last day she was seen, so she'd have needed to clean them unless she was just going to throw them away, and they weren't disposables. Patricia is incredibly shortsighted, according to her mother, and self-conscious about wearing glasses. She always wore her contacts if she could, and she carried a pair of glasses with her in case she had to take the lenses out for any reason. She had spare pairs at work and at home. It was like an obsession. Completely understandable, since her mother said her eyesight was so bad she literally couldn't get from here to the door without help."

"I've forgotten things when I was packing. Important things too."

"Mrs. Farinelli was adamant that she wouldn't have left them. They were always the first things she packed. She also left behind a jewelry box with a few pieces she'd inherited from her grandmother—a diamond ring and a couple of pairs of earrings. Even if she didn't want them, Mrs. Farinelli thought it was strange she hadn't sold them to raise money for her trip." I took a sip of tea. "Then there were her clothes. Patricia had put on a lot of weight and her wardrobe ranged from a size twelve to size twenty. The clothes she took were twelves and fourteens. She would have had nothing to wear for months if she'd been planning to lose weight to fit into them."

"I'll give you that one." Liv stirred her tea, staring at the liquid swirling around her mug. "What are you thinking? That she didn't pack for herself?"

"Pretty much. The whole thing sounds as if it was staged to me. Someone made it look as if there was nothing to investigate and because we're conditioned to see adults as independent and free and not in danger unless the circumstances are obviously sinister, they got away with it."

"Yeah, but who? And if we assume it was the same person who took

Cheyenne, why did he target an overweight nursery manager and a teenager? And how?"

"I don't know why, but I am willing to bet the how was something to do with the Internet. Patricia's laptop disappeared with her so it wasn't possible to recover any information about which websites she'd used. But she was single and not happy about it, from what her mother said. I think someone gained her confidence and persuaded her to trust him, just the same way Kyle convinced Cheyenne to come and meet him. I think the person we're looking for targets women—and girls—who are needy and lacking in confidence and want to be loved. Cheyenne was desperate to be a grown-up and seen as beautiful. Patricia was overweight and lonely. Easy targets for some fake charm."

"It's possible. There's no way to prove it, though." Liv began to say something else, then stopped herself.

"What is it? I promise I won't get cross."

"Well, you're upset about Patricia. You've been talking to her parents—they would say she was perfect. Parents are not good judges of their children. What if she ran away to be with the person who kidnapped Cheyenne? What if Belcott was right and it was like Hindley and Brady—they did team up to attack a child?"

"If that's the case, why would it have taken so long for them to act? She's been missing for eighteen months."

"We don't know they didn't." Liv let that cheerful thought sink in for a moment. "Plus, the fantasy might have been enough for them for a while. Just being together, talking about it, planning it—that could have been part of the fun."

"I take your point about not believing the parents. She was an angel from heaven according to her mother, and her dad said much the same thing. No one is that perfect."

"There's a good chance they don't really know what her life was like either," Liv said delicately. "I mean, most people don't tell their parents everything, even if the parents think they do."

"You're so right. My parents wouldn't be able to tell you much about my love life. At least I hope they wouldn't."

"Did she have any close friends we could talk to? What about the girls from the nursery?"

"Good idea. They were the last ones to see her as well. Worth a chat, I'd have said. I'll see if I can track them down."

"When you have, will you tell me what they say?"

I raised my eyebrows. "Curious?"

"This is twelve times more interesting than what I was doing."

"What was that?"

"Reading the file on a guy named Dave King to see if he had any reason to want to upset John Skinner. It's that thick." She held up her forefinger and thumb about two inches apart. "He's an associate of Ken Goldsworthy. I never thought violence could be so *boring*."

"Not to them," I said simply. "Everyone needs a hobby."

In the end, it was relatively simple to find Meg Spencer, Patricia's second-in-command at the Happy Hoppy Nursery; the mobile number that DS Rai grudgingly dictated to me still worked. I was glad I had started with her rather than Helen McCann, because Helen had moved to Australia, Meg informed me as soon as I mentioned her. Meg was not the sort of person to hold back. She was garrulous to the point where I had to ask her to slow down once or twice, as my pen slid across my notebook at top speed.

"She went about six months after Patricia disappeared. We never actually talked about why she was going, but to be honest with you I think it had a lot to do with Pat."

"Why do you say that?"

"Well, Jamie, Helen's husband, he wanted to move to Australia anyway, and with Patricia going, it was like a sign that she should do something to change her life too. You know, life's too short to stay in one place and wish you had the courage to do something different."

"That suggests Helen thought Patricia had come to harm."

"We all did." Meg laughed a little. "The only people who didn't take us seriously were the police."

"I'm sorry about that. I promise you, we're taking it seriously now."

"It's a bit late for that." She hesitated. "Actually, why are you ringing now? Is there any news?"

"We think Patricia may be involved in the disappearance of a teenage girl."

"Involved? What are you talking about?"

"I can't say anything more at present."

"Well, if I don't know what you're talking about, neither can I." She sounded uncompromising.

"I wish you would. It could be really helpful to us." I dug my pen into the desk, frustrated. "It could help Patricia."

"Obviously I want to help her, but I don't want to get her into trouble."

"That's not what this is about," I said quickly. "The main thing is to find her."

When she replied, her voice was softer. "I never thought that would happen. I thought she was gone for good. I really blamed myself for not asking her more questions about where she was going that night."

Bingo. "Did you think she was going out?"

"Oh yeah. Definitely. She was all dressed up. Put on her makeup before she left and everything. No way was she just going home, which was what she said. Helen and I just nodded at it, you know, because we weren't going to make her tell us what she was doing if she didn't want to."

"And what did you think she was doing?"

"We assumed it was another date."

"Another date? I thought she was single."

"She was." Meg sighed. "Patricia was so unlucky, you know. She never met the right kind of person. She was really shy, but she wanted to get married and have kids. She never even got close to it. She fell madly in love when she was in college but from what she said he was a total nutter—a hippie with long hair who was massively into some animal liberation movement—and he was more interested in little rabbits than a relationship. Pat followed him around hoping he'd notice her and then got arrested on a demo. Typical of her luck, basically. I mean Patricia was not radical in the least. She just did it because she thought it would impress him."

She didn't sound like a very strong character, which made me even more worried for her. Someone like her could be manipulated into doing dreadful things. I passionately wanted to find out that Patricia was an innocent victim, not a collaborator with Cheyenne's abductor.

Meg was bowling along merrily. "So, it took her years to get over him, literally. And they never even went out! She said she could never find anyone who measured up to him." A snort. "I mean, this guy was a total loser. I don't think he ever even got a proper job. Pat just saw the best in everyone regardless of what they were really like."

"Some people are like that."

"Yeah, well, it makes life hard for them. You need a bit of cynicism to get by, don't you?"

"It helps. Did you say she was dating, though?"

"Oh, yeah. Yeah, I did. At least, Helen and I thought she was. She'd done some Internet dating and speed dating and stuff about three years ago but it never went very well. She'd get all excited about meeting someone because his e-mails were nice. She'd imagine it was going to be true love as soon as someone showed any interest in her—she really wanted to meet Mr. Right. But she didn't. They'd never e-mail her again, or they'd be really rude about how she looked, and it completely demolished her confidence. She swore off it completely—said she'd meet someone the traditional way or not at all. But then, a couple of months before she disappeared, she was behaving differently—texting all the time, and dressing a bit better, and making more of an effort with her appearance. We were pretty sure she'd met someone and she didn't want to tell us about it because she'd met them online and she thought we wouldn't approve. Or because she was superstitious about telling us in case it all went wrong again and she felt like a fool."

"Or because he told her not to tell anyone about it." I was thinking about the single message we had to prove Kyle's existence, the insistence on secrecy.

"She'd have done whatever she was asked to do," Meg said dismally. "She didn't have any free will of her own. She just wanted to be loved. And she deserved it, you know? We were so happy to see her going off that night. She had a beautiful dress on, a peacock-feather print, and high heels, and she looked really pretty. They always say that, don't they, about girls who are a bit heavier—'oh, she has a lovely face.' But Pat definitely did."

"I haven't seen a picture of her yet, actually." If DS Rai ever got off his arse and found the file, maybe I would.

"I'll send you a couple now if you give me your e-mail."

I thanked her, surprised that she had offered.

"You're the first person who's acted as if Patricia was a person." Meg's voice had become hoarse and I guessed she was welling up. "If you can find her—if she's okay—tell her I miss her, right? Tell her I can't wait to see her."

"I will," I promised. I hung up and Liv was at my elbow instantly.

"Tell me everything she said."

I dragged my hands through my hair, having given up on trying to maintain the sleekness sometime during my phone conversation with Meg Spencer. "You know, the more I hear about her, the more worried I am for her. And the more furious I feel with Rai for not investigating it."

I opened my e-mail to find that Meg had been as good as her word and had sent a file with three attachments. "Do you want to see a picture of Patricia?"

"Of course." Liv leaned in to look as the attachments downloaded.

"The first two are pictures from Meg's daughter's christening, looking at the file names."

"I take it that's Meg."

I nodded, examining the slight young woman with a tense expression, clutching a baby version of herself who looked comically worried. "Not what I imagined from talking to her. She sounded . . . bigger."

"That happens to me all the time. I can't help picturing people when I talk to them on the phone and I'm never, ever right." She pointed. "That must be Patricia."

In the first picture she was standing at the back of the family group, half-obscured by Meg's husband. She was wearing black, and her sole concession to looking celebratory was the enormous red flower she wore as a corsage. Her posture was hunched, as if she was trying to take up less space, as if she wanted to disappear. She was plump, but nothing like as big as she evidently felt herself to be.

The second one was a candid shot from the same day, taken over someone's shoulder. It was a close-up. Patricia was looking into the camera with a doubtful expression in her eyes, as if she had just noticed she was its target. Her skin was peachy perfect and her eyes were a beautiful chocolate-brown. She was pretty, as Meg had said, but the overall impression I got was of someone who was desperately unhappy, ill at ease with themselves and the exposure of a social occasion.

The third image was also unposed, Patricia caught straightening up from behind a desk. Her mouth was open and I presumed she had been talking when the picture was snapped. This time, there was no makeup and her eyes were hidden behind thick glasses with red and black rims. Her hair was scraped back in a ponytail that cruelly emphasized the roundness of her face, the soft flesh under her chin. In the message that accompanied the images, Meg explained that Patricia hadn't liked to be photographed, and that these were the only three she could find.

"Poor Patricia. I don't know if it's the benefit of hindsight, but she looks like a victim-in-waiting to me."

"Maybe that's what her kidnapper thought too," Liv said soberly. "If he was looking around online, she has 'add to basket' written all over her. It's upsetting."

"It's not just that. I can't shake the feeling that if someone had listened to Patricia's parents' concerns sooner, and had gone to the trouble to find out who took her, Cheyenne might still be alive."

I stared into the missing woman's doe-like eyes in the second picture, wondering who she had trusted and what they had done with her. She didn't look evil to me; she didn't even look as if she had the potential to become evil.

"Come on." Liv nudged me. "You said you needed a drink. I'd say now would be ideal. Sort your head out and start again tomorrow."

I looked around the squad room, suddenly aware that it had emptied around us while I'd been on the phone. Even Godley had left. It was later than I'd thought—almost six—and the energy of the morning had petered out when the post-mortem results came back. There no longer seemed to be an urgent need to follow up on John Skinner's complicated professional life and I could understand why Liv was pushing to get involved with Patricia's case.

"I should probably stay," I said reluctantly. "I do have a few things to chase up."

Liv tilted her head to one side as if she was considering taking offense, then smiled. "Okay. No worries. I just thought you might want a break."

"Well, I do," I admitted. I had a headache and the jacket of my stupid suit was riding up. I tugged it down, annoyed.

"If you change your mind, let me know." She walked back to her desk and I watched her shut down her computer. I was sorely tempted. There was nothing on my desk that couldn't wait until the next day, and I really needed to read DS Rai's file on Patricia before going any further. The flat in Stoke Newington had been cleared out and rented again a few months after she disappeared; the only way I could see what she had left behind was to look at the pictures DS Rai had assured me were in the file. And she had been gone so long that the trail was stone cold. Persuading witnesses to recall where they had been eighteen months before would not be easy. Whenever I tackled it, I would struggle.

"I've talked myself into it."

She looked up from doing up her jacket. "Seriously? Excellent. Where do you want to go?"

"I hardly ever go to the pub, but the traditional drinking place for the squad is the Silver Hook. It's a bit dingy, but it is nearby. And it should be pretty quiet."

"Fine. Let's try there."

It was the obvious choice, but it was also a mistake, as I realized the minute we walked in. The first person I saw was Peter Belcott, who proved to be propping up the bar with Chris Pettifer, Harry Maitland and Art Mortimer. We were not the only ones to decide the day needed to be rounded off with a pint, but we were a few drinks behind the others. And since the others were not the most congenial members of the squad, I smiled at them and moved confidently to the other end of the pub, followed by Liv. There was a booth tucked into the corner, out of their line of sight, and I dumped my coat in it.

"What are you drinking?"

She wrinkled her nose. "Is it too much of a cliché to have white wine?"

"Nope, and that sounds good to me too. Something dry?"

"Sauvignon blanc if they've got it."

"They should," I said slightly dubiously. "I'll get a bottle." It had the added advantage that we wouldn't need to go up to the bar as often. I braced myself and went to order.

Obviously prompted by one of the others, Belcott swung around. "Kerrigan. Aren't you and the lovely Liv going to join us?"

"We're just in for a quiet drink."

"Us too." He was swaying slightly and his eyes were already unfocused. Some beer slopped over the edge of his glass and ran down his fingers. "Oops."

"I think we'll stay where we are."

"You know, Kerrigan, I'm beginning to think you don't like me very much."

It didn't take a great intuitive leap to spot that, not that I would have expected Belcott to be anything but oblivious. I looked at him without answering, waiting until he got tired of staring at me and turned back to the group. He made some remark that was answered with a loud shout of laughter and I felt annoyance prickle at the back of my neck. It wasn't worth a confrontation. But one day, I would properly lose my temper with him, and he would deserve it.

I went back to Liv with the wine in a bucket of ice and two glasses.

"Problem?

"Why do you ask?"

"You've gone pink. And I saw the lads talking to you."

"Belcott was talking to me." I rolled my eyes.

"I think he fancies you," she singsonged.

"I think he hates me and all I represent." I poured. "If you stick around long enough, he might come to hate you too."

"Oh, he can't stand me already, but I'm used to that." She said it as she raised her glass to drink and I couldn't see her face clearly enough to know if she meant it.

"I can't imagine that you're generally unpopular."

"Only with homophobes. They don't seem to realize in advance. When they find out I'm gay, they act as if I was trying to trick them or something." She sipped again, slightly edgy in her movements, and I realized she was nervous about my reaction, which was funny. She was hardly the only lesbian in the police, even if she was more feminine than some I'd encountered. I wasn't exactly shocked by her revelation, more mildly surprised that I hadn't picked up on it, but then I had been cross-eyed with worry that she was going to make a move on Rob.

"Well, you don't fit into the usual stereotype, do you? That's just misleading. The least you could do is wear comfortable shoes."

She laughed and the tension suddenly evaporated. "I really don't try to hide it. I think most of the people on the squad know by now."

"I didn't know. I thought you were interested in Rob," I admitted sheepishly.

"Not even a little bit. I have a girlfriend."

"Do you? Is she in the job?"

Liv nodded. "Back at my old stamping ground in Special Branch."

"Did you get together while you were working in the same team?"

"No. After I left. She had me round for dinner to say good-bye and one thing led to another." Another sip. "Okay—I seduced her."

I leaned in and lowered my voice. "You realize that predatory lesbians are probably one of Belcott's favorite fantasies."

She snorted. "It wasn't like that. She'd just come out of a long relationship so she wasn't looking for another girlfriend. And neither was I, really. But these things happen."

"What's her name?"

"Joanne. She answers to Jo at work, but I like to call her Joanne." She looked blissfully happy as she said her girlfriend's name and I grinned.

"You're properly in love, aren't you?"

"Aren't you?" The dreaminess disappeared. "What's going on with you and Rob?"

I would have put my head down on the table if it hadn't been slightly sticky to the touch. "I fucked it up."

"Come on. It can't be that bad."

"It is. I don't come out of it well."

She filled up my glass. "Have a drink, and tell Auntie Liv all about it."

I did as she said. And then I had another drink, and another, while Liv tried to persuade me that Rob wasn't playing games, that he was a really good person and that he hadn't fallen madly in love with Rosalba Osbourne and forgotten all about me, especially since he'd canceled his date and had gone out drinking with some friends instead.

"He was pretty clear about it. You have to prove that you're willing to give a proper relationship a go."

"How exactly am I supposed to do that when he won't talk to me?"

She looked puzzled. "I don't know him well, but that doesn't sound like Rob."

"I didn't talk to him either," I admitted.

"You're going to have to make the first move. You're going to have to do something that shows him you want to be with him."

"He might not feel the same way."

"That's the point. You've got to take the risk. Make the effort. He's worth it."

The second bottle disappeared more quickly than the first. I reeled up to the bar to get some water and discovered that Maitland and Belcott were the only ones left. Belcott leered.

"Having a nice time?"

"Yes, thanks."

"I didn't know you were into that sort of thing." He put his fingers either side of his mouth and flicked his tongue. I shuddered and looked away.

"What are the chances, Harry?" Belcott said loudly, slurring slightly. "Two women on our squad. One of them's a dyke and the other one's Kerrigan. That's worse than having no women at all."

"Come off it, Peter." Maitland said what I had been thinking. "Don't be an asshole all your life."

"I'm just saying." He sounded injured.

"Well, don't." Maitland turned back to me. "Ignore him. You ladies have a nice time. Here." He dug in Belcott's pocket and came up with twenty pounds. "Drinks are on him."

I risked a look at Belcott who was looking down, apparently wondering what had just happened.

"I can't take it."

"I insist." He held it out to the barman. "Same again."

So we shared a third bottle, which turned out to be my second mistake of the evening. My third was not having anything to eat apart from a packet of dry-roasted peanuts. My fourth was not leaning over far enough when I was being sick in the alleyway outside so I splattered my shoes and the cuffs of my trousers.

When I made it home, much later on, I abandoned my suit on the floor, too out of it to investigate whether dry cleaning might save it. My stomach ached from the acid in the wine and from the physical effort of throwing up. My head was throbbing and I drank two glasses of water, holding on to the kitchen sink to try to stop the room from spinning around me.

"In what sense is this supposed to be fun?" I said aloud, to the no one in my flat. Then I went to lie down and wait for my bed to stop impersonating a roller coaster so I could get some sleep.

Chapter Seventeen

Sunday

The morning after the night before is never a lot of fun, especially if you don't drink much as a rule. I woke up at ten past five with a Saharan mouth and a tongue that seemed to be twice its usual size. Pawing blindly at the bedside table, I discovered I had forgotten to put a glass of water there before I went to bed. I lay back on the pillow, trying to gather the energy to swing my legs over the side of the bed and stand up. Getting up was sadly a necessity. Even if I hadn't needed a drink, my headache was too bad to ignore.

With the power of prayer, I made it to vertical and staggered into the kitchen, holding on to the wall for support. There was aspirin in the kitchen somewhere, I knew. I had seen it in a drawer. Moaning quietly, I rifled through the handfuls of cutlery, instruction manuals and loose bits of hardware that I had dumped in the drawers and forgotten about. The box was in the last one I tried. I took two tablets, washing them down with a pint of water that tasted metallic.

I stood wondering what to do while I waited to feel better. There was no way I was going to be able to go back to sleep while I felt as rank as I did. I curled up under a blanket on the sofa instead and watched the branches waving in the park while I concentrated on breathing slowly and regularly in an effort to combat the nausea. After the first hour, I had recovered enough to risk a bath. After the bath, I managed a cup of tea. After the tea, I checked the messages on my answering machine and experienced a dip in morale as my mother's voice filled my head.

"Maeve, would you ever call home? I've been trying to contact you. It's important. And your mobile phone doesn't seem to be working."

That was a regular complaint. She just didn't like leaving messages on it because I never responded to them. The answering service on my mobile was generic, anonymous. I could pretend she had called a wrong number, or that it had failed to record her message. With my landline, she knew she had reached my personal voice mail. If you listened carefully to the message I had recorded for it, you could hear the lack of enthusiasm in my voice. I had known who would be using it most frequently, and why . . .

The next message was the same, except her tone of voice was shriller. By the third call, she had obviously given up on speaking to me in person.

"It's a good thing it wasn't a medical emergency of some kind as you don't seem to be contactable." There was always time for a telling-off, I reflected, no matter how important the call was. "I was ringing because I wanted you to know your brother has decided he's not going to go ahead with the separation. He says he forgives her."

"Her" being Abby, I presumed.

"I don't know how he can think it's going to last when she's cheated on him once, but he says it's not worth upsetting the kids for the sake of punishing her."

A smile spread over my face. *Good old Dec. True love can conquer all.*

"I can't decide if he's stupid or too romantic for his own good or both. Probably both. Anyway, I thought you'd like to know." She sounded slightly shifty all of a sudden. "And I hadn't told anyone. In the family. So I think we should just forget all about it and not mention it to your aunts. I'm not sure they would understand."

As usual, I was both amused and irritated by my mother, but that was drowned out this time by my relief that Dec and Abby were giving it another try. Dec had far more reason than I did to run away, but he was holding firm. He was too stubborn to give in—too stubborn and too devoted to what he wanted his life to be. I thought Abby was luckier than she deserved, but I wouldn't give her a hard time, for Dec's sake. And also, I had to admit, because Mum could punish her enough for all of us so I could sit back and let her do the hard work.

The last message on the machine was a hang-up. I dialed 1471 to see who had rung me, and recognized the number straightaway. The wayward DC Langton had phoned at ten past eleven the previous night. He had called, but he hadn't left a message. Still huddled in my blanket, I rolled off the sofa and went to find my bag. My mobile phone was right at the bottom, and when I pulled it out, the screen told me I had seven missed calls with six messages. I scrolled through them, seeing two calls from Rob, one from Liv and four from Mum. Liv had left a message with blurry-voiced thanks for a top night out and I would have been amused if I hadn't had a vague recollection of having to repeat myself several times to make the taxi driver understand my address. I didn't want to think about the figure I had cut with my wrinkled clothes and disheveled hair. I was too old to behave that way. And I currently looked at least ten years older than that, with my morning-after complexion.

Messages from Mum I could discount, having heard what was on her mind already. I deleted them without a twinge of guilt. That left me free to torture myself by wondering what Rob had wanted. He had left a voice mail with the second call, at twelve minutes past eleven, just after he had tried and failed to find me at home.

"They seek her here, they seek her there." I could hear the smile in his voice. "I'm very much looking forward to talking to you about DI Derwent now that I've had a chance to spend some time with him. He's all that you said he was, and more." There was a tiny hesitation, and then Rob said quickly, in one breath before he hung up, "I hope you're okay. Let me know."

He had been worried about me. I put my phone down on the table in front of me and spun it like a top, considering what to do. It was almost seven, still too early to call him. But then, that was the reason the text message existed, I reflected, and tapped in a brief one. *Out late. Didn't hear phone. All okay.* It looked a little bit bald. I wavered, then added *with Liv* after "late." It wasn't that I felt I needed to explain to him where I had been, but he had been bothered enough to call. I sent it before I could second-guess myself more than a few hundred times, and threw the phone onto the sofa with a sigh. I hadn't got as far as the door before it beeped.

Glad the hair got an outing.

"Ha," I said aloud, "so you did notice." I turned to go and get dressed with a smile on my face. I still felt like death, but indefinably better. Death after a weekend at a spa. Death following a successful shoe-shopping expedition. Death in love? I shelved that particular line of thought in favor of trying to make myself look like a responsible member of society rather than someone who had been out drinking until the small hours.

There was nothing glamorous about my outfit today: black trousers, a plain black top, a gray jacket. Sober. Professional. In the mirror I was ashen, the bruise on my forehead standing out starkly. I shook my hair over it, glad for once that it was back to its naturally untidy state, and gave up on attempting to improve my appearance otherwise. I would get through the day. I would work hard so I forgot how I was feeling. And I would, eventually, recover.

The one good thing about waking up so early was that I was getting a badly needed head start on the day that would hopefully make up for skiving off work the night before. As I gave the flat one last look and picked up my bag, I reflected that there was one other tiny advantage to being hungover. I couldn't face breakfast, so there was no need to hang around for that either.

I shut the door behind me gingerly, hoping to get out of the house without encountering anyone. I wasn't ready for conversation. I felt as fragile as handblown glass, as brittle as a desiccated leaf. A loud noise could shatter me into a thousand tiny pieces. The house was thankfully still, as silent as the old building ever got. I was growing accustomed at last to its sighs, its knocking pipes and creaking boards, but I still didn't like it. *Maybe a new-build next time . . .*

It was purely because I was on autopilot that I went to check the mailbox as I left—on a Sunday morning it should have been empty. I recalled collecting my post the previous night, getting my key in the lock at the third attempt. Dignified, it wasn't. I made a better job of opening it this time and stared at the contents, confused. I was sure I had emptied it the night before. I might have missed something as inconspicuous as a postcard, but not a padded envelope, even if it was a small one. And it shouldn't have been there.

Something—training, possibly—kicked in. I rooted in my bag to find my phone, then took a couple of pictures of the envelope before I moved it, feeling faintly ludicrous. In a side pocket, I found a pair of latex gloves that I hadn't used at the warehouse. I draped one over my hand to prevent my skin from coming in contact with the envelope as I lifted it out. It was light but not empty: something slid around inside it. The white sticky label had my name and address printed on it in unhelpfully bland Times New Roman, and I stared at it, increasingly unsettled. My name was given as "Detective Constable Maeve Kerrigan—Serious Crimes Squad." No return address. No stamp. No postmark. Hand-delivered. To my home address.

Nine times out of ten, I would just have opened it then and there, but something was making me nervous. I couldn't seem to see past the thought that John Skinner had a history of targeting officers he disliked, that he was more than capable of finding out where I lived, and that he was far from defeated even if he was in custody. And, of course, the kicker: that I was the one who had put him there.

I retreated to my flat, still holding the envelope by the corner, and laid it on the coffee table with extreme care. It sat there, buff-brown and uninformative, as I walked around the room wondering what to do. Ridiculous to think the envelope was booby-trapped. It was too small to be an incendiary device. Gingerly, I felt the edges of the envelope, working out that the object inside was narrower than a matchbox but about the same length. I was not going to call the bomb squad for something so puny. I would just open it myself. Carefully.

I laid out a couple of clean sheets of copy paper to catch any trace evidence that came off or out of the envelope. With gloved hands, I peeled away the edge of the flap, working slowly. It was a self-adhesive envelope and the strip separated with surprising ease, hardly ripping at all, as if it had only been lightly sealed. I pulled enough of it apart to be able to peer in at the contents with the help of my small Maglite. It was empty, apart from down at the bottom where a silvery metallic gleam caught the light. I tilted the envelope so the object slid onto the paper. It was something so familiar, so unthreatening that I almost laughed despite my concern: a memory stick for a computer. Cheap and easily acquired, they could hold vast amounts of information. This one wasn't telling me much at the moment, but all I needed was a computer with a USB port to unlock its secrets. I checked the envelope to make sure I hadn't missed anything, and parceled up both it and the data stick for further investigation when I got to work. I had an extra measure of urgency in my step as I left for the second time. I didn't like that I had it; I didn't like that it had been sent to my home. I wanted to know what was on it and I wanted to spend some time looking at lettings ads. I had a feeling it was getting to be time to move again.

If I had taken the envelope seriously, that was nothing to how the news was received by Godley and Derwent, both of whom were already at work when I arrived.

"This bothers me a lot." The envelope was lying on Godley's desk, the data stick beside it. The superintendent was tapping a pen against his mouth, considering them both.

"Should we have a look to see what's on it?" Derwent was vibrating with curiosity, yearning like a dog on a short lead presented with a tantalizing smell.

"Has it been given the once-over by a forensic technician?" Godley checked.

I shook my head. "Right, well, no one touches it until it's been checked for prints and swabbed for DNA."

"I'll give them a call." Derwent sprang into action just for the sake of having something to do. Godley's office was stuffy and I was feeling slightly faint; I was more than happy to let him make the calls and do the running around. Sluggishly, my brain lumbered into action.

"We should get someone from the IT branch to help, in case it's got a virus on it or something. I don't think we should just shove it into one of the computers out there and hope for the best."

"Bringing down the entire Met computer system would be unpopular," Godley agreed gravely. "Josh, sort that out too."

"Anything else? Coffee? Croissants?"

"If you're offering."

"I was being sarcastic."

"I know," the superintendent said blandly. "Still a good idea. Pop out while we're waiting for reinforcements. You look as if you need something to keep you busy while you're waiting."

With a black look, Derwent finished his phone calls and prepared to go out. I took great pleasure in ordering my breakfast roll and coffee even if he wrote it down with extreme bad grace. Godley asked for fruit salad, which earned him a snarl. But with one of his rare flashes of likeability, Derwent worked his way around the squad room, getting requests from the early birds who were in already. I saw Liv on the other side of the room. She shook her head, pointing at the super-sized coffee that was steaming on her desk. She looked better than I felt, but that wasn't saying much.

I turned back to Godley and grinned. "He'd make a good waitress, surprisingly."

"Hold off on forming an opinion about that until you see what you get. I'm expecting anything but fruit salad."

"It must be fun being able to boss DI Derwent around."

"At times. Not that he listens to me much." The superintendent stood up and stretched. "I should really be giving you a bollocking for opening the envelope. You could have been seriously hurt if it had been booby-trapped."

"I was careful."

"You were lucky." He went over the window and stared out. "Did it occur to you that it might be Skinner?"

"Yes."

"And you still opened it."

"I wanted to know what was inside."

He gave a short laugh. "Of course you did." Still looking away from me, he said, quite calmly, "If John Skinner comes after you, I want you to know that I will do everything in my power to protect you. I will not let him harm you."

"It's a possibility, though, isn't it?" The effort of keeping my voice level made me clench my hands. "He's that sort of person. Vindictive."

"He believes in making people pay for what they've done. But at the moment, he's more focused on finding out what happened to his daughter and punishing the people responsible. I had thought that when he'd worked through that, he might turn around and start thinking about how he ended up where he is."

"Are you worried he'll come after you?"

"Always." His tone was so matter-of-fact that I couldn't quite match it up with what he'd said.

"What will you do?"

"Talk to my wife about it. Discuss the options. Move again, maybe." He leaned his head against the glass. "It's not what she signed up for."

"I'm sorry."

"Not your fault. It's not what you signed up for either." He glanced at me. "Hopefully he won't have noticed you and this is nothing to do with him."

"I'm not scared," I lied. Godley's response was not reassuring.

"Be wary, even if you're not scared now. Listen to your instincts and don't take unnecessary risks. And if anyone sends you a mysterious package again, don't just open it, for God's sake." He came back to his desk. "I've got a couple of phone calls to make."

Recognizing it as the dismissal it was, I slipped out of his office. It was useless to try to settle down to anything else while I was waiting to find out what was on the data stick. I caught Liv's eye as I wandered toward my desk, and she met me there to discuss, in the faintest of whispers, how much her head hurt and how much exactly we had had to drink and who should have called a halt before we got ourselves into that sort of state.

Derwent interrupted us to deliver breakfast, with a scowl, and not long after that the superintendent reappeared.

"Someone from forensics is just looking at the data stick but bad news on the computer support. No one will be available until tomorrow."

"Do you want to wait that long?"

"I do not." He put his laptop down on my desk. "We can use this so if it is a virus, it won't contaminate anyone else. I've disconnected it from the Met's intranet. I see Colin is in. He's probably as qualified as any of us to take the lead."

I was glad Godley's eye had fallen on nice, gentle Colin rather than the team's other resident tech-head, Belcott, who was at the end of the room.

"What is it?"

I explained to Liv what I had found in my mailbox that morning, conscious that the story was attracting attention from my other colleagues. Colin had come over to join us, having heard his name mentioned by the boss. DI Bryce wheeled his chair over, openly interested.

"So where did it come from?" Liv asked.

"Not a clue. I just found it there this morning."

"Yesterday was Saturday. There would have been a delivery of post. It could have come in then."

"No. It wasn't in the box last night. I checked."

"Are you sure? I mean, if you were tired, say, you might not have noticed . . ."

Or if I was smashed. I shook my head. "I picked up my post on my way in. I couldn't have missed the envelope. It's too big."

"And it was in your mailbox in the hall. So whoever put it there had to have access to your house." Without my noticing, Rob had arrived.

"No, not necessarily. If someone put a letter through the front door, anyone who saw it would pick it up and put it in the right mailbox. Chris is really keen on keeping the hall tidy."

"Bet he is. What time did you get back?"

"It was after midnight."

"And what time did you check this morning?"

"Around half past seven. There wasn't anyone else up, as far as I could tell. It must have been put there last night."

"Well, we're looking for a night owl," Liv commented.

"They're all like that. The girl upstairs stays out clubbing until all hours at weekends. Chris always seems to be working whenever I walk past his window, whatever time of day or night it is." I could never help looking through the gap in the curtains, and I usually saw him sitting at his desk, his face shining a ghastly blue-white in the light from his screen. "I have no idea about Brody, but I'm guessing he comes and goes when he likes, and my landlord is basically nocturnal. But as I say, I'm sure they just picked up the envelope and stuffed it in the right box."

"Well, find out which of them did it so we can ask them if they saw anyone deliver it," Derwent ordered.

"That's what I was planning to do," I said sweetly. "It seemed to be the obvious place to start."

Rob had moved around to stand on the other side of the group and now he looked up, his eyes full of amusement. I recalled his message and wished I could talk to him about the inspector now, to hear what had happened the previous day and what Rob made of him.

The superintendent's return prevented Derwent from replying, which was probably just as well.

"Right. We've got the all-clear to handle this." He put the data stick in Colin's outstretched hand. "No prints, unsurprisingly. She'll send the swabs off for analysis. I wouldn't count on getting anything off it, though."

"Well, let's have a look at the files, assuming there are any." Colin stuck it into the USB port and the machine whirred obediently. "Huh. Okay. That's interesting. There's a Word file called 'Dear Maeve.'" He looked up at me. "That's you, presumably."

"You'd think," I agreed. "Go on."

"Then there's a folder of picture files. It's called 'Album One.' And the last thing, in a folder called 'Present' is a video file called . . . well, called that." He pointed. The title of the video file was a meaningless collection of letters and numbers jumbled together. "That suggests it was copied off a website. You'd never name a file that, but a website might host it with that tag."

"Anything else?"

"Not that I can see."

"Okay," Godley said. "A picture paints a thousand words, but give us 'Dear Maeve' first so we know what we're supposed to be looking at."

"What if it's private?" I was trying to sound amused, but my heart was thumping.

"We'll forget we read it. Come on. Open it."

It seemed to take an age for the file to open. I leaned in, aware that all of us were doing the same thing. Rob and Liv had to crane to see from where they were standing, but I had a grandstand view from behind Colin's shoulder.

Dear Maeve,

I hope you don't mind me contacting you out of the blue. I'm afraid you don't know me, but I know you. I hope that doesn't scare you.

I wanted to give you a present to say thank you for all the entertainment. You wouldn't believe how long it's taken me to find something special. What do you get the policewoman who has everything?

I found this and I thought of you. I think you'll like it. I hope it's what you've been looking for.

You need to smile more, Maeve. You're so pretty when you smile. Do you see what I mean?

Maybe not yet. But you will.

With love,
Your admirer.

"What the fuck is he on about?" Derwent said.

I had a deep feeling of foreboding. "Open the images."

Colin selected them and opened them all, so the screen filled with picture after picture, layered on top of one another. As they flashed up in turn, I felt the blood drain from my face. I shouldn't have been surprised—I had seen what was in the letter—but I couldn't quite believe that the images were of me. All of them. Me outside my house, talking to a passing window-cleaner who had nearly taken me out with his ladder. Me in the corner shop chatting to the guy behind the till while I paid. Walking along in the sunshine on the phone, laughing, in jeans and a cotton top. Through my living-room window, me sitting on the sofa, my head turned to say something to someone out of sight. Walking against the wind, my hair flying behind me as I hurried down the street. On the last leg of a run around the park, laughing, and I recalled it had been because "Eye of the Tiger" had just started playing randomly on my iPod and it seemed altogether too appropriate. Not smiling in the rain. And then, suddenly, not in my neighborhood anymore. Not smiling talking to DI Derwent in the street outside the nick. Laughing hysterically with Liv as we left the previous night.

"That was yesterday." Liv pointed.

"Bang up to date," I made myself say. I felt as if my feet weren't properly on the ground. That was shock, I thought. That and feeling ice cold.

Dimly, I was aware of someone taking my hand, putting their arm around me, supporting me as I wobbled. I expected it to be Rob, but when I looked, it was Derwent who was staring into my face intently, concern in his eyes. I felt even more unsettled.

"Do you want to sit down?"

"N-no. I'm fine."

"Sure?"

Instead of answering, I looked across the circle to where Rob was standing, and took reassurance from the fact that he looked as calm as ever. Interested, certainly, but not unsettled. I dislodged Derwent's hand from my arm gently and, with one small part of my mind, wondered how a simple look from Rob could be more effective than all of Derwent's patting and fussing.

"This doesn't sound like John Skinner." There was a note in Godley's voice that I identified as relief.

"Yeah. Just your common-or-garden nutcase. Nothing to worry about." I laughed shakily. No one else joined in.

"He said he'd got her a present. What's the present?" Liv asked.

"The video?" Colin clicked on it and the screen went dark as the file began to load.

The difference between the blank screen and the start of the video was subtle; at first, I didn't realize it had started to play. The light wasn't good, the image darkening to invisibility and then wavering back into some kind of focus. The camera moved and showed us a low ceiling, a narrow, slightly arched space that looked somehow familiar.

"It's the back of a van," Rob said, a couple of seconds before the wheel arch appeared in the corner of the frame and confirmed it.

"What's that on the floor?" Godley asked.

"A tarpaulin, I think." Colin leaned in for a closer look, and then sat back again as the screen suddenly flared with light.

"Oh, Jesus. That's Cheyenne." Derwent sounded distraught. I made myself look back at the screen.

She was lying on the ground, on the tarpaulin, and the skirt of her dress was pulled up high on her thighs. Her hair was over her face.

"Are you sure it's her?" I asked.

"Definitely."

"That's the dress she was wearing when she disappeared," Rob said.

"What is this?" I heard my voice crack.

"This is what happened next." Godley had moved so he could see better and his face was so close to mine I could smell the shower gel he'd used that morning. My mind was twisting away from the fact of what was playing out in front of me, plunging at distractions like a leaping deer. I bit the inside of my cheek hard enough to taste metal, the stinging pain bringing me back to the room, to my job. To the girl lying on the floor and her hair over her face and a hand reaching out to move it away.

"Is she dead?" Liv whispered.

"No. You can see her chest rise and fall." Derwent hadn't taken his eyes off the screen. "Minor injuries."

Cheyenne stirred, and the sound cut in, shockingly loud after the silence that had been the soundtrack before. Rustling, breathing from behind the camera, then laughter as the girl came around, sitting up, staring around her in confusion. She was fourteen years old and alone with someone who clearly wished her harm, but she was John Skinner's daughter too. Fascinated, I watched her pull herself together, draw herself up to a more dignified position and prepare to deal with the situation. When she spoke, it was with the confidence of someone who had never known a threat to fail because it would always be backed up by her violent, dangerous daddy.

"You are in really big trouble."

And the screen went black.

I let air out of lungs that were creaking; I hadn't been aware I was holding my breath.

"Is that everything?" Godley asked.

"I think so. There might be something else hidden on it. Files that have been overwritten sometimes still show up if you look for them. Depends on whether this was a new data stick or one he reused."

"Well, find out. Fast, Colin. We need to know everything that's on there. And where this person found the video footage. You said you thought it came off a website."

"Could be." Colin shrugged. "Could be his own personal video, though, and he's just making it look like he took it from somewhere else."

I found my voice. "It would be a pretty big coincidence that the guy who kidnapped Cheyenne and Patricia would start to focus on me, don't you think?"

"You are investigating the case," Derwent pointed out. "Stranger things have happened."

"No." I poked Colin. "Go back to the images of me. Can you show them as thumbnails?"

A window appeared with the images arranged neatly in rows. I swallowed the panic I felt at seeing them all laid out, not wanting to think about the work that had gone into collecting them, the total lack of warning I had had.

"Right. That one," I pointed at the jogging image, "that was two weeks ago. Long before Cheyenne disappeared. Before I started working on the pedophile case, which was my first point of involvement with this whole mess."

"Are you sure?" Godley asked.

"Absolutely. It was such a nice day that I went for a run, and I hadn't been running for a long time so for the next few days I could barely walk, and I haven't had any time this week. Since I moved to the new house, I have been jogging once, and that was it."

"Okay. So whoever sent you this . . ."

"Is just a local nutcase, like I said."

"Someone who knows you're a copper and what you're working on," Rob pointed out.

I bit my lip. "I sort of told my neighbors what I do. But it couldn't be any of them."

"Couldn't it?" He raised his eyebrows.

"All of those pictures were taken in the street either here or near my house. Someone's been watching me come and go. If they were following me anyway—" I stopped to clear my throat; it had closed up at the thought "—they could have seen where I worked. And it would only take a bit of research to find out what I was doing. I spent the day before yesterday at the crime scene in Brixton, and the discovery of Cheyenne's body was reported in the *Standard*."

"Let's assume it's not directly connected." Godley the peacemaker stepping in to bring order and direction to what was turning into a row. "Let's focus on tracing him as a separate inquiry. I want to know what he knows. Colin, you and Peter Belcott can work together. Track him down for me."

"And me," I said flippantly. "I'd like a word."

"Looks as if all you have to do is keep your eyes peeled, Maeve." Derwent grinned. "Are you sure he's not in here now?"

"That's about all I'm sure of." I couldn't keep the distress off my face even though I tried, and he looked contrite.

"Sorry. I shouldn't joke."

"We should watch the video again," Liv suggested.

"That was my next suggestion," Godley said smoothly. "Colin?"

He played it again, all the way through, this time with an audience of every team member who was at work on a sunny Sunday, which was most of us. I could hear a beat in the background, faintly, when the sound cut in. Music was playing somewhere nearby.

"I think this was at the warehouse. I think that's the sound of the club's music."

Godley nodded, his attention focused on the screen. When the video faded to black, he said, "Again."

The third time Colin went through it frame by frame, stopping when the cameraman's hand entered the frame. The still image was blurry and I frowned.

"Next one?"

The hand inched forward, still distorted by the speed with which he had moved and the poor quality of the recording. When he got as far as touching her hair, his hand lingered for a moment and came into focus, then blurred again.

"Go back to the last frame." I leaned forward. It was his right hand. Something was niggling at me. Someone I had met. Someone I had spoken to. Faces flashed in front of me: Tom Malton, Matthew Dobbs and Carl McCullough, Lee and Drew Bancroft, Ken Goldsworthy, William Forgrave. Malton, open and honest and almost too forthcoming. Forgrave, who had hunted for girls on the Internet. Ken Goldsworthy. *You never get your hands dirty* . . . Dobbs? Derwent had said he was a safe pair of hands. Hands. Whose hand?

In a rush, I remembered. The thumb. The twisted nail. Lee, chewing on it nervously. It was Lee's hand I was looking at on the laptop's screen. And then, with a shiver, I remembered more: Drew so relaxed, so chatty. *I drove the van over with the lighting and sound stuff* . . .

I looked up and found Derwent in the group clustered around the desk. "It's them. It's the brothers. They're the ones." He was looking baffled, much like everyone around him. I couldn't get the words out quickly enough, or think how to explain. "They must have swapped masks to give each other an alibi. And they had a van, Drew said so. *They're the ones.*"

"What are you talking about?"

It felt as if everyone was a million miles behind me. I made myself summon up enough patience to be able to explain what I'd seen, and once I'd finished, Derwent nodded. "Harry, have you got those images you pulled off the Internet yesterday? I want any images where you can see the Bancrofts." Maitland went to fetch them and Derwent looked at me. "You can tell them apart, can't you? You know which one is which."

"They do look different." I sounded as if I was trying to convince myself. "I suppose they were relying on the black-and-white masks to disguise them."

"I imagine it's easier to see the differences when you are looking at them side by side," Godley said. "If they weren't in the same place, people would be easier to fool."

"Especially somewhere dark, like a nightclub in a derelict warehouse."

Derwent tapped the ring binder Maitland had given him. "Come on. Let's all play spot the difference. It's joint enterprise whatever happens, but I want to know which of them took her."

"Well, that's definitely Lee in the video."

"Okay. Follow it through. Was Lee the one who got her out of the club?"

The answer to that, it seemed, was no. Drew disappeared for a good chunk of the evening, his place taken by Lee who had been snapped standing beside the bouncers, black mask in place.

"You can't see his hand in that picture," Godley pointed out.

"It's definitely him. Look at his skin. Drew doesn't have acne, but Lee does. And Lee's bigger. Put that side-by-side with another shot of Drew with Carl McCullough and you can see he's not anything like as broad as the bouncer, but Lee's nearly the same size."

"Lee must have popped out from behind the bar, supposedly to change the beer barrel or something. Then all he had to do was swap masks, come up the other stairs as Drew, make sure he was noticed, then swap back." Derwent shrugged. "Simple, isn't it?"

"Yes, and that makes sense. Drew is the talkative one. If you wanted to charm someone into trusting you, you'd send Drew."

"And they had to get her to trust them so they could persuade her to leave the club without anyone noticing." Godley sighed. "Right. These two need arresting."

"I knew there was something off with them." Derwent raised his fist and bounced the side of it off the desk. "Did you find anything on them on the PNC, Maeve?"

"I didn't look them up." I said it in a small voice, but everyone heard and froze where they were standing.

"Why the hell not? I told you to check them out." Derwent looked absolutely furious and I flinched, not strong enough for a confrontation. There was a general movement away from the conversation as people suddenly found they had urgent business back at their desks.

"I tried, but they gave me the wrong year of birth. Plus their real names are Alexander and Andrew, which they forgot to mention. I only found all of that out when I cross-checked with the DVLA, and then I never got a chance to look them up again because the DS who investigated Patricia Farinelli's disappearance called me back. I thought it was important to find out what had happened to her, so I got sidetracked." I shot a look at Godley, who was looking troubled. "DS Rai in Stoke Newington did a piss-poor job on the case so I had to get the details from her parents and friends."

"Too long. I stopped listening after 'I tried,'" Derwent snapped. "Did you not think checking the Bancrofts might be a priority when you found out they'd *lied* to us?"

"People do lie about their age, you know. It didn't strike me as that weird considering they work in a world where you have to be young and trendy. And if they always use their nicknames—"

"Don't even fucking attempt to defend yourself!" His nostrils had gone white around the edges and a vein was standing out on his forehead. "If you'd done your job properly, we'd have had this information yesterday. We could have arrested them straightaway."

"Well, we can arrest them today." I swallowed. "I'm sorry, all right? I made a mistake."

"So did Marla Redmond's team," Liv pointed out. "They didn't even get as far as spotting they lied about their ages."

"Being cleverer than that lot is not something to boast about," Derwent snapped. "You had a reason to be interested in them and you blew it. You'd better hope an extra day didn't make a difference to Patricia Farinelli."

"Look, I feel bad enough about it already. I know I should have done it."

"There's no need to give her a hard time, Josh. I gave her too much to do," Godley said quietly.

Stung, I shook my head. "It wasn't too much. I should have been able to manage it. Please don't underestimate my abilities because I dropped the ball on this one."

"Oh, I think we've got a fair idea of your abilities at this stage." Derwent's voice was soft, and all the more threatening for that. "Look them up. This time, do a proper job. We'll go and make the arrests, and you can report what you've found when we get back."

"Is this my punishment? Being left behind?"

"No, it's your job. I'm not surprised you don't seem to recognize it. Try doing it for a change instead of swanking around looking for glory."

I turned away and went to my desk, sitting down blindly as tears filled my eyes. I was annoyed with myself, and embarrassed that Godley had seen Derwent give me a well-deserved dressing-down. More than anything, though, I was frustrated that I had let Patricia down, despite all of my disdain for DS Rai. I hadn't behaved much better than him, all things considered.

Out of the corner of my eye, I watched Godley and Derwent shut themselves in Godley's office to plan the arrest strategy. I wished quite fiercely that I could go too, but far more than that I wished that they would find Patricia, and bring her home.

Chapter Eighteen

Sunday

Rob

I sat in the briefing room, listening to what Derwent was saying about the Bancroft brothers with about ten percent of my brain. The rest was pure white noise. It would have been useful if my reaction to worrying about Maeve had been something more constructive, but I was stuck with unreasoning panic. Someone had been watching her. Following her. Tracking her down so they knew her workplace, and what she was thinking about, and where she might go next. Learning her routine. I had heard plenty about stalking before; I had even dealt with a woman who had made a complaint about it when I was first in CID, but I had never understood the reality of it. Someone, for reasons known only to himself, had chosen Maeve to be the focus of his attention, and there was nothing she could do about it except hope that we would catch him and pray that he wasn't violent. I was doing a little of the latter myself. I didn't like that she was out of my sight, even though I knew she was safe in the office. I didn't want to let her move a step on her own.

The thing that really bothered me was that the creep who was watching Maeve was calling all the shots. He had even picked how he showed himself to us. He needed catching, and fast. There was just the small formality of arresting the Bancrofts first.

Godley was briskly dividing the assembled squad members into two teams, one to be led by Derwent and the other by the superintendent himself. I willed Godley to choose me for his team and was rational enough to know that had nothing to do with why he picked me.

"Rob, you can drive my car. I want to stay in touch with Josh and you're quicker than me anyway."

There were positive advantages to having "drive it like you stole it" as a philosophy for life, speeding fines notwithstanding.

"We'll start off in Archway and arrest Drew Bancroft." He handed out maps of both locations, then turned. "Josh, you've been to Lee Bancroft's flat. Can you describe the layout for your team and tell them the strategy?"

Derwent nodded, moving center stage to address the group. He was chewing gum rapidly and blinking very little, hopped up on adrenaline.

"We've got a narrow approach, three flights of stairs. Out the back there's bound to be a fire escape; I want two of you to scope that out before anyone else moves. We'll be letting CO19 do their Action Man routine but I don't want him slipping out the back before we even get a chance to put in the front, so make sure we have it covered from the off." His words were coming out at a rattling pace.

"Who else is in the building?" someone at the back asked.

"There's a shop on the ground floor, an office on the first floor. Flats above that. I don't know how many people live there but the office should be empty on a Sunday. We'll go in hard, grab him, and hope he puts up a bit of a fight, if you know what I mean."

Derwent's aggression was off the scale. I was even more relieved that Godley was in charge of my team. There was no sign of excitement in the superintendent. If anything, he was speaking in a more measured voice than usual, deliberately underplaying the tension. Just an ordinary day out, arresting two abusive kidnappers who had brought about a teenage girl's death. It was practically routine when you thought about it.

"What if they're not at home?" Maitland asked. "Shouldn't we hold off until tomorrow morning?"

"I don't want to wait. Not with Patricia Farinelli potentially in danger. We'll sit on the addresses and wait for them to return if need be. So keep a low profile. Unmarked cars only, and try to keep anything that would identify you as coppers out of sight.

"As Josh mentioned, we'll have support from CO19. They will be armed so make sure you wear your vests."

There was a rumble of amusement at that. The Met police vests were described as stabproof rather than bulletproof, which in practice meant they were thick enough to protect you from nothing more lethal than a determined toddler armed with a wooden spoon. Godley held up his hands.

"I know, I know, but it's the best we've got. Just wear them, okay? And hope the CO19 boys have learned to shoot straight."

Godley ran through what we knew about the flat Drew lived in, which wasn't much. It was off the Archway road, a one-bedroom ground-floor flat. All we had was a fuzzy overhead view of the street with an arrow pointing to the correct property.

"There is a garden but there's no access from there to the street; you have to go through the house. The gardens back onto each other, so we'll have to come at it via the neighbors' houses to seal it off. But it will work in our favor as he can't escape easily that way either. We'll approach it through the front. The armed officers will take the lead. Follow their orders or take the consequences."

"Drew is the talker; Lee is bigger. Don't trust either of them," Derwent said. "They're into bodybuilding and they hang around the kind of gyms where there's sawdust on the floor around the boxing ring to soak up the blood. I would guess they know how to handle themselves in a dirty fight. Don't get too close unless you're prepared to tangle with them."

Godley held up a picture of a plump woman with dark hair and eyes. "This is Patricia Farinelli as she was when she was last seen eighteen months ago. She may not look like this now. We will be arresting anyone in the flats with the brothers as a matter of course, but keep your eyes open for someone who looks like Patricia. We have to take into account that she may be a willing participant in their games, free to come and go as she wishes, so if you spot her in either area, pick her up. It's more likely that she's their captive, and I doubt she was in the Hampstead flat since the brothers chose to meet you there, Josh. Wherever she is, finding her is our top priority after arresting these two safely."

Nods all round, serious faces. No one had taken this case

lightly from the start, but something about seeing the video had made it real for all of us. It was the way Lee had touched Cheyenne. He had treated her like a thing, like she was his to display. He had seemed to be having fun. I was fairly sure I wasn't alone in thinking it was past time for the fun to stop.

"We'll leave at eleven. No need to travel in convoy but stay on the radio for updates. We'll be meeting the armed officers at the rendezvous points I've indicated for both addresses."

We shuffled out of the briefing room, chatting and yawning and generally acting as if we weren't on edge. It seemed to help with the nerves. I walked straight into Maeve who was cutting through the crowd with an unseeing look on her face. In one movement I took her arm, drew her into the small meeting room nearby, and shut the door. I doubt anyone else even noticed. She didn't resist, but when I turned around, she was standing where I'd let go of her, staring into space.

"Are you okay?"

A tiny shrug. "Not really." Her face was as white as paper, her eyes huge and troubled.

"We'll find him, Maeve. You don't have to worry. He's not going to get away with following you around any longer."

"Oh, that." She sounded vague. "I'm sure you're right."

"What else? The PNC check?" I shook my head. "Don't let Derwent upset you. Anyone could have done the same thing. And the chances are it wouldn't have made any difference."

"Lee has a record." She said it clearly, but I could tell it cost her something to admit it. "He was put in a juvenile detention center when he was fifteen."

"What for?" I was hoping for something like vandalism.

"Rape. On a twelve-year-old girl in his school, according to the CRIS report."

"Behind the bike sheds?"

"More or less. The report isn't very forthcoming. There's a note from the officer who investigated, asking anyone who wants to consult Lee's record to contact him, so I'm waiting for him to call me back."

"That sounds serious."

"Yes. I don't think Lee is a very pleasant person." She gave me a tight smile. "So it might have made a difference if I'd looked him up properly yesterday."

"Move on. There's nothing you can do about it now except torture yourself, and there's no point."

"Right." She managed to get a world of sarcasm into that one word.

"You don't seem too worried about being watched."

"I'm trying not to think about it."

"I can't think about much else," I said truthfully. "It bothers me, Maeve."

"What are you going to do? Act as a bodyguard?"

"If I have to." I paused for a second before I went on. I knew what I needed to say, and I knew what her reaction would be. If I pushed her too far, too fast, she would put up the barricades again and I would lose any advantage I'd gained by giving her more space. But I couldn't let that stop me from doing what was right. And in the end, the choice between keeping her safe and persuading her to trust me wasn't a hard decision at all. "I don't think you should stay in your flat on your own. I want you to move in with me."

She looked startled, as if the idea hadn't occurred to her. "Have you been talking to Derwent?"

"What's that got to do with anything?"

"He has all sorts of rules about it," she said vaguely.

"Good for him." I put my hands in my pockets, keeping the distance between us so I didn't seem to be crowding her. "Don't worry. I don't mean that you should move in with me permanently. Just for a while, until we've got him off the streets and out of your life."

"Oh."

"What's wrong?"

"Nothing. It's just—" She stopped. "Nothing."

"No, go on." I was braced for her to say something cutting.

"I never thought you would ask me to move in with you like this. Not for security, or as—as flatmates, or whatever you have in mind."

"I can't win." I sat down on the edge of the table, defeated. "I'm just trying to do the right thing."

"Of course you are. You always do."

I waited, but she didn't say anything else. "Did you have an answer in mind?"

She closed her eyes for a second. "I have to say no."

"Why?"

"I just can't."

"What's the alternative? You move back in with your parents? Try and find somewhere else in a hurry? Stay in some crappy hotel? You can't stay in that flat. I'm not having it."

"Oh, you're not having it. In that case, let me go and pack." Sarcasm. Her eyes had narrowed. I recognized the warning signs. She would be losing her temper in roughly thirty seconds. I wasn't far off it myself.

"I don't understand what's so hard about this. I'm not asking you for anything."

"Maybe that's the reason I don't want to do it."

"Look, what do you want, Maeve? The truth?"

The word landed between us like a grenade. The room was so silent I could hear my watch ticking. Maeve had gone very still. She pushed her hair back and I could tell she was steeling herself for what I was about to say. "Of course."

"You could have fooled me. Don't blame me if you don't like it, though." I took a deep breath. *Cards on the table.* "The truth is, I want you to live with me so I can spend every minute with you. I want you to be there in the evening, all night long and in the morning when I wake up, and if we ever have a day off, I want to spend it with you without even having to think about it. I don't want to waste a single minute worrying about where you are and what's happening to you. I know it's not what you want, so I'll take what I can get, which in this case is peace of mind. I'm not asking you to make a commitment; I'm asking you to be with me because it's safer that way. And you can go whenever you like, if that's what you want."

"All right."

"What?"

"All right, I will come and live with you. But on my terms."

"I'd expect nothing else." I waited, resigned, to hear the conditions. It was enough, I told myself, that she had agreed to the basic idea.

"No half measures. If we're moving in together, it's for real." The color had come back into her face. "I was going to suggest it anyway. Before this came up."

"You were?" I said stupidly.

"It's just that I've been thinking. About us. And I've realized that being with you isn't the worst thing I can imagine. The worst thing I can imagine is being without you."

All I could think to say was, "When were you going to tell me?"

"I was waiting for the right time."

Time. I checked my watch. "Oh, shit. I have to go."

She laughed shakily. "Now this is romantic."

"I really want to kiss you but the blinds are open." The entire team had a grandstand view of us through the meeting-room windows and shutting the blinds was the only thing more likely to draw everyone's attention than sweeping her into my arms.

"Save it for later."

"Your place or mine?"

"Yours, obviously. I have to work out where I'm going to put my stuff."

I couldn't leave her without touching her; I grabbed her hand and pulled her toward me so the solid wood of the door hid both of us from view. It was a brief kiss, but it had all of the weight of a promise fulfilled.

I held on to her for a moment, my cheek against her hair. "Stay safe until I get back."

"You too. Don't get shot."

I had the greatest difficulty in keeping the grin off my face as I left the interview room, and I was certainly the only person in the locker room to be whistling as I pulled on my stab vest.

"Are those yellow feathers I see poking out of your mouth?" Derwent had just come into the locker room, even later than me, and was ripping his tie off, preparatory to getting changed into something a little less formal than a suit for kicking-in-doors purposes.

"Sorry?"

"You look like the cat that got the canary. What's up?"

"Oh, nothing. I just really enjoy arresting people."

He gave that the look it deserved. "Don't kid yourself. You're not going to get close to Drew Bancroft unless it's because you're holding the boss's coat."

"Fine by me," I said serenely. Derwent pulled his shirt off, revealing a torso corrugated with muscle. I was pretty sure he was sucking his gut in to get that effect, though.

"Well, whatever's making you so happy, take it elsewhere." He hauled a navy-blue T-shirt over his head. "Godley's waiting for you."

I finished getting ready in a hurry and made it to the car park on the stroke of eleven, to find the superintendent already in the passenger seat of his car. I jumped into the driver's seat and fumbled for my seatbelt.

"You're late."

"Sorry, sir." I risked a look at the dashboard clock. "Technically, though, I am still on time. And DI Derwent hasn't come out yet."

"Josh is a law unto himself and it's one minute past the hour." He shook his head. "Just drive."

I did as I was told and made time on the journey with some moves that had the boss grabbing for the fuck-me handle above the door, so-called because that's what's going through your mind when you're hanging on to it for dear life.

"I want to get there in one piece, if that's okay with you," Godley said mildly as we had a bit of a close encounter with a lorry.

"I thought you wanted fast driving."

"So did I, but I've changed my mind."

I pretty much ignored him. Driving recklessly was the only way I had to let off steam. Godley's car was a sleek Mercedes that knew what I was thinking before I did and had the horsepower to back it up. We had a temporary blue light stuck to the roof and I took full advantage. I almost wished the rendezvous point was twice as far away; I was having a blast. From the look on Godley's face after I cruised to a stop, though, I was unlikely to be behind the wheel on the way back.

He was out of the car before I'd switched off the engine, conferring with the head of the CO19 team who were waiting to put in the door. I joined them at a more leisurely pace and listened in to the final discussions. We were standing around the corner from Bancroft's address, about a couple of hundred yards away, and the boys in boiler suits toting large semiautomatic weapons attracted a fair number of worried looks from the neighbors.

"We'll run the van into the street so the boys can use it for cover. We don't want your guy to know we're here until we're ready for him."

"Good."

"Any info on weapons?"

"Firearms are unlikely. Beyond that, your guess is as good as mine."

"Well, we'll try for non-lethal force initially."

"Send the guys with the Tasers in first?"

"That's about it." The two men laughed, a momentary relief from the tension that always built up before a raid.

Bancroft's maisonette had its own front door so we didn't have to worry about running across a neighbor in the hall. The plan was to go in fast, zap him into submission with fifty thousand volts if he showed any signs of not cooperating, and then search the place for any trace of the missing woman. Simple. And as Derwent had said, I would be doing nothing more taxing than standing around.

It was sort of hard not to envy the CO19 guys their firepower. I joined a little group of our lot who were cooing over the MP5s. Moving to CO19 would be fun, I thought, doing my fair share of perving. Spending all day kicking in doors and taking down targets had its good points.

Since the main thing we had to remember was not to get in the way, Godley and I hung back a bit once the order came to move, watching the scene from a distance. The CO19 team had the procedure refined to an art: they slid around the corner, invisible in their unmarked van, and slipped out to their positions without anyone so much as twitching a curtain in Bancroft's road. I heard rather than saw the moment when they put the door in: one shouted warning and a single blow that sent the door crashing back. They wouldn't be used to doors that weren't reinforced, I reflected. It was probably in bits.

The silence stretched for an uncomfortable minute while I wondered what was going on. I wasn't the only one.

Godley was patting his pockets, looking for something. "I left my radio in the car," he said at last.

"Me too."

"What use are you?"

"You didn't say I had to bring one. You just said I had to drive."

Maitland was behind us and he had his earpiece in. He reached forward and tugged on Godley's arm.

"Boss. Something's wrong."

"What is it?"

"It sounds as if they've found a body."

We started to run at the same moment, pounding down the street hampered by our heavy, unwieldy stab vests. Godley was fast; I only had to hold back a little bit to let him get there first. He almost collided with the CO19 team leader in the doorway.

"What's going on?"

"There's a DB in the bedroom. Looks like your target. The rest of the place is clean. No sign of any other occupants." The officer was pale and he rubbed a gloved hand over his mouth before he went on. "He was shot. Afterward."

"After what?" I asked, but Godley didn't wait to hear. He shouldered through the gang of armed officers in the narrow hallway and pushed into the bedroom. I was right behind him, reckoning that if I didn't step on it, I would never get inside.

"Ah, Christ." Godley sounded disgusted and as I came around the door, I saw why. Drew Bancroft—at least, I presumed it was him—was spread-eagled on the bare white-painted floorboards of his bedroom, naked, and very dead. His face was a mass of injuries, the product of a beating as determined as any I'd ever seen. The pictures I had seen of him showed a handsome, cocksure man with white, even teeth. All of that was gone, obscured by blood that was still fresh enough to be bright red. His knees were slightly bent, his elbows too, so that his hands lay by his shoulders, and his limbs were held in that position by the nails that had been hammered through his palms and feet. His mouth sagged open, presumably because whoever shoved a gun into it and shot the back of his head off, hadn't bothered to close it again afterward. The splatter of blood and brain and bone fragments fanned out from the top of his skull like a Jackson Pollock knockoff.

"Smell that?" I turned to Godley. "Cordite. This is recent."

He was still staring at the floor, too much in command of himself to react by retching, as Chris Pettifer was behind me, but unable to tear himself away from the somewhat surreal dismantling of the body that was lying in front of us, the unmaking of what had been close to physical perfection.

"Skinner." It was said almost to himself.

"Huh?"

He made himself look at me with a palpable effort. "This is John Skinner in action. What did he say? There'd be a reckoning?" He pointed. "There's your reckoning. Justice, Skinner-style."

Maitland, crowding in the doorway behind Pettifer, got there a second before I did. "What about the other one?"

"The other one?"

"Lee Bancroft," I said, already starting to move, anticipating what the boss's reaction would be. "If they started with Drew . . ."

"Lee would be next. And Josh was running late." He checked his watch as he strode toward the door. "His team won't have got started yet."

But when they did, there was a good chance they'd be walking into an ambush.

"Harry, see if you can get through to the CO19 commander—tell him what's going on here." Godley took his phone out and started looking for Derwent's number. I made a path for him through the armed officers who were clogging up the hall, watching where he was going so he didn't have to.

"Do you want me to get the car?"

"We'll both go." He had the phone to his ear. "He's not picking up."

The two of us went flat-out to get to the car, and this time I decided getting there as quickly as possible was more important than being diplomatic. I'd left my radio on the dashboard tuned to the main set, the force-wide channel. It was a habit I'd picked up in uniform so I could keep track of serious incidents running on my patch, mainly so I didn't blunder into the way. It was always good to know what else was going on.

What was going on currently, I discovered when I picked it up and tucked the earpiece in, was bedlam. At first, all I could hear were odd words, the rest drowned out by background noise and a flat, repeated crack that could have been fireworks. The voices were loud which was both unusual and worrying: sounding like you were bothered was something most coppers tried to avoid, and it was a fairly clear indication that the shit was hitting the fan somewhere.

Then, at last, something that made sense.

"Trojan four two alpha, urgent assistance, urgent assistance, shots fired at police on Hampstead High Street."

I looked across the roof of the car to Godley, who had just got there. He didn't bother groping for his own radio, which was off.

"What's happening?"

"Shots fired at the other team. The CO19 commander has just given permission to fire back. It sounds fucked." There was no other word for the chaos that was coming over the radio.

"Anybody hit?"

"Don't know."

"Go."

I ducked into the car, aware of Godley doing the same on the other side. He appropriated my radio and ripped off the earpiece, turning the volume up so we could both hear what was going on. The siren wailed as I punched through the traffic toward Hampstead. On the radio, the air was alive with increasingly senior officers trying to take control of the situation, local units working out which roads to close, and the armed officers yelling updates over the rapid, loud popping that was a full-on shoot-out in progress.

Godley was completely silent beside me and I had to concentrate on the road so I couldn't risk a look at him.

"Are you okay?"

"That rather depends on what happens." I could hear the edge in his voice. He had the ultimate responsibility for the operation. If someone was hurt—if someone died—he was the one who would have to explain it to the bosses, the squad, the police complaints commission and the officer's family. He was entitled to be a little bit tense.

"Chances are they're outnumbered and outgunned. The Armed Response lads do this all the time. It won't take long to get them under control."

"Maybe not." Godley was silent for a second. "How did he know, Rob?"

"Who? Skinner?"

"Who tipped him off? Or his boys, anyway. We didn't even know until an hour ago."

It had to be someone on the team—that was the obvious answer. I knew Godley would have worked that out too, so I didn't bother to say it.

"Let's assume for the sake of argument that it's not you." Godley sounded a little more like himself. "Where do I start to look for the leak?"

"You don't. Let the DPS handle it. Whoever's done it needs kicking off the force."

"I don't like letting the DPS in until I know who they're looking for. They're like foxes in a henhouse when they get excited. I want to limit the damage, not cause more."

"Well, you still don't start to look for the leak yourself. Get someone you trust to do it."

"Who should I trust?"

"Do you want me to volunteer?"

"Not everyone would want that job," Godley said quietly.

"In case I find it's someone I like." I shrugged. "Too bad, basically. If they're wrong, they have to take what's coming. I'll nose around. You can handle it as you wish."

Every armed response vehicle on duty was racing toward the scene, calling out for authority to ready their weapons. I let two go past us—they did have guns, I reminded myself, and we didn't. The passengers in both cars were doing the same thing: sorting out the weaponry. It was definitely an occasion for breaking out the submachine guns they carried in the cars' safes. I winced at the thought of the firepower that was going to be concentrated on one small area; the potential for collateral harm was altogether too high. A stray bullet—ours or theirs—hitting someone it shouldn't became more and more likely as every second passed.

And it could be counted in seconds too. From the first burst of firing to that moment had only taken a couple of minutes. We weren't far off now, racing along the edge of the Heath.

"At least it's close."

Godley didn't respond. He was concentrating on the radio, where a breathless voice was saying, "Trojan four two alpha, ambulances required. Gunshot wounds. One conscious and breathing, injury to left arm. Second not conscious, not breathing. We're doing CPR."

"Have you got a defib kit available?" the dispatcher checked.

"In our vehicle."

"Ours or theirs?" I asked.

Godley shook his head.

I looped through the cordon a local uniformed officer was holding open for us, traveling down the wrong side of the road to pull in a safe distance from the scene, behind the CO19 command vehicle. The gunfire had stopped, I realized after I turned the engine off, and with it our siren.

"Come on." Godley took off, running for the doorway of Lee Bancroft's building. On the pavement outside it, a figure lay on the ground. An officer knelt by the head, holding it still as other officers took it in turns to do chest compressions and mouth-to-mouth. They were sweating heavily under their armor. As we approached, one of them looked up and shouted, "Where's that defib?"

Jesus. Not good at all.

Derwent moved out to intercept us, his face tight with worry. I was still looking past him, trying to see the guy on the ground. With an almost shameful sense of relief, I realized he wasn't anyone from the team or the firearms unit. I didn't recognize him. It was a fairly safe assumption that was because he wasn't one of ours. As we got closer I could see the ground was veiled in ice-green fragmented glass from the shop window. The panes that hadn't shattered were starry with bullet holes and I hoped the shoppers and staff had had the sense to hit the deck when the shooting started.

"Josh, talk to me," Godley rapped out.

"One of them is dead, or on his way." Derwent looked back at the guy on the ground, at the blood that was drenching the pavement. "Three in custody."

"Our lot?"

"Mostly okay. One of the firearms guys got winged. Two of them managed to trip over one another and fall down the stairs in the confusion. They've just got bruises, twisted ankles, that kind of thing. We were too far away to be in any danger."

Godley breathed out slowly. "Bancroft?"

"He's down. Not shot," Derwent clarified quickly, seeing the look on Godley's face. "He was beaten up pretty badly before we got here."

Three ambulances turned into the street in convoy, blue lights whirling. The paramedics jumped out, loaded down with their kit, and went running past us to take over from the CO19 officers' increasingly labored efforts at CPR. The officers stepped back, breathing hard, absolutely knackered.

"Where's the officer who got shot?" Godley asked.

"They took him to hospital themselves. Didn't bother to wait for the paramedics. It was a through-and-through." Derwent pinched his arm, indicating the track the bullet had taken through the officer's muscle. Getting a hole that size put in your flesh tended to sting just a little, but it wasn't anything like as complex or debilitating as a shattered shoulder might have been.

"Any reason why we need to stay out here?"

"Not really. Lee is still upstairs—that'll be where those paramedics are heading. And the three gunmen haven't come out yet."

"They'll be waiting for vans to transport them," I said.

"And uniforms. You don't want them to say they picked up gunshot residue off the firearms blokes if there's any doubt about who fired what."

"It sounds as if inside is where I need to go."

We walked toward the door, passing close to the bloodstained figure who was evidently not responding satisfactorily to the paramedics' attentions.

Godley was staring at the man on the ground. "Is that—?"

"Felix Crowther. Yep."

"Who's Felix Crowther?" I asked.

"One of John Skinner's buddies. Last I heard, he'd retired to Spain."

"I bet he wishes he'd stayed there," Derwent said darkly. "What a fucking mess."

I stood back to let him go ahead of me and caught a glimpse of his face as he turned into the building. He looked strung out, the excitement of earlier having soured to something less positive. I couldn't really see what there was to be so upset about. Okay, so the operation had gone badly, but it wasn't Derwent's fault. It wasn't Godley's fault either, but he would be carrying the can if anyone had to take responsibility, so all in all, there wasn't much for Derwent to be chewing his lip over. Then again, I was aware I was preternaturally imperturbable, able to rationalize almost everything to the point where I didn't get too fussed about much. Except Maeve, I admitted to myself with a secret grin as we took the stairs two at a time. I definitely got fussed about her.

We passed walls pitted with holes on the way up the stairs, plaster crunching under our feet. The door to Lee Bancroft's place was standing open, splintered around the locks where they'd kicked it in, and the flat was in about as good a state as you'd expect given that the trapped gunmen had shot wildly around themselves as they tried to find a way out. We trooped in to find three men lying on the floor amid the dust and debris from the fight, hands cuffed behind them, with bags over them to preserve the gunshot residue on their hands. They were fairly effectively incapacitated, I would have said, but no one was taking any chances: they had a cordon of armed officers who were obviously itching for an excuse to go for their weapons. The men on the ground were heavily muscled, clean-cut types, and Derwent pointed at them in turn.

"Laurence Murray, Wes Roberts and Phil McKenzie. Lower down the pecking order than Felix, but trusted members of the Skinner family nonetheless."

"New since my time," Godley commented. "They'd have been in school when I was after John's lot."

Derwent laughed. "Reform school, maybe." He leaned down. "Not so clever now, are you, lads? I haven't heard a word out of you. Presumably you're going to keep your mouths shut until you find out what the boss wants you to say, because I can't see how you'd be able to talk your way out of this one."

Not a flicker of a reaction from any of them. I was surprised that the inspector even bothered to taunt them. They were professionals, not the sort of shite who you could goad into revealing backchat. Besides, there were many, many witnesses to them trying to shoot their way out of the building. They were screwed, no matter what they said or didn't say. It was kinder just to leave them alone so they could contemplate the sentences they would most likely receive. Life sounded about right, for possession of a firearm with intent to endanger life and the little matter of more than a few counts of attempted murder.

"You know, I'm beginning to think Ken Goldsworthy might be on to something. Skinner's throwing away resources like they're weighing down his balloon. If he doesn't put a stop to it, he'll be stuck for decent muscle to carry on his businesses."

"And Ken can step into the gap." Derwent shook his head. "Hard to imagine John letting it all go just like that."

"Maybe he doesn't feel he has anything to work for anymore." Godley sounded sober, and I guessed he was imagining himself in the same situation. Skinner was as irrational and angry as any bereaved father, but a key difference was that he had the assets to act on his emotions. Murray, Roberts and McKenzie, not to mention Crowther downstairs, were just collateral damage, as they seemed to be starting to realize.

"Knock, knock. I've got three taxis downstairs for the gentlemen on the floor." A cheerful uniformed inspector from the local force nodded to Godley. "All right if we take them away?"

"Fine by me."

We watched as the men were hauled to their feet and moved with exaggerated care through the doorway and down the stairs. It would be absolutely ideal if we could avoid any accusations of police brutality that might muddy the waters of what was a crystal-clear case of being caught in the act. Fortunately, the local police seemed to have got that memo.

"Where's Lee?"

"In the bedroom." It was one of the armed officers who spoke in a voice that rumbled all the way up from his boots. "He needed a nice lie-down after Pricey shot him."

The man he indicated gave us a sheepish grin and patted his Taser. "No one argues for long."

"What did he do?" I asked, frankly curious. "Try to fight his way out?"

"When we got here, he was being punched about by two of the lads who've just left. We broke up the party, but one of them had said something to him about his brother having put up more of a fight. As soon as things calmed down, he asked what he'd meant."

"And the joker with the red hair told him they'd shot him dead," the other officer interjected. "So he went a bit mental."

"He wasn't trying to attack us," Price explained. "He was trying to get at them. But he wasn't very interested in listening to reason."

"When did you shoot him?" Derwent asked. "Shouldn't he be up by now?"

"The paramedics say he's concussed. Not because of being shot. Because of what they were doing to him when we got here."

Godley moved to the back of the flat and pushed open the bedroom door so he could look in. "How's he doing?"

I couldn't hear the response, but the superintendent grimaced and turned back to us. "Hospital. Who wants to babysit?"

Derwent melted away like snow on a summer's day, muttering something about wanting to check up on what was happening with processing the gunmen.

"I suppose that leaves me."

"Thanks, Rob. You can give me a call when the doctors say he's okay to interview."

"Right you are," I said, resigned to a few hours of sitting about doing nothing.

"I'll let you have someone else to keep you company. What about Chris?"

I groaned. "Pettifer only talks about Spurs, boss. You wouldn't do that to me, would you? Can't I have Maitland?"

"All right. But I wouldn't have thought he was that much better."

"He's not, but at least he bores on about Arsenal. I can just about cope with that."

I hoped to God Maitland didn't find out I was the one who'd nominated him to spend the rest of the day in a hospital corridor. I hoped it even more fervently when I heard him on the subject all the way there, after Lee Bancroft had been scraped onto a stretcher and bounced down the stairs. He had looked, as Price observed to me, like "hammered shit," his face battered, his eyes dilated and full of confusion. Godley had swept off in his Merc to update the brass and explain why half of Hampstead High Street had had to be closed. Derwent was nowhere to be found. The rest of the team had wished us well and got down to work, ripping the two brothers' flats apart in search of any clues that might lead us to Patricia Farinelli. Because unless Lee cooperated, we were still at square one when it came to finding her, alive or otherwise.

I endured forty minutes of Maitland moaning while we sat outside the room where Lee Bancroft was recovering. Eventually I sent him off in search of a sandwich and a coffee. The hospital claimed it had a Marks & Spencer outlet, complete with café, but its location seemed to be a closely guarded secret. I was anticipating a vending machine tea at the very best, and gave him a round of applause when he returned in triumph with a tray of cups and a bag of food.

"Good work, mate." I dived in. "Can I have the all-day breakfast?"

"No you can't." He reached over and snatched it. "I get first pick. Caveman rules. I hunted it."

"So you did. It actually didn't take you as long as I was expecting."

"Oh, well, I had a bit of help." He ripped open the packaging and wadded half of the sandwich into his mouth in one go. Around it, he managed to say, "Liv Bowen told me where to go."

"Liv's here?" She hadn't been on either team, now that I thought about it. I was pretty sure I hadn't seen her since the nick.

"She's downstairs. With Kerrigan."

I stopped what I was doing. Downstairs was A&E. "Maeve? What's happened?"

"I didn't see her. I was just looking around and Liv came up out of the ground. She said she'd come in with Kerrigan. I didn't ask why— Where are you going?"

I was halfway down the corridor already, moving fast. I didn't bother to answer. The only thing I would have said was the only thing that was going through my head.

I knew I shouldn't have left her.

Chapter Nineteen

Sunday

MAEVE

Previously, I would not have thought that it was possible to be elated and despondent at the same time. I wandered down the hallway, trying not to catch my colleagues' eyes for two very different reasons: I was mortified by forgetting to look up the Bancrofts on the PNC, and I didn't want anyone to ask why I was stupid with happiness. There was a time and a place for floating around in a haze of bliss, and this was definitely not it. I gathered myself together, making a very conscious effort to forget about Rob while I concentrated on sorting out the mess I'd made.

My stomach went into free fall every time I thought about Lee Bancroft. The moment I saw the conviction on Alexander Bancroft's PNC record would stay with me for a long time. The PNC tended to be blandly uninformative on the details; the "method screen" gave the officer in the case two lines to say what had happened. I couldn't have said why, but the bald description raised the hairs on the back of my neck. "The offender raped a twelve-year-old female at Evanston School, Enfield." He had been fifteen. The very fact that the officer had requested the file be kept in the general registry for longer than the regulation seven years told me that he had taken it seriously, that he had been worried about Lee's potential to become a repeat offender—that he had seen him as dangerous.

The case's unique reference number included the code YE, which told me that Edmonton was the police station where the complaint was handled. I had called up, hoping to track down DC Tony Stone, and wasn't surprised to hear that in the previous eleven years he'd moved on. In fact, Tony Stone had moved around quite a bit as his career progressed, ending up all the way down in Croydon as a DI. I called Croydon, hoping he might be on duty, but of course he wasn't. By dint of begging I managed to persuade them to give me a personal number for him, and rang his mobile only to be told by a pleasant-sounding woman that Tony had taken the kids to football and had left his phone at home by accident. She'd get him to give me a call, she promised, and with that I had to be satisfied.

There was, in fact, nothing for me to do. I had read the report on the central Crime Reporting and Incident System, which was by no means as informative as I could have wished, and I had requested the file from the general registry. There was precisely no chance that it would appear on a Sunday, and I would have to be very optimistic to count on getting it the following day. All I could do was wait for DI Stone to get back to me, and hope his wife remembered to pass on the message.

In the meantime, I tried to stay out of the way of the officers who were heading out to arrest the brothers. I didn't want to think about it. Derwent was right; I hadn't done my job properly and I didn't deserve to go with the others, but it still burned. Loss of face was one thing; loss of Godley's trust was another. I would apologize—I had apologized—but I didn't expect anyone to forget about it until I had proved myself all over again.

I sloped back into the squad room once I calculated they were likely to have left, and found it all but deserted. The only desk that was occupied belonged to Liv, who was working away industriously.

"Why didn't you go with the others?"

She turned in her chair. "I wasn't feeling too good, funnily enough. I volunteered to do the paperwork. The CPS are going to need case papers if they're going to rush through our request for authority to charge."

I pulled a face. "Most people would run a mile from that sort of job."

"I don't mind it. I like filling in forms."

"That's unnatural."

"It appeals to me. I have a tidy mind." She turned back and kept working, stopping occasionally to sip water. Clearly she was still pinning her hopes on rehydration to make herself feel better. I smiled wryly. I had started to feel more human as the day went on, right up until the moment when the arse fell out of my world. And that was without even thinking about the fact that I had somehow acquired a creepy admirer. Which was all he was, I told myself sternly. I was irritated by the photographs, and a little unsettled, but not scared. But I was still glad Rob lived in Battersea, all the way across the river from where I currently lived.

I sat down at my desk and put my mobile phone in the middle of it. There was no point in staring at it until it rang. I knew that.

I couldn't take my eyes off it.

"Everything okay?" Liv came over to my desk.

I explained what I was doing and she nodded. "I'm sorry. If I hadn't dragged you out for a drink, you'd have got around to looking them up."

"Don't even suggest that. I made a decision to go out. You didn't force me. You just provided the opportunity for me to skive off work and I did the rest myself." I shook my head at her, pretending to be annoyed. "This is why women don't get ahead. We take responsibility for other people's fuck-ups. You should be taking advantage and trying to suck up to Derwent while I'm in the doghouse."

She gagged. "Do you mind? I'd appreciate a bit of warning before you suggest something as disturbing as that."

I grinned. "Even so—"

"Even so, I'm still sorry."

"Okay. Completely unnecessary apology accepted."

She looked at me with a slightly puzzled expression. "You haven't said anything about the pictures—aren't you a bit freaked out?"

"Yes and no. I'm obviously not thrilled that someone's been following me around, but most of that is annoyance with myself for not spotting him. I mean, it shouldn't be that difficult."

"They're pretty good at hiding themselves, though. It's not like he was wandering around with an SLR or something—you know they have all sorts of tricks to disguise camera equipment. And most of the pictures were taken in your neighborhood, so you wouldn't have thought it weird to keep seeing the same person around the place."

"Yeah, but I didn't see anyone. I haven't even had a tingle at the back of my neck. My intuition has conked out." I was trying to make a joke of it, but it did bother me that I had been so oblivious.

"Well, you have got a lot on your mind."

"I'll have to make room to watch my back."

"Seriously, though."

"Yes, Mum."

The phone in front of me hummed, vibrating against the desk and I snatched it up. "Kerrigan."

"Tony Stone. You were looking for me." He sounded pleasant, infinitely calm and not at all surprised to be tracked down on a Sunday. It was part of the job, especially if you had years of experience behind you. Criminals re-offended. Cases recurred. You never really left any of them behind, not the big ones. And the bad ones, I was starting to realize, followed you around like a comet's tail, unfinished business you couldn't forget.

"I'm sorry to bother you, but I've got a case where you arrested one of the main suspects as a juvenile, and there's a note on the file that you wanted to be contacted if he ever came to our attention again."

"Oh yes?" His calm manner had sharpened to interest. "Who's that, then?"

"Lee Bancroft. Alexander Bancroft, officially—I don't know if he was going by Lee when you dealt with him. It was up in—"

"Enfield. Yes, I remember. Must have been in 'ninety-six. No—nineteen-ninety-seven."

"That's right. The file says he raped a twelve-year-old girl."

"Just hold on a second." I heard footsteps and a door closing. "Right. I didn't want to talk about it where the kids might hear. Alexander Bancroft." He sighed. "I knew he'd come back some day. What's he done?"

I told him what we suspected, about Cheyenne and Patricia and the possibility that she was still alive.

"Absolutely nothing you're saying surprises me. Maybe just the fact that it took this long for him to crop up again."

"What happened in Enfield? What did he do?"

"Alex—he was Alex then—was a bit of a troublemaker in school. Andy was the opposite: butter wouldn't melt, but actually he was always up to mischief. He just never got caught. Alex was disruptive, challenging authority, always getting into fights. The head was one of those do-gooder types who wanted to reach out to him, especially because of his home life."

"His home life?"

"The parents were dead—they died when the boys were eleven and thirteen. There was a history of domestic violence and drug abuse. The two of them had separated and got back together again more times than the boys had hot dinners. Eventually, Mum had enough, said she wasn't going to take him back this time and she wanted a divorce. Dad strangled her, hanged himself. The boys found the bodies."

"Jesus. If you weren't a bit off-balance before, you would be after that."

"Oh yes. There's plenty of background there to explain why Alex turned out the way he did. Not that I think he wasn't responsible for what he did. Lots of kids have traumatic childhoods and don't turn into violent rapists, but it did help with the mitigation when he came to court." He hesitated. "Where was I? Oh yeah. The head. Vita Mountford. She had a bee in her bonnet about Alex. Thought she could give him some stability, a bit of discipline, bring him round. She made him stay after school three afternoons a week so he could do his homework in her office and do chores around the school instead of just having detention. She wanted to separate him from Andy because he had a tendency to let Andy do the talking. She wanted him to start thinking for himself. Which was a mistake, let me tell you."

"Who was the girl?"

"Carly Mountford. The head's daughter. Not a very confident girl, not very streetwise. Little thing, barely spoke when I interviewed her. He got her alone in an unused classroom and barricaded the door. He kept her there for over an hour, until her mother finally tracked them down and phoned us. During that time, he raped her repeatedly and beat her black and blue. The level of violence was shocking, even to me."

"Punching? Kicking?"

"That and biting. For fun, according to him. He left marks all over her body."

I was starting to see why the case had worried Stone so much. "He bit her for fun? Aged *fifteen*?"

"He said he liked it. Ordered her about, made her do things for no real reason, just to control her. I asked him about it in interview and he said he liked telling her what to do."

"So he cooperated."

"He was very forthcoming. He said he'd wanted to do something like it for a long time. He'd been waiting for an opportunity. I asked him why he'd chosen Carly and he said it was to teach her mother a lesson about trusting people."

"Jesus."

"I don't remember ever meeting a teenager who was so obviously dangerous. He was totally matter-of-fact about what he'd done. There was nothing behind his eyes, when you looked. No feeling at all for the girl. He thought it was funny. That's why it stayed with me, I suppose. I could see a mile off that he wasn't going to change."

"How long did he get?"

"Five. Out in two and a half."

"Is that all? Even given the level of violence and his reason for choosing the girl?"

"That's all. He had the sob-story background, and he did plead guilty. The judge was in the mood to believe in happy endings. Mrs. Mountford left the school and I believe the family moved to the States not long after. She had a total turnaround. The woolliest *Guardian*-reading liberal you ever met, but if we'd had the electric chair for Bancroft, she'd have flicked the switch herself."

"Not that surprising, is it? I presume she felt guilty about him being there in the first place."

"Indeed she did. Not a nice case."

"Did you ever get the same sort of feeling from Drew—from Andy? That he was dangerous?"

He sighed. "I've got to be honest on this one. I wasn't sure. He seemed very shocked by what his brother had done. He wrote Mrs. Mountford a letter of apology, even, but I didn't let her see it. Nothing would have made her feel better and I didn't like the thought of him trying to manipulate her, even if he was genuine. Better leave well enough alone. Then I got a call about five years ago from someone in the GMP. Andy was at university in Manchester, and someone had accused him of kidnapping their daughter. They saw Alex on the PNC and wanted to know the story."

"Kidnap? What happened? I didn't see anything when I looked him up."

"Andy was never charged. The girl was located and said she was fine. She said she had chosen to break off contact with her parents. They were seriously concerned that he had undue influence over her and that he'd stolen from her. She said it wasn't true—she'd voluntarily given him her savings, which included a nice little inheritance from her nan. It was a five-figure sum, if I recall correctly."

"Wow. Not bad for a student."

"Indeed. She'd dropped out and got a job as a barmaid, and Andy was pocketing her cash too. The whole thing stank, to be honest with you, but there was nothing they could do when the girl was so definite that she had no complaints. People can be stupid when they're in love, and she was in love. And Andy was pretty plausible when he was interviewed, so the case disappeared."

"What do you think?"

"I think they're both trouble. I think Andy is better at hiding it. That's all part of the fun for them."

"Who looked after them when their parents died? Were they taken into care? Fostered?"

"There was a great-uncle, Michael Bancroft. He had a big house just outside Enfield, in the middle of nowhere. He took them in. Didn't want to see them go into care, he said. They ran rings around him. He was devastated when Alex was convicted. Eventually he admitted he couldn't cope with Andy either and social services got involved."

"What happened to Alex?"

"He did his time. By the time he came out, he'd turned eighteen. The two of them kept in touch with Michael and moved back in with him once they were old enough to leave the care system."

"I'm surprised he let them move back if they were so hard to control."

"I don't think he had a lot of choice. They bullied him something chronic. He used to say blood was thicker than water. He was a lovely man. He'd be able to tell you what they've been up to since they last came to our attention."

"That's not a bad idea." I tapped my pen on the desk, considering it. "The thing that worries me is that we know about Cheyenne, and we know about Patricia, but there's a gap, isn't there?"

"There is indeed. Neither of those two boys was the patient sort. I can't imagine they were sitting on their hands."

And at some stage Andy had become Drew, Alex had become Lee, and they had started lying about their date of birth. Nothing as dramatic as a change of surname, nothing that required an official stamp of approval, but camouflage, nonetheless. I wanted to know when the change had taken place. I wanted to know if they'd had something else to hide.

"Do you know how I could get in touch with Michael Bancroft? Do you remember his address?"

"You'd have to check the voters' register. It was somewhere north of Enfield, that I do remember, but it was in the sticks. A big house, falling to bits. Funny place for two teenage boys to end up. It was an old man's house. But they said they liked it." He thought for a second. "Bonamy Lodge. That's what it was called."

I thanked the DI for his time and he wished me luck. "Let me know what happens, if you get the chance. Alex Bancroft is one of those people— you sleep better for knowing they're a long way away from you."

I promised I would and hung up. The voters' register was a quick and easy way to confirm that Michael Bancroft still lived at Bonamy Lodge, and once I had the postcode I was able to get directions to it in a couple of seconds. Directory inquiries broke the bad news that the landline was out of service. The drive up to Enfield cut straight through North London, and

if I hadn't been so completely in the doghouse, I might not have bothered
with it, given that I would be going on spec. But I needed to do anything
and everything to make myself look better in the eyes of the bosses. If that
meant dashing around on a wild goose chase, so be it. I turned to see Liv
tidying her desk with the air of one who has finished a task. "Done?"

"All ready for the boys when they get back."

"In that case, do you feel like taking a trip with me?" I explained quickly
where I wanted to go, and why.

"Sounds like fun. What are we waiting for?"

I piled my things together and stood up. "Absolutely nothing. Let's go."

There was something liberating about fleeing the office. I should have
taken a bit more time, though, because I might have noticed that my phone
was perilously low on battery. Ten minutes into our journey it began to
beep despairingly.

"Shit." I picked up my bag and shoved it at Liv without taking my eyes
off the road. "Make it stop whining, for God's sake. Can you have a look in
the glove box and see if my charger is in there?"

"I have and it's not," she announced a couple of seconds later. "Bad luck."

"I lent it to Derwent a couple of days ago. I usually charge my phone
overnight, but . . ."

"Yeah, I know. You were distracted. I've got mine."

"Good for you. Did you bring a radio?"

"Yes." She waggled it on the edge of my vision.

"Okay. So at least one of us is behaving professionally."

Liv was poking at the radio handset. "The only thing is, this one isn't
working."

"You're kidding."

She turned up the volume so I could hear the static. "That's the main set."

It should have been constant transmission to and from the control room,
not featureless fuzz. She went through the channels. *Click . . . click . . .
click . . .* Every one was white noise. "Sorry. I knew it was playing up, but I
thought it would be okay."

"Well, I didn't bring one at all." I sighed. "Never tell anyone about this.
We'll get a reputation for being dim birds who don't remember to check
their equipment."

"Er, and you're saying we're not? We've got one phone between us and no
radio. I don't think we should be patting ourselves on the back."

"All right, I wasn't going to go that far. I'm just warning you not to give anyone a reason to think we're bimbos. They don't need much excuse. No unforced errors."

"I'll try to remember."

"I bet Special Branch wasn't like this."

"Are you kidding? It was twenty times worse. At least Godley treats you like a human being. My last boss was a total pig."

We spent the remainder of the journey swapping horror stories. It was hard for anyone who wasn't in the job to understand the pervasive culture of chauvinism, the lip service that was paid to equality. By its very nature policing was a profession that attracted conservative-with-a-small-c types, those who appreciated traditional values that included women knowing their place. It didn't do to be too sensitive about that sort of thing. It was too easy to get a reputation for being humorless, for being touchy, for being a pain. So you learned, even if it didn't come naturally, to laugh when you were mocked, to give as good as you got, and to be on your guard against giving anything away. I took it in my stride. Liv had found it tougher to get used to.

"For the first few years, I never wanted anyone to find out I was gay. Then I decided there was no point in hiding anymore."

"Yeah, but why should you tell people? I don't tell everyone what I do and who I sleep with. Why should you?"

"Because it has to do with who I am. And it keeps the creeps at bay."

"But you must get men offering to show you the error of your ways."

"Oh, obviously. Just for my own good, so I realize what I'm missing out on. Then there are the ones who seem nice enough, but they're generally working up to asking if they can watch sometime, or suggesting my girl-friend and I might like to spice things up by trying a threesome."

"How tempting."

"I haven't found it too difficult to say no, but never say never."

"Oh, I think you can say never in some circumstances."

She snorted with amusement. "Speaking of never saying never, did I see you and Rob having a quiet moment together earlier? Anything you want to tell me?"

"Not really." I couldn't hide the smile that spread across my face, though, and she clapped her hands.

"Thought so."

"Jesus, you're like a witch. How did you know?"

"I watch body language. You both looked like you were trying too hard to be serious when you came out of the interview room."

"Did anyone else notice?" I was mildly disturbed that we had been so obvious.

"I really doubt it. They were all fired up about arresting the Bancrofts."

I turned my wrist so I could see my watch. "They'll have done it by now, probably. All over. They might have found Patricia."

"Or her body."

Liv was right, but it still made my mood plummet. I couldn't stand to think of her poor parents. My phone call would have given them hope for the first time in years, and it would be my responsibility to take it away again if the news wasn't good. Not for the first time, I cursed DS Rai. If he'd only done a better job and paid more attention to his own case, I could have left the Farinellis alone until there was some real news either way. The car was silent for the next few minutes, until we reached the outskirts of Enfield and found the right road out of town.

"We're looking for a big house set back from the road. Bonamy Lodge is the name. It was falling to bits ten years ago, according to DI Stone, so it probably won't be too grand."

"Got it."

The road was lined with hedgerows and it was hard to see houses until you were more or less on top of them. I nudged the car along the road, slowing down and speeding up until Liv muttered something about needing a sick bag.

"There's not a lot I can do."

"You could maintain a steady speed that isn't too fast so I can actually read the house names—ooh, there it is." She pointed across me.

I wrenched the steering wheel around and the car shot through the narrow gates painted with the house's name. Gravel crunched under the wheels but it was a long time since the driveway had been looked after; green weeds had seeded across it and I stopped on a large bald patch right outside the front door which seemed to be where every visitor to the house parked.

"This is cozy," Liv commented, peering up.

"I'm not familiar with that definition of cozy." The house was a brooding Edwardian lump, gray and forbidding in a coating of pebbledash that did nothing to make it more homely. It was gabled left, right and center, as if the architect had been stuck for inspiration and scattered them rashly where the design looked too plain. Time had not been kind to it. The woodwork was weathered and peeling, the roof gappy where slates had fallen off and had not been replaced. A length of guttering on the right was sagging under the weight of a young sycamore tree. The windows were dark and dusty. It was starting to look as if I wasn't going to get to talk to Michael Bancroft after all.

We both got out of the car and I went up to the front door. The doorbell was dead, so I rapped with the knocker. It sounded too loud. Behind me, an occasional car swished past, and birds were singing in the tall evergreen trees that lined the borders of the property, but there were no other sounds. The trees were overgrown, seriously unkempt, and did a good job of screening the place from the road and its neighbors. I was on the edge and tried to work out if it was lack of sleep or delayed reaction to the news that I had been being watched that was causing my nerves to jangle.

There was no reply to my knock; I sort of hadn't expected one. I stepped backward, shading my eyes as I looked up at the windows on the first floor for any signs of life.

"What do you think?"

Liv had crunched across the gravel and was standing on tiptoe, peering in through a window. "Not much in the way of furniture. It looks derelict."

"Maybe he's moved since the last time the register was updated."

"Maybe he's dead."

I frowned at her. "That's your answer for everything, isn't it?"

"People do die, Maeve." She started toward the side of the house. "I'll check around the back."

"Okay." I crossed the gravel to the window at the other side of the front door and shaded my eyes to see what I could of the interior. It was a dining room, a large and shadowy room with a dusty table in the middle surrounded by scroll-backed chairs. There was nothing to say the room was in use, but the fact that there was furniture at all was a hopeful sign. I returned to the front door and knelt down to peer through the letterbox. I was lucky; there was no draft excluder and I had a clear view of the parquet floor, the square-edged wooden staircase, the stained-glass window halfway up the stairs that cast a reddish glow over the interior. I sat back on my heels, frowning, and that was how Liv found me when she came back.

"I've gone all the way around and I haven't seen anything to make me think there's someone living here."

"Rubbish bin?"

"Outside the back door, empty."

"Note for the milkman?"

"Now you're reaching."

I stood up. "Okay. Have a look through there and tell me what you think."

She bent down and pushed open the flap of the letterbox so she could see in, much as I had. "A whole lot of nothing."

"Right. Look down."

"Two flyers for fast-food restaurants and a leaflet that looks to be advertising the services of a cleaning company. I think he should phone up. He looks to be in dire need of a good clear-out." She let the flap fall and turned to me. "Am I supposed to be interested in any of that? It's just junk mail."

"Exactly. What's the first thing you do every day when you get in from work?"

There was a glint in her eye as she opened her mouth to answer and I held up my hand. "Let me be completely clear, I'm not just curious about how you say hello to your girlfriend. I mean, what's the first thing you do when you unlock the front door?"

She thought for a second. "If I'm home first, pick up the post."

"And?"

"The junk mail."

"Every day. Handfuls of it. Even allowing for the fact that we're in a reasonably rural area, you can't tell me that the stuff in there is more than one or two days of deliveries."

"Huh. You're right. So who's been getting rid of it?"

Instead of answering, I knocked again, listening to the sound echo through the house as the reverberations died away. We waited for a full minute, but there was no noise from inside.

"I'd really like to get in and have a look around." I leaned back to look up at the windows again.

"Well, why don't you? You've got your Asp in the car. A quick knock to the kitchen window and a leg up for me, and Bob's your uncle."

"I'm sure you're not suggesting we should break in. We need a warrant. The only exception to the rule I can think of is section seventeen of PACE: 'saving life or limb.' And I'm not aware of either being in jeopardy."

Liv leaned in, her ear to the wood of the door. "Did you hear that?"

"What?"

"I thought I heard someone call for help."

"Yeah, right."

She raised her eyebrows. "Do you want to go in or not?"

I did, as it happened. "You must have excellent hearing. Where's this window?"

"Get your Asp and follow me."

I got my Maglite as well as my extendable baton and walked around to the back of the house where a small window by the back door had a useful rain butt underneath it.

"Are you sure you'll fit through there?"

"Positive."

"Stand back, then." I shielded my face with one arm and hit the window in the center, a sharp tap with the end of the baton that sent cracks across the glass and knocked a few triangles of it to the floor inside. No one came running at the sound of the blow, or the tinkling chips of glass as they landed. I ran the Asp around the edge of the frame, knocking out the jagged edges as best I could. It wasn't even close to safe.

"You'll tear yourself to ribbons on that, Liv."

"I'll put this over the windowsill." She had found a sack, a rough-looking thing that had once held coal. "Good thing I decided to wear black today."

"Me too." I was craning to see in through the empty window. "I don't think this kitchen has been cleaned in recent memory, and I'm fairly sure the rest of the house is in a similar state."

"Let's have a look." She elbowed me to one side and laid the sack over the edge of the window.

"Do you need a leg up?"

"I can manage." She clambered onto the rain butt and perched on the windowsill for a second, before slipping inside with a small thud and a crunch of broken glass. Her voice sounded hollow when she spoke, echoing in the sparsely furnished room. "I'll open the back door."

I went around and waited, listening to her fumbling to draw the bolts and turn the key in the door. The lock was stiff and uncooperative. From the cobwebs spun across the door, no one had used it for a long time, and when Liv finally got it open, she had to drag it back across the floor. The wood made a shrieking noise against the tiles that set my teeth on edge. I leaned my shoulder against it and pushed as she pulled, and between the two of us we got the door to open wide enough that I could slide through the gap. The air that greeted me was unexpectedly fresh and cold. I looked around, noticing the vent in the wall that was breathing a chilly draft on the side of my face, the gap at the edge of the tiles where the skirting board didn't quite meet the floor. The house was far less solid than it pretended to be. The wind tossing the conifers outside moved through it with a whine that might almost have been a lament.

"The bulb is dead." Liv flicked the wall switch up and down a couple of times, then moved to the worktop where a small jug kettle was standing. It sighed into action as soon as she turned it on. "Okay. So there is electricity. Just no light."

"Not bright in here, is it?" I turned my torch on and spun around slowly, picking out the gas cooker complete with a frying pan on top of it, the base still filmy with grease. There was a cup on the side by the sink and I leaned over to look inside, seeing a brown tidemark. "Someone drinks tea. Or maybe coffee."

"Recently?"

"It's not moldy." Nothing was, in fact. "This doesn't make sense. Someone has been here, and recently, but the house is completely neglected."

"Well, we're in now. Let's have a look around."

We were talking in low voices, even though we had made enough noise breaking into the place to get anyone's attention. I found myself tiptoeing as I followed Liv into the hall and I made myself walk properly, confidently, as befitted a police officer on official business.

Liv went to one side of the hall and I took the other, opening doors and cupboards. Inside, the rooms looked even more pitiful, neglected and unused.

"What do you think of this?"

I crossed the hall to see where Liv was looking and found a small, over-furnished sitting room. The walls looked like a jumble sale waiting to happen—random pictures and tapestries hung at odd heights. The shelves of a bamboo whatnot that lurked in one corner held a vast collection of ornaments and outright junk: old batteries, a hairbrush, a pair of glasses lying lens-down with the arms folded in like a dead beetle's legs, a sheaf of envelopes, a few assorted keys, a metal bracket long-divorced from whatever it had held. An ancient television sat on a low table, a red light announcing that it was on standby. A blanket lay folded on the sofa in front of it, beside a half-eaten packet of crisps. The air smelled of cheese and onion. I picked up a crisp experimentally and found it was soft, giving a little as I pressed it between my finger and thumb. It suggested the packet had been open for a while. The sofa was cold, the cushions ridged in their positions.

"It looks as if someone's been using this room, but not for a few hours at least. Maybe yesterday or the day before."

Liv nodded. "Upstairs?"

"Yeah. I'll go first." I really didn't want to, which was all the more reason to force myself. Liv had taken the lead in getting into the house in the first place; I owed it to her to take my turn.

The stairs creaked, of course, and I went up them slowly, past the stained-glass window. The landing was square, shadowy and smelled of drains; I wrinkled my nose at Liv and saw her react as it hit her too.

"Yuck."

All of the doors were closed. I tried the one nearest me and discovered a bedroom, the walls decorated in bilious green paper, which was ripped. A splatter of something that might once have been soup decorated one wall. A wafer-thin pillow sagged at one end of the bed and a coverlet was thrown haphazardly over the foot. There was nothing on the nightstand beside it except for a dark-pink porcelain lamp with a tasseled shade.

"Classy," Liv commented. I moved in far enough to open the wardrobe with a wary finger, seeing nothing but empty hangers. There was a smell of mothballs that I found oddly reassuring; better that than an infestation. The floorboards groaned under me as I turned to leave and I pulled a face as I made a long stride to reach the relative safety of the hall.

"If I go through the floor, call an ambulance."

"I will if I have any reception." Liv took out her phone and thumbed it on to see. "Two bars. I'd probably get through. Where are we again?"

"Bonamy Lodge, also known as Bancroft's House of Horrors. Imagine what it must have been like ten years ago." I opened the next door to discover a dilapidated bathroom, the walls tiled in bleak white, the sink gray with dirt. "Not all that different, I'm guessing."

Liv poked her head around the door beside the bathroom. "A loo. I'm not going near it."

"That must be where the smell is coming from."

"Yeah, I suppose." She sniffed. "It's by no means fresh in there, that's for sure."

I was laughing at the expression on her face as I tried the next door. The door stuck a little and I shoved it with my shoulder, stumbling into the room as it gave way. The curtains were drawn and it was hard to see much at first; I had a vague impression of a double bed, a chest of drawers, a dressing table with a three-fold mirror where I saw myself in triplicate recovering my balance. The coverlet had fallen off the bed, the sheets slipping sideways as if someone had jumped out of it in a hurry and left it in disarray. I turned and ran the torch over the furniture, picking up a reflection from silver-backed brushes and the glass in photo frames on top of the chest of drawers.

"That's Drew. That's Lee." I went over for a closer look, seeing skinny and awkward juvenile versions of the confident men I'd met. Both had features too large for their faces in the pictures; it had taken them time to grow into their appearance. Lee looked uninterested, Drew was smiling widely. "This must be Michael's room."

When Liv responded, her voice was shaky. "Down there. There's something . . . down there."

I shone the torch where she was pointing and realized with a spasm of horror that the tumbling bedclothes were draped over a shape that lay on the floor beside the bed, not three feet from where I was standing. It was a long, thin shape that was somehow unmistakably human, even before I saw the waxy yellow hand reaching out under the bed, pleading for mercy that hadn't been shown. I moved forward, holding my breath, and shone the torch down on the side of the body's head. Michael Bancroft, I presumed, and there was no doubt that he was dead. Not recently, either.

"There's no smell of decomp."

"It's dry in here and pretty cold." I leaned closer. "I don't want to step on Glen Hanshaw's toes, but it looks as if he's mummified."

"Not much insect activity inside the house. Especially if it happened in winter."

"Yeah, and I wouldn't even be too sure that it was this winter." I stepped back delicately, watching where I put my feet. "We'd better call it in. Godley will definitely want to make sure this isn't murder."

Liv was holding her phone, looking troubled. "If he hasn't been drinking coffee and watching TV, who has?"

"Good question." I left her standing in the hall, dialing 999, and carried on to the next room, also a bedroom, this one as untouched and unlovable as the first we'd found. One for Lee, one for Drew, and Uncle Michael dead in the middle. Happy families. Maybe the brothers liked to come back and stay. Maybe it was a home from home for them.

I had got back to the top of the stairs. I looked around the landing, wondering what I was missing. I ran through what I had seen room by room: the kitchen, the dining room, the small sitting room, the hall, the bedroom—the small sitting room. What was it about that? The keys. Everyone had old keys hanging around their house. The glasses. Upside down. You wouldn't leave your own glasses like that: the lenses might scratch. Dumped was the word that occurred to me. Black arms, folded in. Dust on them. There a long time. Forgotten.

Liv was giving the dispatcher directions to the house. I waited until she rang off. "Did you see any outbuildings when you did your tour? Sheds?"

"No. There's nothing but fields behind the house. There was a garage on the left, but it was empty."

I looked around again, seeing the unhelpfully blank doors, a bad landscape on one wall, an ugly opalescent light hanging down from the middle of the ceiling like a deformed Christmas bauble. My eye tracked upward along the line of its chain, to the ceiling rose that was splintered, to the square hatch beside it that led to a loft.

"Did you happen to notice a sturdy chair on your travels?"

Liv went into the third bedroom and came out with an upright wooden chair. "This do?"

"Perfect." I positioned it under the hatch and hopped up, stretching as high as I could to push against the hatch with my fingertips. I could just reach it. Not for the first time I was glad to be tall. I tried all four sides, hoping it was a pressure-release catch, but nothing moved.

"Try the middle. It might just lift up."

I did as Liv suggested, pushing hard, and almost toppled off the chair when the hatch gave way. The smell of drains was instantly stronger and I coughed, but I still managed to push the hatch away from the hole and get hold of the ladder that was poking over the other edge. I drew it down and reached to get a foot on it.

"Can you hold it steady for me?"

Liv grabbed hold of the bottom. "Be careful."

I was looking up, at the gray daylight that was illuminating the room above. There had to be skylights, or dormer windows. The beams overhead looked as if the pitch of the roof allowed for a proper room, not just a loft space. I didn't like going up the ladder, especially not when it meant that my head would be poking up through the hatch for a couple of seconds—I could feel myself tense at the thought of how vulnerable I would be to attack—but at least I wasn't climbing into darkness. I stuck my torch in my pocket and went up the remaining steps fast, without giving myself time to think. I checked through 360 degrees as soon as I was clear of the hatch, seeing piled-up junk, boxes, old suitcases, the ordinary detritus of life. The light came from a window in each of the four walls. It was actually a nice space, I thought, with a vague memory of Brody's flat overlaying the reality of the room in front of me. I levered myself out and straightened up, still wary of banging my head.

"It's okay," I began to say to Liv, who was climbing after me. "There's nothing up here. There's—"

The words died on my lips. Upright, I could see across the attic, over the tops of a dusty bookcase and a pair of tables stacked one on top of the other. Away in the far corner, by the window that looked out over the back of the house, there was a radiator. And by the radiator, there was a mattress. And on the mattress, there was a body, this time with long dark hair, a body dressed in a gray sweatshirt and black tracksuit bottoms, a body with bare dirty feet. She was lying curled up, huddled in a tight ball, a bit of an old blanket thrown over her shoulders. I saw the empty water bottle, the plastic containers empty of food, and I noticed the red plastic bucket that was the source of the smell. I heard Liv exclaim behind me, but I didn't respond. I couldn't. She was thin, painfully so, but I knew she was Patricia, even though I hadn't seen her face, even though she had changed out of all recognition physically.

And I knew I was going to be making the phone call I had dreaded. She was not moving. She was limp. Lifeless.

As usual, we were just too late.

Chapter Twenty

The spell broke at last as my brain started to function again. In the face of death, there was always professional duty to distract me, and I walked around the piled-up furniture to reach the huddled body, intent on securing the scene and getting a good look at Patricia before Liv called the dispatchers back. We would need another ambulance but otherwise we were ahead of the game. The scene-of-crime officers who were on their way to deal with Michael Bancroft could handle two scenes; Glen Hanshaw would be able to manage two dead bodies.

"You'll need to call Godley," I said over my shoulder. "He'll want to know."

"Is she . . ."

"Dead? I should think so." There wasn't as much as a drop left in the water bottle. I wondered how long it had been empty, how long she had survived. *Three minutes without air, three days without water, three weeks without food.* That was the rule I had always believed, though Glen Hanshaw had scoffed at it when I mentioned it to him, on the grounds that the water and food requirements didn't take into account the variables in environmental conditions, or the underlying health of the individual. Patricia's underlying health was unlikely to have been great, all things considered.

I reached out to touch her neck, to check for a pulse, moving her hair to one side in order to do so. It reminded me all too much of the video I had seen, of Lee's casual handling of Cheyenne, and I had to control the tremor in my fingers as best I could. Emotion was not helpful, I told myself sternly. The anger could wait.

I moved my hand, aiming for the hollow to one side of her windpipe, but just as my fingertips grazed her skin, without warning, she moved. Her eyes came open and she sat bolt upright in the same moment. I overbalanced as

I flinched, sprawling back inelegantly. Behind me, Liv made a noise that was nearly a scream and I had enough spare mental capacity to be glad that I had been breathless with shock, too startled to cry out.

Patricia was looking at me with a dazed expression, as if she was drugged. I recognized her instantly, even though her skin was dull and drawn, her cheeks hollow. Her lovely eyes were shadowy and half-closed. She wasn't quite in touch with reality, I thought. I doubted she knew Liv was even there and I stayed where I was, leaning back, almost afraid to move in case I startled her. She put a hand up to rub her eyes and I saw the medium-weight chain that snaked around her wrist. I followed it to the old-fashioned cast iron radiator, to where the chain was wrapped around it and ended in a heavy padlock, and I felt anger twist deep within me. They had left her enough chain to reach the bucket, but no more. Her wrist was rubbed raw in places where the metal had dragged against her skin.

She looked at me then, and her eyebrows drew together in a frown.

"It's okay, Patricia. We're police officers. You're safe now. Everything's going to be all right." I said it over and over again in a gentle tone, hoping the meaning would sink in. Behind me Liv moved away, toward the opening in the floor. She climbed down the ladder to the hall and I heard her on her phone, updating the control room in a matter of fact voice. I couldn't hear the words and I was glad of her tact, glad that Patricia didn't have to hear herself being discussed. She was swaying like a tired owl, her eyes glazed.

"Can you talk, Patricia? Are you in pain?"

She touched her mouth. "Thirsty."

"I've got water." There was a liter of it in the car; I'd never been so glad to have a hangover. "I'll get you a drink when my colleague comes back. I'm Maeve. Her name is Liv."

She nodded but her eyes were still vacant and I doubted she had understood what I said.

"You're safe now. Everything's going to be all right."

A smile touched her cracked lips, parted them and showed me black gaps in the previously neat symmetry of her teeth.

"Liv will be back soon. She'll stay with you. I'll get you the water."

"Thank you."

It was an automatic response but it still made my throat close up; she was able to be polite, even now, even after all she had been through.

"Lee and Drew—they're under arrest. They can't hurt you any more."

She looked baffled and I recalled belatedly that the brothers had two sets of names. "Alex and Andy?"

Nothing.

"The men who took you."

Comprehension dawned. "I didn't know . . . names."

"They never told you?"

"I thought Vincent, for one. That was the name on the profile." She stopped and coughed a little.

"Don't try to talk."

She ignored that. "What did you say? Lee?"

"And Drew. Short for Alexander and Andrew. Bancroft is the surname."

"Which is which?"

"Lee is the bigger one. Drew is the talker."

"Nasty and nice. But they were both nasty." Distress touched her face for a moment and then faded again. We were back to the zombie-like composure, and I was distinctly relieved to hear Liv on the ladder.

"They're on their way. Five minutes. The last time estimate was an hour, so we've gone up the list." She sounded breathless, overexcited. I made my voice slow and quiet when I answered.

"That's good. Did you get hold of the boss?"

"Yes. He'll meet us at the hospital."

"Do you mind staying with Patricia for a bit? I'm just going to get something for her to drink."

"Sure. No problem." She looked past me to the woman on the mattress, and then looked away. She perched on the edge of a trunk, about ten feet from Patricia, and I wondered if she was scared to talk to her, too scared to get too close.

I stood up slowly, making sure I didn't crowd Patricia and trying not to loom over her. "I'll be back very soon."

I wasn't altogether sure Patricia was aware I was leaving. I left her and Liv sitting in silence, both of them staring into space. Liv wasn't finding it easy to deal with a real-live victim. I wasn't exactly used to it either, but it was a distinct improvement on the usual dead body. I ran down the stairs at breakneck speed and took the direct route out to the front, unlocking the main door and leaving it open on my way back so the ambulance crew could get in quickly.

On my way across the hall it occurred to me to take the keys from the television room, just in case any of them fitted the padlock on Patricia's chain. I leaned around the door and picked them off the bamboo whatnot in the corner. As an afterthought I returned and flipped over the glasses, catching my breath as I recognized the black and red stripes on the sides. If I had looked at them properly earlier . . . she would still have endured eighteen months of captivity, I reminded myself. I would just have known she had been there at some stage. And since I had been well on the way to believing her dead, it wouldn't have made much difference at all. A glint caught my eye and I looked down at the base of the whatnot, seeing the end of a thin silver chain. I drew it out carefully and was somehow not surprised to see, when the end finally emerged, an oval medallion sparkling with diamonds. Cheyenne's Miraculous Medal. I left it where it was, to be collected with the other evidence, but my jaw was clenched as I left the room. A trinket, to be thrown aside with the others. To be thrown away like the girl herself.

Back at the foot of the ladder I stuck the glasses in one jacket pocket, the keys in another, put the water bottle under my arm and climbed slowly, wary of falling. It would be just like me to lose concentration, slip and end up in hospital again.

Liv was still sitting where she had been when I left, her arms folded around her knees as if she wanted to be certain no part of her would come in contact with Patricia. It struck me that she was particularly fastidious in her grooming—her clothes and hair were always immaculate—and perhaps that was because she devoted quite a lot of time and effort to staying away from dirt. And Patricia was far from clean—not that she had had much chance to be anything else. Her hair had the soft dullness that comes from never using shampoo; half-moons of black ringed every fingernail. When I had been close to her, I had been able to smell her, despite the stinking bucket and the years of dust that blanketed the attic, rising in clouds at every step. If the only water she had was in the two-liter bottle that lay empty beside her mattress, I could see how washing in it would not be a priority.

I went slowly as I approached her, and stopped a couple of feet away. She had turned around a little, facing more toward the wall, and I wondered if the presence of strangers was upsetting her.

"Here's the water." I crouched and held the bottle out to her. She pawed the air blindly before she came in contact with it, but once she had it safely in her hands, she popped the top off and drank greedily.

"Take your time," I cautioned. Too much water could be as bad as too little, or so I had been told. She paid no attention anyway, gulping at it as two thin streams snaked over her jaw and ran down her neck.

"Are you hungry?" Liv had come to stand beside me, looking down at her. "Do you want something to eat?"

"She shouldn't have anything until she gets checked out," I muttered.

"I'm not hungry." She held the bottle up. "More water."

"Do you think the tap water is okay?" Liv leaned forward and took the bottle gingerly. "I could run down to the kitchen."

"Yeah, I wouldn't trust the stuff in the bathroom. See if there's anything left in the kettle, maybe. And don't fill the bottle." The last bit was in a low tone that Patricia wouldn't have overheard. I hated to ration her, but I didn't want her to make herself sick. "Shouldn't the paramedics have arrived by now?"

"They've got to find the place," Liv pointed out as she walked away. "It's not easy even if you know what you're looking for."

"Where are we?" Patricia blinked up at me. "Is this England?"

I didn't laugh. "We're just north of Enfield."

"Enfield—London?"

"Still within the M25."

"I don't . . ." She trailed off, looking upset. "They told me not to run. They told me there were no neighbors, that I'd die of exposure, that no one would understand me. I thought it was somewhere far away. Iceland or Norway or something." She swallowed. "I could have gone home, if I'd run."

It was a long speech, and reassuringly coherent. The water seemed to have revived her. "They might have hurt you if you'd tried." I fished in my pocket for the keys. "Besides, they've got you pretty well tied up."

"This is a new chain." She rattled it, pulling as hard as she could, apparently oblivious to the metal links digging into her arm, though the sight made me wince. "They upgraded it. Said I was too precious to lose after what happened with the new one."

"The new one?"

Her face went still, her mouth a line. She looked defensive, and frightened. "I don't want to talk about her."

"About Cheyenne?" I didn't imagine it; the name sent a shudder through her narrow frame. She rattled the chain again, more urgently, and I started sorting through the keys I had found. "One of these might work."

The padlock was new, though, and the keys I had found were all old, the metal tarnished. I had grabbed all that I could see on the whatnot, without thinking about whether they might be appropriate or not. Now I laid them out on the mattress, discounting the two sets of house keys immediately. There were three possibles and I set to work to test them. Patricia was bent over, peering at the keys.

"Where did you get these?"

"Downstairs. There was a pile of them in the TV room."

"I don't know that room. I only went in the kitchen and the bedrooms." She laid a finger on one of the key rings that held a Yale and a Chubb. The fob was a plastic mouse with most of the paint rubbed off; I could just about make out a jaunty smile. "Those are mine. My keys to my flat."

It wasn't her flat anymore, but I hadn't the heart to tell her that. "Did you give them to either of the brothers?"

"They were in my handbag, I think, when I went to meet him." The still face again, the withdrawal. *Don't push, Maeve.*

I played around with the padlock for a while, but reluctantly had to admit defeat. "No joy with the keys, I'm afraid, but we can get the fire brigade to cut you free. They love a chance to get out their cutting equipment." I was checking my pockets as I spoke, making sure I hadn't overlooked a key, and my fingers brushed against the glasses. "Oh, I think these are yours too."

"What are?"

I held them in front of her, moving them closer when I realized she couldn't see them clearly enough to know what they were. Between blank incomprehension and recognition there was a split second; it barely took longer for her to snatch them out of my hand and slide them onto her face. She blinked a few times, looking at me and past me and craning to see the end of the attic room, then she rose up onto her knees and stared over the windowsill at the fields that stretched away into the distance.

"Where were they?"

"Beside the keys."

"Downstairs?"

"Yeah, in the television room." I was distractedly gathering up the keys again, and her voice had been so casual that I had no warning at all. I didn't notice the moment her composure crumbled, but it gave way like a dam wall bursting. She collapsed as completely as if her sinews had been slashed and by instinct and pure luck I managed to get my arms around her before she hit the ground. She lay against me and wept, holding on to the frames of the glasses as if she was afraid I would take them away again. I could feel her ribs through the thick cotton of her sweatshirt and the knobs of bone that tracked a stegosaurus spine. There was no flesh on her at all; she was as frail as a ninety-year-old.

When she had recovered enough to be able to speak again, she managed, "I asked . . ."

"For the glasses?"

A nod. "It was the only thing . . . I kept asking for. At first, I asked for lots of things, but I stopped. I knew there was no point. But I kept asking for something to help me see. *He* said he was sorry they'd lost the glasses. *He* said he'd get me another pair from somewhere, that he never stopped looking for my own pair. *He* said all I had to do was what he wanted, and make him believe I liked it."

"Lee did? The big one, I mean?"

"No." She screwed her face up in disgust. "The other."

As if she had recollected herself, she pushed me away. I became aware of noises downstairs, of Liv's voice and the tramping feet of officialdom. A pleasant-faced, gray-haired paramedic was the first person up the ladder and she nodded to me before focusing on Patricia.

"Let's have a little look then, lovey."

I moved away a little to give her some privacy. I was glad beyond words to hand her over to someone who knew what they were doing.

"Where are you going?" Patricia's voice was high with panic.

"Nowhere." I came back to where I had been standing. "I'm staying here."

"What was your name again? I'm sorry. I've forgotten."

"Maeve."

"Don't leave, will you?"

"I won't," I promised, meaning it. I would stay for as long as she needed me, until someone who loved her was able to take my place. It felt like the least I could do.

"I'm bored."

"There's no pleasing you, is there? Dramatic hostage rescue, a woman saved from the edge of death, a simply disgusting corpse and the finest coffee this hospital can provide." Liv handed it over and I took a gulp even though I knew it would be too hot to drink.

"Ow."

"Steady on, thrill-seeker. At least blow on it."

"I need the caffeine. I'm starting to fall asleep." I put the cup down on the floor and fanned my mouth, then slumped down another couple of inches in the chair. "The only thing that's keeping me going is taking bets on the next injury to come around the corner."

We were sitting in a corridor in a busy part of the A&E department and as ever I was amazed by the variety of ways people could find to damage themselves.

"If you feel sleepy, go for a walk." Liv checked the time. "Godley should be here soon. And I doubt the doctors will be that much longer with Patricia. The paramedics seemed to think she was in reasonable nick."

"That's why we were allowed to come here, isn't it? Because it wasn't an emergency. But I still think it might take them a while to run through all of the tests, given that she hasn't seen a doctor for over a year." Godley had asked if Patricia could be brought to the casualty department of a specific hospital in North London—because, it transpired, Lee Bancroft was there already, and he wanted to keep tabs on both of them, rather than having to shuttle between two places.

Liv sat down beside me and leaned her head back against the wall. "Just take advantage of the downtime, if you can. You should get some rest. Patricia is pretty intense."

"Do you blame her? We're the first friendly faces she's seen for a long time." I shivered. "I can't even begin to imagine what she's been through. Just the fact that she survived is incredible."

She didn't answer straightaway. She was poking at her cup, rolling the edge of the cardboard, and frowning.

"What?"

"Nothing. It's just—you don't think she was in on it, do you?"

"She was chained to a radiator, Liv. She's skin and bone."

"We made a lot of noise when we got to the house. We rang the bell, broke a window—and she was asleep upstairs the whole time."

"In the attic. I didn't hear the ambulance crew arrive. I only heard them when they were at the foot of the ladder."

"Okay, fair point. But she could have run up there, put the chain around her wrist and pretended she was asleep."

"Did you see her? Did you see her teeth? That's not the sort of thing that happens to someone who's a willing participant in whatever games the Bancrofts were playing."

"I just think it's worth keeping in mind that she might not be completely innocent. We haven't had anything like an explanation from her for the DNA on Cheyenne."

"And she didn't want to talk about her," I admitted. "But I think that's normal, really. Whatever happened, it wasn't pleasant."

"Godley will get it out of her."

"Oh, he'll charm her. Where is he, anyway?"

She shrugged. "On his way? I suppose he might start off with Lee. He's not doing too badly, by all accounts."

"Whose accounts? Who have you seen?" If I sounded twitchy, it was because I felt twitchy. Liv and I had been sitting in the corridor for hours. I was desperate for something to happen, a new face to appear, a bit of interesting information to while away the time. I would not have done well in the attic, it occurred to me. I doubted I would have made it through eighteen days, let alone survived for months.

"I met Maitland by the lifts. He was looking for the café too. I steered him in the right direction."

"That was nice of you."

"Wasn't it?" she said sedately. "It was worth my while, though. You'll never believe what we missed by not going on the arrest."

Briefly, she told me what she'd found out from Maitland about the shoot-out, and Drew Bancroft's horrible death. I shuddered.

"I've seen enough tortured men in the past week to last me a lifetime. I'm just glad I missed that one."

"I bet Patricia is pleased about it too," Liv said slyly. "If you hadn't gone to interview the uncle—"

I interrupted, uncomfortable with the ifs and but-for-the-grace-of-Gods. "Who else is here?"

"It's strange you should ask that." She raised her eyebrows meaningfully, looking past me.

When I turned, I saw Rob hurrying toward us, concern on his face. I stood up and went to meet him.

"Hello. What's up?"

He put his hands on my shoulders, scanning my face. "Are you okay?"

"Never better. Why?"

"Miscommunication. Don't worry about it." He gave me a lopsided smile.

"You looked like it was the end of the world," I said, not unreasonably.

"When you're in hospital, it tends to be."

"Oh, ha ha."

"You know it's true."

"I know nothing of the kind. Aren't you supposed to be minding Lee? I take it that's what you're doing here."

"I left Maitland in charge of the shop. He should be able to cope. How about you?"

"We found Patricia Farinelli." I couldn't stop myself from beaming; I still couldn't quite believe it. "She's alive. She's okay. More or less."

I described how we'd found her. When I'd finished, Rob said, very softly, "That bastard."

"Huh?"

"Godley asked Lee where Patricia was, just before they carted him off in the ambulance. He said there was no point in looking for her. He said she was dead."

"She would have been in a couple of days," Liv pointed out.

"He's looking at a whole-life sentence anyway. Patricia's testimony won't make any difference to that. Why would he want her to die?"

Rob shrugged. "Because he's evil. Because he doesn't think she deserves her life. Because he thinks it's funny to lie to us. Take your pick."

"All of the above, I'd have said."

"And you're probably right at that."

"He wanted her to die slowly and painfully, for no reason." I shook my head. "It's hard to shake the feeling that it's a shame Skinner's boys didn't get to finish the job."

"No faith in the criminal justice system to punish him enough?"

"None whatsoever."

Rob and I were still standing in the middle of the corridor. He looked up and down it. "I should get back."

"Okay. See you later."

He waved at Liv and turned as if to go, then doubled back and took my face in his hands. "I'm very glad you're not a patient this time."

"Me too." I said it with feeling.

He leaned in and kissed me, a kiss that went on until Liv cleared her throat. "Guys . . ."

I was expecting her to make some sort of quip, but when we looked around, she was looking exceedingly uncomfortable. Rob moved away from me smartly, and as I looked over my shoulder, I realized that he had seen what I hadn't: Superintendent Godley coming toward us, closing fast. He would have had to be blind and stupid to have failed to notice what we had been doing, and he was demonstrably neither. I braced myself for what he would say, miserably aware that there was nothing we could say in our defense.

But it seemed that our dressing-down was going to be deferred. All business, he asked, "What's happening with Lee?"

"Nothing much. He's sleeping it off. They found he had a cracked bone in his arm, so that needs seeing to. I think it'll be tomorrow before we get to talk to him." Rob sounded completely calm, as if he had nothing to be flustered about, and I wished for a tenth of his composure.

Godley switched his attention to me. "And Patricia?"

Before I had to answer, a nurse appeared at my elbow. "Are you Maeve? She's asking for you."

"Can we speak to her now?" Godley asked.

"If she wants to talk to you, she can, but she might be a bit dopey. The doctor's given her something to keep her calm, because she kept trying to take out the drip." The nurse looked around at us. "She's in a bit of a state, isn't she? What happened to her?"

"You don't want to know," Rob said pleasantly, but in a way that forbade any follow-up questions. The nurse shrugged and bustled away.

Godley nodded to Rob. "You should probably get back to Harry. I'll come up when we're finished here. Maeve, do you want to go in first and see how Patricia is? Let her know we're here and we'd like to talk to her, but leave it up to her. If she doesn't want to be interviewed, I'm not going to force her."

"No problem." I headed for the door to her room, aware of Rob walking in the other direction. I would have given a lot to be able to talk to him at that moment. But, making a huge effort, I pushed it to the back of my mind, along with the demoralizing thought that my career was once again in trouble. Or as Derwent might have put it, heading for the shitter. All the more reason to play a blinder with Patricia. I squared my shoulders and knocked on the door, then opened it without waiting for a response.

She was sitting up in bed, looking smaller and frailer against the piled-up hospital pillows. They had given her a hospital gown to wear in place of her filthy clothes and it swam on her, emphasizing her fragility. Her head seemed to be too big for her narrow shoulders. Her face was pale, her lips bloodless, and the Valium they had given her had made her eyelids sag behind her heavy glasses.

I pinned a smile to my face. "How are you feeling?"

"All right." There was a noticeable lag before she answered, as if thoughts were taking a long time to filter through the drug-induced fog. She lifted up one stick-like arm, the wrist bandaged where the chain had damaged it. "They've put a needle in me."

"They're just giving you fluids because you were dehydrated."

"I don't like being tied up." She shook her arm weakly, making the plastic tubing rattle against the bed frame. It was uncomfortably reminiscent of the way she had agitated the chain.

"The drip is on a stand with wheels." I pulled it away from the bed a little and showed her. "When you feel better—when you're strong enough—you can get up and walk around with it."

She leaned away from the pillows to see, then sat back against them with a heavy sigh.

"Are you tired?"

"A little." She ran her hands over the sheets. "This is strange."

"Hospitals always are." I knew that wasn't what she'd meant, but I wanted her to feel that everything was normal—that *she* was normal. A matter-of-fact breeziness that was wholly unnatural seemed to be the only way I could talk to her. "Do you feel strong enough to have a chat with me and a couple of my colleagues, Patricia?"

Her hands stilled. "What about?"

"About the past eighteen months."

"Since they took me?"

"Exactly."

She looked down, considering it. "Eighteen months. Is that how long it was?"

"Give or take a few days."

"I tried to keep track, but it was hard. They wouldn't let me make any marks on the wall or the floor. They checked, now and then. If they found anything . . ." Her voice trailed away and she balled one hand into a fist, miming a punch.

It was such a basic human desire to want to keep track of the passage of time, such a fundamental need to keep order. They had even taken that away from her.

"So would that be all right? It's just Liv, who you met earlier, and my boss, Charles Godley."

"Is he scary?" She whispered it.

"Not in the least." I crossed my fingers as I said it, but I meant it. He wouldn't be scary as far as she was concerned. I must have convinced Patricia, because she nodded her agreement. I wasn't feeling quite so sanguine as I went to the door to summon him and Liv. I was dreading seeing something unfamiliar in his eyes—judgment at the very least, disappointment if I was really unlucky. But as far as I could tell, he was exactly the same as normal as he followed Liv into the hospital room and stood at the end of the bed.

"It's nice to meet you at last, Patricia. I'm sorry that we have to bother you by asking questions at this stage, but it's very helpful for us to know what happened before we speak to the gentleman we have in custody."

"The gentleman?"

"Lee Bancroft."

"The bigger of the two brothers." To Godley, I explained, "Patricia didn't know their names."

"Where's the other one?" She looked absolutely terrified, tranquilizers notwithstanding.

Without hesitating, without fanfare, Godley said, "He's dead."

"Are you sure?"

"I saw his body." He didn't add anything else and I willed Patricia not to ask how, or when.

Her face twisted and she gave a tiny wail that raised the hairs on the back of my neck. "He's dead. He's really dead."

"Yes, he is."

For the second time I saw her cry, but this time they were silent tears that slid down her cheeks from behind her glasses, dripping off her jawline. She didn't seem to notice.

"Are you all right, Patricia?"

"It's just that I dreamed of him dying. I wanted him dead *so badly*. And now you're telling me he's gone, and I just . . . I hated him so much."

"Sometimes hate keeps you going when nothing else will," I said quietly.

"Yes. You're right. That was it. I wouldn't give him the satisfaction of breaking down."

"Why did you hate Drew so much?" Godley asked.

"Because he was the one who tricked me in the first place. He was the one who wrote the e-mails."

"On the dating website?"

She nodded. "He made me believe he was someone else."

"Vincent," I said, and she nodded again.

"He was so charming in his e-mails. So funny. I didn't want to meet because I knew it would ruin everything." She laughed bitterly. "I thought about that a lot. How I'd been right without knowing it."

"How did he persuade you?"

"I told him I was too fat and ugly to date anyone. I sent him a picture of myself that was really unflattering—it was the only one I had. He told me I looked beautiful. He told me he could see the beauty inside, and that was what mattered." Two more tears slipped down. "I printed that e-mail. I carried it around with me. I'd read it on the bus, or when no one was looking at work. It made me feel so special. It made me trust him."

"That's what it was designed to do," Godley said quietly. "It wasn't your fault you were taken in."

"Yes, but then—then he made me trust him again. He made a fool of me *twice*. But that was later."

"What happened when you met him?"

"He was everything I'd hoped he would be," she said simply. "Totally attentive. A proper gentleman. We met in a bar and I thought people would stare at us because I was so fat and ugly and he was so beautiful. It was as if he knew I was uncomfortable. He'd arranged a table for us at the back, a booth, so I wasn't on show. I assumed it was him being thoughtful, but later I realized it was so no one would remember seeing us together."

"Did you spend the evening together?"

"No. Just two drinks. But the second one was spiked with something. He'd asked me if I'd told anyone about him, if I'd said to anyone where I was going. He checked, first, to make sure it was safe to kidnap me. And I made it so easy for him."

"You mustn't blame yourself," I said quickly. "He knew what was going on—you didn't."

"I should have known he was too good to be true." She gave a long, quivery sigh. "He said we should go for dinner. He said he knew a nice restaurant. I was too out of it to think about whether it was a good idea or not, but even if I'd been totally sober, he would still have convinced me. I wanted to believe he was for real."

"Did you go to a restaurant?" Godley asked.

"No. He told me it was a drive and he wanted to take his van because he didn't like leaving it parked on the street. He hadn't been drinking because he was supposed to be driving home, he said, so I didn't see anything wrong with letting him take me to the restaurant. But he didn't. He said he had to get something out of the back of the van, and when he opened the doors, he pushed me in. The other one was waiting there and he hit me so hard, I blacked out. When I woke up, I was in the house."

"In the attic?" I asked.

"In a bedroom. The one with the green wallpaper. I couldn't think where I was."

"Were you tied up?"

"No, but the door was locked. When it opened, it was the other twin who was there. He beat me again, and then he raped me." She said it dully, as if it was just routine. "That happened every couple of hours. No food. No water. I thought I was going to die. I wished I would. Over and over again. And then—then the other one didn't come back for a while. The next time the door opened, it was Vincent. I remember it so clearly—I was lying there, on the floor, and he came in with a tray. He picked me up and sat me on the bed, he gave me water, he fed me and put disinfectant on my cuts. He was loving. I thought he was going to save me."

"More manipulation," Godley said.

"Oh, definitely. I realized that a long time later. But at the time, I thought he was my guardian angel. He left the tray behind when he went—and I begged him not to leave me, you know, I really did—and when I recovered enough to look at it, there was my passport. I couldn't understand how it had got there. I knew I hadn't had it with me when I was at the bar. The next time, when Vincent did the same thing after—Lee, you said?—after he'd attacked me again, he left a little clock by the bed. It was my clock, from my nightstand at home. I worked it out, they'd been in my flat. They'd taken my things. I asked Lee about it when he came in again and he said it was his brother's idea. Vin—Drew—said he thought it would be nice for me to have my things around me."

"Did you ask him about the glasses?" I said.

"Then and every time I was in the same room as him. He said he was looking for them but that they'd lost my handbag. He gave me to under-stand that if I was nice to him, he'd look after me. If I . . . did things for him . . . he would do things for me. I thought he might help me escape if I convinced him I liked him, so I did what he wanted. Anything." She sobbed, once. "It was easier with the other one because he never gave me a choice. With Vincent, I was the one making the moves. And I hated myself for it when I realized that was the game. He was like a cat, playing with me. He'd make me think there was hope just to crush me again."

"What did they do about food for you?"

"After the first month or two, they stopped coming every day. They'd leave some food and water, but I never knew when they would be back, and there was never enough anyway. I had to guess how much I could eat at one time. They loved it when I had nothing left—they thought that was funny." She half-smiled. "They took me downstairs once, to the kitchen. They made me cook them a meal. I hadn't eaten for two days and I was faint—I felt sick, actually, not hungry, so I didn't care. But it was that sort of thing, all the time. Cruelty because they could be cruel."

There was no hint of self-pity in her voice and somehow that made it worse.

"How long did this go on?"

"Until a couple of months ago. They'd got tired of me. I was thin, and my teeth were terrible, and I was dirty—they didn't let me wash properly anymore because they hardly ever touched me so it didn't matter if I was clean. It was too much trouble to take me down to the bathroom. I knew they were up to something because Drew was excited, full of energy—he hadn't even spoken to me for weeks. Then he told me they had good news for me. I'd be so pleased when I heard it, he said. I thought they might let me go. Or kill me. I honestly didn't care."

"When did you find out what it was?"

"Last week. Before the girl arrived. Drew told me it was almost time. He made me change the sheets on the bed in the green room. He said I was going to get a friend." She turned her face away from us and closed her eyes. "I couldn't stand it. They were doing it again, right in front of me. Making me a part of it."

"Did you know when Cheyenne arrived?"

"The girl?" A wry smile. "I couldn't have missed her. She screamed the place down. On and on. They thought she'd get tired, but she trashed the room. Lee was too strong for her, though. She was quiet after he'd been with her. But it didn't last." The calm voice ran on, recounting atrocities as if they were normal life. The truth of it was that for her, they had been. "In the end, Drew sent me down to talk to her. Through the door. I told her to go along with it and they would hurt her less."

"What did she say?" Godley sounded deeply disturbed, but he was still in command of himself.

"She asked me what had happened to me. I told her. She asked me how long I had been there and I said I was sure it was more than a year, but I couldn't say for certain."

"What happened then?"

"She cried," Patricia said simply. "She didn't scream again, that I heard. She just gave up. And the next morning, Drew came and told me she was dead. I thought I'd broken her heart."

"She had an asthma attack," Godley said. "Not your fault."

"No? But I was the last person to talk to her." She sighed. "I wished it was me."

"How did your DNA get on her hand?" I couldn't resist asking it. "Your saliva was on her palm."

"That's right. I hoped you'd find it. They made me bathe her and wrap her up, you see. They didn't want there to be any traces of them or the house on the body. So when I was drying her, I licked her hand. I tied her hands together, to protect it." She held her wrists up to demonstrate. "I knew no one was looking for me. I knew what they'd done to stage my disappearance. The only thing I could do was hope there was enough evidence to make the police suspect them."

"You made us aware that you were in trouble, Patricia. You did well." Godley's voice was gentle.

"Did it help to catch them? Was that how you knew they were guilty?"

"Not quite." Godley hesitated for a second, as if he wasn't sure how to go on. "Did you ever see anyone else? A friend of the brothers? Or friends?"

"No. No one." She was definite.

"Not their uncle? It was his house."

"No. But I didn't go into all the rooms. Just the attic, and the green bedroom, the hall and the kitchen. And never on my own. Was he there?"

"In a way," I said cagily, not wanting to tell her about the corpse that had been her nearest neighbor for months.

"Did they ever use a video camera to record you?" Godley asked.

It wasn't my imagination; her entire body stiffened. "How did you know?"

"Some other evidence that came to light. Not you. Cheyenne."

"Yes," she said, with some difficulty. "In the beginning. And if they were doing something *creative*. They liked to show off."

"But who saw? Who were they showing off to?"

"The other members of the club." She said it as if we should know what she meant. "On the Internet."

"What club, Patricia?"

"They were members of a website that was for freaks and perverts. The worse stuff you could put up, the further you went up the ladder. *He* explained it to me once. They had top privileges, he said."

"What was the name of the site?"

"I don't know."

"Had they kidnapped anyone before you?"

"I don't know."

Godley tried another few questions, but it was clear that Patricia was strung out, too tired to think. Besides, she had told us all she could remember, of that I was fairly sure. I leaned over and put my hand on his arm while she lay back with her eyes closed.

"I think we should quit while we're ahead. Give her a chance to get some rest."

"Agreed." He raised his voice a little. "Patricia, we're going to leave you in peace. You are a very brave young lady and you must not feel guilty about anything you did from start to finish. You did what you could, and what you had to do, and you've survived. That's something to be proud of."

She nodded, but I could tell she didn't believe him.

"It will get easier, in time."

"I hope so." She sounded exhausted.

"Do you think you might be able to sleep?" I asked.

"I think I will." She looked up. "You've been so nice. Thank you for being here."

"For nothing." As I said it, there was a soft tap on the door. I looked at Godley, then at Liv who went to open it. Patricia was watching dully, her eyes half-closed already; I doubted she was even trying to hear the low-pitched conversation in the corridor. I was, but then I knew who to expect. I could hear Keith Bryce's voice, which meant he was back from the airport. He had made good time.

Godley had gone to the door after Liv, and now he turned. "Patricia, you have some visitors."

She frowned as if trying to imagine who that might be. Godley nodded to someone I couldn't see, and the next minute there was a rush of feet as a small, square, gray-haired woman shot into the room, closely followed by a slim, tanned, elderly man who had a smile locked on his face. Mr. and Mrs. Farinelli, recently arrived from Pisa, I presumed.

At the sight of them, Patricia's eyes went wide, and then her face twisted as she dissolved into tears. Mrs. Farinelli was sobbing too, her arms wrapped around her daughter as she kissed her hair over and over. Patricia's father had taken one hand and was stroking it, over and over, crooning to her in lyrical, rolling Italian. There wasn't a dry eye in the house, including my own.

After a couple of moments, I moved toward the door, judging that the Farinellis deserved some time alone.

"A happy ending," Godley commented once we were all in the corridor and the door was closed behind us.

"Of sorts," I said. "I don't think Patricia's going to find it easy to get over what's happened to her. Being with her family will help, but—"

"She'll need time," Liv said, finishing off my thoughts. "And counseling. It's such a terrible story."

"We need to find out more about that site."

Godley looked at me quickly. "You noticed that too? I think it's likely we've just found out where the video came from."

"Was that really what motivated them though? Membership of a website?" Liv sounded puzzled.

I shook my head. "The website was just another game. What motivated them was old-fashioned wickedness, pure and simple. I wish I could find it in me to be sorry Drew's dead, but I'm not."

"Don't worry," Godley said grimly. "After hearing Patricia's story, neither am I. Who would have thought John Skinner would be useful after all?"

Chapter Twenty-one

Monday

Rob

It took the rest of Sunday to winkle Lee Bancroft out of the snug little billet he'd found for himself at the hospital. The doctors were far more punctilious than I would have been about looking after his welfare, and Lee had all of the old tricks I would have expected from someone who had spent a fair bit of time inside. He claimed headaches, nausea, sensitivity to light, a pain in his neck that came and went and ringing in his ears, and by five o'clock that afternoon I was fairly certain it was all lies. We had interrupted Skinner's retribution at an early stage, and although they had thrown him against a few walls, the damage they had done to him was reasonably superficial. He was a dedicated bodybuilder, as fit as a butcher's dog, but to hear him talk he was an invalid on the brink of total physical collapse. Godley was as annoyed as any of us, but rightly wary of handing him an advantage when it came to his defense. We couldn't interview him until the doctors had signed him off and his solicitor had agreed he was fit to talk to us, so there was no alternative but to wait.

After two other officers turned up to relieve us, Maitland and I trailed out of the hospital. On the way to the car we occupied ourselves with speculating on what might ail him next.

"A pain in his tum-tum."

"Dislocated toenail."

"Sticky eyeball."

"Itchy sinuses."

"Earache."

"Face-ache."

"Bumhole-ache."

"I don't think you're taking this seriously, Harry."

"You're right. I should be more understanding." He didn't sound terribly contrite.

Neither of us was pleased to leave Bancroft behind. There was always a chance that he might decide he'd recovered sufficiently to be interviewed while our backs were turned. Maitland, of course, didn't have an evening with Maeve as consolation, and he was mordant company all the way back to the nick.

Without making a big deal of it, I turned down the chance to go for a drink with a few of the lads, sorted out what was on my desk and headed home. Maeve was working, head down, and I didn't attempt to get her attention. We had agreed that she would meet me at the flat, and I didn't want to hassle her by checking she was still coming, but I wouldn't have laid any money that she would actually show up. As the minutes ticked by, I paced from room to room, wishing I had told her I'd meet her at the station.

It was with a mixture of relief and incredulity that I eventually heard her knock on the door. I pulled her inside.

"Where have you been?"

"Finishing up at work." She put her arms around my neck. "I wanted to make sure I'd done everything this time so no one could accuse me of not doing my job, by which I mean that asshole Derwent. But I'm here now."

"Yes. Yes, you are." I grinned at her, seeing the same elation on her face that I was feeling. I had expected nerves—I had expected her to try to back out, if I was honest—but there didn't seem to be any question of that.

"I bought a toothbrush on my way back, but that's about it as far as belongings go. I really need to go back to my flat and pack a bag."

"Not without me. Tomorrow, after work." I shook her gently. "Promise me, Maeve. Don't set foot in your old neighborhood without me."

"Why would I? You can carry my things for me."

"Yeah, make a joke out of it."

"What else am I supposed to do? Don't get me wrong, I am more than pleased to be here. But the circumstances are pretty far from ideal, don't you think? And I don't really have the option of hiding out while I wait for whoever took the pictures to be caught."

I could acknowledge the sense in what she was saying without feeling in the least bit reassured. "Just be sensible about it. That's all I'm saying. He knows you know about him now. He knows we'll be looking for him. If he's going to do anything more than watch you, now is the time to do it."

"I had worked that out, thanks."

"Did anyone follow you from the station?"

"Rob, for God's sake, I wasn't looking over my shoulder the whole way."

"Maybe you should have been."

"That's what he wants. That's why he announced himself. He wants to upset me. He wants to change my behavior. He's driven me out of my home already—it's just a lucky accident that I have somewhere better to be."

"Look, I don't want to start with an argument—"

"Then don't." She let her bag slip off her shoulder and leaned back against the wall, looking drained. "I know what you're worried about and I'd be lying if I said I wasn't bothered. I am being careful, I promise you. But I don't want to let it poison everything. I don't want to live in fear of someone who is basically a coward. I am not going to give him the satisfaction when he hasn't even got the nerve to confront me himself."

"Well, don't taunt him into being brave, will you? I can live with a timid stalker."

"Me too. And since I don't seem to have a choice about it at the moment, that'll have to do." She stood on her tiptoes and kissed me. "What's for dinner?"

"Oh, I see. Like that, is it?"

"Well, why else would I move in with you?"

"Someone said something about wanting to be with me and how it wouldn't be the worst thing in the world. That was you, wasn't it?"

She shrugged as she sidled past me, the picture of innocence. "Do you know, I can't quite recall."

I went to work the following morning with a smile on my face, a few minutes behind Maeve. She had insisted on getting a head start so no one would guess we had started our journey together. I hadn't the heart to tell her it was probably the worst-kept secret in the Met; Liv had worked it out within minutes of joining the team, and she could hardly be the only one. There were natural hazards to working in a room full of coppers and not having any privacy was one of them, but I let Maeve have her solitary journey. When I arrived I greeted her with a cheery "Good morning" in case anyone suspected we had done that part of the day several hours earlier, and in quite a different way.

Godley waved me into his office as soon as he saw I was there.

"I'm just going to interview Lee Bancroft."

"Can I sit in?"

He looked apologetic. "Best not. I want to keep the room clear. Just me and Pettifer, him and his solicitor. You can watch on the monitors."

I was sorry to miss out though I didn't argue. I got on well with Godley, but he was still a superintendent and it was useful to keep that in mind, I found. I had never known him to pull rank—he was confident enough not to need to—but the rank was there nonetheless, and he'd reached it for a reason. I nodded instead and tried to look as if I didn't mind.

"Have you had a chance to think about the leak?"

"I have."

"And?"

"I've got some ideas," I said. "Leave it with me. I want to talk to the guys who processed Murray, Roberts and McKenzie yesterday. I also want to check what personal effects Felix Crowther was carrying when he was brought to the morgue."

"Why?" Godley was being uncharacteristically abrupt and I recalled that he was personally interested in this, that whoever had passed on word about the Bancrofts was probably the person who had given Skinner the superintendent's home address.

"I will tell you, you know. But you might as well wait until later, when I've got facts rather than ideas."

He considered it for a second and I knew he wasn't happy, but he let it go. "All right. I'll mind my own business."

"It will be today, boss. We'll know one way or the other by this afternoon."

"You sound very sure."

"I have a reasonable idea of who was responsible. Don't you?"

"I think so. There's an obvious candidate." He went and looked out of the window, his back turned to me. It wasn't like him to be so rude, but it was entirely in character—and understandable—to be upset about being betrayed. And there was no mistaking it; the person who had passed on Godley's personal details had done so in the full knowledge of how they would be used, and why, and to possess them in the first place he had needed Godley's trust. However you cut it, they needed catching and they needed to be punished for what they'd done. I was looking forward to playing my part. It almost made up for being relegated to the cheap seats for Lee Bancroft's interview.

I was far from being the only one who wanted to know what he said. The meeting room was crowded, the chairs all full by the time I made it in there, having spent an interesting half-hour on the phone and a further twenty minutes haring around the nick sorting a few things out. I took up a place at the back of the room, which happened to be my preference anyway. I liked being able to make a quick exit.

Right at the front, Derwent was making a big deal out of shushing people as Godley and Pettifer took it in turns to ask a stony-faced Bancroft to explain what he'd done, and why, and how many times. "We want to be able to hear what he's got to say, not what you got up to last night."

I found Maeve's face in the crowd and raised my eyebrows, enjoying the fact that I could see the blood rise to her cheeks from the other side of the room.

Up in the corner of the screen there was a box that showed the police side of the room, and although the image was small, I could read the interviewers' faces quite clearly. They were far too professional to show their distaste in any obvious way, but knowing them as I did, I could see that they were increasingly fed up with the lack of cooperation they were getting from Lee, who was on his third "no comment" since I'd walked into the room. His voice came all the way from his boots and he looked bigger, if anything, on-screen. His solicitor, whom I knew to be a man of average build, was about half his size.

Lee's clothes had been bloody after his run-in with Skinner's thugs, but someone had got hold of a clean T-shirt and jeans for him. The T-shirt clung to his pectoral muscles and looked tight on his arms.

"Look at the size of him," Ben Dornton marveled.

"He's not that big. The camera adds ten pounds. Everyone knows that." Maitland was a hard man to impress, but in this case he was taking the piss for the sake of annoying Dornton, who fell for it from a height.

"Ten pounds? You wouldn't see ten pounds on that body. He's a giant."

"That's pure beef," someone else commented. "Not an ounce of fat."

"He didn't do it all the hard way. He had a couple of different types of steroid on the go, from what I saw in his flat."

"You're just jealous, Rob." Maitland lolled in his chair, his head tipped back so he could see my reaction upside-down.

"Oh, definitely. I want to bulk up. I must ask him where he gets his T-shirts."

"Only if you want to look like a boy-band reject," Liv said tartly.

"For the last time, shut up." Derwent glared around at us. "If you're not interested, get out."

"You're not missing much." Keith Bryce was standing beside me, his hands in his pockets. "He hasn't said anything interesting yet, has he?"

"Not specially. Unless you count 'no comment.' But that doesn't mean he won't." Derwent turned back to the screen, watching it with the sort of intensity that had to be exhausting to maintain.

On the monitor, Godley was becoming, for him, irate. "You told us Patricia Farinelli was dead. That was a lie. She was alive at the time, but she wouldn't have been for long. Were you prepared to allow her to die? Was that what you wanted?"

Lee looked through him, a half-smile on his face.

"Tell us how you selected your victims."

"No comment."

"Was it you or your brother who came up with the idea?"

Silence, but Lee's gaze switched from the back wall of the room to Godley's face.

"He was the talkative one, wasn't he? He was the charmer. You're just the muscle. Without him, you don't have anything to say for yourself, do you?"

"Have you found out who killed him yet?"

"He speaks," Bryce murmured, and when I looked around, he was smiling.

Pettifer leaned on the table. "We're asking the questions, Lee. You're under arrest on charges of kidnap, false imprisonment, attempted murder and multiple counts of rape. You might like to think about that rather than worrying about us doing our jobs."

"Which of them did it? Which of them shot him?" Lee's shoulders were bunched up around his ears with tension. "Have you even bothered to find out?"

"It hasn't been a priority for us," Godley said quietly. "We've been more concerned with your victims than your brother. If we could clear up a few things about them, then we can concentrate on Drew."

"Victims?"

"Cheyenne Skinner."

He made a movement that was pure impatience. "We didn't kill her. She died."

"You raped her."

A laugh. "She just tried to play hard to get. I wasn't having that. She liked it."

"That's not what we've heard. And not what the forensic evidence suggests."

"She didn't like being kept."

"You made a mistake with her, didn't you? You thought she was older than she was. You thought she lived alone, so you could make her disappear like you made Patricia disappear. You must have been very annoyed when you found out the truth."

"It was unfortunate."

"Why didn't you let her go?"

"It was too late for that."

"You'd already raped her. You'd beaten her up. Withheld food from her."

"She tried to push the boundaries all the time. She needed to learn the house rules."

"I can't believe Godley's getting him to talk," Maitland said.

"It's the same thing he did with Skinner." Maeve was still looking at the screen. "He wanted us to find his daughter so he told us everything we asked. Just goes to show everyone has something they love, no matter how bad they are."

"The house rules. What were they?" Godley asked.

Lee shrugged. "Do what you're told."

"Patricia did what she was told, didn't she? It didn't seem to do her much good."

Lee looked away again, his expression bored.

"Why don't you want to talk about Patricia?"

"I don't see the point."

"Her evidence is going to put you in prison for life," Pettifer said. "You should be telling us your version. Give yourself a chance in court."

"You're not interested in helping me. You're just nosy." He shifted in his chair. "I'm thirsty."

Pettifer poured him a glass of water from the jug behind him and pushed it across the table. "So what if I am nosy? Tell us about Patricia."

"I don't know anyone of that name."

"Okay. Let's call her the woman you kept hidden in your uncle's house for eighteen months. Let's call her the one you starved and terrorized to the brink of death. Does that help to jog your memory?"

"It's just not ringing any bells." The mocking smile was back on Lee's face.

"Are you saying that you don't think of her as a person, Lee?" Godley's voice was quiet. "You didn't treat her like one. You treated her like a slave. Would it help if we called her the slave?"

His smile broadened. "Your word. Not mine."

"What would your word be?"

"When I talked to it—which wasn't often—I called it 'cunt.'"

He had said it for effect and he would have been delighted by the reaction it got from the team. I was not under the impression I was surrounded by choirboys, but there was a rumble of disapproval all the same. I glanced across at Maeve, whose lips were pressed together tightly. She had told me a little about finding Patricia, and about the story she had told Godley. I had gathered that Maeve was deeply bothered by what had happened to her and I knew that she was trying not to show how upset she was. It was chilling to hear a person dismissed in those terms, but it was hardly a surprise to find out Lee felt that way.

Godley hadn't so much as flickered. "Why do you feel that way about her?"

"Don't waste your time and mine."

"You used her. You treated her like she was worthless."

"It stopped being fun. So it got replaced." Lee turned to his solicitor. "Can we stop this now? I've got a headache."

The solicitor raised his eyebrows and Godley shook his head. "A few more questions. Then we'll take a break."

Lee folded his arms with the air of one who had finished cooperating for the time being.

I leaned toward Bryce. "Are you interested in this?"

"Not specially," he murmured.

"Can I have a word, then? Outside?"

He was too experienced an officer to ask any more questions; he moved past me toward the door with neither haste nor fuss. I followed him a couple of seconds later, checking my watch as if I had somewhere else to be. It was a wholly unnecessary bit of pantomime—while Lee Bancroft was in interview I could have worn a gorilla mask and streaked the squad room without attracting any attention whatsoever.

Bryce had gone into the small meeting room and I followed, shutting the door. There was absolutely no point in mincing my words.

"The boss is pretty sure there's a leak from this squad. Someone's been keeping Skinner informed about what we've been doing."

Not a muscle moved in the long face. "That sounds likely. He has always been well connected."

"The obvious question is who."

"Yes, it is." The heavy-lidded eyes stared into mine. He was giving nothing away for free.

"The boss asked me to do some sniffing around."

"He must think very highly of you."

I smiled a little. "I don't think that's why. I haven't been directly involved with this case, or with Skinner. He can be pretty sure it wasn't me."

"If you say so. There's a lot of other people it could be, though."

"Anyone in particular?"

"You first."

He was going to make me say it. I braced myself. "Have you ever wondered about Josh Derwent? You've worked with him for a long time."

Bryce's shoulders sagged an inch. "Ah. I hoped you wouldn't have thought of that."

"Well?"

"I never wanted to think he might be on the take. He's a good lad. He works hard, in his own way."

"He's been up to his neck in the case. There aren't many people who would be better placed to pass on information to John Skinner. And Godley trusts him. They have a friendship outside work. He would have been one of the few to have known his address."

"He would. Have you talked to him?"

"Not yet."

"What about the boss?"

"I need evidence."

"Yes, you do. What are you thinking?"

"When Crowther was shot at Lee Bancroft's flat, he was carrying two phones. One was his own iPhone, for personal use. The other was a cheapie job that he was obviously using for work. I got the telephone intelligence unit to download the messages off it and bingo, that's how they were communicating with the person in this squad. So if you don't mind helping me have a look through Derwent's things, we might be able to find the phone he's been using to communicate with Crowther."

"Won't he have dumped it by now? Given that it all went tits-up yesterday?"

"Possibly. But it's his means of communication with the Skinner gang. He's not going to want to abandon it without having an alternative lined up, and I doubt he's had time. They'd have to give him the new number to use and Skinner has been running out of staff. My betting is that Felix Crowther was in charge of the intel—that was his reputation, wasn't it?"

"He was probably the brightest of them," Bryce allowed. "That's not saying much."

"All things considered, it's worth having a scout around. But I need to be quick, and I don't know him well enough to be able to explain it if he found me looking in his desk or his car."

"I get the picture. You want me to do that."

"I'll check his locker."

"What if he has it on him?"

"Would you take that risk?" I half-smiled. "Anyway, he's in his shirtsleeves and his trousers are on the snug side. I can see how many coins he's got in his pockets. If he's got a phone in there, it's too small to be visible with the naked eye."

"Fair point." He shook his head. "I don't like it."

"If I'm wrong, he'll be none the wiser."

"If you're right, he's in a lot of trouble."

"Not of my making."

"Maybe not." A deep sigh. "I'll help. But I hope you're wrong."

"Honestly? So do I." And I meant it.

"Josh? Can you come in here for a moment?"

"What's up?" Derwent breezed in, kicking the door shut with a back-heel. He looked around the room, at Bryce in one chair, at me leaning against a filing cabinet, at Godley who was sitting behind his desk, his fingers laced. "Who died?"

"Sit down." Godley waited until Derwent had flung himself into the vacant chair, his fingers tapping on his knees. I had never seen anyone so wired who wasn't on drugs and I found myself wondering about that for an instant, then put it out of my mind. *Concentrate on the things you can prove . . .*

"Josh, you know as well as I do that John Skinner seems to have had access to the information we possessed all through this case. Rob has been looking into the likelihood that someone has been leaking that information deliberately."

"Makes sense." Derwent looked at me expectantly. "Found anything?"

"Yes."

Godley's head snapped up at that; I hadn't told him. I was watching Derwent. The fidgeting hadn't stopped, even for a second. It was a good cover for giveaway twitches he wouldn't have been able to hide otherwise, and I couldn't pinpoint anything that made me sure he was guilty.

Derwent raised his eyebrows. "Don't keep us in suspense. Who was it?"

"You."

"What?" He stopped dead for a second, his mouth open. "What the fuck are you talking about?"

Bryce was looking down at his feet. Godley's face had gone white. I was not the sort of person to enjoy the theater of unmasking a villain; quickly and quietly I explained what I had learned.

"This case was obviously of particular interest to John Skinner, but it's not the only one that's been compromised by leaking information, from what I've heard. You and DI Bryce worked for Superintendent Godley on the task force that targeted Skinner some years ago. He was always ahead of the game. You never managed to catch him in the act, no matter what you tried. No one is that good. He was acting on inside information then, just the same way he was on this occasion."

Derwent had folded his arms. He was smiling, incredibly. He seemed to have decided not to take it seriously. "Skinner has a habit of corrupting people. You can't be sure there wasn't someone crooked on that task force and someone else on this team. Why does it have to be the same person?"

"It doesn't. But it has to be someone who Superintendent Godley trusts." I risked a look at the boss. "You invited DI Derwent to your home on numerous occasions, boss. That's true, isn't it? He knew your wife and your daughter's names. He knew a lot about your family."

"I was close to my team in the old days. I've got into better habits now."

"Keith fits both of those criteria too," Derwent pointed out. Bryce's eyebrows twitched in surprise.

"DI Bryce didn't react strongly at the sight of Cheyenne Skinner's body. I was there when you ran out of the room. You had a visceral reaction to it, and it surprised me at the time. It's what I would have expected from someone who knew the victim."

"Are you telling me I shouldn't be upset about the death of a fourteen-year-old girl?" His voice was harsher—he was getting angry with me. I preferred it to the mocking levity, on the whole.

"I am saying that it was an unexpected reaction from someone who presents himself as being an old-school copper. The boss has a fourteen-year-old daughter. I'm sure it was hard for him to see Cheyenne's body. But he stayed in the room."

"You're a dickhead. You think you're being clever, but you don't know jackshit about me."

"What is there to know?"

"I have personal reasons for being upset at what I saw in the warehouse. Those reasons are not relevant to this discussion."

"With respect, they are if they go some way to explaining how you behaved."

"With respect, fuck yourself sideways."

"What about the shooting yesterday? When we got there, the action was all over. Three in custody, one down. None of our lads shot. You weren't responsible. You had been well away from the action. But you were sweating like a horse when we were talking to you."

"I don't like shooting," Derwent muttered. He looked ashamed of himself, but defiant. "I was in the army before this. I was in Northern Ireland in the nineties, right at the end of the fighting, and it fucked me up, the things I saw. I left after that—couldn't deal with the stress. I don't like being around CO19 at the best of times and I can't deal with gunfire."

Bryce raised his head. "It's true. He's always been gun-shy."

"Then you went to the trouble of telling the three thugs to keep their mouths shut in interview. I bet you felt a lot better after that."

"What are you talking about?" Derwent's forehead crinkled as he tried to remember. "I was just putting them under pressure. Softening them up."

"Why bother? They weren't going to break down because you told them they were screwed."

"It's what I do," Derwent said simply. "That's how I get results. I'm not the quickest at outthinking people in an interview room, but I'm good at pushing them around."

"Literally." I tried to keep any hint of my personal feelings out of my voice for the next bit. "What happened when John Skinner was arrested? How did Maeve Kerrigan get injured?"

"She fell."

"She had help."

"I did push her. But I was terrified she'd get shot. I don't like women being in harm's way. I'm old-fashioned like that."

"She said you went to restrain Superintendent Godley even though there were two men fighting your fellow officers. You went to help Skinner. Were you trying to get him out?"

"Through a million and one CO19 boys? I'd have to be suicidal." He looked at Godley. "Boss, I could see you'd lost it. If you'd done serious damage to him, that would be it. End of career. No question about it. I had to stop you, but for your own good."

Bryce looked sorrowful. "Josh, I can't believe it."

"Because it's not true." Sweat was standing on Derwent's forehead, darkening his hair. "Charlie, you've got to believe me."

If he'd hoped using Godley's first name would remind him of their friendship, he'd miscalculated badly.

"I can only believe the evidence," Godley said tonelessly. "It doesn't matter if I'd prefer it to be a mistake." He looked at me. "What else is there?"

I nodded to Bryce and he put a phone on the desk in front of Godley. It was still attached to strips of electrician's tape. "I found this in Josh's car, stuck to the underside of the passenger seat. It matches the number that sent the messages the TIU found on Crowther's mobile phone."

"I've never seen that before in my life."

Godley slammed his hand down on the desk. I suddenly understood why Maeve had been so unsettled to see him lose his temper; it was an unnerving sight. "Stop *lying*. You've been found out, Josh. You've lost. Just admit it."

"I'm not going to admit doing something I didn't do."

"The fucking phone was in your car, Josh. How did it get there if you didn't put it there?"

I was very glad there was a desk between Derwent and Godley. It was the only thing saving him from a punch in the face, or worse.

"I don't know, all right? I don't have a fucking clue."

"I do." After Godley and Derwent shouting at one another, my voice sounded absurdly calm and quiet.

"What do you mean, you do?" Godley was glaring at me.

I turned to Derwent. "You were right, earlier. There was another person who had the same access to the boss—who was around when you were working on catching Skinner the first time. Keith Bryce."

Bryce had his hands on the arms of his chair, his fingernails digging into the upholstery. "What's this game, Langton?"

"I asked you to help me search DI Derwent's car and desk." I ignored the choked outrage from Derwent's direction. "I told you I couldn't do it myself because I didn't want to risk getting caught. I lied. I'd already carried out a quick search in both locations so I could be sure the phone wasn't there. I was pretty sure you were the leak, so I gave you a nudge to see if you would try to implicate someone else. I told you I was looking for the phone. I don't know where you had it—I think you probably had it hidden about your person, in fact, as you suggested DI Derwent might have done that with it. You wear very baggy clothes—frankly, you could have a fax machine in your jacket pocket and we'd be none the wiser. I wanted the phone and I wanted to know that you were the only person who could have put it where it was discovered. And you fell for it."

Godley was looking thunderstruck. "But the things you said about Josh . . ."

"All reasons to suspect him. But I believe his explanations." I turned to Derwent again. "I'm not sure you'll forgive me for any of this, so I might as well say it. You're obnoxious. You come across as a total asshole, but you're too much of an asshole to be subtle.

You draw too much attention to yourself. Your colleague, on the other hand . . ." I looked at Bryce ". . . you'd forget he was in the room half the time. I know who I'd rather enlist as my spy."

"Keith . . ." Godley was back to white-lipped distress but the anger had ebbed away. "Why?"

I didn't expect him to get an answer, but they had a long history, the pair of them, and maybe Bryce still had a conscience in there somewhere.

"I'm sorry, Charlie. I don't even have a good excuse. It was money." He spread his hands helplessly. "I gamble. Always have done. On anything. Racing, football, two flies crawling up a wall— it doesn't matter to me. I've made thousands, but I've pissed away tens of thousands. Elaine doesn't know. She'd kill me if she did and I don't blame her. We almost lost the house seven years ago. Skinner got in touch with me and offered to pay off my debts. I said no. He said he'd give me a regular retainer—mad money, he called it. All I had to do was tip him off now and then. No harm done. He would let us make arrests so none of us looked bad, but he wanted to stay out of jail. If he did, I'd be better off." He looked piteously around the room, seeing no sympathy. "I know it was wrong, but I thought he'd be running his empire anyway, even if he was locked up. What difference did it make if he was free or behind bars?"

"You should have quit."

"I realize that now." He shook his head. "I never wanted to give him personal information about you, Charlie. He was just so good at getting it out of me. A question here or there. A suggestion. A threat, sometimes. He played me like a Stradivarius."

"You're making my heart bleed." Derwent had bounced back remarkably quickly. He was staring at Bryce with total loathing. "I can't believe you were going to fit me up."

"On the scale of betrayal, I think putting my family at risk is a touch more serious," Godley pointed out mildly.

"You're right. You're right. Sorry." Derwent had the grace to look abashed. "What happens now?"

"You can go," Godley said to Derwent. To me, he said, "Thanks, Rob. I appreciate it."

"Do you want me to call DPS?"

"I'll do that myself."

Bryce was huddled in his chair, his eyes wet with self-pity. "I need to call Elaine. They'll be searching our house. I need to explain."

"For old times' sake, I'll let you use this phone." Godley lifted the receiver, back in control of himself, icy reserve in place. "Once I've called DPS and told them what you've done."

I followed Derwent out of the room, wondering if I should risk an apology. He got a safe distance down the corridor, then turned to confront me.

"You frightened the shit out of me. I thought I was getting fitted up good and proper." He grinned. "No hard feelings, though. I'd have done the same thing if I'd thought of it."

"You couldn't be in on it, I'm afraid. You had to believe I really thought you were guilty if you were going to be convincing."

"Did you tell Charlie it was me?"

"He didn't know anything. He needed to be convincing too."

"I thought he was going to kill me."

"Me too," I admitted. "But I would have stepped in."

"I wouldn't have needed any help." He pulled his shoulders back, broadening his chest. I wondered if he was even conscious of doing it. It was so much a throwback to the apes it was almost ridiculous. The missing bloody link, alive and well and policing London with maximum offensiveness.

I shook his hand, then and there. Much to my surprise, I was getting to like him.

"You would have to be completely insane to ask Derwent to be your inside man. He'd wear a T-shirt advertising the fact just to show off." Maeve was never going to be a member of DI Derwent's fan club, no matter how much I tried to convince her he was all right. "I still can't believe it was Bryce, though. He's so . . . nondescript. How did you work out it was him?"

"Process of elimination." I turned in a circle, checking in all directions for signs of a stalker before I followed her up the steps to her front door. "And just the fact that he is a nothing. Skinner's not stupid. He recruits the people he needs. A not-too-ambitious career policeman with a gambling habit is pretty much ideal."

"I wonder what Derwent's freak-out was about, when he saw Cheyenne's body." She was fumbling in her bag for her keys.

"Good luck finding out. He wouldn't even tell us to save his job."

"One of these days he'll let something slip." She slotted her key into the lock, but the door opened before she could turn it. She stepped back on top of me, more jumpy than she would admit. "Oh my God, Walter, you scared me."

Her landlord was standing in the doorway, his face pained. "Maeve, I've got to ask you to leave."

"I was going to. I mean, I wanted to give you notice."

"You aren't welcome in this house anymore."

"Why not?"

He pushed the door open properly, and I could see a little group huddled on the bottom steps of the stairs. There was the lush nanny with a hulking, beardy boyfriend scowling behind her, and a good-looking man who had to be the actor.

"Where's the other one?"

Walter looked at me with something approaching disgust. "If you mean Chris, we don't know."

Maeve had walked into the hall and was staring through her front door, which was standing open. "What happened?"

"We got raided, darling." Brody jumped off the step and went to join her. "They ripped your place apart. Do they not like you?"

I pushed past him to see what he was talking about. "Holy shit."

The walls were riddled with holes, long tracks in the plaster-work where a wire had been followed, plotted and removed. Every item of furniture of any size had been dismantled and arranged neatly in a pile: the sofa was the principal casualty. Maeve's personal belongings were stacked against one wall of the sitting room. I found myself thinking it would be handy for packing, but I managed not to say that. Maeve was moving through her flat slowly, dazedly. I shadowed her, wary of getting too close. Shock first, then anger; she was as predictable as Christmas.

The kitchen was a wreck, the doors hanging off the cupboards. The bathroom walls were perforated in several places, with tiles missing or cracked. The bedroom was the worst of all: in many places the walls were down to the bare lathes, and plaster dust lay thickly on all the surfaces.

Maeve finished her tour of inspection back in the hall, where Walter and the others were waiting. "Who did this?"

"The police. They had a warrant to check the premises for surveillance equipment. They did the same thing in the other flats. I'm going to sue. And you've definitely lost your deposit."

"How is this my fault?"

"They said someone had been watching you. They said they needed to check that your flat wasn't bugged. Then they said they needed to check the other flats."

"What for?"

Walter shrugged. "They didn't say."

"Did they do the same thing everywhere else?"

"More or less." His face was pinched. "I tried to stop them."

Maeve turned to me. "Belcott."

"Colin Vale was working on it too," I reminded her. "He must have thought this was necessary. He wouldn't have let Belcott get away with this out of spite."

"Is he the tall one, with glasses?" Szuszanna piped up. "He was nice. The other one, not so nice."

Maeve had closed her eyes. "I can't stand the thought of him poking through my stuff. It's worse than being burgled."

"For me too," Szuszanna said crossly. "I watched."

Maeve was too concerned with her own trauma to have much time to listen to Szuszanna. "I would have liked a bit of warning. A phone call would have been courteous. I might have wanted to be here—you never know. I can just see his smug little face. He must have loved it."

I had moved away a little and was ringing Colin Vale's mobile. "Hello?"

"Colin, I'm at Kerrigan's address." *Please don't ask me why.* "What happened?"

"Cameras in the walls and items of furniture. The whole place was wired up—sound, pictures, everything. Upstairs too." He sounded harried. "We've traced the cables to the flat on the ground floor, the one opposite hers."

I looked up; I was standing outside Chris's door. "Did you get in?"

"No. We needed the resident's permission to search and we didn't get it so I had to go off for a warrant. We think he left via the fire escape as soon as we started to knock through the walls in Maeve's place."

"You didn't get her permission before you searched her place, did you?"

There was a tiny pause. "She knew we were investigating. Belcott said we could take it as read."

"Did he indeed?"

"She would have said yes."

"She might." There was little point in torturing him about it. "How are you doing on that warrant?"

"I'm sorting it out right now." A tiny pause. "Is Maeve there?"

"She won't be for long."

"Good." He sounded infinitely relieved. "I don't want to be there when she finds out about the cameras."

I looked across to where she was arguing with Walter about her deposit. She was jabbing a long finger into his chest. Fierce was not the word.

Into the phone, I said, "Nor do I, mate. Nor do I."

Chapter Twenty-two

Tuesday

Maeve

I was in no state of mind to be reasonable on Tuesday morning when I flung open the door to the office.

"Where's Belcott?"

He raised his hand from the far end of the room, where he was lurking behind his computer. "Ah, Kerrigan. We've been expecting you."

"Don't try to be funny." I stalked the length of the office and stood beside his desk, my hands on my hips. "You have a lot of explaining to do."

"Why I am so very attractive to the opposite sex?"

I closed my eyes for a second and shuddered; it wasn't entirely for effect. *The very idea . . .* "I was actually wondering why you didn't tell me you were going to search my flat. I say search. I actually mean fuck it to oblivion."

"It was all necessary—" he began.

"I don't believe you. It looked as if squatters had been living there for six months. How you did all that damage in one day, I can't imagine."

"It was the best way to find what we were looking for."

"Which was?"

"You have to have worked this out by now. I thought you were a shit-hot detective, Kerrigan." He smiled up at me maliciously. "Use your intuition."

"You took out wiring."

"And a whole lot more." He looked past me. "Hello, Rob. Didn't you tell her?"

"It's nothing to do with me."

I looked around to see Rob leaning up against a desk behind me, a neutral expression on his face. He had been quiet the night before, but I had put it down to exhaustion.

"What didn't you want to tell me? For fuck's sake, Belcott, I am beyond tired of the twenty questions game. Talk. Now. Or your nostrils and this stapler are going to get to know one another a lot better." I picked it up and waved it under his nose menacingly.

He leaned out so he could see past me. "As a matter of interest, do you think she's beautiful when she's angry? Because I'd get your eyes tested if so, mate."

"Stop talking to Langton. Talk to me. This has nothing to do with him."

"I wouldn't say that." As if he had tired of baiting me, Belcott sat up straight and nudged his mouse to bring his screen to life. "Okay. I know you think I set up the search of your flat to piss you off, but actually, we had good reason. The video your one-member fan club sent you was taken from a website that we traced yesterday. It's called Zabolagee.com."

"That doesn't mean anything to me."

"That's actually the point. The founders came up with a name that wouldn't bring them up in casual searches—it's word-of-mouth personal recommendation only, and the site is members only."

"How did you find it?"

"I've got a mate at CEOP who let us in on a few tricks for matching the file to the website," Colin Vale said, coming forward to stand beside Belcott, as if he felt he should be there to support him. Collective responsibility and all that, though Belcott would probably have left him to drown if the situation had been reversed. "We managed to get through into a few of their password-protected areas. And then the hosting company was persuaded to be helpful and gave us access to IP addresses for contributors."

"They were shitting themselves. Said they had no idea what was on there. I did say *most* of it was perfectly legal—I think that was when they started to throw information at us." Belcott sounded smug. He did have a way with words, if that way was to make you feel physically sick.

"What was on there?"

"The majority of what we could see was the standard stuff you'd expect on a BDSM website—that's bondage, domination, sado-masochism," Belcott explained, seeing the frown on my face.

"I'm not sure what I would expect. I don't spend a lot of time on that sort of website."

"I'm not saying I do, but generally it's your usual fake dungeon environment with submissives performing for their mistresses or masters. Pain, humiliation, obedience—that's what gets them their jollies. Zabolagee is structured around levels of mastery, if you see what I mean. So at the entry level, you have the willing participants, consenting adults, a bit of light whipping." Belcott seemed far too fluent in talking about it. I was starting to understand why Colin Vale was looking so sick.

"It goes all the way up to where your boys were, the top. That's actual slavery, torture, rape. Snuff films too, it seems. We couldn't get access to them but the techies are working on it."

"What did you see?"

"Rape where the victim is obviously drugged or unconscious. Rape where the victim is conscious and resisting. Serious violence." Vale's voice shook. "I found it tough, to be honest with you."

"The second level up is where the content isn't too sick but the participants aren't necessarily willing or aware. Cameras in shop changing rooms and gym locker rooms, spying on ladies in the nude without their knowledge. Up-skirt photography. Stalking an individual and taking pictures of them going about their business over a period of time ranging from hours to years." Belcott paused for effect. "That's where we found the section devoted to you, Kerrigan. It was labeled with your first name."

"Well, that explains why Lee asked me how I spelled it." I was still trying to sound nonchalant even though it made me shudder to think of my stalker's surveillance pictures being shared with his fellow perverts. "He must have come across it."

"I'm sure it was popular." Again, Belcott looked past me. "Wouldn't have thought it of you, Rob. It was a real eye-opener when we started watching the film clips."

I suddenly felt cold. "Film clips. From inside my flat."

"You and Langton going at it like bunnies. It was good of you to leave the lights on—that night-vision camera work gives me the creeps. It always reminds me of a nature documentary and that's not what you want when you're thinking about knocking one out."

"I don't believe you."

"Do you want to see? The site's been pulled by the host company but I took the precaution of downloading the clips to my machine. I was thinking of raffling a look at them to raise money for the next Police Dependant's Trust appeal." He turned the monitor around and showed me the files on his desktop. Each had a thumbnail picture and I could see enough to know that Belcott had seen far more than I would have wished. "Want to see more?"

"You absolute fucker."

"I got them taken down. I've protected your honor, Kerrigan. You should be on your knees thanking me." His manner left me in no doubt about what I was supposed to be doing while I was down there to show him my gratitude and I took a step toward him, not really sure how much damage I could do in a room full of police trained in restraint techniques, but willing to have a go nonetheless.

"All I need to do is click and everyone can see what I've seen. Gather round." He aimed that at everyone else in the team. "Roll up, roll up for the greatest show on earth, if you like watching a bit of old-fashioned shagging."

"That's it. I am going to hurt you." I stepped around Belcott's desk, the red mist preventing me from thinking about the consequences. I wanted to rip his head off.

Rob was too quick for me. He bent down and unplugged Belcott's computer. "Plug it back in and regret it, Belcock. I'm having it wiped by IT under my supervision."

Colin Vale was nodding enthusiastically. "That's what I told him we should do."

"Spoilsports." Belcott grinned at me. "Never mind. I've got my memories."

It would take buckets of bleach to make me feel clean again. I moved away from him, my fingers still twitching with the desire to do him some serious violence.

"Did you trace the wiring to Chris Swain's flat or did something else tip you off?" Rob asked.

I had to give him credit for still being able to focus on the case; he was presumably as bothered as I was about the invasion of our privacy, and the ramifications which were only just beginning to sink in. Our relationship was common knowledge. Godley might have ignored the kiss he'd seen at the hospital if he was feeling kind, but when the entire squad knew about our relationship, he couldn't exactly turn a blind eye. One of us would have to volunteer to bow out. I was listening to Colin Vale's answer, but most of my brain was dealing with the realization that I had run out of road.

"We had our suspicions that someone at Maeve's house was involved because the IP address for the person who posted the material came back to somewhere near there. We weren't able to pinpoint it before we went to do the search." A nervous glance at Belcott. "We both felt it was more important to find out the level of intrusion into Maeve's personal space and whether it was common to other flats in the same building."

"And?"

"The flat above hers was also wired extensively, as was the top floor. It was clear that the wiring stemmed from the right ground-floor residence. Nothing was found in the flat directly above that—it's the landlord's, I believe."

"So he was spying on Szuszanna and Brody as well as me." I was still feeling nauseous. "I thought he was friends with Brody."

"Maybe Brody didn't mind," Rob suggested. "Actors perform. Maybe he liked being watched."

I pulled a face. "Don't. At least Walter's private life will remain a mystery. But he must have known what was going on. I think he tried to warn me about it. I thought it was just that he didn't like you."

"Big of him. Presumably he was worried that interfering with a copper was a risk too far."

"Oh, I'm sure it wasn't for any noble reason that he wanted to stop it. Walter and I never really became close, but I wouldn't suspect him of having many of the finer feelings."

Rob looked back to Belcott. "How did you let Swain go? Were you in too much of a rush to get warrants for the whole place?"

"We just assumed it would be someone off-site. And he knew as soon as we started knocking on walls—I mean, we couldn't do it quietly, could we? He was gone before we'd traced the first set of wires to his flat."

"For fuck's sake—"

"Don't pretend you'd have done it differently," Belcott said warningly. "It's not our fault."

"But it was our best chance to arrest him." Rob was glowering and I realized all of a sudden that he was truly worried about Chris Swain. The thought was about equally comforting and disturbing.

"Once the Bancrofts got nicked, he must have thought it was only a matter of time before he got caught so he ran. They were major figures on the website—heroes, for what they had done with Cheyenne and Patricia and the others."

"The others?" I asked.

"We think they did the same thing to at least three other women, based on what we could see on the site. But we can't get at all of it. We're just going on comments made by other users."

"Oh, no." I leaned against the nearest piece of furniture, suddenly weak. I had feared it, and DI Stone had more or less expected it, but it was still devastating to have our suspicions confirmed. And currently we had no idea how to trace them, dead or alive, or even who they had been. I imagined three other families like the Farinellis, waiting for their own miracle.

"The site included a forum where users exchanged gossip, tips, that sort of thing. We were concerned that the news about what had happened to the Bancrofts would drive other contributors underground. There was evidence to preserve. We didn't hang around."

I rallied. "You wanted a chance to look through my underwear drawer, Belcott. Don't dress it up."

"We missed Swain by minutes." Belcott actually looked a little bit ashamed. "The more I find out about him, the more I regret it. He was one of the founder members of Zabolagee.com. He had access privileges at every level, which is how he found the Cheyenne material. Why he sent it to you and drew attention to himself is a mystery when he could have watched you more or less at will for as long as he liked. But from what he wrote about you, I'd have to say he was pretty far gone."

"I thought he just had a crush. He was pathetic. I didn't take him seriously."

"You should have," Colin Vale said seriously. "He has a penchant for drugging and raping women. He doesn't like it when they fight."

Rob was looking at me. "Do you remember the night you had a drink with him and Brody? You seemed a bit out of it when I got there."

"I'd had a bang on the head," I pointed out. "I'd just got back from the hospital. I was entitled to feel a bit strange."

"Did you finish your drink?" Colin Vale asked.

"I just had a few sips." I was thinking about it and coming to a very disturbing conclusion. "Oh shit. No wonder he was pissed off when I wouldn't stay. And then you turned up, Rob." I started to laugh, slightly hysterically. "Poor Chris. That didn't go his way at all."

Rob didn't look as if he found it funny. "What are you doing about finding him?"

"We've got a trace on his known credit cards and bank account. We've notified the police forces in areas he's been known to live, where he has friends or family. There's an alert out to all ports and he's been circulated as wanted on the PNC in case someone stops him somewhere. He dumped his mobile so we don't have live cell-site, unfortunately, and he didn't have a car. It's as if he was ready to drop off the face of the earth."

"He probably was. He must have known this day would come," I said. "He wasn't stupid."

"We'll track him down." Godley had emerged from his office without my noticing. Of course, he would know all about it already. It was an active investigation under his command. But I still blushed to the roots of my hair at the thought of what he now knew about me, and what he might have seen.

He looked at me levelly. "Don't allow yourself to worry about Swain. You've got the full might of the Met at your back and we won't stop until he's in custody. You have my word."

"I'm sure he's got enough sense to stay well away from me."

"Maeve, you're the first mistake he's made," Rob said gently. "I don't think he has a lot of sense where you're concerned."

"Very reassuring."

"I want you worried. And careful. And in one piece."

I was embarrassed by the frankness with which he spoke, but then there was no reason to hide anymore. Just like that, I made up my mind.

"Could I have a word with you, sir?"

"Now, Maeve?" Godley checked his watch, looking hassled. "I'm just on my way to interview Lee Bancroft again. We're still trying to work out who they took before Patricia. She certainly wasn't the first, but Lee isn't willing to cooperate."

I backed down instantly; it wasn't a conversation I had really wanted to have anyway. "After that."

"Fine." Godley began to walk away, then stopped. "Have you spoken to Lee?"

"Not since the initial interview. Before he was a suspect."

"Want to give it a try? It can't hurt for him to see a fresh face."

"Of course." I could feel Belcott's death stare on my back as I walked out with the superintendent. *Suck it up, you little creep.*

"He's been asking about you." Godley sounded embarrassed and I suddenly knew what was coming. I got in first.

"You want me to flirt. Act the bimbo."

"Hard questioning isn't getting us anywhere. You're better than that, obviously, but—"

I smiled, but without humor. "'The end justifies the means,' as DI Derwent would say."

"Machiavelli said it first."

"I doubt he meant it the way Derwent does." We had reached the door of the interview room. I took off my jacket and undid a couple of shirt buttons, then shook my hair free from its clip, hating Godley for asking me to do it, hating myself for not saying no. If I got Lee to confess, it would be worth it, I told myself. "How do I look? Unprofessional?"

"Wildly so." Godley handed me a folder. "Pictures of possible victims. They disappeared in the right time frame; no sightings since." It was a depressingly fat folder.

"Thanks." I took a deep breath, then let it out slowly. "I'm ready."

Godley opened the door, saying to me over his shoulder, "I still don't think it's a good idea—oh! Mr. Bancroft. You're here already." Another anxious look in my direction. "I didn't realize." *And the Oscar goes to . . .*

I took small steps as I walked into the room instead of my usual leggy stride. I looked nervously at Lee Bancroft, glanced at his solicitor, then stared at him again with all the acuity of a rabbit gazing at a pair of headlights.

"Mr. Bancroft. Or—can I call you Lee?"

"Maeve." He smiled. "It's nice to see you again."

"Let's get this interview started," Godley snapped, pretending to be irritated as he poked at the tape recorder.

"You've been watching me," I said very softly, my eyes as big as saucers. *This is for your ears only, Lee. I want to talk to you and only you.* "I had no idea."

"We enjoyed the show. And we enjoyed meeting you." Another smile. "Sometimes simple pleasures are the best."

"Is that what it was? A simple pleasure?" I allowed myself to look distressed, biting my lip. "I just didn't have any idea."

"Stop chatting, Maeve, and do your job." Godley switched on the machine and recited the preamble, sounding bored, as if he was rushing through it. He flung himself into a chair beside me and I barely acknowledged his presence, staring into Lee's eyes as if I had been hypnotized.

"You might as well begin."

"Oh. Okay." I opened the folder and closed it again, flustered. "We wanted to ask you about some other missing women." I looked at Godley quickly, as if for guidance.

"Who else did you kidnap?" the superintendent demanded. "We know there were more, Lee. It wasn't just Patricia and Cheyenne."

"No one worth talking about."

"There were three of them, weren't there? We've found references to them on the website. Three women who we haven't traced. What happened to them, Lee?"

"I have nothing to say to you."

Godley had been leaning on the table; now he sat back in his chair with an air of resignation.

"Maybe . . ." I sounded hesitant. "Maybe you could tell me what happened. With the women. So I can understand. I want to understand."

He gave a tiny shrug, as if he was annoyed by the question but amused enough to indulge me. "They suffered from built-in obsolescence. We had our fun and then we were done with them."

"If they were alive, they'd have complained to us about what you did. Wouldn't they?"

"Maybe. Some of them liked it."

Of course they did. "I really need to know who they were, Lee. For their families. For my own sake—I'm under a lot of pressure here." I flicked my eyes sideways to where Godley was sitting. *Please help me because the big bad boss is bullying me. Only you can save me . . .*

"I'd like to help. But I don't recall."

"Maybe these will jog your memory." I opened the file again and laid three photographs in front of him. "Pick out the women you recognize, Lee."

He shook his head, but it was a no that meant "I don't recognize anyone," not a refusal. I laid out another three pictures.

"What about these?"

The pictures were of variable quality, some blurry with enlargement, others pin-sharp studio portraits. One was a wedding photograph and it made me feel physically sick when Lee laid a finger on it. "That one. I think her name was . . . Sadie."

"Sally," Godley said. "Not Sadie. She was twenty-three."

Lee nodded. "Separated from her husband. Looking for fun."

"What did she find?"

"That there was a certain pleasure in being obedient." His tone was terrifyingly matter-of-fact.

"Where is she now?"

He gave Godley a cold stare for interrupting. "You'll have to find her, won't you?"

"We need some idea where to look, Lee. She could be anywhere. Did you leave the body somewhere, as you did with Cheyenne? Did you bury her? Burn her? Dump her in water?"

"We buried her."

"Where?" Godley again.

"You'll have to work it out."

"Did you keep her at your uncle's house?" I don't know what put it into my head; maybe because they had seemed so comfortable with death, with corpses, with their own slaves in their own world. "You didn't want to part with her, did you? Not when you owned her, body and soul. Even though all you had left was the body."

"Not stupid, are you?" He didn't look pleased at that idea.

"It was a lucky guess." Godley glowered at both of us. "Where at the house? Outside?"

"Somewhere away from the house itself," I said softly. "Somewhere that wasn't overlooked so the neighbors didn't see you bury her. But somewhere you could see easily so you could keep an eye on her."

He smirked instead of answering and Godley nodded, making a note. We would search the ground for signs of disturbance, for traces of decomposition in the soil. We would find her. If I was right.

"Will you look at more pictures for me?"

"Pictures of you?"

I didn't have to fake the heat that came into my cheeks. "Please, Mr. Bancroft."

"Lee."

"Lee, then. What about these? Take your time."

"Her. Linette." He tapped a picture of a pretty girl with very short hair. "She was Drew's favorite."

"That's two. Who was the third?"

Lee leaned across the table and grabbed the folder, pulling it out of my unresisting hands. He leafed through the remaining pictures in a bored way before stopping. "Angela. She was the oldest of them. That was the problem. It took too long to persuade her to fall into line."

"What happened to her?" I said, not really wanting to hear the answer.

"I can't recall." Lee gave me a tight smile. "I don't think it was very interesting. She's not around anymore, anyway."

"You told us Patricia was dead too." Godley sounded angry. "How do we know you aren't lying again?"

"I've told you where to find the bodies. Dig." He was still staring at me.

"Why did you return Cheyenne's body and not the others?"

Lee looked past Godley at the blank back wall and sighed.

"I think I know."

"Would you like to share with us, Maeve?"

"Because they never really owned her." I looked nervously across at Lee.

"That's right, isn't it? You didn't want to keep her because she wasn't yours. So you put her back where you found her."

"More or less. She was a mistake. We didn't like mistakes."

"Why didn't you bury your uncle too?"

"He died naturally. We needed the house but he'd left it to charity. We couldn't tell anyone he was dead, so we just left him there and pretended he was still knocking about. If we'd got found out, we'd just have lied and said we didn't know he was up there. Seemed fair enough. If we'd buried him, we'd have had a lot more explaining to do."

"Very clever," I said, dropping the wide-eyed look and allowing just a little of what I really felt for him into my voice.

"Right. I'm going to stop this interview so we can brief the SOCOs who will be investigating the scene. Interview stopped at oh-eight-forty," Godley said.

As soon as the tape was stopped, I asked, "Why did you say Patricia was dead already? Why did you lie about that?"

"Because it was dead as far as I was concerned. It had no interest for me."

"'It?'" I stood up, aware that my knees were trembling. "Let me tell you something. Patricia is braver than you'll ever be. Patricia survived. And do you want to know something else? Patricia never talks about you. She talks about your brother, but she doesn't say anything about you. Patricia barely knows you exist, and she certainly doesn't care."

"That's not true."

"I'm afraid it is. She didn't even know your name." I walked to the door. "You know, she hasn't even asked where you are or what's happened to you. You'll rot in prison and she'll go and live her life, and I don't think she'll think about you at all."

I was halfway down the corridor, doing up my buttons when Godley caught up with me. "Well done."

"For sneering at him?"

"For getting him to confess."

"It wasn't difficult, was it?"

"I hadn't managed it," Godley said simply. "You did well."

"I did my job just the way Derwent and Belcott assumed I would. That doesn't make me feel brilliant, to be honest with you."

"You worked out what that creep needed to hear—and how he needed to feel—to get him to talk. You flattered him. You let him think he was in control. And you've probably got the names and locations of three women's bodies, which is the whole point of what we're doing here. You've given them back to their families. That's all we can hope to do at this stage, but it's worth doing well."

"Thank you." His praise made it so much harder to do what I needed to do, but I had no choice. "Can we have that chat now?"

Godley nodded and led the way to his office, standing by the door to shut it after I went in. I waited for him to sit down, then took my place opposite him as I had so many times before.

"I'm more sorry than I can say about this, but I would like to request a transfer to another team."

He frowned. "Really, Maeve? I didn't expect you to want to leave, but of course I understand your decision in the light of what's happened to you since you've been working with me."

"It's not that." I couldn't stand to have him think that. "I've loved every minute of it. I just think it's time to go. I have personal reasons." *As you know very well.*

"If your mind is made up, I will respect your decision, but I hope you'll think again. I'd be sorry to lose two of you in the space of twenty-four hours."

"Two of us?"

"DC Langton came to see me yesterday and requested a transfer."

"Yesterday? I don't understand—" I broke off, confused. "What did he say? Why is he leaving?"

"Personal and professional reasons," Godley said. As usual, I couldn't tell what he thought. "If you need more details, you'd better ask him."

I turned and saw Rob on the other side of the office watching us, his arms folded. He was chewing his lower lip, a habit he had when he was on edge. And just like that, I flipped. Rob must have seen the look on my face because when I flung open the door of the office, he was already making his way across the room at speed to intercept me.

"What the hell do you think you're playing at? Why are you leaving?" I didn't bother to keep my voice down even though we were the center of attention. There didn't seem to be one of my colleagues who had anything better to do than watch us argue, but I was too angry to care.

"I have a better offer elsewhere."

"Bullshit."

"It's true. My old DI is with the Flying Squad, now at Tower Bridge, and a DS job has opened up on his team. Godley's put in a good word for me.

You know I was waiting for something to come up, and it doesn't get much better than that."

I knew he'd been waiting for a sergeant's job; he had passed the exams months earlier. The Flying Squad dealt with robberies—investigating them and preventing them by pretty much any means necessary. It was full-on, high-pressure stuff and Rob was made for it.

I looked at him dubiously. "So this has nothing to do with us."

"I didn't say that."

"You love this job. You wouldn't be leaving if it wasn't for the fact that we're involved."

He thought for a second, then shrugged. "Probably not."

"And no one would have found out if it wasn't for me, so I'm the one who should go."

"Maeve, stop being stubborn for a second and think about it. I quit yesterday. Before anyone saw the film clips."

"So why?"

"Because I want to do this properly. I don't want to hide and pretend and lie anymore." He pulled me into his arms and I let him, though the catcalls that rang through the squad room made my cheeks burn. "I want everyone to know."

"It's not a good enough reason to sacrifice your career."

"Who's sacrificing anything? I get promoted, remember? Which makes me senior to you and it would be nice if you could start doing what I say for a change."

"No chance," I said automatically and he laughed.

"Didn't think so."

"I still don't think . . ."

He shook me, gently. "Maeve, just shut up, for once in your life. Believe me, it's worth it."

Before I could argue, he leaned in and kissed me. There was a time for fighting and a time for giving in. I ignored the wolf whistles, applause and shouts of "get a room" as I wrapped myself around Rob, all doubts forgotten.

And behind us, a soft clack announced that the superintendent had closed his blinds.